MW00834514

Sparrow Alone
on the
Housetop

Sparrow Alone on the Housetop

Jean James

and

Mary James

Edmond, OK

Sparrow Alone on the Housetop

Copyright © 2011 Jean James, Mary James, and 4RV Publishing

Cover art copyright © 2011 by Aidana WillowRaven and 4RV Publishing

Book designer Mandy Hedrick

All rights reserved. Except for brief excerpts for reviewing, no part of this book may be reproduced or transmitted in any form or by any means, electronic or mechanical, including photocopy, recording, or any information storage or retrieval system, without permission in writing.

Inquiries should be addressed to:

4RV Publishing LLC

PO Box 6482

Edmond, OK 73083

http://www.4rvpublishingllc.com

ISBN-13: 978-0-9826594-8-9

Printed in the United States of America

Chapter 1

The stars burned like white fire in the midnight-blue sky. The hush of the night was broken only by the gentle gurgle of water around her body as she glided across the glassy pond. Near the deeper, cooler center, she rolled to her back and sent ripples in all directions. With the yielding water for a pillow, she floated away the day's heat, face to the dark heavens above. A heady scent of night jasmine filled the air, and Anne breathed deeply of the perfume she loved so well. Deep within she longed for someone, anyone, to share the moment. The longing at once made her feel forlorn, forgotten. It was the loneliest of moments.

The sleeping world around her offered poor company as her thoughts drifted back to her homeland. Though she loved these mountains of South Mexico and the ragged Indians of her mission, deep inside she missed home. Such admission would have seemed strange to the Anne Sumner of two years ago, the Anne who had defied father, wealth, and power, to step into this poverty. But in the blackness of night, the years and miles between her and her former life mounted up into eons of time and distance.

Would the village ever be self-sufficient enough for her to leave? Frail, both spiritually and materially, Tutlu could be blown away with the slightest breath of trouble. A few renegade tears coursed down her already-wet cheeks as weakness took sway, but she splashed them away along with her melancholy mood and climbed ashore refreshed.

She managed a desultory laugh at herself. Didn't her own choice keep her a willing prisoner of the tiny Indian village? Hadn't her own hands freely renovated the miserable patch of forest, with its two dozen discouraged, poverty-ridden families, into a prospering village? The village had no real claim on her. She could leave if or when she chose. She had no one to answer to but God and her own overly-developed conscience, now that her church back in the States had failed in their support.

"And that was the best thing that could have happened to us," she reminded herself for the hundredth time.

She pushed aside the mosquito-net door of her weathered, canvas tent and hurried in ahead of a few persistently annoying bloodsuckers. Not bothering to towel dry, she slipped into a loose, cotton shirt and stretched out on her narrow cot for the second time that night.

Although cooler now, sleep still eluded her. She stared wide-eyed at the mildewed ceiling and mentally listed the morrow's tasks. The distant hum of an aircraft interrupted her thoughts. She jerked upright in bed. It wasn't time for *their* moment of glory yet, but a small tingle of excitement crept through her. More contact with the outside world would encourage everyone.

Only minutes later, she arose to the dim light of dawn and hurried to dress. She grabbed a cold ear of roasted corn and ate it while she headed for the nearly completed runway. The monumental task of converting the sixteen hundred feet of narrow, rutted trail into something wide, smooth, and straight enough to accommodate a plane had required huge effort, but its accomplishment lay only a day distant.

Anne hefted the axe from where she had sunk it into the wood of a large stump the evening before. Through three hours of yesterday's heat, she had chopped and dug around its roots. Conquest loomed close now. One hour's work should see it defeated and lying on its back. She waved good morning to Ruben, who already worked on another stump not far from hers.

"Anne, I finally beat you to work."

"I should have come out sooner. I guess I should have worked all night. We have to finish this today."

"I thought you *did* work all night. Your chopping sang me to sleep.

We'll make it in time. See, our help comes."

He was right. Villagers trickled out, a *quick* trickle this morning. They were excited, too. By ten o'clock every able-bodied adult worked, and even the children put aside studies and play for this all important day.

When the last root gave way to her axe, and while she struggled to wrench the stump from its hole, the sound of an approaching airplane drew her attention. She wiped her wet, dirty forehead with her sleeve and gazed up, realizing it would be like this on the morrow when they would all watch the skies for their plane's arrival.

A small plane actually did come into sight, cruising much closer and lower than usual for the few agricultural planes that took that route. While Anne continued to gaze skyward, the plane dropped to where she could see the pilot. He waved to her, and she waved back, wondering why he flew so low. He began to circle their village.

"Oh, no! Malinali, quick, get everyone out of the field. I think he intends to land. It must be our plane. He's early, a day early. Run. I'll try to stop him."

While the plane made its second circle, Anne rushed to move children and tools. She ran back to the airstrip, waved to him, and pointed to the stumps and many holes in the narrow stretch of rough dirt. He waved back and smiled. Did he mean to land anyway? She had to stop him. She waved him away more violently and shook her head as he descended closer and closer. He waved again.

"Don't land. We're not ready. Tomorrow. Come tomorrow," she hollered, her words lost amidst the shouts of the villagers and the sound of the plane. With a determined grin on his face, the pilot started to touch down. She watched in horror as the plane bounced all over the uneven ground. The villagers didn't understand and cheered gleefully.

She ran toward the cavorting plane, positive something terrible would happen in the next few seconds, but it still took her totally by surprise when it did. She plunged into the large hole of Ruben's stump. Her foot went down deep beside the taproot, and her chin hit hard on the ground. A pile of loose dirt slid into the hole along with her, filling her shirt and shorts and even her mouth. When she tried to climb out, her left foot wedged under the root, and she couldn't make any progress except to bring more dirt into the hole. She wiped the dirt from her eyes in time to ascertain the plane had landed safely after all, and she was the only casualty.

"A-Are you okay?" the pilot shouted and ran toward her. She suffered the most humiliating moment of her life when he stepped halfway into the hole to render aid.

"I'm fine. I can get out."

"Do you always play in the dirt like this?"

He plunged his hand down through the loose dirt, found her booted foot, and pulled it free. In spite of her protestations, he proceeded to push and drag her out of the hole. A final shove to her posterior set her free of the pit and landed her ungracefully on her hands and knees. He scrambled up and held out his hand to her, which she ignored and bounded to her feet on her own.

"That was a b-bad fall. You sure you're okay?" His gray-blue eyes reflected the daring exhibited in his landing.

"You're not due till tomorrow, tomorrow morning. We're not ready."

She refused to acknowledge the torturing throbs in her ankle. Why further broadcast her clumsiness by showing him she was in pain?

"I c-came today," he said simply, with perfect English and a slight stutter. "Do you want me to leave and c-come back tomorrow?" He slapped the dirt from his pants and gave her a teasing smile.

"Welcome to Tutlu. Look over your runway and see what else needs done to it. I have to change clothes."

In spite of twisted ankle and wounded pride, she straightened her back and exited like a true dignitary, not one limp, though the echo of her ungracious words followed her back to her tent. She peeked out only to see the villagers all group around the plane and pilot. Now, after she had done most of the work, her triumphant moment of waving him in to land would never happen on the morrow.

The thought gave her sufficient cause to stay in her tent and sulk, but instead she tossed down an aspirin with a swallow of tepid water and searched for a more attractive outfit than the one originally intended for *plane-landing* day. She had expected Fritz, or some pilot like him – a grizzled, tobacco-chewing, older man with bad teeth. This man wasn't old or bad looking. From his speech she guessed he might be from the States.

She threw on her best shorts, swallowed a second aspirin, and hurried back to the runway. The pilot gave the children turns in the cockpit while he laughed and talked with the adults. His Spanish was passable, equal with her own. All the villagers could speak that language, though their native tongue was a Mayan dialect. She hadn't yet mastered the Mayan, and only Ruben spoke English fluently, so she usually communicated with them in Spanish, too.

When the pilot saw her, he immediately came to her side. Though not a tall man, he still had a couple inches on her. He looked at her ankle, the inevitable question in his concerned eyes.

"What does the landing field need?" She picked up a medium-sized rock from the runway and threw it into the woods. "Will it work for you? Can you land here every Friday afternoon?"

"I'd t-take out that big stump you embraced earlier, so my ground crew has no more mishaps. The rest I can live with."

"We haven't leveled it all yet. You were due here tomorrow morning."

"Now I've saved everyone a whole day's w-work, and you can leave it like it is. I've seen it now. I can avoid the lumps. I land on worse all the time." He glanced around, and when she didn't render a quick answer, he called out, "Work's done. You can play now." He looked back at her and grinned. "Right?" The villagers close enough to hear laughed and spread the word to the others.

Anne was exasperated. She couldn't leave the runway like that. It wasn't *in* her to do something halfway. But she couldn't disappoint them in this their long-awaited moment of victory. She would no doubt have to finish the task herself, working a few hours every day until it suited her. She took in the pilot's cocky bearing and could tell he enjoyed the situation. He looked at her playfully. Everyone looked at her, and she felt like a slave driver.

"We'll take a break while the plane is here, but the pilot can't stay long."

"I c-can stay all night."

"Hush. Let them hear that, and they'll want to celebrate. They'll stay up all night, and I'll have no product for you to pick up on Friday."

"What product do I transport for you?"

"Fudge."

"Fudge? C-Candy? You're kidding."

"So far it's been a rather primitive operation. We've had to sell it in

5

little outlying towns on market day. But I drove to Mexico City last month and found enough customers to buy all we can make. The factory's going to ship it along with their other truck deliveries."

"Sumner Chemical factory? The place I fly for? I didn't know they did c-candy. I thought they only dealt in fertilizer and all those inedible farm chemicals."

"They ship produce, too. They ship anything they can cheat from the locals and turn into a profit. Since their planes fly directly past here on their way to the farms, I figured it wouldn't cost much to have one drop down on its way back and pick up the fudge. The plane would be empty, and our insignificant bit of fudge would be no trouble. They said to expect a plane on Friday since a pilot delivered the farm payroll that day. You're no doubt the pilot they meant."

"J-Jim Orr."

She waited, then asked, "Or who? You mean it will be Jim ... or you, one or the other of you? Or won't it be you at all?" She felt slightly disappointed.

"I'm Jim Orr – O-r-r. I'm your pilot. J-Just me. What do they call you?"

"Anne Sumner." She purposely mumbled the last name in hopes he wouldn't hear it.

"Anne *who*?"

"Anne Sumner. But you can call me Anne. Everyone does," she added, again hoping he wouldn't register the last name.

"Sumner, like Sumner Chemical? The same as the b-big boss? Mr. Money Bags? You related?"

"Sort of. He's my father. Look, I'd better ..."

"Your father? Anglin? Anglin Sumner's daughter? I know that man. He's not your father. We're talking about the same man, aren't we? Has four or five of these chemical p-plants and a corporate office building in Houston tall enough to knock planes out of the sky? Ships these poisons all over the world and buys slave labor, m-myself included? Keeps a bullwhip in his belt and dares anyone to get in his way? You mean *that* Anglin Sumner?"

"He doesn't own a bullwhip. I've never seen him with one."

"It's there, just the same. You've never been stung by it?"

"I've been stung."

"You do have his eyes, darker though." He suddenly peered past her toward where the end of the runway disappeared into the woods. "Company's coming."

"Company?"

"A vehicle. Sounds like a Jeep."

The sound grew louder, and everyone's attention turned toward the trail. Within minutes an ancient Jeep rattled into the clearing and came to a sliding stop not far from the plane. Before the dust-caked driver had time to kill the motor, a woman screamed and rushed through the crowd calling, "Isdel, Isdel." She reached the Jeep before any of the rest and tugged at the lone passenger slumped in the back.

"What is it, Zafrina?" Anne called.

"My son, Isdel." Zafrina sobbed and tried to revive the half-conscious young man.

Anne recognized the Jeep's passenger: Zafrina's oldest boy who worked at the Sumner farms some fifty-five miles west of Tutlu. He seldom made it home to the village. Jim and the Jeep's driver carried Isdel to a grassy spot in the shade, where he stretched out and groaned. He breathed noisily and with much effort, his face ashen in spite of his dark skin.

Zafrina and the driver spoke so rapidly Anne couldn't follow the entire conversation. Ruben helped by explaining, "He says Isdel's awfully sick. Flu or something. Many of the farm workers are ill, though not as bad as Isdel. To help Isdel, he took one of the farm's Jeeps and drove him here. He has to get back before someone finds out."

"How sick is he?" Anne asked the driver before he could pull away.

"He thinks he will die. He wanted to go home. I was sick, too, but I'm okay now."

"How long has there been sickness?"

"Since two days ago. It happened all at once, in the morning. I must go now."

Anne turned back to Jim and the hysterical mother who knelt beside her now unconscious son.

"I can fly him back to the factory, Anne. There's a hospital nearby. She should come with him. We'll make Isdel comfortable in the cargo area while she packs."

When the frantic mother understood their plans, she sobbed, "I can't leave."

"She has four younger children here, and her husband's dead," Anne said as she put her arm around the distraught woman. "Come, Zafrina. We'll find someone to take care of your children. I'll help you pack, and we'll pray for Isdel and for your safety."

In less than five minutes, Anne returned with Zafrina. The woman carried only a small straw basket for luggage, and Anne pressed a few bills into her trembling hand before she boarded the plane to join her son.

"Jim, I'll pay for this. If it's sickness, like the flu or some virus, Sumner won't be responsible for it."

"You shouldn't have to pay. I'll tell Sumner it's work-related. It won't cost your dad anything."

"It *would* cost him. Sumner Chemical is its own insurer. It's like pulling teeth to get them to pay claims from the fund they've set aside for that. I know. I worked in the Houston office. An argument over insurance claims prompted Dad to ship me off to work at his plant down here. I'm just thankful you're here to help us."

"I'll be back Friday for your candy." With a quick wave, he scrambled into the plane and managed an almost gentle departure in spite of the rough runway. Zafrina's pale face stared at them from the window.

Anne watched until the plane became a speck in the distance, watched until even the speck disappeared. The brash, likable pilot held her thoughts for a minute, but her concern over Isdel and other possibilities darkened her mood. Had an epidemic hit? Was Isdel's the *only* serious case? It seemed strange that everyone became sick the same morning. It didn't sound like a virus, but the driver could be wrong.

She turned to the people who stood about in small groups, quiet and uncertain. "We'll not work any more today. Tomorrow we prepare a great amount of fudge, so rest now, and please don't forget to pray for Isdel and Zafrina."

When all the people had wandered back to the village, she put on her work clothes, took up the axe, and started work on the root that destroyed her self-esteem. When that was conquered, she followed Jim's airplane tracks and worked that area as level as possible. The sun had set when she finished the job to her satisfaction.

Lace-ups and socks were shucked at the hard bank of the pond, but the rest of her clothes needed a bath worse than she did. She plunged into the dark water and swam to her favorite spot, a point that jutted out at right angles to the rest of the pond and created a secluded nook hidden from the eyes of the village. Shaded by trees on three sides, the water stayed cooler at that end. She loved to splash away the hours there.

They also kept their fish traps in that sheltered point of the lake, and sometimes Pacal, Malinali's ten-year-old son, helped with them. She had taught him how to swim and sometimes they'd enjoy the water together. Most of the others, children and adults, only waded.

When she finally swam back to the shoreline closest to her tent, Malinali walked up.

"We cook fudge tomorrow?" Malinali's English didn't compare to Ruben's, but she often tried to use it when she talked with Anne. She seemed to realize it pleased Anne to hear her native tongue at times.

"Early in the morning. We'll cook all day. And Friday morning we'll wrap it and get it ready for the plane."

"Airplane man like runway?"

"He said it was good."

"You make better. No take rest. You should ask help."

Anne hadn't wanted anyone to notice her runway work.

"I tried to clean it up – so no one would fall into that hole."

"We have big fire and music. You want come?"

"Thank you, but I'm so tired I believe I'll go to bed. Don't let them stay up too late."

"I promise. Buenas noches."

With days crammed full of physical labor, come dark Anne craved sleep, just sleep, but the villagers never failed to invite her to their nighttime gatherings. They loved their times of music and play, more frequent now as the village prospered. They were forlorn get-togethers at best but a beginning. She remembered a time of no bonfires, no music or celebration. With a full heart, she kneeled and prayed her thanks:

Thank you, Lord, that you blessed this mission so wonderfully. You took care of us when all else failed and there was no place to turn. You gave these people joy and are bringing them, one by one, into your fold. Thank you.

9

Chapter 2

The entire village rose early the next morning, ready to prepare their largest batch of fudge to date. Anne expected a trying day. At least Ruben had lit the long, narrow bed of charcoal.

"Someday, Reuben, we'll get another source of fuel for cooking."

"But God gave us all these trees – for free."

"Yes, but it takes extra work to make the charcoal, and the heat's too intense for those who tend the pots. We need stoves."

Reuben left for more charcoal, and she hurried to help with the cooking. For a while she fluttered from one operation to another: measuring, stirring, pouring, and cutting. Fudge was temperamental. But in spite of the confusion of twelve separate pots, each of which had to be removed at the perfect second, stirred until the correct instant, and finally poured and spread with the speed of lightning, it amazed her how few batches ruined.

At that instant, a large, flying grasshopper landed in the pot she stirred. Should she scoop it out and say nothing? The temptation held sway, until an eager little boy ran to look in the pot.

"Wow. That's a big bug. Come see the bug."

"It's a grasshopper," Pacal explained knowledgeably.

When half a dozen more children ran over, she gave up the pot. Within minutes, the pot was returned sparkling clean. She asked no questions. She only hoped the grasshopper hadn't been devoured with the fudge, though her old Herter's survival book claimed they tasted delicious when fried. She totally respected Herter's opinion, as her ragged copy of the book attested, but she had yet to test that bit of information.

"We've worked fast," Malinali said and continued to stir her pot. "Only one ruined batch. Twenty-five more and we can wrap them. It's only noon."

Ruben tapped her on the shoulder and drew her attention away from the huge pile of fudge.

"Hear? Jim's plane?"

"Jim? Is it Jim? He's not due till tomorrow afternoon."

"Maybe he brings news of Isdel."

"That would be thoughtful. I've been anxious."

The plane followed the exact path of its first landing and glided in smoothly, making her glad about her extra work. She, along with half the village, ran to meet him.

"I hope you're not here for the product. It won't be ready till tomorrow," she said as Jim climbed out with a wide smile and a wave for everyone.

"You have till t-tomorrow night. I stopped today because I don't make the trip tomorrow. They paid the workers early and gave them two days off because of the illness."

"How is Isdel?"

"About the same. He slips in and out of consciousness, and the doctor says Isdel's lungs are affected. I told his mother I'd check on her kids."

"They're doing fine. Have there been any other serious cases at the farms?"

"Don't think so. Looked normal there. My plane needs maintenance. Can I do that here? That'll save me a special trip back tomorrow, and you might need a professional taster – you know – someone to test the product."

"You'll have to join the rest of the kids." She pointed to the ragged assemblage, from naked baby to teenager, who now surrounded the large pots. "They all hope for the inevitable spoiled batch or broken piece. You won't taste much candy, but you're welcome to stay. And there are men here who can help you with your plane."

"I'll find one. But I don't have to start this instant. Do you want to get rid of me? Can't I help make c-candy?"

"I doubt I could stand one more untried worker. Oops! I forgot my kettle." She ran to the large unattended pot and quickly tested its temperature. "Oh, no! It'll be brick hard when it cools."

"Is it ruined?"

"Maybe not. It didn't burn. If I add water and extra butter, it may come out soft enough. Close call, though."

She yanked the pot from the fire, threw in the extra ingredients, and stirred frantically. Jim took the paddle from her and applied his own vigorous strokes to the dark, sticky mass.

"Now what do I d-do?"

"Better let me do it. Fudge making can be tricky."

"I can do it. Tell me what —"

"*That pan!*" she interrupted. "Pour it into that big pan. Quick! Scrape the sides as you go. Hurry! It has to be all at once, or it'll set up before I can spread it out."

"Ouch! It's hot."

"Here. Use a potholder. Hurry. It's setting up."

"D-Darn. It g-got me again. How do I hold it and scrape at the same time?" He fumbled the pot from side to side.

"Like this!" She jerked it from him and started pushing the fudge out onto the pan. It mounded high into an ugly, shapeless glob.

The happy cheers of the children told him his interference had ruined that batch. She sighed and looked at it in disgust.

"Can't you reheat it? Melt it again?"

"It'd come out grainy. I don't want an inferior product. It might hurt future sales."

"Where's m-my chunk?"

"Get in line."

He looked back in amusement at the long line of children awaiting their piece of the spoiled batch. Everyone laughed when he squeezed into the front of the line. When the spoiled fudge vanished and work began again, he came to her.

"Will it cost much? That ruined fudge, I mean?"

"No. We either grow the ingredients ourselves or trade with my other mission. Between the two places, we're well-supplied. The few items we don't have, we trade for in the nearest village."

"What other mission?"

"I help at Capaso, too. It's about thirty miles down that trail there. They make part of the fudge you'll pick up. Theirs is stacked in my tent."

"I know Capaso. You forget, I fly over these places all the time. But that's a Catholic village. I thought your mission was Protestant. Isn't that a conflict of interest?"

"I give both villages Jesus Christ, and there's no conflict. Neither village has a preacher or priest. Reverend Sergio comes to Tutlu twice a month, though he's terribly overworked with the care of his own missions. Padre Juan visits Capaso a couple hours each Sunday, but that's all the spiritual help they receive, outside what I can render."

"I've met Padre Juan. His church is over by the farms, isn't it? I didn't know he had any others."

"That's his home church. Capaso's a mission he takes care of. It's too poor to have a full-time priest, but we *are* building a small church there."

"Who supports your missions? Churches?"

"The Tutlu mission *was* supported by my church back in Houston; that is, they supported it while they were still thrilled with the idea of aiding a village in such dire condition. However, relieving that condition kept me too incredibly busy to go home with the glowing reports they expected. When their support dwindled to almost nothing, I kept on as best I could. That was when I found Capaso. Their squalor equaled Tutlu's, and I couldn't resist helping them, too. I never used any of the church support money, just spare time and effort, but my church discovered my heresy and discontinued all support. Hence the fudge."

"Wasn't that a might callous – deserting you like that?"

"More like a blessing. It scared me at first, but I knew I couldn't desert these people. I surveyed the natural products of the two villages and found our answer: fudge. Who would have thought something so simple would work? A fudge factory."

"You can't call a few blackened pots and a campfire a fudge factory, Anne. Candy factories have stainless steel sinks and smooth counters, not log platforms."

"The log counters work nicely and were free. And it isn't every fudge factory that has an airplane come pick up their product. I think we've become pretty high-class. Now we need to clear a landing field in Capaso."

"Maybe there's a place to land without any clearing."

"You could never land there. Absolutely."

"I can land anywhere. Let's go there now and have a look-see. Come on."

"I can't leave now."

"Sure you can. Give them a chance to run things. What will happen when you find a third village and don't have time for them anymore?"

"No. No more villages. I know my limitations."

"Do you now?" He gave her a searching look. "Well, if you won't fly now, my plane needs a couple of hours of work. Let's make a mechanic of you."

"Who do you think maintains that old truck most of the time?"

"Good. Let's get started. You can hand me tools and stay clean."

After a few minute's labor, Jim looked around at her studiously. "You don't look like him," he finally said.

"Who?"

"Anglin Sumner. He flew in yesterday. Some kind of mess in Honduras he had to look into. I heard him ask whether Anne had been b-by the factory. He meant *you*. I realize that now. I'm surprised he'd help in something like this – the shipping, I mean. But you *are* his daughter. All I'm saying is ... evidently he's not what he seems."

"He's exactly what he seems. There's not a subtle bone in his belligerent body. And I pay for this shipping. He doesn't know I'll ship through him. *Does* he?"

"Sure he does. Why would it matter?"

"Because he disapproves of me. He considers my work the biggest joke in the world. My sister and brother have lush offices back in his Houston complex and rake in the dough. I'm one step from being disowned. That's why I didn't want him to know about my distribution plan, though he makes a profit from it. I hope the warehouse manager made the money angle clear to him."

"I'm s-sure he did, but I heard Anglin brag about your business venture. He said, 'The next time I come down here she'll be shipping national. She's like me. Everything she touches turns to gold.' That was *you* he spoke of, Anne."

14

"I ... I can't believe that."

"Those were his words, not m-mine. Maybe you *should* ask him for help."

"I'd never ask. And he'd never give it."

"Well, 'scuse me, ma'am," he said with a pronounced southern accent. "Y'all don't need ta get yoh back all up." The perfect drawl mocked her. "I reckon we'uns bettah mosey unto safah ground, foh yoh send me home with no dinnah."

"How'd you do that? You didn't even st-stu ..."

"Stutter? Were you trying to say stutter? Must be contagious."

"I'm sorry."

"Ye mustna' blame yersel', koind leddy." He grinned at her and continued with the new brogue. "Ef I pretend ta be onyboody ither than mysel', I niver fret ma talking. My tongue is always riddy for onythin."

"Scots?"

"Of coorse."

"That's amazing."

"N-Not so very. I stuttered so badly when I was a boy, my parents enrolled me in an acting class in hopes it'd help."

"Did it?"

"It showed me two things – that I could memorize anything I read and that I could keep from stuttering if I played the part of someone with an accent. After a while I lost my stutter totally."

"B-But you s-stut ..."

"There you go again. I told you it was contagious. Speak up. I'm n-not ashamed of it. Yes, I stutter at times now. It came back when I piloted in the Gulf War."

Full of interest, she waited to hear more.

"The close calls in the air didn't bother me, but, when I lost two friends on the ground, my old stutter returned. It just came. I don't know why. The m-military lacked sympathy regarding my problem."

"Couldn't you have pretended you were back in acting class?"

"Too late. Everyone knew I had no accent. My superiors felt I might be misunderstood over the radio, so I was grounded for the duration. If it hadn't gone on my record, I'd be flying a jet instead of crop dusting here in no-man's land."

"That's so unfair. Do you work solely for my father?"

"I'm on his payroll, but I work for a few other places around here, on the side. I make deliveries and spray for them. Hey, someone called you."

"It's Malinali. I'll run see what she wants."

Anne returned shortly. "They're wrapping the fudge. They want to finish today so they can play tonight."

"Great idea. Let's have a fiesta. You get to work and help me."

"Sorry, I'm needed now."

"You think you are. I bet we could fly over to the coast right now, have a great time, and come back tomorrow for the fudge."

"That would never work. I have to be here."

He looked at her doubtfully.

"Once, during fudge-making time, I drove a child to the medical clinic. I was gone only a couple days, but it caused disaster. The men carried the fudge, and anything else they could find, to market and traded for pulque. A week went by before they'd all straggled back to the village and two weeks before we had any fudge to sell."

"Weren't they remorseful? Will you never trust them again?"

"How can I? No one stands up to the troublemakers and drinkers. Everyone goes along, afraid they'll miss the fun."

"But what if something happened to you? If they don't learn to rely on themselves, this will all go back like before."

"Not everything."

"Everything. They'll turn your fine log outhouses into charcoal to trade for pulque."

"They might at that, but those aren't outhouses. They're bathrooms. Come see."

"You mean there's a septic tank here?"

"Of a sort. It was one of my first projects. I bought empty, fifty-five-gallon drums from the Sumner warehouse, dug a long, deep trench for them, and laid them end-to-end. There's about two feet of dirt on top."

"A lot of digging."

"The digging was easy, compared to cutting tops out of metal drums with chisel and hammer. It's not a great sewer system, but at least it's a safe distance from their drinking water."

16

"Does your drinking water come from that pond?"

"I like to think of it as a *small lake.* Come, I'll show you around." She couldn't contain her eagerness. They rarely had visitors.

"We get our drinking water here, where the spring seeps out. It's above the level of the lake and can't be contaminated. We use the lake water to wash clothes, water the crops, and flush the toilets."

"Then you have running water?"

"Y-yes."

"Where's your pump and generator?"

"It's a different kind of *running water*. See those plastic drums on top the bathhouse? Well, we *run* to the lake, fill our buckets, *run* up that ladder to the roof, and pour the water into those drums. A hose runs from the drums to the toilets and lavatories. That's our *running* water. It takes plenty of running to keep it going. And now I have to *run* back to our fudge, or we won't have a shipment this week."

"I didn't hear anyone call you."

"I thought you wanted a fiesta. It'll require preparation, you know."

"Get to work." He shoved her off in the direction of the outdoor kitchen and called after her, "I'll get my own help."

A short time later, she noticed the children had left their stations at the fudge pots and had gathered around the plane, along with a good many of the men. The sound of cheers drifted her way, followed by the unmistakable sounds of a scuffle. She ran to the circle of bodies that enclosed the scene and discovered Ruben and Jim struggling in the dirt, literally ripping each other apart. Heavy punch followed heavy punch as they tore into each other – a violent fight that registered no malice.

The spectators all laughed, but she couldn't understand the amusement. She shoved her way to the front for a closer look. The two men regained their feet and resumed pounding each other. Drenched in sweat and dirt, with his shirt half ripped off, Jim dove at Ruben and sent them both sprawling in the dust again.

"Ruben! Jim! Stop! What on earth are you doing?"

They looked around startled. Jim's hand darted out and took something from Ruben's shirt pocket as the two men pushed away from each other and stumbled to their feet. They stood at attention before her, suddenly two long-lost brothers. Ruben had his arm across Jim's shoulders, and they both smiled ludicrously.

"What's the matter?" she asked.

Jim straightened still more and replied, "He t-took my ... my ..."

"Hat. I take his hat," Ruben helped out.

He pointed to Jim's hat on the ground and gracefully stooped and picked it up, placing it on Jim's head. They both turned simultaneously and walked off together, arms thrown carelessly over each other's shoulders.

The bottle of liquor hadn't eluded Anne's eyesight; neither had the new bulge in Jim's hip pocket. She wanted to laugh. On the other hand, she hated the stuff and couldn't abide another temptation for her villagers. To make matters worse, other men followed them into the woods. A larger scuffle threatened.

With no time to be ladylike, she ran swiftly toward the retreating backs and snatched the bottle. The villagers immediately stood back and grinned. She had won. They wouldn't cross her. But Jim was a different matter. Fun and determination spread over his face as he started toward her. She turned and ran, startled he would dare.

He was close behind when a hole tripped her, for the second time, and she fell flat on her face. Jim simply sat on her and held her left arm in a loose hammerlock behind her back. The villagers laughed, Jim laughed, but she still had the bottle in her right hand underneath her. She managed to loosen the cap and let the liquid leak onto the ground. She felt it soak into her shirt but didn't care. When Jim reached under her to reclaim the bottle, she gave it to him, then lay there on the ground and laughed hysterically.

The smell of burnt fudge assailed everyone's nostrils at the same time. Muddy and reeking of whiskey, she jumped to her feet and rushed to the fudge. All the ladies had left the pots to join in the fun. Quick work saved half of it, but six batches overcooked, two of which burned so badly the pots would require tedious scouring. She still laughed, in the midst of this new calamity, and couldn't resist squeezing more fun from it.

"These would have been our last batches, but now we're short. We might as well start twelve more. There won't be time for anything tonight except wrapping." A groan followed her announcement and told her how much they had been looking forward to the night's festivities. "Or," she hesitated until there was silence, "or we can use these overcooked batches for our fiesta tonight. It will take about six of you to wrap the rest of the fudge that goes to market, and the rest of you get meat, vegetables, fruit. Hurry. Ruben, you help Jim with his plane, and don't steal his hat again."

Jim walked over to her. "Judging from the shock on their faces, I don't believe their ruler ever loosened up that much before."

"I'm not a ruler. I'm a ... friend."

"Yeah? Convince *me*, Anglin Sumner's daughter. Better go change clothes." He looked wryly at her alcohol-soaked shirt. "Preacher might come today."

A couple hours later, when Jim wandered back to the cooking site wiping his grease-covered hands on a rag, she commented, "I didn't realize they could move so fast. Maybe I should have a fiesta every fudge day."

"Now you're talking. Everyone's not as strong-natured as you. Some people need fun. Sanitation and education are important, but they need to laugh, too."

"Jim, I do more than that." She couldn't keep the hurt from her voice. "When I first came here, they didn't even eat regularly. The men drank every chance they could get. There was no laughter, no music, no dancing. They lived in drunkenness, sickness, and poverty. No one in the village even owned a blanket for warmth at night."

"I'm sorry. I didn't mean it like it sounded. What I'm trying to say is, maybe *now* it's time to fiesta."

"And what makes you think we don't fiesta all the time?"

"Ruben told me. He said sometimes the people have music at night, but you never come. He said you never play; you work, work, work. You sleep, you get up, and you work – sometimes all day, sometimes all night."

"I don't ask *them* to work all the time. I should be allowed to choose how I spend my own time."

"I'm through with the plane," he said, changing the subject. "What can I do?"

"Get some fish for the fiesta. Help Pacal check the fish baskets."

"Fish baskets?"

"Basket traps. I made them myself, modeled them after ones in my Herter's book. There's a log raft over there, and each basket has a float marker. Pacal knows what to do, but remember, he's only ten. His mother doesn't want him to drink."

"You're snooty. And condescending. Did you know that? You may be out here in the jungle, dirt on your nose and sweating like a pig, but you're still snooty ... Surely there aren't any fish in that puddle."

"It's stocked with bass, catfish, and trout. It *was* only a puddle, but thanks to a natural depression below the spring, it's a small lake now. We cleared brush from it and dammed up that narrow point down there. We're still adding to the dam to make it stronger."

"That's a big thing to pull off. How long did you say you've been here?"

"Two years. But we've accomplished more than that. Things were in a pitiable state here when I first found them."

"How *did* you find them? They're totally hidden here in these mountains. How would *anyone* find them? Why'd your church send you to a spot like this?"

"I sent myself. When I worked in Dad's plant here, I rode in the company helicopter back and forth to the farms. The pilot often dropped down to villages for cocoa beans and vanilla beans. I saw the terrible poverty of this village."

"And you were looking for a cause."

"Definitely not. But I couldn't look away when confronted with one."

"Who flew the helicopter? Fritz?"

"He's the only one they let fly it."

"They let me. I'm a better flyer than Fritz, and ... and he's a drunk and a lady's man to boot. Did he ever make a pass at you?"

"Of course. I may have dirt on my nose and sweat like a pig, but I'm still a charming pig. Now go find some fish. I have work to do."

Meat soon roasted over the last of the coals from the fudge making, and tortillas kept warm in a large, earthen canister. Small pumpkins and fresh ears of corn awaited roasting, and a nearby log table held an inviting display of oranges, papayas, mangos, and avocados. On one end of it, sat a massive pile of irregularly-shaped chunks of fudge the children had cut by themselves. A pot of coffee by the fire sent out its fragrance.

Jim looked in wonder at the banquet spread out for the evening's feast.

"Wow! Where did it all come from?"

"We either grow it, trade with Capaso, or buy it with fudge money."

When twilight fell, a central bonfire and lamps on the food table provided light. A rickety guitar and a couple of handmade drums comprised the extent of the villagers' musical possessions, but those did their best to lend a festive air to the gathering. Merry laughter and talk filled the air, and some danced. Jim joined the latter group, doing his best to keep time with the sometimes erratic beat. That sight delighted everyone, and the sounds of revelry increased to a low roar.

Anne envied his naturalness. She could never unbend that far. She could work for them, nurse them, teach them, and pray for them, but she couldn't play with them. She saw it as her lack, not theirs. Finding it difficult to stay awake, she silently slipped away to her tent.

Weariness racked her body, but her plans for the remainder of the night afforded her only a few minutes rest. Fully dressed, she dropped onto her cot and fell asleep instantly. Less than an hour later, Jim's voice called from her tent door. She didn't stir, not even when a flashlight beam searched the tent's interior, but, when she heard his footsteps retreat, she groggily pulled herself from the cot.

During what remained of the night, she would replace those ruined batches of fudge. Her small cooking fire couldn't be seen from the village, and earlier that evening she carried all the necessary supplies into her tent. The hours that followed whirled by in an exhausting rush. At two in the morning, she placed the empty pots aside for washing and started on the wrapping. She knelt on the tent floor for that backbreaking work and doubted she would ever be able to straighten again.

The odor of coffee and roasted meat wafted on the early morning air, and a soft hum of music still came from the village. The henequen net across her doorway swung open, startling her, and Jim stepped in burdened with food.

"You've worked long enough. I brought the fiesta to you. Some of this is hot, so stop now and eat."

"Thank you. I don't have much left to do. How did you know I was awake?" She took the plate of roasted meat and breathed deeply of its rich smokiness.

"I've checked on you five times. I decided enough was enough."

"It's our first shipment. It shouldn't be short. But I didn't want to ruin the fiesta and quell their excitement."

"Do you do this sort of thing often?" Reproving eyes, dark gray in the lamp's dim light, searched her face as she sat cross-legged on the floor eating with her fingers.

"What? Make fudge? Yes, every week." She licked her fingers innocently.

"You know what I mean. You ..."

"This tastes wonderful. I didn't realize how hungry I was. I'm glad you didn't bring any fudge. I've seen enough for one day."

"That was all gone, even before you were."

"There, I've eaten the hot food. Now I've got to finish this wrapping before I fiesta any further. I'll enjoy it more if the work's done."

"Let me help."

"We'd get in each other's way. Anyway, I had your help once today. Remember?"

He didn't argue but sat back on her cot and rummaged through her books. Herter's drew his interest first. He leafed through it and now and then read something aloud. When he had exhausted that book, he took up her Bible.

"Where's the best place to read?"

"In your airplane, possibly."

"Very cute." He pulled some slips of paper from the Bible and started to read them.

"Those are private." She reached for them, but he pulled away from her.

"Nope. Nothing's private. You're a public servant. No skeletons in *your* closet."

"I don't even have a closet. But some of those papers have personal thoughts."

"But if they're *your* thoughts, why'd you need to write them down? They were already in your head. You must have written them down so others could share them."

"I wrote them down to remind *myself*, because noble thoughts aren't always there in your brain when you need them."

"Ah. *Noble* thoughts. Since they're noble, you'll of course want to share them, being a public servant and devoting your life to helping and bettering people like me."

Anne threw up her hands in despair. "Go ahead, read away. Help yourself."

Grinning easily, he leaned back on her cot and examined all her notes. When he ran out of slips of paper, he flipped through her Bible.

"You don't have any aviation magazines lying around anywhere, do you? Any good mysteries? Reading material's about as scarce as money in this neck of the woods. I used to spend all my spare time reading."

"Sorry."

"Anything about planes in here?"

"I don't remember any reference to airplanes in the Bible. Maybe something on flying. Try the concordance in the back." When she saw his look of helplessness, she showed him where to look and went back to her work.

Minutes later his voice reminded her of his presence.

"I've found some. Let's see, 'dead flies cause,' ump um, wrong k-kind of fly. Ah, here's one, 'he did fly upon the wings of the wind.' Find that one for me."

"It's in Psalms. Look for the number they show."

"Come on, Preach. What's more important, that fudge or me?"

She took the Bible and quickly found the place. "Here it is, in Psalms, like I said."

He read aloud, "'He bowed the heavens also, and came down: and darkness was under his feet. And he rode upon a cherub, and did fly: yea, he did fly upon the wings of the wind.' I like that, 'fly upon the wings of the wind.' And here, too, 'He made darkness his secret place; his pavilion round about him were dark waters and thick clouds of the skies.' He's got it right. That's how it is when you fly at n-night. Who said it?"

"David, King David. He wrote most of the Psalms."

"He must have flown."

"Not that I know of."

She worked on while he continued to search the pages of her Bible. The thought pleased her. In a short while he again broke the silence.

"Listen here, 'For by thee have I run through a troop; and by my God have I leaped over a wall.' That's still David, isn't it? I like how he talks."

"I'm through wrapping. I'll put these pans to soak by the lake and finish my feast before I turn in. You'd better get some sleep, too. I don't want you to fall asleep in the cockpit and wreck your plane with all our fudge aboard. It's already three o'clock."

When she returned, Jim was gone, along with her Bible and one of her candles.

She laughed to herself. His taking the Bible somehow cheered her. His interest in it seemed genuine, and he had gone straight to some of her favorite passages. Remembering his fight with Ruben over the bottle of liquor, she decided he was an interesting heathen. He displayed such enormous confidence in himself, and yet another side of him peeked out at times.

Chapter 3

The sun shone brightly when she stepped from her tent the next morning, but the village slept on. She noted the amount of wood sacrificed to the night's festivities and decided to replenish some of it while waiting for the village to awaken.

With no other fuel available, they could never get ahead, so she chopped wood every morning before the day's heat became extreme. She had split only a few chunks when she saw Jim climb from his plane. Proud of her adeptness with the axe, this boded a great opportunity to show off. Long ago she had learned that accuracy and technique played a more important part than strength, though she certainly wasn't weak and was even a wee bit vain about her athletic shoulders and arms. Quickly choosing a dry, short log with straight grain and no knots, she made ready to bring the axe down the instant Jim came near.

"Let me try a hand at that. You shouldn't do it. It's a man's job."

"I do this all the time. This is my last one. Then you can have the axe if you like."

She brought the axe down on the wood and split it crisply. While she split the two halves into quarters, a vile plot formed in her mind.

"Time for me to pay for my dinner," Jim said and grasped the axe.

Anne innocently glanced at the pile of log rejects, *unsplittables,* the village had dubbed them. "I'm working on this pile over here, if you want to try your hand at it. But it's not necessary, honestly." She winked at a couple men who had walked up.

She watched him position a log on the chopping block. She winced as he brought the axe down with enough force to lift his feet off the ground. The axe dented the log and bounced off. He tried again, and again, and finally managed to split it into ragged halves. His face had turned red and he sweat profusely. Like magic, a ring of men surrounded him, all with expectant grins.

Anne knew she'd assigned him the pile of knotted and lightning-struck log sections they had all abandoned, but who could resist tricking someone so cocky? Afraid she would laugh out loud, she drifted away to watch from a distance. Amazingly, he finished the chunk and reached for another. Self-reproach assailed her, and she wandered back to join the growing ring of spectators. She was pondering how to confess the hoax when he looked up at her.

"I guess I'm not as good as I thought I was," he said humbly. "I'd better practice awhile. I'd hate for a woman to beat me at anything like this."

She looked around at all the smiling faces and couldn't bring herself to ruin their fun. She left again, only to come back an hour later and find him still at it. Each time he brought the axe down, they cheered as if they watched a bullfight. Only a few chunks remained. He showed his exhaustion but didn't stop. When he started on the last log, she cheered along with the rest as blow by blow he conquered it, but she quickly slunk away to her tent after that.

From her tent door, she watched him shed shoes and shirt at the lake bank and dive into the water. She ventured out and dared call from the water's edge, "There's something I must tell you."

"I can't hear you. Come on in."

He didn't need to ask twice. She slipped off her shoes and leaped ungracefully into the water. Swimming all the way around the lake, she took her time getting to him.

"I see you swim as admirably as you chop wood."

"I swim all the time. It's the only way to fight this heat."

"I'll bet you built this lake for yourself, not for the villagers at all."

"I'm afraid you've found me out. And that's not all I'm guilty of."

"Really?"

"Those logs you split were discards, logs nobody could split without rattling all their teeth loose. You split a year's worth of rejects."

"Anne, I'm not stupid. I could see the old axe marks on them, all over them."

She looked at him quizzically and burst out laughing.

"You *are* stupid." She laughed hysterically. "You half killed yourself. You ..."

He pushed her under before she could stop laughing, and she came up coughing.

"I swallowed ... a gallon. It's all right. I forgive you. I've never learned to keep my mouth shut when I swim."

After a short, violent water fight and a brief chase, they both swam for shore. It felt good to laugh with someone. She hadn't realized how much she missed that. They had hardly dried out when it was time for him to leave.

"Would you try to get more news about this illness?" she asked as he boarded his plane. "I'm worried about Isdel and about my villages. Did the doctor diagnose it as flu? Were there other cases at the hospital besides Isdel's?"

"He said it appeared to be flu. I ... he ... Isdel's not at a hospital. Your dad arranged for a private home where his mother could stay with him. A d-doctor sees him there, the doctor who takes care of the farm workers."

"Amos Fields, you mean?"

"Yeah, Amos."

"He's not a doctor. He's a medic, a poor one at that, and my father's pawn. I've had run-ins with Amos before. Now I *am* worried. I should drive to the farms, I guess."

"Let me check first. I'll drop by and let you know if there's sickness."

The next morning she found a weighted message on the ground outside her tent. It confirmed there were no new cases of illness. After breakfast, she discovered he'd kept her Bible. The missionary part of her hoped it wasn't by accident. Relieved about the illness, she waited till after Tutlu's Sunday morning service to drive to Capaso. She stayed long enough to help make their fudge and drove back to Tutlu Monday night. Upon arrival, she learned that Jim had brought Isdel and Zafrina back, and he would come on Friday and stay over again.

At Zafrina's house, she found a pale Isdel propped up on a homemade cot. His labored breathing proclaimed the seriousness of his sickness.

"How do you feel, Isdel?" Anne asked.

"Bad here." He rubbed a thin, claw-like hand over his chest, indicative of pain.

"He sleeps all day, all night. Always tired," Zafrina added.

Anne hadn't needed that information. Tiredness was written all over the lean, slumped body, the gray face, and the listless, sunken eyes.

"It's good to sleep. He needs to build his strength back up." She felt his forehead. "He has fever. What medicine did the doctor send?"

"No medicine."

Anne went to her tent for some aspirin. When she returned, the mother brought out a small, grimy sheet of paper. It contained only a few lines of instruction, which simply said the patient should rest and take plenty of liquids. It was signed "Amos Fields." Anne seethed inside. Was Amos the only person who checked Isdel? Why had Anglin arranged for Isdel to stay in a house? Sumner Chemical couldn't be held liable if Isdel had only contracted flu.

Anne checked Isdel daily and prayed with him. His condition showed no noticeable upturn, but Zafrina refused hospital care for him. Anne didn't press it.

Friday afternoon Jim's plane hovered into sight above the trees and promptly dropped down to their runway. Welcoming cheers turned into a roar when someone broadcast that Jim had brought ice cream. It was melting, so with much hilarity everyone sat down under the trees and dug in.

"What a kind thing to do. Will you let me share the cost?" Anne asked. "Ice cream's expensive. This is a wonderful treat, an unbelievable treat."

"I didn't pay for it."

"Where on earth did you get it?"

"From the plant. That's why it's about melted. I was leaving with the payroll when I saw a room full of goodies awaiting some sort of Sumner shindig. There were drinks, cakes, cookies, and two vats of ice cream. I decided they only needed one ice cream, so I slid a vat into a black plastic trash bag and carried it out like a janitor. At the hanger, I packed it with ice from the ice machine and took off.

"Jim! I can't believe you'd ..."

"I want you to know, there came a minute when I was sorely tempted to take the ice cream and payroll and head north. That is, until I remembered I hadn't returned your Bible." He grinned and handed it to her. "So here I am. David would be proud of me."

"David? Oh, *that* David."

"Yes, *that* David. And if I hadn't had a fast plane that could 'fly upon the wings of the wind,' this confounded ice cream would have melted long before I got the payroll delivered. I would have looked like one of those jets with the white stream trailing behind, and everyone within a hundred miles would have known who stole the goods."

"I'll not tell. I'll just count it as part of the Sumner inheritance I'll never receive."

"Can I count on you to not tell one more thing?"

"*What* one more thing? Go on."

"Your dad and everyone else back there think I have a Scotch accent. I was afraid you might accidentally give me away. I used the accent to get the job. When someone sees you have a handicap, they think they can get you for less. They look down on you, too. Your dad's hard enough to work for. What would he be like if he thought I had a weakness somewhere?"

"Dad hates weakness. He'd likely use that whip. But yours isn't a weakness."

"Anglin would think so. Especially stuttering. It sounds weak, indecisive."

"I'll never tell, don't worry. Have you heard any more news about the illness?"

"Not here. There's some sort of health problem at his farms in Honduras. Heard him talk on the phone with someone about it. But nothing new here."

When night time came, she laughed with them, ate with them, and watched them dance. When Jim got up and made merry with them, she wished she could toss away her reserve and join them. She stayed until late, and, when she finally rose to slip away, Jim stepped out of nowhere. He rested his hands on her shoulders and waltzed slowly to the fast Latin rhythm of the guitar and drums. She laughed and followed as best she could, stumbling over the uneven ground and over a decidedly unwaltzable rhythm.

When they reached her tent, he followed her in and rested on the cot while she lit a couple of candles and a kerosene lamp. She picked up her returned Bible. He had used it, indeed. The pages in the Psalms section must have been turned a hundred times.

"Jim, I have some cheap Bibles here. Why don't you take one? I have too many English ones, and they're wasted. My church sent them. I tried to explain to them that few people here speak English, much less read it."

"And?"

"They said everyone should know English, and I should teach them to read it. I've managed to get some Bibles made up in their native language, and I also bought some in Spanish. Anyway, take one. They're not good quality but should last a while."

"Okay. And give me a marker for Psalms, one like those you have there."

She took her best bookmark and slid it into his Bible at Psalms.

He promptly pulled it out. "'Blessed is he that considereth the poor: the Lord will deliver him in time of trouble,'" he read aloud. "That's sweet, but don't you have something a tad more m-manly? I saw better stuff than that in there."

"I have a few more. I make them up as rewards for the children." She handed him a small pile of colorful ribbons. "Most of these aren't from Psalms."

"I want one from Psalms." He grudgingly picked up and discarded one after another. "This one's good: '... they shall mount up with wings as eagles; they shall run, and not be weary; and they shall walk, and not faint.' I'll take this one until you get something better."

"That's Isaiah."

"Who's Isaiah?"

"He's past Psalms. You'll find good books in between, too."

"I'm still working on Psalms. Can I mark this Bible up like you did yours?"

"Of course. It's yours."

He suddenly looked at her seriously. "Don't you get lonely?"

"How could I get lonely with all these people here?"

"You don't have a friend, do you?"

She raised proud, sad eyes to his and spoke impulsively. "I'm overwhelmingly lonely, every night, when I fall exhausted into my cot. It lasts about thirty seconds, and then I'm asleep because I'm worn out."

"Don't you miss your family? Your home in the States?"

"I miss the States, but I have no *home* there. I miss the ocean. And I miss my horse. I've wanted to bring him down here."

"You can't talk to a horse."

"Of course you can. And he talks back. Sometimes he's amazingly eloquent."

"If you care for him that much, you should find a way to have him with you."

"The money's needed for more important things than my whims right now. He stays at a lovely stable with green pastures all around. He's probably forgotten me."

"I doubt it. You haven't forgotten him. I know I'd feel lonesome without my plane. And it doesn't ever talk with me, that is, unless it needs repairs." He wiped his hand across his forehead. "Whew. It's hot in this tent. I think I'll take a swim. Is that permitted, or is the pool closed at this hour?"

"Of course it's allowed."

"I'll go change clothes in my plane. You'll swim too, won't you?"

"At *night*?" She tried to look aghast. "In *that* lake?"

He studied her dubiously for a minute before leaving.

In a short while, he returned to find Anne swimming about in the lake. She swam to the far end of the pool, and he followed with swift strokes.

"At night I swim ... mostly over here." She gasped and wiped water from her eyes. "It's further from the village, more private."

"So, you do swim here at night. You wanted to scare a greenhorn."

"My mistake. You obviously don't scare easily and definitely aren't a greenhorn. I swim here almost every night." The roar of an airplane overhead interrupted her words. "That's one of my father's planes. I hear them sometimes at night."

"This time of year we spray and dust heavily. When there's plenty of moonlight, we spray at night. That way we don't lose time when work's going on in nearby fields. I've passed over here many a night and looked down at your pond gleaming in the moonlight. I never imagined a beautiful siren swimming in it, or I might have dropped down sooner. Now I'll be tempted to come down for a quick dip."

"That would wake the entire village. They'd wait at the water's edge, and when you came out they'd expect a fiesta. There'd be no *quiet* dip, that's for sure."

"I'll cut my motor and glide in."

"On this terrible landing field? Wouldn't it be impossible to maneuver at night?" She half-hoped he would say otherwise.

"Piece-o-cake. You watch for me. If I don't have time to stop, I'll still drop low so you'll know it's me if you're in swimming. That's a promise."

The next hour became a magical time of gliding through shimmering water, splashing, and laughter. Midnight breezes brought the distant sounds of the fiesta accompanied by the fragrance of wood smoke.

When the village grew quiet, Anne stepped from the water with regret. "We'd better say goodnight. If the villagers have gone to bed, it's later than late."

Next morning Jim came to her tent door while she still lay in bed.

"Hey, this is no morning to play lazy. Let's check out Capaso before everyone's up. Come on. Hurry."

Quickly donning shorts and tank top, she ran out and climbed aboard his plane.

In the early light of dawn, they circled above Capaso. All her improvements showed to advantage. A picturesque, little village now nestled on the same mountainside where a squalid, depressing camp once stood. She hadn't realized its beauty until that moment and couldn't help the pride that welled up in her heart.

Jim circled the area four times and dropped low enough to terrify her.

"This'll be a tough one. See that stretch of trail there on your left? It's about half a mile below the village. I need a wider spot at the far end to taxi around. Don't want to hold up traffic, you know."

She laughed at the mention of traffic. "We'll get on it right away. Maybe both places can increase in production, though I don't know if I can make fudge six days a week and still do my other work."

"Trust them to do the fudge. They need you more in other ways."

"I ... don't know. I don't want to rush them if they're not ready."

When they returned to Tutlu, Ruben stood beside the plane with solemn mien.

"Pacal told everyone you'd run off with Jim. They decided to eat the fudge."

"What! Oh, no!" Anne stumbled in her haste to reach the ground and would have fallen except for Ruben's quick reflexes. He landed her safely and laughed uproariously.

"I kid. I kid you. The fudge is okay."

"Oh, Ruben, how could you?" And she laughed, too.

While the villagers loaded the fudge into the plane, Anne stepped aside with Jim.

"He absolutely fooled me. That's the first time anyone here has played a trick on me. I think you've been a bad example. They've learned it from you."

"They didn't learn it. They've always had it, a sense of humor, I mean. You've unbent a bit lately, and they don't find you so unapproachable."

"I'm not unapproachable," she said, her feelings wounded. "I've had no time to fraternize. I'm fighting a battle of survival."

"Maybe the battle's won. Maybe you could ease out of the front line an inch or two. I know there are forgotten villages. Your two would be among the worst, considering their location. But take it easy, or you'll break."

"I'm not breakable."

"Okay, Anne the Rock," he said as he climbed into his plane. "Have it your way. But when I tempt you to cut class, see if you can resist."

Late in the night, Anne awoke to the sound of a plane buzzing her tent. Half awake, she staggered to her tent door in time to see a plane circling for another pass. It came in low, and when it passed directly above her, a bag descended from the cockpit and landed at her feet. She stared at it only a moment before she grabbed it and rushed into her tent, lighting the lamp by her cot.

She ripped open the package and gasped at sight of a can of salted cashews and a box of chocolate-covered cherries. She cried for joy. Seated on her cot, she devoured all the nuts and most of the candy, saving only two of the chocolates for morning. She had meant to parcel the goodies out, make them last a week or two, but couldn't help herself. She stared at the last two chocolates and cried again, then popped them into her mouth. Finally, she found the note: *Psalm 78: 24: And had rained down manna ... Man did eat angels' food – Jim*

She smiled. It had surely been angels' food but there would be the devil to pay. She crawled into bed with a wonderful sick feeling and awoke Sunday morning with stomach cramps. She only smiled again.

Later that day, she drove to Capaso and learned that Padre Juan had extended his stay. He would dedicate the rustic, little church and would stay till Monday morning.

"The church is charming. How is it possible? Last week there was nothing, and now I see this delightful building, so perfect in every way," he said in his quaint, precise Spanish.

"The whole village worked. They've been eager for you to see it and are overjoyed you'll stay overnight in the little room they built for you. They'd like your permission to celebrate this evening."

"A fiesta would be fitting in such a case. I will be honored to attend for a while."

News of the fiesta caused much excitement, and Anne suddenly realized she had never made such a request of them before. She blessed Jim for his advice.

That night they outdid themselves with good things to eat. They fixed a comfortable seat near the fire so Padre Juan could join in the festivities. It felt strange to see the serious, sad-faced, little man smile and even laugh at times. He sang along with their songs as much as his asthma would allow. He had been transferred to this deserted sector because his lungs could no longer tolerate the air of Mexico City, but now he cared for two parishes and looked forever tired.

Everyone got a late start on the fudge the next morning, and Anne had to stay until Tuesday morning because they hadn't wrapped all of it. On her return trip to Tutlu, she exceeded any former speed record, anxious to see if Jim had been by. When she arrived, Pacal rushed to tell her of the newest airdrop.

Sure enough, there sat a package on her cot. She tore it open, and a beautiful mantilla tumbled out. With awe, she studied the soft, black wrap. It had been woven through with threads of silver and gold, and the same threads formed a long, rich fringe along it edges. The attached note said: *Next time dance more, but don't step in any stump holes – Jim (Psalms 68-13)*

She searched for the reference in her Bible and found: "Though ye have lien among the pots, yet shall ye be as the wings of a dove covered with silver, and her feathers with yellow gold." She was laughing when Malinali came through the tent door and rushed to admire the shawl.

"Oh. Magnificent. It is from Jim?"

"He sent it as a joke, hinting we should have more fiestas. He's teasing us."

Malinali caressed the shawl and smiled knowingly. Finally, she looked at Anne and laughed. "Yes, but he gave the mantilla to *you*."

Anne had no ready reply, so she changed the subject.

"Malinali, sometime soon I want to double our product. It'd mean maybe three days of work each week, but that should give the village a good income. I'll buy stoves, and we'll use bottled gas. That will make everyone's task easier. Will you tell me when you think everyone's ready for that?"

"Right away. We can cook more fudge right away. If we had stoves and more pots and trays, we could make three times as much and still only work two and a half or three days. Some of the men could cook, too. Even Pacal can wrap."

She surprised Anne with the enthusiasm and confidence she exuded. Overnight she had become a businesswoman.

"I believe you're right, Malinali. If we did that, everyone in the village could receive a wage, even the older children. We'd take out a percentage for improvements, and the rest of the profits could be divided so everyone had personal money to spend."

"If you do that, *all* the men will want to help. No one will work in the gardens or gather wood or build."

"Everyone would be paid for the work they do."

"Only yesterday, Xunan told me she wants to study to be a doctor. And Pacal says he will be a boat captain. It feels good to wake in the morning to our beautiful village. Songs and flowers burst out everywhere

I walk. You made these things happen."

Anne was taken aback at the praise and emotion of the other woman. "Everyone worked hard to accomplish these changes. I've simply helped get the projects started."

"You may say as you like. I know what I see. We all know." She started to leave but turned back for a last thought. "You should wear the mantilla Friday night. Wear it for Jim."

Alone again, Anne sat down on her cot and picked up the mantilla. It contrasted ludicrously with her ragged wardrobe. Arranging it on her head and around her shoulders, she waltzed over to glance at herself in the tent's small mirror. The deep blue of her eyes sparkled with a purplish cast when she turned this way and that to get the shawl's effect, but her cotton shirt ruined the end result. She rummaged through her scant box of clothes and brought out a black tank top. She laid it beside the mantilla and laughed. It would have to serve as her evening gown.

Soon another idea struck, and she dug out a piece of white sheet she'd saved for rags. She wrapped it around her, just under her armpits, tucked in the loose flap at the top, and tied a red scarf around her waist. It might pass for a strapless evening frock, but it looked strange with lace-up boots. She laughed again, slung the mantilla around her shoulders, and danced around the tent until she heard the sound of someone coming. She tore off the costume in time to greet Pacal at her tent door.

"My mother told me about the beautiful mantilla. May I see it?" Anne's little buddy asked excitedly. He smiled and ran one small, grimy finger through the trailing fringe.

"So soft. I will buy my mother one of these."

"Yes. That would be wonderful."

"Momma said to tell you they will start the fudge in the morning. They want to make more this time and want to finish quickly, so all day Friday they can fix the fiesta. Momma said to tell you that."

Anne was surprised at the sudden spark of ambition. "That sounds great. Tell her we'll start in the morning."

When Jim arrived late Friday afternoon, the fudge lay stacked and waiting. They had doubled their output and were exceedingly proud of the accomplishment. With all the laughter and singing, it had felt like a fiesta all day, though the plane's arrival marked the real beginning of festivities.

Anne rushed to change clothes. She had argued with herself for three days about whether or not to wear the shawl when Jim came. Now he had arrived, and there had been no time to change the sheet into a dress. In desperation, she wrapped it around her like a long skirt, tying it at the waist. The black tank top looked strange with it, so she exchanged it for a white one and pulled the mantilla around her shoulders. She had broken a strap on her sandals, so she went barefoot, as many of the villagers did. She felt utterly ridiculous and didn't stop to look again in the mirror. Halfway across the landing field, she lost her nerve and turned to go back, but Jim had espied her.

"A g-goddess in white. Must be a vision or altitude sickness," Jim stuttered.

"I'm wearing a bed sheet. But thanks. The mantilla didn't go with my khaki shorts."

"It certainly looks better on you than on your mattress – the sheet, I mean."

"Am I supposed to thank you for ... That was supposed to be a compliment, wasn't it?"

"It looks good. You'd likely look even cuter in the pillowcase. You could try *it* next time."

"Next time I'll stay in my tent."

"Anne, I'm sorry. Really, you look n-n-nice."

"Why do you always stutter on the wrong words?"

He promptly went into an exaggerated accent. "Ye air loike a wonnerfoo morn, all white an' guld. I'm na tae be troosted around ye, ma bonnie girlie."

"Never mind. Stutter away."

There was something different about the people that night, a certain pride, like they knew they earned their rest. She resolved to stick out the evening, no matter how tired she felt. Leaning back against a tree, she partook of the generous supply of food and watched their games and dances, amused that Jim joined them in everything. When she grew sleepy, she drank cups of scalding coffee from the blackened pot by the fire. The next thing she knew, someone was shaking her.

"You'd fallen asleep," Jim said close to her ear. "It's almost morning. I'll walk you to your tent."

"Umm. What a wonderful scent of flowers. I never smell them till I'm out here at night. Guess I'm too busy during the day to notice."

"When are you going home?" he asked after a few minutes.

"Back to the States? I ... I don't know. I never thought I'd work here forever. Do *you* plan to stay here forever? Work for my father ... *forever?*"

"Ha. Him? I hope not. But a job's a job. I'd rather work for myself, of course."

"You've got a license to fly in the States, haven't you?"

"Sure. And I go back often, on your father's business. Come with me next time."

The idea excited her. "Do you stay long? I'd like to see my horse."

"Just your horse? You must have a lovely family. They all take after Daddy, eh?"

"My sister takes after Dad, but my brother's okay, just a might weak when it comes to drink. My mother's remarried and lives in Oregon. Dad used her money to get his start and then discarded her. I keep in touch, but I don't believe she misses any of us much."

"I think I know your sister. Has dark brown hair like yours, not bad looking, but leans toward the hard side? Her name's Angel, isn't it?"

"That's what most everyone calls her. Her name's Angeline, after Dad. He wanted to name all of us after him and came as close as he could. My brother's named Anglin Fredrick, but at his choice we call him Fred. When I came along, my dad couldn't find any more variations, so I'm just Anne, the least and last of the flock."

"Well, Miss Least and Last, get things in shape so you can leave for a few days. You're coming with me the next time I fly back to Houston, if it's only to see your horse."

"I can't leave while Isdel's sick. He hasn't improved since he's been back, and I wouldn't want to be away if he needed emergency care."

"I won't make the trip for a while. We've got a heap of spraying to complete the next couple weeks. You'll hear us flying over night and day when we go to the warehouse for supplies. I'll drop down if I can."

"Remember, I'm at Capaso Sunday afternoon and Monday. We'll work on both the airfield and fudge this week in Capaso."

"I'll buzz them every time I pass. That'll stir them up. I'll drop a note and tell them we'll have a big fiesta when it's completed."

"That ... that might be a good idea."

"It's a *great* idea. I know exactly what to say. I'm taking off, now. There's enough moonlight. Remember to watch for me this coming week."

When she arrived at Capaso Sunday afternoon, half the village was out working on the landing strip. Padre Juan came to meet her as she climbed from the truck.

"I didn't tell them to work on Sunday, Padre. I'm sorry."

"Is all right. I gave them my blessing. But you misinterpreted the scripture."

"Scripture?"

"The scripture in the note you had the airplane drop." He brought out a folded sheet of paper, still tied to a rusty bolt, and handed it to her.

Anne read the large, clear words: *Clear runway, fast. Mathew 3:3 'Make his path straight.' Plan for big fiesta and airplane rides for everyone when runway is built.* It was signed *Anne.*

She laughed. "He must have used the concordance. I showed Jim how to use the concordance, the scoundrel. And now he's found the New Testament."

The priest looked at her dumfounded and added meekly, "I'd like to be here when ... I've never been in an airplane. Could ... will the fiesta be on Sunday?"

Tears streamed from Anne's eyes as she tried not to laugh. "Yes, it will be on Sunday, both the fiesta and the rides."

She told herself it would have to be Sunday. Many of Capaso's men worked on her father's farms, some twenty-five miles distant, and Sunday was their only day off. Some didn't even bother to make the tedious trip every week, nine miles of which they walked and fourteen of which they spent in the back of an open truck.

All day Monday Anne worked on Capaso's fudge and on clearing the runway. Both jobs progressed amazingly fast. Jim passed low over the trees and waved to them twice. Before leaving Capaso, she told the people about the new fudge plans. Such swift progress worried her a bit, but Jim had hoisted the idea, and Malinali had pushed it over the wall.

Late Monday she headed back to Tutlu, still tickled at Jim's *note from the heavens*. At least he used his Bible, no matter how devious his reasons. During his last visit to Tutlu, she had seen the Bible lying in his cockpit amidst a pile of scattered notes. Who would have thought his note would create such stir at the mission? And Padre Juan wanted an airplane ride! She could hardly wait to tell Jim.

The sun still burned hot when she arrived home. Twice that night she thought she heard Jim's plane, once directly after swimming and once near dawn. Evidently he was working that night.

For a few days and nights, Jim's plane and another small plane passed overhead every now and then. She could easily distinguish his plane in the daytime, even when he didn't pass low. Its polished, silver body sparkled brightly in the ever-glaring, summer sunshine. Apparently those two planes did most of the work, and Fritz probably piloted the other plane.

Thursday night Anne lay uncovered on her cot, courting sleep unsuccessfully. Though deeply tired from the long day of fudge making, the heat kept her wakeful. Usually nights were bearable, no matter how hot the days, but occasionally it didn't cool off till late. She dozed fitfully for an hour and awakened to a loud noise that registered vaguely in her half-awake brain. Abruptly her mind cleared enough to realize she'd heard a plane.

She jumped up and rushed through her tent door in time to see blinking, yellow lights disappear into a blue-black sky, too distant to identify the plane. With lamp in hand, she searched carefully the area around her tent. Jim wouldn't fly low at night except to drop something, but she found nothing. Disappointed, she returned to her tent, only to find it still uncomfortably warm. Slipping on shorts, she headed for the water to cool off.

The lake looked lonely, now that she had shared its night mysteries with Jim. Half-heartedly, she swam to her favorite end and dove below into the cool depths. When she surfaced, the air seemed full of the robust odors of nature, pungent enough to overpower the heady perfume of the jasmine. She swam and frolicked and relived that once-upon-a-time night with Jim. It seemed so long ago, but in less than twenty-four hours she might swim there with him again. The thought thrilled her. She stayed longer than usual, hopeful he might circle back, but finally gave up and returned to her tent.

All at once exhausted, she dried off and went directly to sleep. Later in the night, she awoke with a sore throat. Her clock showed two in the morning. When she sat up and reached for a drink of water, she felt dizzy. That was unusual for her because she never suffered health problems. There wasn't time to be ill, she told herself and fell asleep again.

At seven in the morning, she awoke again. Her throat, her whole mouth, burned like fire. When she sat upright, a strong nausea assailed her, and she barely made it outside in time to avoid vomiting in her tent. *Influenza* was her first thought, concern for the village her second.

"Don't come too close," she called to Ruben, who headed in her direction. "I don't feel well. It may be the flu. Can you take care of things for me today? Keep everyone away from my tent, but tell me if anyone else is ill."

She groaned over the effort those few instructions cost her and slumped weakly back to bed. The air felt too heavy to breath, inadequate for anything except sleep. Near noon she awoke but had become too dreadfully ill to get up. Abdominal cramps made further sleep impossible. While she thrashed about, a thought made itself heard over her pain – no fiesta for her that night. Disappointment rolled over her more intensely than her illness, and she realized how much she looked forward to Jim's visits. Finally, exhausted from the increasing pain, she sank into fitful sleep.

"Okay. No sleeping allowed on fiesta day," she heard through the pall of her misery. Jim had arrived. Her clock showed four in the afternoon.

"No fiesta ... for me. I've caught ... something. Don't come near." She turned her head and saw him in her tent doorway.

"It's nice to know you're concerned about me."

"You'd spread it ... to the villagers. I'd have an ... epidemic on my hands." She had tried to speak teasingly but knew she fell short, so short the last words sounded like a groan.

"All right, you've convinced me of my worth. Don't flatter me any more, or I'll get bigheaded." When she didn't come back with a ready retort, he asked seriously, "Do you need a doctor?" Ignoring her quarantine rule, he came and placed his hand on her forehead. "You're warmer than you should be but not extremely hot."

"Maybe I'll get over it ... quick. Hate to miss the fun."

"I'll bring you food."

"No. No food ... No food.

"Okay. I'll leave you alone for a while. But, if you're not better in the morning, it's the doctor for you. Can I get you anything?"

"No. But check ... if anyone's sick. If it's what Isdel has ... could be bad. He's not better."

The night hours wore on intolerably. She slept seldom, and dawn found her much worse. Too sick to wash, she attempted to put on fresh clothes, but that effort proved beyond her energy, too. She crawled back onto her cot just as Jim came through the door.

"You look worse. How do you feel?"

"Stomach cramps ... throat burning up." She stretched out and thought he was gone but abruptly felt his hand on her forehead again.

"Your skin's yellowish. Breathing heavy, aren't you?"

"Hadn't noticed," she lied.

"When did this start?"

"Thursday ... No, Friday. Early Friday morning ... woke with a sore throat."

"Tell me what to pack. You're going to a doctor."

"It's a bug. I'll be ... well tomorrow."

"That's fine. Tomorrow you can be well. Today you go to a doctor."

Too sick to argue, she groaned and rolled over on her side with her back to him. Sounds of his poking around in her tent registered hazily in her mind before she drifted off to erratic sleep again.

The next thing she knew, he had lifted her from the cot, blanket and all. She stared up at his stern face.

"Jim, I ..."

"Hush. Save your strength. I took your bag to the plane."

Too weak to argue, too weak to hold on, she let him take her to the plane. He slid her into the passenger seat and strapped her in, tucking the blanket around her. In another minute, she felt the plane lift off and knew she wouldn't enjoy *this* ride. Slumped down in the seat, she fell asleep but awoke at times when someone adjusted her position. Once she thought someone gave her oxygen, but it was all vague, more like a dream.

Sometime in the day, or was it the night, she was carried on a bed. She saw a plane and yet not a plane or not Jim's plane. Once Jim knelt beside her and assured her he was the one piloting her.

She asked no questions and didn't care where she was being taken.

The next time she roused, she was being carried on a bed again, or was it a cot? It tipped crazily, and she wondered why she didn't fall out.

"Where?" she gasped in barely a whisper.

"We're in Houston, at a hospital," Jim explained. "Don't talk."

She didn't want to talk. When they carried her into the medical facility, she wondered, foggily, if hospitals came in all sizes. The blur of people coming and going, the constant pain in her abdomen, and the torture of being turned this way and that all faded at times into periods of darkness. Finally the darkness took sway.

Chapter 4

Sometime later she awoke again. A doctor stood beside her bed, Dr. Wildermuth, according to his name tag.

"Do I ... have the flu?"

"We're still assessing your condition. We know that your liver and kidneys are affected, but we think we have those under control."

"My arms, hands," she paused for a breath, "y-yellow."

"That's to be expected, but they're better today." He listened to her heart with his stethoscope. "Take a deeper breath."

She tried and coughed. "It's ... not easy to ... breathe."

The doctor left, and within minutes a nurse came in and raised her bed to a semirecumbent position. It helped.

Time sank into vagueness again. In what may have been days, or only hours, Dr. Wildermuth stood there beside her bed again. She looked up at him questioningly.

"You've had damage to the parenchymal cells in your liver and tubule cells of your kidneys. We believe we caught those problems in time and damage is minimal."

"I can't breathe."

"Your lungs are affected, of course. We're trying to arrest that condition. If it becomes worse, we'll put you on oxygen."

"What day is it?"

"Tuesday. You were brought here on Saturday. This is your fourth day at the hospital. You're doing well, under the circumstances."

"Four days? Isn't that ... long for a virus?"

"I'm putting you on new medication." He didn't answer her question but wrote on his sheet and left the room.

Shortly after the doctor left, Jim stepped into the room.

"It's about time," she said, so faintly she could barely hear her own voice.

"Shh, I'm not allowed in here. I've waited for a chance."

"Am I so sick?"

"You're sick. How do you feel?"

"My stomach's ... bad, and it's hard to ... talk." She laid a hand on her chest, signifying the problem.

"Still not breathing well?"

She nodded.

"Don't try to talk. I'll be here in Houston a while. I'm piloting your dad's jet for the time being. I'll check in on you later."

"The villages? The fudge?"

"Fritz will make the pickup. Don't worry. It's good for them to try things on their own. If they fail, you can pick up the pieces when you're well."

"Is there sickness?"

"Haven't heard anything about Tutlu. I'll see what I can find out."

"It's strange being back ... in the States. Not how I envisioned ... my trip home. Does ... does my father know?"

"He had you brought here. He's paying for this."

"I must get up ... find work to pay him." A sense of urgency overwhelmed her for a second. "I can't owe him."

"Sure. Let's go out and get you a job. Where'd you put your clothes?"

She smiled weakly. "Okay. I'm beat ... for now."

"I'll be back. Rest."

The next morning the abdominal pains subsided, though her lungs remained the same. She tried to sit up but could endure it for only a minute. Later that day, when she had the room to herself, she attempted to walk around the bed. After a couple of shaky steps, she collapsed on the floor and had to rest there a good while before she could pull herself to her feet.

A nurse came in at that moment and helped her climb back into bed. She stared at the unsympathetic ceiling while her thoughts cried out in anguish, over and over again: *When will I be well? Where is God?*

The week wore on, and sleep consumed twenty-two hours out of every twenty-four. Her few minutes of wakefulness were spent in extreme apprehension over the villages. She must do something, help them if they needed help, but there was no strength in her. Desperately, she struggled to stay awake but would inevitably fail, only to awaken later in a deep abyss of guilt. At times, the mental torment made her wish she could fall sleep and never rouse again to the worries of this world.

She missed two of Jim's visits, found only a note saying he hadn't wanted to wake her. If anyone else had visited, they left no word. Desolate loneliness consumed her, yet she dreaded seeing anyone she knew, with the exception of Jim. How could she converse with her sister or brother? And she would rather die, right then and there, than face her father in her present state of weakness.

When she discovered a notepad and pen Jim had left for her, she felt wretched, indeed. Evidently he planned for her to write, not talk. Discouraged and discomfited at her invalid state, she forced herself to be more active. Three times she tried to stand and take steps. Each time she grew faint and suffered terrible weakness. She noticed slight improvement in her body's adjustment to less oxygen, but drawing in that oxygen exhausted her more quickly than anything else.

When she missed a third visit of Jim's by being asleep again, she took the notepad and began to scribble thoughts and words she wanted to say to him:

Please wake me. I don't want to sleep my life away.

I can't seem to help myself.

It's strange, this disease I have. It feels similar to how it is when you've driven for a long, long time, and your eyes won't stay open no matter what you try. And the back of your neck, your head, your entire body becomes numb with drowsiness. You think how delicious it'd be to close your eyes for an instant, to let happen what may. Even if you slammed over an embankment, or smacked into a tree, you wouldn't feel anything because you'd already be deep in sleep. And the temptation lingers. It travels up around your groggy mind, until you suddenly remember your duty.

You remember the passengers, who trust you with their lives, and you remember those in the other vehicles, whom you might endanger. You remember the friends and acquaintances of those people, who would also be affected if you gave in to your weakness. And last of all, you remember the ones who love you, if you are so lucky, the ones who would sorrow over your passing.

So you struggle on, and slap yourself in the face, and look for a place to pull over and snatch a few minute's rest before you go on. And you go on ... and on ... and on, because you must.

I'm working hard, so very hard, to go on, to conquer this. I'm tottering on the brink, and if I stop fighting, it will consume me. I want to be awake. I want to talk with you. I must talk with you. I must know what's going on. I won't let the villagers' hope be destroyed by ...

She fell asleep while still writing, but Jim sat beside her bed when she awoke, and the page of thoughts had been removed from her notebook. Glancing up at him, she saw an edge of paper sticking from his shirt pocket. She had meant to rewrite it into an actual letter before giving it to him. It had no salutation or signature, but he knew it was his. She sighed and felt satisfied. He hadn't tried to wake her but had waited for her to waken on her own.

"I must leave here. I need money. Have to find ... work somewhere."

He only nodded and patted her hand. He sat beside her bed, saying nothing, and soon she fell asleep again.

He visited twice again and woke her both times but never mentioned the letter. By the end of the week, she insisted the hospital release her. She deplored getting further in debt to her father, and there didn't seem to be any progress in her condition. Besides, there were less expensive places to rest than a hospital bed.

The doctor, still noncommittal, evaded every question about the longevity or seriousness of her illness but finally agreed to release her on Monday morning, her tenth day in the hospital. Jim picked her up in a company car.

"Thank you for coming." During her hospital stay, she had learned to halt every few words or talk at a snail's pace, if she wanted to talk at all. Her entire life must run slowly.

"Where to?" Jim asked sternly, obviously disapproving of her release.

"Sumner Chemical. I hate it, but I have to see my father. I left word I was coming."

"Good. I planned to take you there no matter what you said. Now we won't have to argue."

During the ride, she rehearsed a dozen different speeches for when she came face to face with her father. Too proud to let him witness her breathlessness and fragility, she must somehow conquer it, no matter what the cost in pain. She dreaded the impending meeting more fiercely every moment and wished Jim would slow down.

When they pulled into the large complex, she didn't recognize it. Not sure at first what was different, she finally realized the old apartment building next door was gone, and Sumner had expanded into that region.

"Dad must have bought the adjoining property," she said slowly. "He bullied the owners for years to sell out. They would have been glad to, if Dad had offered a decent price. Guess he finally persuaded them."

She tried to walk tall and straight as she entered the impressive building, so familiar yet so different. Anglin wasn't there but had left word her old job awaited her if she wanted it. She could take it easy and work as much or little as she liked. Anglin's secretary handed her a sheaf of papers denoting what her father wanted accomplished. A glance through the detailed sheets confirmed she was no charity employee. She would be her own boss and have her own office. That satisfied her immensely.

Once outside the intimidating reception office, she hugged the wall for support and could have cried in thankfulness. She looked up at Jim happily. "I have a ... job, my old job, public relations. I'll show you my office. Could you bring me that elevator over there?" She tried to laugh at her joke, but the laugh sounded pitifully weak.

"Anyone can see you're running on sheer nerve. I can carry you, Anne. There's no shame in it."

"Shh! Someone might hear. I can make it."

She took his arm for support and held tight until they reached her office. When Jim closed her door behind them, she collapsed onto a short, puffy sofa that sat across from her desk.

"So much for a job, though I'm disappointed in your dad. I expected a more fatherly response or at least a charitable one. You haven't seen him since you've been back, have you?"

"He doesn't want to see me any more than I want to see him."

"You're not fit to work. Where will you live?"

"Here, in this room. I have no belongings. I'd be too tired to go back and forth to an apartment. If anyone complains, I'll flash my ... name in their face. I'm not proud of it, but I'm ... still a Sumner."

"Don't talk so fast. Take it easy. How can you stay in this office? Just a room?"

"It's bigger than my tent, and it has a bathroom and shower ... luxury to a girl from Tutlu. Besides, I move slowly now. It will take twenty-four hours a day to accomplish eight hours of work. I know what he wants done. I'm to run his new campaign to make Sumner look good to the rest of the world. It's a public relations job requiring loads of advertising. He hasn't made the effort since I worked here before. I guess he's ready to boost his image."

"I don't think you're up to it. It exhausted you to *say* all that."

"I'll do it. I won't be sick ... forever. I'll save money, fast, and get back to Mexico. Just don't tell Dad I'm not a long-term employee."

"All right, I'll help you play your game, against my better judgment. And don't you forget I'm a different Jim from the one you knew at Tutlu. At Sumner, my Scots heritage will be more prevalent." He winked at her.

"You mean your accent? How do you remember to keep it up all the time?"

"I don't, but no one's noticed so far. Guess they think I'm becoming more Americanized."

"Someone's bound to ask you questions about where you're from."

"Sure, but that's no problem. My mother was born in Scotland and had a heavy brogue. I lived there for a while, too."

"If you fly back to Mexico for any reason, will you check for sickness in the village and look in on Isdel? I believe I have the same illness. I hope it doesn't last as long for me."

Jim stared out the window for a minute, and she thought he wouldn't answer. Finally, he met her eyes and said, "You're tough. You'll make it. Can I get you anything for your new apartment?"

"Could you sneak my bag up here? And maybe a pillow and blanket? The office kitchen should have food, but I have this unbearable craving for fast food. A hamburger. I'll pay you back with my first paycheck."

"I'm not Anglin Sumner, Anne."

"I'm sorry. Here, take these and make copies. They're keys to the building and to my office. I'll tell the watchman you're to come and go as you please."

"Ah! The power has gone to your head."

"Of course."

"Well, don't bother to tell anyone anything. I already come and go as I please, and I can get any keys I want."

"Ah! The power has gone to your head, too. I guess they've grown lax around here. In that case, my door will be locked most of the time. I intend to sleep around the clock without interruption. Give me a warning tap before you let yourself in."

"How about an SOS – ditty dit, da da da, ditty dit."

"Rather tedious, don't you think? How about just the *S*, you know, for *Sumner*?"

"Okay, Miss Ditty Dit. I'd better leave before you make me a doorman. How do you want your hamburger, Miss Sumner?"

"Big."

"And do you need clothes? Remember, I packed your suitcase. You're wearing the only outfit suitable for this office."

"I left a box of clothes in my tack room where my horse is stabled. They may not all be out of style."

"We'll worry about it tomorrow. Don't get up. I'll lock the door behind me."

Tired to death, she tried to realize she was actually back in Houston and part of the corporate scene again. Nothing seemed real, not even the semi-luxurious room. She curled up on the too-short sofa and never stirred until "ditty dit" sounded at her door, waking her from a sound sleep. She struggled to a sitting posture while Jim deposited a hot, weighty bag, fragrant with promise of burger and fries, on her lap.

"Um, it smells wonderful. I can now appreciate being back in the civilized world. You can't imagine how good it is to be out of the hospital."

"You have an appointment with Dr. Wildermuth tomorrow afternoon. I promised to bring you back. That's the only reason they released you. You're still in a bad way. You know that, don't you?" He put her suitcase and a new pillow and blanket in the office closet.

"Of course, I know I'm sick. Aren't you going to eat with me? This is great."

"I can't stay. Have a job to do for Daddy. I'll stop back this evening, if I can."

Before he could leave the room, a tall, well-built woman stopped his progress at the door. Anne immediately recognized her sister, Angel. Like the office building, something appeared different about her, something more worldly-wise, more expensive, and much harder. At first glance, she reminded Anne of herself, maybe the dark hair or the way she stood, but beyond that the resemblance dwindled. The smile was too large and false, the teeth whiter than teeth were meant to be, and the nails were long enough to gouge the heart out of any nonsuspecting victim. Her regal coiffeur must have cost more than Anne expected to make in a week, and it shouted to the world, "Woe to you if you dare muss even one well-placed strand." In spite of everything, some things never changed. Anne was still assimilating the picture when Jim took the bull by the horns, wielding a faint accent.

"Angel, I brought your Annie back to you. She's under the weather, so don't stay too long."

"Come see me later, Jim. We have business to finish." Angel smiled at him and poked him playfully in the ribs.

Jim winked at Anne and gave a crocodile smile behind Angel's back before he closed the door on the two women.

Anne tried to erase the surprise from her face. She hadn't realized Jim and Angel were that well-acquainted.

"Are you here to stay?" Angel asked. The words lacked warmth, but Angel had never been a warm person.

"I'll attempt to earn my keep while I'm here," Anne evaded.

"Why bother? Dad has plenty. Apparently you've given him guilt qualms, if that's possible. You should play it for all it's worth."

"I don't need to play. It's an effort to sit here, to talk."

"I believe you. You look terrible."

"I'm surprised at all the changes here," Anne said, putting the conversation on a less personal basis. "I see Dad finally got hold of the land next door for expansion. How'd he persuade them to sell?"

"Expansion? Oh, I'd forgotten how long you've been gone. Yes, the apartments burned to the ground. Some tramp living in there set it on fire.

51

Dad's old warehouses on that side burned at the same time."

"What about the tenants in the apartments?"

"The building had been condemned. Dad *did* manage that much. Tenants were all vacated before it happened."

"Did Dad lose much?"

"Insurance covered it. He keeps a separate policy for his real estate. He lost nothing, possibly gained. You know how it is. Everything Dad touches turns to gold."

"The Sumner family motto," Anne replied.

"I came to invite you to a party I'm throwing tonight, but you don't look up to it."

"I'm not, but thank you anyway."

"Well, don't work too long. I'll see you tomorrow."

Weary clear through, Anne rose to lock the door behind Angel. With the new pillow and blanket, she made a bed on the floor behind her desk. The thick, cushiony carpet proved more satisfactory than the inadequate sofa. She slept soundly till six in the evening when Jim returned.

"Is Chinese okay?"

"Oh, joyous day. I planned to steal instant soup from the kitchen and drink all their coffee milk. But Chinese, wow. I've seen enough beans the past two years to last a lifetime, but a bean sprout's a new creature. And you brought fortune cookies. Come, sit here with me. It's great to have my appetite back."

"Good acting, but you can't fool me. You know you belong in a hospital, don't you? The doctor told me that's where you should be."

"My fortune cookie say, 'Best eat Chinese while hot.'"

"Okay. Be stubborn. But let me know when you feel well enough to visit your horse."

"To-Tomorrow," she choked. "Tomorrow?"

"We'll see," he said noncommittally and took his carton of food. "I have to leave now. I'll take this with me."

He said goodbye, and Anne finished her dinner alone. When she returned to her bed on the floor, she fell asleep instantly. Near midnight she awoke. The office building felt eerie when she peered out her door into the empty hall. Hungry again, she headed toward the kitchen to search for a late snack. If she husbanded her strength, she might be able to work an hour or two before needing another nap.

When she passed her brother's office, she noticed a dim light shining from under his door and heard the unmistakable sound of a computer game. Fred obviously hadn't changed. He worked enough to get by. The rest of his time he spent with computers, playing games till late at night, usually with a bottle for company. She wouldn't begrudge him that. Countless times he had helped her through computer problems. He might be lazy, but he could certainly whiz through computerland.

She tapped lightly at the door. After a couple of minutes, the door cracked open, and Fred's bleary eyes appeared in the opening. He immediately opened it wide.

"Hi, Anne. Give me one minute to shut this down."

She took a chair and waited. Their family reserve kept her from throwing her arms around his neck, but she hugged him with her thoughts and smile. How good Fred looked, weak, loveable Fred. He would sit here in his office for thirty more years, or however long Dad had left on earth, and then take his inheritance and spend the remainder of his days somewhere else. He would, no doubt, live for the same things he lived for now: computer games, liquor, and an occasional woman friend. He chose those friends from the lower realm of society – low-class women to her dad and Angel, working girls to the rest of the world. Angel had stopped inviting him to her parties, said he disgraced her with the type of company he kept. Anne guessed she now inhabited a lower rung of disgrace than even Fred, to Angel's eyes anyway, but it gave her something in common with him.

"How's it going?" Fred asked, obviously too embarrassed to mention her health. Not having seen each other in over two years, awkwardness prevailed. "You look tired."

"Tired and sick, Fred. Too sick to work, but I needed a job. Excuse me. I have to talk slow – no breath." She all at once knew she could be honest with Fred. "So here I am. I work an hour and sleep four. For the time being, my office will serve as an apartment, and in a minute I'll raid the office refrigerator for tomorrow's meals. Don't tell anyone."

"No one's business, any of it. But you're welcome to come home with me, you know."

"Thanks, but this is easier for me right now. I don't have energy for more."

"Wait here. I'll rob the kitchen for both of us. Play my game for me while I'm gone. I've saved it, so it's okay if you get killed."

"Gee thanks, Fred." She sat down at his desk and fiddled with his laptop for a while. In a few minutes he came back with a tray.

"Sandwiches, coffee, and for you, a glass of half-and-half. You need to build yourself up."

"But they'll wonder where the coffee cream ran off to, come morning."

"*Morning* has arrived. And I filled the bottle back to the top with water."

"Fred, they'll know there's something wrong with it."

"No, they won't. I do it all the time. After all, it *is* half-and-half. If I mix half water with it, it's whole milk, right?"

"You win." They both ate silently. She was glad he drank only coffee. He no doubt remembered how she felt about alcohol.

"Do you still handle Dad's overseas sales?" she finally asked.

"I didn't for over a year, but a short while ago I went back to it."

"What *were* you doing?"

"Dad put me in charge of Sumner's insurance fund. Some fun job." He winced at remembrance of it.

"I used to call it Dad's savings account."

"It's not all his money. Remember the shareholders. Anyway, the job proved too cutthroat for me. With any of Dad's money at stake, people aren't allowed to file claims against it. I told him I wanted nothing more to do with it. Now I'm back here where I wanted to be all the time. This is simpler. We have products for sale. Should anyone desire to buy them, I name a price, and they say 'yes' or 'no,' thus allowing me to get back to more worthy pursuits, pronto." He gave her a sheepish grin. "Angel carries the insurance bag now. Dad hung it on her diamond-studded shoulders."

"What does she think of that?"

"She's passionate about it. Suits her to a T. She asked Dad for a percent of all the money she saves by crushing claims – off the record, of course. I hope I don't slip on the stairs and break my leg."

They both laughed quietly.

"She's a lot like Dad," Anne finally said.

"No. She's a *little* like Dad. Has his corruptness. You're the one who's a *lot* like Dad, bullheaded, stubborn, ready to stand up to the world if it gets in your way, or to walk over it if it remains obdurate. That's why you and Dad don't get on."

"I think you've been drinking too much. I'm nothing like him. Nor are you."

"We all have a little of him in us, whether we like it or not."

"I'm about beat, Fred. I'm going back to my room so you can work." They both looked down at his game at the same time and laughed again. "Also, Fred, I have to write some letters to Mexico. I'd rather not have prying eyes notice them. Would you mind if I used your home address for replies?"

"If I can contribute anything – money, lodging, transportation, half-and-half, *anything* – please let me know. You're the only one in this family who ever did anything worthwhile." He looked down, moved by his own words.

"Thank you, Fred. I'll need help. I don't see any improvement in my health, but I force myself to keep on. It scares me somewhat, that's all. Goodnight, Fred."

Chapter 5

At six in the morning, she awoke to a deserted office building and headed straight for the kitchen. A few minutes of rummaging in cupboards and refrigerator supplied her with an armload of edible items, which she carried back to her office. It pleased her to know she could stay hidden away all day, work and sleep on her own schedule, and not have to waste breath on curious visitors.

By the time others arrived for their day's work, Anne had written letters to Malinali, Padre Juan, and Rev. Sergio. She was gravely worried about the villagers. Did they make the fudge? Did the right people get hold of the money, or did the wrong people drink the profits? Did any of them have the same illness she had?

"And what *do* I have?" she asked herself. "What's wrong with me anyway? Why won't anyone tell me?" Exasperated and anxious over her slow recovery, she wondered when she would get back to Mexico. How long could she bear to sit there with no strength to even walk to the post office and mail her letters?

Putting them in a drawer, she settled into her public relations planning. A couple of times someone tried her door knob, but no one knocked, and she didn't bother to get up and unlock it. At eleven, she took a peanut butter-and-cracker break, followed by a nap on the floor behind her desk. Later on, Jim's familiar knock disturbed her sleep. He came quietly into the room and locked the door behind him.

"How're you doing? I brought sandwiches and a salad. Have you eaten?"

"Snacked, thank you, but you don't have to feed me, you know."

"Your father paid for these."

"I'm not my father's charity case. Why'd you let him?"

"Don't get hot about it. He doesn't know. There's a board-meeting luncheon, and I just brought your share because I knew you wouldn't want to attend."

"Where is the ice cream?" she laughed. "Really, Jim, this stealing could become a bad habit."

"Not stealing. He's your father."

"I gave up any right to Dad's money, or to a position in his business, the day I quit Sumner and started my mission work against his wishes."

"Well, you work for him again, so eat up."

"You brought Thousand Island dressing. I like bleu cheese."

"Should I go back and see what I can find?"

Jim walked to her desk and dialed a number.

"Fred," his clear voice rang out with a faint hint of Scots ancestry, "sorry to interrupt the meeting. Could you send some packets of bleu cheese up to Anne's office? I got the wrong kind."

Anne looked at him astounded, certain he didn't know Fred, and even more certain he faked the call as a joke. A minute later Fred knocked loudly on her door. He came in with an amused look on his face and half a dozen packets of dressing in his hand.

"Fred! Were you in the meeting?"

"Sure. Jim called my cell phone. Old Mrs. Sherp, who sat next to me, heard Jim over the phone. Her eyes bulged so much I thought they'd knock her spectacles off. I told Dad I had an important call from a buyer and would have to leave for a few minutes. Everyone in the room looked at me when I walked to the lunch table and picked up six dressings and left the room."

Jim slapped him on the back, and the two of them laughed heartily. Anne looked at them both horrified. Fred straightened his tie with dignified mien and stated, "I must return to the grown-up-kids' discussion forum and international-decisions meeting now. Enjoy your dinnah."

"I didn't know you were acquainted with Fred," Anne said when she and Jim were alone again.

"Fred? Sure. Last night, when I came back here to check on you, I met Fred going out. He said you'd eaten and had gone to bed, so we hung out for a while."

"I wonder where," she replied sarcastically.

"Not where you think. We went to a café. Now aren't you ashamed, Preacher Woman?"

"Yes."

"And indebted to me?"

"Of course."

"Good, because I don't want any argument when I take you back to the doctor today."

"I'm through with doctors."

"Sorry, Daddy's orders. He's the one who signed for your release and took responsibility for you. You might get me sent back to Mexico if you cause trouble."

"Do you know when you'll ... go back to your work in Mexico?"

"Who knows? Right now I'm k-kissing up to Daddy and flying the corporate beauty."

"Do you mean the jet or Angel?" she asked in jest.

"Both. Sis likes me. I'm the family pilot, bodyguard, shoe shiner, Scotch butler, and all-around bloomin' idiot."

Taken aback that her joke turned out to be truth, she was careful to hide the uncomfortable feeling the thought gendered.

"Since when did Angel acquire a taste for paupers?"

"She likes my accent."

"*Fake* accent, you mean," Anne said with undisguised resentment. "What if someone asked your family about you? Would they lie for you?"

"My mother's gone. Dad's still going strong, but he'd never give me away."

"Well, don't give yourself away. You might forget at the wrong time. Maybe you should talk Scots all the time, to me, too."

"Good idea. Get yer wee butt intae me limo, lassie. It's toime to gang awa' tae the doctor man."

"If you speak like that, *no* one will believe you. I hope I'm never

58

nearby when you have to talk much. I'm liable to break out in laughter. I'll pay a visit to the good Dr. Wildermuth this one time, but I wish I could afford a different doc."

"I'm sure he's the best money can buy. Your father chose him."

"No doubt. But he acts too vague. Either he doesn't know what's wrong with me, or he's hiding facts. I'd like to be a fly on his shoulder when he writes in my file."

"Ask to see it."

"I told him I'd like a copy of my medical records, but he said he'd have to clear it with my father. It didn't make sense to me. I'm not a minor. But I didn't press the point since my father's paying the bills. Guess I'll try to read it while I'm in there."

"That's the spirit. Go to it."

"I will, but I need your help. Why don't you come into the waiting room with me? When I've been in his exam room for a few minutes, you go outside and call him on your cell phone with a question, some sort of emergency question. If he leaves the room to talk with you, I'll look at his notes."

"You are devious, aren't you? Maybe you're in the wrong line of work. Okay, I'll think of something."

An hour later, Anne sat nervously through the exam and waited for Jim's call. She asked numerous questions about her condition, received no satisfaction, and grew more uneasy at the doctor's continuing noncommittal attitude.

"I don't think I breathe any better. Sometimes I think I'm worse."

"You don't have any more nausea or stomach cramps, do you?"

"N-No, but I'm weak."

"Your color's good. I'll start you on supplemental oxygen now. At this point it can only be a help."

"You mean, like keep a tank with me? I might as well be in the hospital or ... or in a n-nursing home."

"It's not as inconvenient as it sounds. I'm prescribing intermittent use at this time, for times of overexertion. Many people use oxygen therapy ..."

"I can't do that, not while I hold down a job."

"There are tiny cylinders available for people on the go. I'll recommend a large tank for your home and small, portable tanks you can carry in a purse, if you like."

"Maybe I *am* better. Let's wait until my next appointment." She let the receptionist set up an appointment for the coming Friday afternoon, but she had no intention of keeping it. The job of recovery had landed squarely on her own shoulders. The doctor hadn't offered any new suggestions or new medicine.

In the hall she found Jim waiting.

"A fine help you were."

"S-Sorry. It didn't work." He made no explanation. "When did you want to see your horse?"

"Now!" she gasped. "Right this instant. I need a friend."

Out of the corner of her eye, she saw Jim flinch. Her words had stung, as she had intended. She felt a traitor, but she wouldn't take them back. She had noted a subtle change in him lately. He belonged to her dad and Sumner now, and Sumner included Angel.

Wordlessly, they drove to the lush Sumner stables. A piercing whinny greeted her when she entered the large barn. Tom-tom remembered her, much to her pleasure. He pawed impatiently and whinnied again. She hurried to him, hid her face against his soft, warm neck, and cried silently for a few minutes.

Tom-tom lost patience with her and bent his rubbery neck around backward, playfully mouthing her clothes with extended lips. She shoved him away and mopped the tears from her face before Jim could see them.

"Behave yourself, Tom-tom. I have few enough clothes for the office. If you want to eat me, wait till I wear something old."

She mopped her face a second time and turned sheepishly to Jim, who had walked over.

"He looks good, doesn't he? My father keeps Homer here to tend the horses and exercise them everyday. I could never afford a place that would give him this kind of care. I pay a pittance, hardly enough to cover the feed. See, I do accept some charity from my dad. I think, soon as I'm well, I'll save up enough money to take Tom-tom back to Mexico with me. I could put in an area of pasture for him with my own money."

"Now you're talking. He'd be handy there in that terrain, better than your truck."

"I could ride him to Capaso every week."

Somehow, it felt like they both talked make-believe. When would she get well? Dr. Wildermuth scared her, made her feel so hopeless. He never spoke of recovery.

Slumped against the rail, too tired to stand any longer without support, she still refused Jim's help when he came to her. After a few minutes, she was able to make it to a nearby bench, where she dropped down hopelessly. With her head on her knees, dry sobs shook her body. When Jim laid his hand on her neck, she struggled to gain control. Even that kind of crying required more oxygen than she could draw through her affected lungs. A haze enveloped her mind, and she grew dizzy and faint. She sat very still, trying not to lose consciousness. When the fog slightly cleared, she concentrated on breathing and wished for some of the oxygen the doctor had recommended.

"Are you all right? Can I take you back to the doctor? The hospital?"

It seemed hours before she could answer. "Rest," she managed to say. She continued to relax until she could find enough air to speak. "Will I ever be well? The villagers ..."

"Don't think about anything. Where's that faith you speak of? Can't God take care of your villagers until you've recovered? Doesn't He know you're ill?"

"Will I ever get ..." She couldn't speak her fears again without crying, and there wasn't enough oxygen for more tears. Finally, after a few more minutes of rest, she said, "Thank you. I'm totally faithless."

"No, you're sick and rightfully scared. You have me a mite scared, too. I don't want you to argue with me, just listen for once and do as I ask. I'm going to pick you up and carry you to the car. You'll be able to rest more comfortably, and, when you feel better, we can talk."

He didn't wait for her answer but lifted her in his arms and carried her back to the car, gently sliding her onto the front seat.

"Do you want me to lower the seat back so you can recline more?"

"No. Gravity pulls against my lungs, makes it harder to breathe." She leaned forward against the dash. After half a dozen attempts, she managed to partially inflate her lungs with an unsatisfactory yawn. Soon she accomplished more short yawns but waited a good while before she attempted to talk again.

"It must be infection." She talked slowly and paused often. "The doctor didn't say so, but that must be it. Maybe I need to build myself up. Thank you for bringing me to see Tom-tom."

"Why not take a short vacation from work until you're stronger? Let your dad help. You should sit at the beach, or under a tree, until your body recovers."

"Maybe," she answered thoughtfully. "Dad owns a hunting cabin. No one ever goes there."

"I meant somewhere around people, somewhere you could get help if you needed it."

"If I had a cell phone, I could work from there for a couple weeks. I don't need the office equipment right now. I could take Tom-tom."

"You haven't strength for that, not for the care of a horse. Go to a health spa or a resort, some place that befits a daughter of Anglin Sumner."

Too tired to argue, she remained silent. Let him think he had won. But the cabin idea appealed to her, and she intended to investigate its possibilities.

"Have you heard anything about the villages?"

"Does it matter? You're too weak to do anything. Concentrate on yourself and your health."

Again silent, she mentally planned how to check on the villages without his help. It looked like she couldn't count on anyone's help for matters important to her.

"Would you get my box of clothes from my tack room?" she asked meekly. "I need a change, or everyone will think I own only one outfit."

Back in her quiet office, she wrote three more letters to Mexico before she indulged in a nap. Afterward, she settled to the business of her real job, the one that paid for her survival. She could enjoy the work if she fully believed in Sumner. It had seemed a noble calling, once upon a time, to tell how Sumner made it easier for all those Third World countries to feed themselves and better their lives. Those were her fresh-out-of-college feelings, back when she first started her public relations job there. Hired now to the same position, older and less gullible, the job loomed much more difficult.

Even during her first stint at Sumner, it hadn't taken long to discover Sumner's unlovely side and to learn how distasteful it could be to inform the world about nonexistent virtues. When she admitted to her dad she didn't have the *three C's* type talent a Sumner job required, the ability to *connive, cheat, and cover up*, he promptly sent her to the plant in Mexico. With their prime troublemaker gone, Sumner could proceed, unrebuked, on its unvirtuous path.

She had accepted the transfer, with its new, less-compromising position, almost happily. After all, Sumner's Mexican operation carried on more business than the home company in Houston. From their south-of-the-border location, they handled all the overseas trade. They shipped chemicals from their plant to the costal ports of Veracruz and Acapulco and then to buyers all over the world. South Mexico also supplied all the natural resources they needed, and those resources came cheap, almost as cheap as the land and labor, with few restrictions to complicate matters.

Inevitably, she saw more evidence of Sumner's dirty underpinnings at such a large operation. She soon realized her calling wasn't at Sumner but at the lowly village of Tutlu. Poor little Tutlu, caught in the highlands between her father's agricultural holdings and his large chemical operation. How she missed it. It seemed so long ago.

Now she had a difficult chore ahead and couldn't be critical or nitpicking. No big corporation was perfect. Maybe all companies stooped to questionable policies and dealings at times. She would give Sumner the benefit of the doubt and not be judgmental. Her new campaign would be to picture Sumner as it *should* be. If she succeeded, maybe the company would try to live up to its new reputation. That would be her crusade while recovering strength enough to return to her villages.

Finally inspired, she wrote page after page and was deep in thought when someone tapped at her office door two hours later. She took her time, in hopes the visitor would give up and leave. When she eventually opened the door, Fred stood waiting. Instantly pleased, she motioned him in, and they sat down on the small sofa.

"Did I wake you? I knocked quietly so you wouldn't hear me if you were asleep."

"I was awake, earning my paycheck. But I sleep lightly. I'd hear you, even if I were asleep."

Fred grinned. "Oh, by the way, I've knocked three other times since Jim brought you back. You never answered."

"Okay. I used to sleep lightly. I guess nothing's the same."

"I came to ask how the doctor's visit went. How are you, according to him?"

"*Him* won't tell me anything. My first paycheck goes for a new doctor, that is, if I'm still this sick."

"You don't believe you're better, do you?"

"Honestly, I don't know. Maybe it's my impatience. If Dr. Wildermuth would say I need two months to get over this, I could live with that. Or if he told me what was wrong with me, I'd feel better."

"Let me pay for another doctor. I have plenty of money. Think of it as money I won't use for drink." He looked at her so wistfully, she considered his offer.

"Can I pay you back?"

"Am I your brother or not?"

"I wouldn't want Dad to know. I could use a different address."

"Good enough. When do you want to go? I'm ready whenever you can arrange it."

"I'll call about an appointment. Don't tell Jim either."

"Our secret."

After Fred left, Anne called Dr. Logan, a specialist she had looked up earlier. Even though it was late in the day, she reached the receptionist and, due to a cancellation, was able to secure an appointment for Thursday afternoon. She called Fred with the information and went wearily to sleep.

In the evening, she awoke to the sound of someone in her office. Rolling to her back, she glanced up at Jim from her bed on the floor.

"I've worked today," she said proudly. "Look at that copy on the desk. Doesn't it sound fantastic? It should give Sumner a real facelift. I believe I'll earn my keep."

Jim sat down at the desk and studied her printed inspiration while she gazed up at him expectantly.

"The writing's fine. Reads like a novel."

"And? Is that all? You didn't like it?"

"Like I said, it reads like a novel, pure fiction. Maybe even a fairy tale. Your hero doesn't exist."

"Sumner Chemical, you mean." She sat upright on the floor, disappointment and battle in her eyes. "I wrote the truth. It's difficult to find something praiseworthy in the company. I think I did well. They do give jobs to the ultra-poor, they do help Third World countries improve their agricultural output, and that raises their standard of living. I don't think my father's company hurts anyone – much."

He laughed at her.

"Sure you do. You saw it clearly when you worked here before. You saw it clearly a couple weeks ago when you worked down in Mexico. I think this third-floor office has gone to your head. It's the altitude no doubt."

"I-I need a job for a l-little while … until I'm well," she quavered, close to tears. "I can't battle the world right now, or Sumner. Besides, this isn't as high an altitude as Tutlu. I simply envisioned what Sumner *could* be. How else can I do my job?"

His criticism of her work had unnerved her. She turned away to hide her frustration.

"I'm sorry," he said, laying his hand on her shoulder. "What you wrote is fine. Don't pay any attention to me. I've had a bad day."

"I didn't lie."

"Of course not. Daddy will love it."

"Maybe it will spur him on to be more like I portrayed him and the company," she said, facing him hopefully again.

"Sure it will. It'll bring out the best in him." Laughter hid behind his eyes as he spoke the words she wanted to hear. She looked at him dubiously.

"You're humoring me. You don't think there *is* any best in him."

"I don't think there's any best in me either, but sometimes you about convince me otherwise."

"What have you been doing?"

"Brown-nosing Daddy, flirting with Angel, drinking with Fred, and flying arrogant big shots here and there."

"You'd be better off in Mexico. You'll be corrupted."

"It's great to fly here in the States again. It's what I've always wanted. Your dad's good for something. I'll add a line about him to your copy here."

She got up and took a seat on the sofa while he leaned over her desk to write.

"Will you stay here?" she asked softly. "When I go back, I mean." The thought sent a great wave of loneliness over her that dwarfed her worst times in Mexico.

He looked at her for a long moment.

"I don't know. Your dad treats me favorably. It won't last. There'll be a price attached, one I can't pay. I'll end up fired and back in no-man's land."

"Surely your whole life, your future, doesn't revolve around my father. You might not be able to pilot a jetliner, but there must be other good piloting jobs. You own your own plane."

"Yes, but for the time being I'm dependent on Sumner. That could change," he added thoughtfully, not offering an explanation. "It's eight-thirty. I'd best leave and let you sleep."

She wanted to talk with him awhile, but pride kept her from telling him. He hadn't been gone two minutes before she made up her mind to ask him to stay. Why not ask him to take her out somewhere? She hurried down the hall to the end by the elevators. Breathing heavily, she studied the parking lot from the window. His car was parked there along with Fred's and another one. She slid the window open, in readiness to get his attention if he came into view.

All at once he stood below her but not alone. Angel had hold of his arm. The third car in the lot must be Angel's. The twosome headed straight for it, laughing and talking animatedly. Anne held her breath. Was he politely walking Angel to her car? But no, he took the proffered car keys from Angel's extended hand. After opening the passenger door for her, he walked around to the driver's side and got in. A sob caught in Anne's throat. She quickly slid the window shut and returned to her office.

Bitterness consumed her for a minute. How could Angel, who had whatever she wanted, take possession of her one friend? She sat at her desk and started back to work on the promotional package with hot, dry eyes. Hours later, dead weary, she remembered Jim had written something on her other sheet. She picked it up and found scripture at the bottom, in Jim's writing. "Psalms, of course," she said out loud and laughed. But when she read his words she didn't laugh.

Behold, he travaileth with iniquity, and hath conceived mischief, and brought forth falsehood. He made a pit, and digged it, and is fallen into the ditch which he made. His mischief shall return upon his own head, and his violent dealing shall come down upon his own pate.

Chapter 6

The amazing fact he had memorized the entire scripture took second place to the scripture's content. What possessed him to memorize that particular one, she wondered. It didn't sound uplifting, gallant, or even joyous. Was he accusing Sumner of falsehood and violent dealing?

It took a long time to fall asleep. Jim's scripture upset her nearly as much as his driving off with Angel, but weariness eventually won its battle, and she slept deeply.

Later in the night, when she awoke and stared around the room, there sat Jim on the sofa, obviously deep in thought. She silently studied him through half-shut eyes. He never looked in her direction but continued to lean forward, his forearms resting on his thighs while he gazed intently into the darkness. She couldn't face him that moment. He would sense her resentment and know she had seen him with Angel. She could never hide her turbulent thoughts from him. When his head turned in her direction, she controlled her breathing and became deathly still. Within minutes she heard him close the door behind him.

At the hall window, she again watched him leave, this time alone. From the looks of the parking lot, everyone had gone home. Now past midnight, she wondered if Jim and Angel had been together all that time or if Jim had occupied her sofa longer than she suspected.

The big new Sumner addition across the way drew her attention. The impressive structure now filled the spot where the old apartment complex had stood. The additional land area had made it possible for her dad to put in a runway and keep his planes there. Before the acquisition there wasn't room enough for landings and takeoffs. She understood that problem well, after her own work in Mexico. The adjacent hangers housed three commercial planes and her father's little jet, all visible from the window.

The old apartments next door *had* been an eyesore, worse than Sumner's own deteriorated warehouses. Her dad had voiced more than once his intent to tear down those old buildings. The fire conveniently took care of it and also gained him the property he coveted. Everything did appear to go perfectly for the rich, or as her father bragged, everything he touched turned to gold.

A small voice inside whispered of how interesting it would be to know more about that fire. The voice hinted of more, much more, but she tried to silence its implications, realizing Jim's writing had given them birth. After a short mental battle, she convinced herself she should look up the record of the fire in the archives because it might give her more ideas to present in her brochures. She could write something about turning disaster into progress or decay into beauty. Only half-fooling herself, she headed for the room where the older files were kept.

Not sure what heading it would be under, she searched randomly at first. Coming upon a file marked "Demolition Bids," she leafed through it. Her father had accepted bids from two different contractors to demolish the group of warehouses the fire had destroyed. She thought at first the bids were to remove the debris caused by the fire but soon ascertained the bids were for taking out the standing building. She wrote down the date and names of the bidders, curious if any of the bids had been accepted. Nothing in the folder indicated so.

In an insurance folder, she found information on the fire, including an old newspaper clipping with pictures and a story. Too tired to stay longer, she took the file back to her office and locked herself in.

Reclining on the sofa, she studied the contents. The fire occurred about a month after the demolition bids. Her father had collected from the insurance company for the destruction of the warehouses in the fire.

Instead of paying for demolition, Anglin had been paid a significantly large sum for the loss of the buildings.

The newspaper article said the fire appeared to have been started by a homeless man who lived in the empty, condemned, apartment building. The man, identified as Arron Briggs by a medical tag around his neck, had perished in the fire. No family had been located.

Further reading disclosed that the apartment owner had made plans to refurbish the building and have the condemned status removed. Evidently, he had intended to renovate rather than sell to Anglin, or at least until the fire destroyed such an option. If he knew Anglin instigated the move to have the apartments condemned, that would have produced strong feelings. No doubt the man collected an insignificant amount of insurance on his lost building because of that. Did her father take advantage of the situation in order to make his deal? Anne hated her thoughts but couldn't stop them.

She became curious about what Anglin had paid for the property and when he had obtained ownership, but she was too tired to investigate further. With the file hidden under papers on her desk, she went to sleep.

Later in the morning, she awoke and had barely put her bedding away before someone knocked at her office door.

"Just a minute. I'm coming," she called.

"Don't bother. I have a key," Angel answered and opened the door. "Do you work twenty-four hours now? I saw your light when I left last night, and you're here ahead of me this morning."

"My work speed still operates below par, so I stay longer. But I'm progressing on the new campaign."

Apparently Angel didn't know about her living arrangements, Anne thought with relief. Angel was so caught up in herself, it was easy to evade or fool her.

"Why trouble over it. Get out and have some fun. You've lived like a gopher for years. You're above ground now. Take advantage of it. Jim told me your village doesn't even have electricity and that there are no towns within reach. How did you stand it? You should live it up now."

"I'm not well enough to live it up."

"Rudy still talks about you. Why don't you and Rudy come along with Jim and me tonight, and we'll go out to dinner. Dinner's not strenuous, and Rudy would jump at the chance. I'm sure he's free tonight. If not, I'll make him go anyway. And you know Jim, don't you? He was the one who flew you back here. You should feel comfortable."

Mention of Jim stabbed her heart. The nerve of Angel to suggest she be Rudy's date. Angel knew she and Rudy broke up long before Mexico, and Angel knew why. Rudy had only been after a position in the company. When he realized Ambitious Angeline could prosper him more than Assiduous Anne, he followed Angel around like a lap dog. Of course, Angel soon tired of him, a habit of hers with boyfriends, but it was grossly insulting for Angel to think she would touch him now. She had the utmost contempt for him. She looked at her sister disdainfully, until she realized she hadn't answered her question.

"Yes, the pilot who brought me here – Jim Orr, I believe. But, if I had enough energy to go out to dinner, I assuredly wouldn't waste it on Rudy."

"Rudy's done well for himself. He bought the property next door after the fire. Of course, he bought it for Dad, with Dad's money, but he's the one who suggested it and made it work. Then he merged his little company with Dad's. Dad's given him an excellent position."

"I thought you were attracted to him at one time?"

"You know me. I wear a man out quickly."

"This J-Jim, he's not the type you usually go for, is he? A pilot? A crop duster?"

"Since when have I gone for a certain type? And who says I've gone for him? We've been out for coffee. He amuses me. That's more than most guys do. And I like his accent."

"Y-Yes. His accent." Anne suddenly realized Angel didn't know the Jim she knew. She wondered how well Angel knew the fake one. "So you plan to amuse yourself with him for a while?" Anne couldn't resist asking.

"Could be. Maybe I'll speak to Daddy about promoting him or something. He's smart, knows how to play the game."

"You're ready to corrupt him? Buy his soul?"

"He knows more about corruption than I do. I can tell he's been around."

Anne winced. "I thought him rather naïve and warm-hearted, like he might actually have a conscience."

"Naïve? Never! You're the only one who's naïve. But don't worry. I can take care of his conscience if he develops one, which I doubt. You have a fairy godmother impression of him because he rescued you and saved your life. Daddy should reward him for that, don't you think?"

"Is my life saved? I don't exactly feel such assurance yet."

"Of course you're saved. Money can buy a new body if you need it. Daddy will see to that."

"I rather liked my old one."

"Well, let me know if you change your mind. About going out, I mean. See you later."

Anne felt genuinely depressed after Angel left. She had to get away for a while, as soon as she could get a couple of paychecks under her belt. She calculated possibilities in her mind. If she concentrated on the work that required office equipment, she could maybe finish in a week and a half. Fred would drive her to the Sumner cabin if she convinced him it would speed her recovery. She craved the privacy, the loneliness, of that woodsy, deserted spot. No one ever went there anymore, except during hunting season. With a definite goal in sight, she set to work at a more strenuous pace and was hard at it when Jim came late in the day.

"You're overdoing. You're paler than usual."

"Is that possible? I thought I already looked colorless. I've worked more hours today than usual, but it feels good."

"It might feel good to your mind, but your body disagrees."

"I'm tired of listening to my body. It says the same old things."

"Like 'Give me rest and don't work me so hard'?"

"No, more like 'Give me air.'"

"I hoped you'd say that. I have an oxygen tank in the hall. I'll put it in your closet."

She rose to her feet angrily. "I told the doctor I didn't want it. I'm not that desperate. I'll get well on my own, with the air everyone else breathes."

"It's for an emergency, in case you overdo," he said and stubbornly took it to the closet.

She sat down unhappily, too breathless to argue further. He made her feel like an invalid, a pale, listless invalid who had to rely on an oxygen tank. The thought made her terribly unhappy. On the verge of harsh words, she mentally kicked herself for being so foolish. It shouldn't matter, it didn't matter. Nothing mattered except her work in the villages and getting back quickly.

Jim looked at her thoughtfully. "I meant to ask you out for a while, but you look all in."

"Angel already tried to arrange that. She said you and she were going to dinner, and she'd fix me up with Rudy, a castoff of hers. I declined."

Jim laughed heartily. "I'm sure I heard resentment or jealousy." He laughed again.

"I haven't time for games. I have real work waiting, and I'm trying hard to get well and get back to it. Whether you play around with Angel, or not, it doesn't interest me."

"I haven't seen Angel. Would you like to take in a movie, as an old friend from Mexico, you know?"

Anne choked when a lump instantly rose in her throat.

"If I could sleep an hour first."

"Sleep three. I'll be back later. That suits me better, too."

Anne slept two hours and spent the remaining time on her appearance. Exhausted, after trying on three different outfits, she slipped into the closet to study the oxygen system. She indulged in a small banquet of tanked air until near time for Jim to arrive. It helped. She sat composedly and waited.

When Jim came through the door, he immediately sniffed the air.

"You tried the oxygen."

She knew she blushed scarlet. "I-I wanted to see how it worked ... for an emergency."

"How *did* it work?"

"It helped. I'd rushed around too much, and it helped me recover more quickly. If I'd known you could smell it, I'd never have experimented," she admitted honestly.

"I can't smell it. How could I smell oxygen? It's just air, isn't it?"

"I think I hate you. I won't go out with you now."

"Sure you will, unless you're too tired. If so, I'll rent a movie to watch in here."

"I'll go. I need a change."

"Wait. I'll see if Angel and Rudy are ready." He turned toward the door, then turned back quickly and looked at Anne with laughter in his eyes.

She realized at once her mouth hung open.

"Just kidding. Don't get angry." Before she could refuse to go again, he grabbed her arm and pulled her with him out the door.

"Do you want to go in somewhere to eat, or would you prefer takeout we could eat in the car?"

"Takeout sounds good."

She expected a hamburger place, but instead he stopped at an elite French restaurant, one that surely wouldn't have takeout. Still, he returned in a few minutes with an elaborate spread.

While arranging the entrées on the dashboard and inadequate front seat, he announced smoothly, "Bouillabaisse, filet de rouget barbet aux légumes, and mousse au chocolate."

"Ah, so now we're French?"

"Whatever it takes."

The conversation didn't flow naturally as in times past. Every subject seemed a no-no. She didn't want to talk about her health or Mexico or Angel.

Finally he asked, "Did you like my addition to your composition the other night?"

"You mean the scripture you wrote on my paper? How on earth did you remember it, every word of it?"

"I told you I could memorize anything. I'm glad to see it interested you enough to check it out."

"You insinuated Dad was dishonest. I know he's hard, but you implied more."

"Yes? So?"

"Was there a reason? Something you know?"

"Is there something *you* know and want to know if I know it, too? You defend your dad out of one side of your mouth and are skeptical out of the other."

"I've always considered him basically honest, in spite of shortcomings in other directions, but ..."

"But you have doubts?"

"I ran across some things, and Angel made some revealing

statements. I wonder about the fire, the one that destroyed the apartment building next door to Sumner. Dad wanted the property badly and used his influence to get it condemned. The owner didn't like Dad and wouldn't sell to him, but Dad got it through an arranged buyer, after the fire."

"And you ask me if he's honest? Does that sound honest?"

"It's as honest as Dad's ever been. It's the same with many businessmen I know. But it's not his business dealings I'm concerned about. I can't help but wonder about the fire. I know it's terrible to think ... to think Dad could have something to do with it. I must be crazy. He's not capable of arson. Is he?"

"He's your dad. You should know," he said noncommittally, his face a mask.

"Darn it, I know that. But what you wrote implied more. Maybe you know him better than I do. Maybe I'm too close to him. I found some papers, old contractors' bids for demolition of a group of run-down warehouses on his property here. Shortly after the bids were made, those warehouses and the apartment building next door to them burned. Dad needed the next-door property for expansion purposes. The fire not only gained him that, but it also got rid of his derelict warehouses, saved him a demolition fee, and gained him insurance money."

"These papers, the ones you found, were accidentally left on your desk?"

She looked at him guiltily for a minute while his serious eyes searched hers. When the seriousness changed to laughter, she couldn't keep from laughing, too.

"At night, when everyone had left, I investigated. I wanted new material to stimulate my thinking for my promotional theme."

"So you went directly to the old files to check up on a fire. Great promotional idea."

"Shut up. I don't know what I was looking for, but I found suspicion. And you hinted as much. Do you know something, anything, about Dad I don't know?"

"Nothing you won't know by tomorrow at the rate you're investigating."

"Jim, I'm serious."

"Sure, what do you want to know?" he asked too jovially, too agreeably.

"Never mind. I can see you won't tell me anything. I guess you're corrupted, a Sumner pawn."

"I was never a saint. But I think I'm a better person since I've known you, Anne," he said seriously.

"Do you think my dad's capable of burning property, his or someone else's, to gain his ends?" she burst out. "I'm not asking if he did. I just want to know if you think he's capable of such dishonesty."

"Of course he is. Don't ask me why I say that. And don't be angry that I consider him less than virtuous."

"When he sent me to the Mexican branch of Sumner, I had misgivings about Sumner's business dealings. Now the doubts creep back, multiplied. I'll become worse than before, if I stay here. Dad will ship me off somewhere further away than Mexico before you know it. But I couldn't hold down any other job right now, and I'm not strong enough or rich enough to go back to Tutlu."

"You're breathless, and you're starting to slump. Let's save the movie for next time and get you home."

Anne slept a nine-hour night and awoke with barely enough time to clean up before the office force arrived. She worked diligently and took only one short nap before Fred came by in the afternoon to take her to her doctor's appointment. Jim hadn't come in, and she was glad he wouldn't know about the new doctor. No one would know about it. She felt guilty about the appointment and guilty about letting Fred pay for it, but she was desperate to speed up her recovery.

Dr. Logan, red-haired and bearded, turned keen eyes on her when she entered his office. His rumpled Bermuda shorts and tall, lanky frame didn't fit the surroundings, but she felt immediate confidence in his ability and intellect. His manner was decidedly different from her other doctor, different from any doctor she knew. After giving her a thorough medical exam, he wasted a good fifteen minutes asking questions about her work in Mexico. She talked, and he wrote notes on the sheet in front of him. He showed interest in what she told him about Isdel and about the similarity of symptoms in their two cases.

"Tell me about the twenty-four hours before the symptoms

occurred. Let's see." He looked down at his notes. "Friday morning you woke with nausea and a sore throat. How did you feel Thursday night? Did you do anything different that night? Or during that day?"

"Same old schedule. We make fudge every Thursday."

"Were you sick at all Thursday night?"

"No, not till morning. I felt hot, restless, like I am many nights. I took a night swim to cool off."

"A swim?"

"I swam most nights and usually a couple times during the day."

"What time did you swim?"

"About ten or eleven o'clock." Her mind flashed back to her sudden awakening that night and the retreating airplane lights. It seemed so long ago. "I went to bed after I swam. Woke once in the night with a raw throat. By morning I felt awful."

"Is the water pure where you swim?"

"It's a lake, or I should say pond, we made ourselves. It's spring fed and reasonably clean. It's maybe not pure enough for drinking water, but we're careful with sanitation. We've had it for over a year. Some of the villagers drink it, in spite of my best efforts, but no one has ever become ill from it. I usually swallow some when I swim, but I've never been sick, ever."

"Do you use any chemicals for anything? Pest control? Farm chemicals?"

"No. We can't afford any. We live totally organic at the village."

"You mentioned that this," he looked down at his sheet, "this man, Isdel, worked at the farms, some distance from your village."

"Yes, fifty-five miles. They use chemicals there for crop dusting and such. But we use nothing at our village. We don't even own a can of bug spray."

"Have there been any new cases? You said a number of people were sick when Isdel came down with his problem, but no one severely, correct?"

"That's right. They closed the fields for two days because of the flu or whatever the problem. Only Isdel became seriously sick. I've written twice to find out if there's any more illness but haven't heard back yet. My village doesn't have ready access to mail delivery."

"I want to know anything you find out, as soon as you receive word. Don't worry about whether you have an appointment. Call or come in. I want you to find out the state of the villagers' health. If you don't get a letter from them by tomorrow, try some other means of communication. Meantime, I've scheduled you for more tests at the hospital, and I want to see you here at nine thirty in the morning."

"I-I'll try. I'll be here."

"Is there someone to drive you, to look out for you?"

"Yes. I'll be okay."

She was embarrassed to impose upon Fred, but he was more than willing to see her through the hospital ordeal. After the tests were finished, she spent the night at his house.

"Let's hope he has good news," Fred encouraged next morning on their way to Dr. Logan's office.

"Don't get me wrong, Fred. I do want the truth. But I can't help being scared."

Dr. Logan met her at the door and offered her a chair. He again sported rumpled Bermuda shorts that looked decidedly similar to yesterday's pair. His mien came off much graver, and that didn't help her nerves. She clenched her cold hands together to avoid wringing them. The seat in his office felt cold, too, and she tried to sit arrow-straight and look like a well person. It didn't fool the doctor.

"I'm surprised you get about at all."

Those weren't the words she wanted to hear. They definitely didn't produce a calming effect. She didn't respond. Her body began to shiver, and her voice wanted to follow suit.

"You know, don't you, that you have extensive lung damage, extreme proliferation of pulmonary connective tissue?"

She stared at him blankly. She didn't *know* anything, except she had no energy and couldn't breathe. Was she supposed to say something? He looked at her like he wanted her help.

He started in again, "We are dealing with pulmonary fibrosis, a progressive cyanosis."

"That doesn't sound like flu," she answered, embarrassed at the shakiness of her voice.

He shook his head in negation.

"I haven't established yet the cause of your illness, but your condition is severe, extremely severe. I'm surprised no one has discussed this with you."

"How severe?" a meek little voice asked. It didn't sound like hers, but it came from somewhere in the depths of her.

"Irreversible, in most cases." He hurried on as if to drown out the sound of his words. "You find it difficult to exercise, walk, or even move around." He said it as a fact, not as a question, and looked at her closely.

Chapter 7

The shock of his words left her speechless at first. Finally she croaked, "Yes. That's how it is. Is there ... anything I can do?"

"Oxygen therapy may help. We'll attempt to arrest the condition, which probably won't be possible. Our main efforts will be against complications that will arise from this condition. The first one is hypoxia. The oxygen may help that.

"Like I said before, I'm not certain what caused your condition, but the results are there for anyone to see. It's been close to fifteen days since the symptoms occurred. I'm sorry I can't be more encouraging." He looked down, no longer able to meet her eyes. The totally human expression on his face surprised her.

"Something felt incredibly wrong, but no one would tell me anything. Have the conditions been getting worse for fifteen days while some quack ..."

"I'm sure your doctor knew of the damage. It's totally visible. He, no doubt, did what he could for the condition."

"Why didn't he tell me? What can I do?"

"I can't say what you'd like to hear. We can fight it with oxygen; possibly later we'll go to diuretic therapy, maybe digitalis."

"For m-my lungs?"

"To help you survive the complications that will arise."

"Am I going to die?" She looked at him straight on, stiff, cold, and dry-eyed.

"There have been a few cases, less serious cases, where the victim experienced a reversal. That's not likely in your case."

"What can *I* do?" she asked again, helplessly.

"Stay as healthy as you can. Get plenty of rest and listen to your body. I'm sorry. I can't advise more at this time. We'll look into every possibility when I have all your results back."

"That's okay." She felt like she should say more but didn't know what. Finally, she said, "Thank you," and stumbled out of his office.

She waited in a daze for the receptionist to set up a return appointment.

"We'll see you at 10 in the morning, day after tomorrow. The doctor will have the rest of your test results by then."

Anne nodded but had no intention of keeping the appointment. She had given them a false phone number and address. She knew what she needed to know and was through with them. She wanted to break down and cry, but that would have to wait. Death would have to wait, too, until she took care of some important matters. In the restroom she splashed cold water on her face, over and over again, while she rehearsed a speech calculated to convince Fred all had gone well.

"He explained my condition, plain and simple," she told Fred. "I have lung damage. I'm to rest, take care of myself, and not expect a speedy recovery. I have to admit I'm relieved, Fred. Thank you for bringing me."

"Do you have a return appointment?"

"N-No. He said I could make one if any complications arose," she lied glibly.

He studied her a couple of times. She could see the troubled expression on his face, but she stared straight ahead and tried to look cheerful.

"It's time for a health campaign," she said with a bright smile. "By the end of next week, I'll have completed two major projects for the company, and I'll have two paychecks. I'll go up to Dad's camp in the hills. The doctor thought it a good idea." She blushed with the absurdity of the lie. "I can work on my job there and get more done than at the office. But I'll be outdoors in the fresh air, and it should help me get my strength back."

"Sounds good to me. But there's no one there. There's no electric, no running water, no phone. Who would help if you had an emergency?"

"I'll get a cell phone. The spring runs close by the cabin, and there are kerosene lamps. It's not cold yet either. Summer's dragging into fall this year. But I don't want anyone to know I'm there. Not anyone. I'd rather everyone think I'm at some resort. Maybe I should say I'm at a health spa. That would be most honest."

She asked herself why she worried about honesty at this point of her duplicity.

"Could you keep it a secret, Fred? I believe it'd help me wonderfully." She looked at him pleadingly.

"I'll take you there, but only if you agree to call me every evening."

"It's a deal. I'll get things in shape here at the office, so I'll be able to leave."

"Don't overwork this next week. Nothing's that vital. Rest and get stronger, or I'll be afraid to leave you at the cabin."

"Don't worry. The work's nearly done. Can you take me there after work next Friday?"

"Sure. No problem."

During the next week, in between times of office work, Anne planned her retreat. She called Homer at the stables and arranged for him to bring Tom-tom to her dad's hunting camp the day after her arrival there. An old, log corral beside the cabin would do nicely for him. She made a list of necessary food and supplies. She'd get Fred to stop at a couple of places on their way to the cabin, so she could buy what she needed. In her box of clothes she found jeans, boots, and some other outdoor clothes. She packed them in her suitcase along with an old swimsuit for use in the small lake beside the cabin. Just the thought of it rested her, and she sighed audibly.

She refused to think about what the doctor had said. If she dwelt on it now, it would unnerve her, make her unfit for anything. At the cabin she could let herself go and face what lay ahead.

Early in the week, Jim came in, checked the oxygen tank in her closet, and left. It instantly angered her. No one had a right to know how much she used it. Maybe she could still get the small portable system the doctor had recommended. Promptly she checked with the medical supply store listed on the oxygen system and found she could order a portable system on her father's account since Dr. Wildermuth had prescribed it. She immediately availed herself of their smallest system and a bunch of spare tanks and about fainted at the price. Someday she would pay her father back for all of this. Meantime, the tanks would be used only for the most urgent situations. No need to think beyond that.

The cabin would be her trysting place, a place to meet with death and life and find which had the stronger claim on her. The thought came by itself and surprised her. She hadn't resigned herself to death at all. She wanted to get well. But she couldn't think about it there at the office, not with all the bustle of people and business around her. Such matters belonged to remote, lonesome spots where one could cry or laugh, and only God and nature would hear the sound.

In the meantime, she derived a degree of pleasure out of the fact she no longer used the large cylinder in the closet. It delighted her when Jim came in Wednesday evening and looked surprised when he found the gauge unchanged. He didn't say anything about it but sat down as if he planned to stay awhile. She used the opportunity to convince him she had improved.

"I believe I'm much better." She smiled and sat straighter than usual. "I've worked all day and don't feel half-bad. Haven't had to use your oxygen," she lied and hated herself for it. She'd never stooped to lying until this illness. They might be half-lies, but they gave her guilt pangs. "Haven't seen much of you lately."

"Anglin's had me flying all over creation, and Angel considers me her personal pilot when Daddy doesn't need me."

"That must be so unpleasant," she said facetiously, not able to keep the resentment totally out of her voice.

He gave her one of his long, questioning looks that always made her blush. While she tried to think of something more to say, he came near and kissed her fully but gently on the lips. His hand trembled where it rested on her arm, and the realization disturbed and confused her. He turned and left.

Minutes flew by. She sat and stared at nothing while tears streamed down her face. The sound of Angel's voice through the closed door brought her back harshly.

"Anybody home?"

"Coming." She violently mopped her face dry and hurried to unlock the door before Angel could use her key. Anne made a mental note to buy and install a second lock on the inside of her door, one of those simple slide-across ones that didn't require a key. She could use it during the daytime hours when Angel roamed the building.

"Hi, Angel," she said genially.

Angel brushed past her and found a seat on the sofa. Anne, already braced for a disagreeable visit from her untactful sister, decided to put on a show of good health. She had always prided herself on her strong will, but it would surely be put to the test before the week's end, she thought, turning her attention to Angel. One could only wonder what she wanted this time.

"Didn't I see Jim just leave your office? I came from the elevator and thought I saw him close your door."

"Oh, yes. He regularly checks the gauge on my oxygen tank. I suppose he'll be taking it back soon, now that I don't use it."

"I didn't know you used oxygen. You *are* an invalid, aren't you?"

"I've been in a bad way ever since I got here." She smiled and tried to look vivacious. "It's nice to be on the road to recovery."

"Glad you're better. Got to go now. See you later."

With that announcement, Angel rose and took herself out the door. Anne rushed to close and lock it behind her. Angel hadn't bothered to cover up her reason for the visit. Her curiosity had driven her to find out why Jim had been there. Before Anne could give the incident more thought, her office phone rang.

"Do you feel up to a visit tonight?" Jim's voice asked over the line. "We could go somewhere."

"I have work to catch up on. I'm behind schedule," she fibbed. She couldn't be around Jim with so many conflicting feelings and thoughts, not with Angel's hold on him, and her own new awareness of her physical state. And thoughts of that kiss, that strange, uncomfortable kiss, still lingered.

"Hang the work. I can't come till about eight. Is that too late?"

Anne didn't answer for a minute. She wasn't sure what she should answer.

"Anne, I need to see you."

"Eight's fine."

"Don't dress up. I won't have a chance to change. My life ceases to be my own anymore." He sounded bitter.

"Like I said, a pawn of Sumner. I knew it'd come to that. Don't worry, I feel it myself. Not up to a fight yet, but I'll gain steam. See you at eight."

She had taken her first big step. Both Angel and Jim thought she was recuperating. Could she manage the tricky task of convincing her body? She just wouldn't listen to it any more but instead would abuse it till it hollered uncle.

After a short nap, she donned white shorts and a white halter top, the same ones worn many times in Mexico when her body exuded health. The mirror told her she had lost weight, along with most of her suntan. Her face looked especially pale, and she slumped, too. Straightening her posture made her cough, but she maintained the stance in spite of it and saw immediate improvement. She applied makeup carefully, intensifying her color, but in the end washed it all off and applied only pink lipstick. Armed with a new purse containing a new oxygen canister and wielding newly renovated willpower, she sat down on her sofa to wait.

Jim breezed in five minutes early and looked as if he had run to get there. His eyes showed he approved of her attire. He reached out his hand, and she took it, letting him pull her up from her seat. She faked a miniscule bounce of energy and deplored the fact it no longer came naturally.

He kept hold of her hand as they rode the elevator down. His car was parked at the sidewalk by the front door. She got in and never thought to ask where they were going. It didn't matter. They must have driven for half an hour before Jim's voice finally broke through the night's quiet.

"What're you thinking about?"

"About loneliness. Remember the time in Mexico when you asked if I was ever lonely or homesick? I've discovered something new, now that I'm supposedly home. I'm still lonely, and it has new depths to it, especially at night. My office seems not so much different from my tent. It makes me wonder what *is* my home and where *do* I belong."

"Are you lonely now?"

"N-Not so very."

"Why?"

She was irritated at him for pressing the issue, but she couldn't, at that moment, be less than honest.

"Maybe you make the difference, though I don't know why."

"Maybe I'm home."

"If you're home to me, what are you to Angel?" She hated herself for asking, even as she said the words.

"I'm the new sports car in the garage." His brash words came much too quickly.

"There have been a few sports cars before. Sometimes the garage becomes so crowded they have to park in the street."

"Would that be called catty?"

"It might, but then she's my sister. I know her well. If I wanted to be catty, and still honest, I'd say you were closer to being a new pair of shoes than a new sports car. She's had many, many shoes." She sat there with tongue in cheek and waited for a reaction.

"Now that definitely rang catty. For your information, I'm neither sports car nor shoes. I'm the new game she's trying to learn how to play."

"Why aren't you teaching her tonight?"

"How do you know I'm not?"

He pulled to a parking spot by the ocean, adjacent to a beach shack and eatery. A number of people milled around, proving the spot's popularity. They got out and found an empty bench. Anne sat stonily silent. Jim laughed and shook her shoulder.

"I'm sorry. But you're so close-mouthed. You hold your feelings in so well, I like to get your dander up. It's the only time I can get a glimpse inside you. But I always regret it."

"Now it's my turn to ask why."

"Because you're so honest, so clean. It humbles me. Most people are lies. You're not. I don't mean you're not deep, you're enormously deep. But the deeper I see, the truer and finer you appear. I guess I should have realized it'd be that way, if only because you were down there, doing what you were doing, and by your own choice. I've met other missionaries, dedicated ones. I've yet to meet one who would stay and *work* to support their mission if no organization supported them financially. How many missionaries do you know who would do that?"

"Not many," she said thoughtfully, "but I do know of *one*. He had nineteen missions in Mexico, and, when he didn't have the outside support to keep on, he repaired musical instruments, like violins, for the money to continue his work. He's dead now, but he's proof there are much better people than I'll ever be. He and his wife worked down there for thirty years."

"Ah. You said a lot there, 'He and his wife.' That makes an enormous difference. You worked all alone. That makes you more of a hero to me, no matter what you say. Sorry, but I've assimilated some of that Bible you gave me. He probably had an easier time doing nineteen villages than you had doing two – the widow's mite, you know."

"Thank you for the praise. Yes, I can see you've read beyond Psalms. I'm glad. This is a pleasant spot. Ah. Breathe that salt air."

"I remembered what you said about missing the ocean, back when we were in Mexico. I thought we'd walk on the beach."

"I'd love that," she said happily but a wee bit scared she wouldn't make a good showing. "No running or swimming yet."

"You sit here, and I'll get you something." He disappeared into the adjacent building and came out pushing a beach wheelchair with large rubber tires.

Anne's spirit cried out at the thought of Jim pushing her in that contraption. She would not allow it, ever! She couldn't let him picture her an invalid.

"I don't need that," she choked. She promptly rose from the bench and walked off toward the ocean, her back to him. Mortally afraid an uninvited tear might slip out, she hurried to get beyond the lights. Within minutes Jim came up beside her, minus the chair. He took her arm, slowed her down, and walked beside her.

"I'm sorry. I'm not bright. Earlier today when I reserved the chair, it seemed like a good idea."

She couldn't talk about it. "The ocean's wonderful. I want to walk in the water."

"Sit down here on the sand with me for a minute. We'll take our shoes off."

In a few minutes her breath came easier, and she settled back and looked out at the ocean. "I love this. I could stay here all night. I can breathe this air."

"No doubt. You're not breathing Houston smog. But we can't stay here all night because I have to be back by eleven to take up the jet. We can come back here some other time, though."

Anne was both disappointed and relieved at their shortened date. At least she knew exactly how long to play healthy and vivacious. With a forty-five minute drive back to the offices, that left little time for the beach. She would survive it if it took a week to recover.

They sat and gazed at the dark waves rolling in. Finally, Anne broke the silence.

"Thanks for bringing me here. All my cares have become less pressing, insignificant."

"They're not insignificant."

"Sure they are. I'll slowly mend, and I'll go back and pick up the pieces. I'm impatient, worried about the villagers, and ... I feel the water calling."

She bounded up with her best show of energy and walked to the water's edge. The foamy water swirled around her ankles.

"It's warm. I wish I'd brought my suit. How I miss swimming." She turned toward him, wondering how well he remembered the night they swam in Tutlu.

"No swimming yet for you. Those waves would knock you over. Let's head back. We can pick up something to eat at that little shop."

They took their food to his car and rolled down the windows to enjoy the breeze.

"Have you heard anything new about the villages? No one answers my letters."

"I'm sure you would have heard from someone if you were needed. No news should be good news."

Abruptly, his cell phone rang. He glanced at it and turned it off. "I miss the peace of my old job."

"Has the new job turned into permanent?"

"Who knows? Excuse me while I run into the restroom here. Don't drive off and leave me."

The second his door closed, Anne dove into her purse for oxygen. She didn't feel the need of it with the wonderful salt air all around her, so full of oxygen from the ocean, but she wanted to be ready for the rest of the evening. A moment later he reappeared. She watched him slide his cell phone into his pocket and knew he had returned the call.

"I'm called to work sooner than I expected. We'll have to go back now. I'm sorry. There were things I wanted to ask you."

"Maybe on the way back?"

"No. They'll wait."

He talked little and acted slightly evasive on the homeward drive. Anne kept up her show of energy until safely behind the closed doors of her office. When she felt certain he had left, she hurried out to the hall window that gave a view of the runway and hangers. Jim had driven to that area and parked his car beside another one, *Angel's*. She watched him open Angel's door and walk with her into the hanger.

Her chest felt like it had withstood an actual blow. She staggered back to her office and sat down on the floor for a while. She didn't cry. She couldn't. Jim's job involved flying Angel and her dad anywhere they wanted or needed to go. But that didn't make it easier on her. Wasn't she a Sumner, too? Why not demand Jim fly her back to check on her village? But the village had nothing to do with her work at Sumner, and it wouldn't be honest.

Her resentment and jealousy didn't last long. They were replaced by a disquieting thought. In her own way she behaved worse than Angel. All evening she had lived a lie and led Jim to believe she had gained ground on the road to recovery. Was that fair to him?

Chapter 8

The minute quitting time rolled around Friday, Fred found her more than ready for her venture afield. When she had picked up her paycheck earlier that day, she notified the office of a possible two-week absence.

"I can't get used to wages, Fred. It seems like too much money after slaving for pennies in Mexico. I should eat well these next two weeks, anyway. And thank you for the cell phone."

Fred accompanied her into the grocery store, but, when he suggested a motorized shopping cart, she refused and obstinately walked behind her cart. Halfway down the first aisle, she realized her folly. She leaned on her cart for the rest of her shopping spree, but she had fun on this first trip to a well-stocked grocery after so long doing without. Fred laughed at some of her purchases.

"But I've only eaten fast food and office fare since I've been back. I want to grill a hot dog and toast marshmallows. I want to fry bacon and eggs."

"Shouldn't you stick to canned fare? It might be hard to keep supplied with ice."

"I'll keep the perishables in the spring."

At the cabin, Fred insisted she rest while he checked things over. He filled two buckets with spring water and brought in an enormous stack of firewood from the shed. With a can of kerosene he had brought, he filled a couple of lamps and lit them. Finally he put away her purchases and started a fire in the fireplace.

"This will be hard for you," he stated. "I don't see how you'll do it. There's not a two-week's supply of firewood left in the wood shed, and you can't carry water. It's chilly here at night, too. Fall's here."

"The air's great. I feel better already."

"I'll get someone to help you. The folks up the road used to take care of things here and keep us supplied with wood. I'll call and arrange for someone to come by twice a day."

"You do that, and I'll go straight back to the office and kill myself with overwork and bad air. Give me their phone number, Fred, and I'll call them if I need anything. It's too late to bother them now."

She didn't intend to call, ever. She came there for privacy. An old axe leaned in the corner by the wood box, and it would be part of her plan to get well, or to get on with whatever lay in store for her. She knew she wasn't reconciled to the outcome the doctor had predicted, but, on the other hand, she wished she'd asked him how long she might survive. All her thoughts were a jumble of contradictions as she wavered back and forth between depression and hope.

"I brought two extra batteries for your phone, since there's no way to charge it here. Would you like me to stay the night, this first night anyway?" Fred asked, breaking into her thoughts.

"I'm fine. I'll call you in the morning. I'll call every day. Now I'm going to curl up here and gaze at this great fire you built, until I fall asleep."

She stretched out on the sofa in front of the fire and pulled a blanket around her. When Fred finally left, she breathed a sigh of relief. She had waited forever for this moment, the moment she could break down and give in to the emotion she had struggled with ever since Dr. Logan's diagnosis. But before the sound of Fred's car motor had faded and before her tears could find an outlet, she fell asleep.

All too soon sunshine flooded the room, waking her from a deep, dreamless sleep. Birds outside sent forth music from all the trees, but she felt too tired to enjoy it. She made a trip to the outhouse, noting it couldn't compare with the one she built in the village, but surprisingly it had a large mirror in it. No doubt Angel had brought that item of civilization.

When she noted how slumped she looked, she resolved to stand straight, no matter the cost. After washing her face and taking a drink of cold spring water, she crawled back onto the sofa. She might have slept the day through if Fred hadn't called two hours later.

"I'm sorry, Fred. I'm having such a good time I forgot to call. It's grand here, with warm breezes and all these oxygen-giving trees." She was glad he couldn't see the gray face and drooping shoulders she'd viewed in the outhouse mirror. "You've not told anyone where I am, have you?"

"Everyone figures you're working in your office, except for a couple of people who think you're away at some fancy health spa. I doubt anyone remembers we have the cabin. No one's used it for years. Call me every evening, or I'll come get you."

"I'll call, and don't worry. I'm fine."

If breathless and tired and sick to her stomach denoted fine, then she was fine, she told herself and crept back under her blanket. She slept until a piercing whinny woke her. Homer had arrived with Tom-tom. Behind his pickup truck, he pulled a shiny, silver horse trailer containing one excited horse that pawed in impatience to be let out.

Homer put Tom-tom in the corral, which had entered the last stages of deterioration. One rail was missing, and two other's looked as if they would break at a light touch. The thought of repairing them in her present condition dispirited her. Tom-tom played the devil with rails. He would try them all within thirty minutes, and he wouldn't be sympathetic with her weakness, either. Besides that, there would be the water trough to fill every day.

Some of her perplexities were answered when Homer brought out a long rope and ran it around the insecure spots of the corral, threw in a mineral block and a bale of hay, and filled the water trough from the nearby spring.

"Is there anything else you need? I'm leaving the trailer here. There's some extra rope in case that old corral gives way. I threw in a couple of saddles and all the other tack you'll need. I'll leave the grain and hay inside it and park it beside the corral."

"Thank you, Homer. We shouldn't need anything more. I'll call you when I'm ready for him to go back."

When she said goodbye, she led him to believe that everyone, including Anglin, knew she was camping there with her horse. If she acted the least bit secretive, he would go straight to her father and tell him. Anglin signed his paycheck.

For a while she leaned against a rail and watched Tom-tom devour the thick, tall carpet of grass and weeds that filled the corral. The camp obviously hadn't been used for a good while. It gave her a glad feeling to see Tom-tom there, to have him with her again, but it also brought sadness. What might become of Tom-tom if … She couldn't complete the thought. It hurt too much. She rubbed his searching, quivering nose and gave him a marshmallow.

Returning to the cabin, she lit a tiny fire in the cookstove and heated some soup. After dinner and a short rest, she checked on the firewood situation. The cabin bin contained enough for two days, with maybe another two day's worth in the shed. She would have to add wood to the supply every day if she wanted to enjoy a fire in the evenings. Physical labor sounded more appealing than delving into the uncertainties of her tomorrows.

Close around the cabin, she found an abundance of dry sticks and limbs that would burn readily and not require much work. She gathered an armful of small pieces and carried them to the cabin's open porch. In a patch of sunlight, she sat back and slowly broke all the wood into fireplace and cookstove length. The tiny pile of firewood that resulted gave her more satisfaction than all the hard work accomplished in the office during the past two weeks.

When she deposited the bundle into the cabin's half-empty woodbin, she made up her mind to use only the wood she gathered each day. The four-day stockpile could be saved for an emergency or to keep Fred from worrying in case he came by. Of course, only the cookstove required wood. She could always crawl under her blankets on cool evenings, but a warm blaze at night would feel good, like an old friend giving cheer.

Before settling for the night, she went outside to check things over. Tom-tom hadn't touched his hay yet and wouldn't until he had devoured all the grass in the corral. He seemed well-satisfied for the night. Maybe things wouldn't be so difficult after all. She might not be ready to carry a full bucket of water yet or chop firewood with an axe, but she could work up to those tasks gradually. It wouldn't be hard to keep Tom-tom's water trough full, and a gallon of water a day should be sufficient for her own needs. Even if her health didn't improve, she could get along if she didn't weaken her body too much. The realization brightened her.

Carrying only a quarter bucket of water at a time, she leisurely topped off the horse trough. When that was finished, she gathered a few more sticks and carried them into the fireplace, lighting a small fire. Hunger arrived unannounced, and she downed six hotdogs, blackened over the fire, followed by a cup of hot tea. As an afterthought, she put a potato on to bake in the coals.

Never knowing when she dozed off, she awoke later to find the fire out except for a few red coals. Hungry again, she dug the potato out of the ashes. Though charred on the outside, it looked perfect inside. She bolted it down with salt and butter and felt strangely like she wanted to cry when it was gone. Opening a can of baked beans, she ate them cold. At the rate her appetite had improved, her canned fare would soon be gone, and she'd be left with only eggs, bacon, and a few staples. Of course, there were fish in the lake. That thought made her mouth water. Tomorrow she would check what tackle the cabin afforded. With some line and hooks, she could set a trot line or maybe make a fish basket like the ones at the village.

When evening came, she reprimanded herself for getting sidetracked. She'd come to the cabin to rest and sort out what remained of her life, not to practice wilderness survival techniques. She fell asleep thinking she should face her future and awoke thinking only of fried fish. Her lungs hurt worse than usual but not bad enough to keep her in bed.

Skipping breakfast, she rummaged through the storage room and found a tackle box with adequate supplies, some old cane poles, already rigged, and one rod and reel. Satisfied with the equipment, she dug for worms behind the cabin and found enough to supply her needs.

Choosing a spot on the lake that evoked memory of past success, she took a minute to manufacture a cork out of a piece of twig. Fish rose all over the surface, and she rushed to bait her hook. She would satisfy her hunger with her own two hands. The instant she dropped her bait in the water, she had a strike. She set the hook into the jaw of a medium-sized bream and flung it ashore with primitive glee.

Hurriedly, she slid the fish onto a cord stringer and rebaited the hook. By the time the sun had lightened the sky to a soft coral-gold, there were five nice brim and one catfish on her stringer. Sitting on the bank, she cleaned the fish and took time to put together a makeshift trotline out of four hooks. Baiting the hooks, she tossed the line a short ways out from shore, securing the end to a nearby bush.

Frying the fish proved harder work than catching them. The heavy, cast-iron skillet tried her present ability, but she managed to slide it around and successfully fry all six fish. She ate them all, though she had meant to save a couple for evening.

When she stepped outside again, Tom-tom pawed and whinnied for attention. She gave him grain and noticed he'd taken the grass down considerably during the night. His bulging sides gave evidence of his satisfaction with his temporary home. By tomorrow he would need hay. She took time to replenish his water before going inside for a long nap.

Ravenously hungry upon awakening, she wondered whether she might run out of food altogether. Though her health seemed the same, or possibly worse, her appetite had grown immensely. With visions of more fried fish, she checked her trotline. The bait had been nibbled off three of the hooks, but the fourth hook had caught a catfish. She baited and set them again before going in search of firewood. With the aid of an old canvas bag from the store room, she improvised a way to easily transport the wood. She fitted a rope handle to it and dragged the wood behind her instead of carrying it. It worked well and enabled her to get a nice supply with minimum effort.

All day she fished, ate, and gathered wood. By evening she had stacked enough wood to guarantee a substantial fire that night. However, in the excitement of her success, she inevitably overworked and fell asleep that night totally beat.

Morning arrived with a vengeance. She suffered enough pain and fatigue to dwarf her last days at the office. If she was experiencing a natural reaction to the increased demands on her body, then improvement should manifest itself when her old fitness returned, she told herself. But if this new weakness signified the illness taking its toll, it scared her to think what might come next. It took all her willpower to drag herself from bed.

Munching a cold biscuit, she went straight to the old axe that tempted her every time she looked in its direction. Upon examination, she found the head snug but the edge blunt. When a quick search turned up no file of any type, she decided the axe would do for her needs. She hefted its familiar weight and set forth to the nearest fallen pine. Even with the dull edge, it took only one blow to knock off a two-foot chunk of the decaying wood. When the sixth chunk dropped defeated on the ground, she, too, dropped flat on her face on the forest floor and thought she would never rise again. Close to losing consciousness, it scared her enough to keep her there a good fifteen minutes.

Finally, she rose to her knees and smiled to herself. Pulling herself to her feet, she gave a trembling blow and knocked off another chunk. The light, rotten logs would burn poorly, but they would last longer then twigs.

After a short rest, she took care of her daily chores and spent the rest of the day fishing. Before she knew it she had waded into the warm water, fishing all along the shore. An overpowering urge to slide into the water and float around consumed her. Evening had almost arrived, but the sun still gave off some warmth. She waded deeper, to where the water level rose over her chest, but, with the added pressure against her lungs, she couldn't fully inflate them.

She moved back into shallower water and splashed herself clean. Finally, sitting at the water's edge, she let her mind drift back to another pond and another time. When the distant hum of an airplane interrupted her reflections, the atmosphere around her seemed to swirl with nameless emotion. Her tears, held at bay for so long, flowed in a torrent down her face. No longer was it aching lungs crying for air but an aching heart crushed into the depths. She let desperation sweep over her, drown her, swallow her up in its fury, but, after it had done its worst, she still had hold of a small tendril of hope. She didn't know how long she sat there, remembering and trying to forget, but, when she finally rose stiffly from the water, the sun had left and evening chill had set in.

Chapter 9

When she tried to climb out of bed Tuesday morning, her body revolted. She expected as much, knowing she had overdone physically and mentally the day before. Just when she decided she might never get out of bed again, a loud thump sounded against the cabin wall, along with the decided clang of a metal bucket rolling off the front porch. Dragging herself to the door, she was greeted by the sight of Tom-tom chomping grass around the cabin.

She tied him to a tree and went to examine the corral, only to find two more rails down. After repairing it with rope, she reinstalled her unhappy horse. Tom-tom looked longingly out at the green grass, so close and yet so far. She recognized that look and knew there would soon be more broken rails.

Tom-tom raced excitedly around the corral a couple of times, kicked out his back legs and bucked, then finished off with a vigorous roll in a dusty corner before coming to her. He nuzzled his soft nose against her fingers, searching for a treat. Would she be able to ride him, she wondered. Just the thought of saddling such a spirited animal seemed a monumental task. But ride or not, she welcomed his company. She had missed him terribly in Mexico.

After a while, she pulled herself away from Tom-tom and chopped firewood with the axe. She found that if she rested after each blow, she could hold up to the work much better. Her patience needed development. Physical tasks would have to be done at a slower pace, the same as when she talked. She gave one swing with the axe and rested before rendering another blow. Within an hour, she had twelve logs scattered about, and she felt no worse than at the beginning. Yet it saddened her. Less than a month ago she could have cut all twelve in one minute.

Come evening, she settled in front of the fire with her Bible for the first time since her sickness. She wanted to face God and talk with Him as of old. She had hardly prayed since the illness hit. Prayer came harder when your body and mind were so far down. She knew she would have more understanding, henceforth, of people in that condition.

Her Bible fell open to Psalms. It would most likely always fall open to Psalms, since Jim had used that section so thoroughly that first night. Tears threatened again. She hated remembering. Why did everything hurt, and why was she so full of everything?

Jim hadn't called since she had been there. He probably gallivanted somewhere with Angel. He might as well spend his time with her. What future could he find in hanging with an invalid missionary? A year from now she would no doubt be gone, perhaps much sooner. Even as the thought came, a part of her wouldn't accept it. Part of her still wanted to fight, and that part didn't want to give up her one friend. She wanted him beside her, if it were only for a year or a month or whatever. He didn't belong with someone like Angel.

Honesty came easier out there alone in the woods. She read in Psalms for a long while, and, when she finally slid under her blankets to sleep, she knew God was still there, had been there all along.

Tom-tom waited patiently to be rescued the next morning. His front legs were outside the corral, and he had a rope wrapped around one fetlock. Smart enough to understand his dilemma, he stood rock still and waited to be extricated. After setting him free, she haltered him and put him on a picket line she tied between two trees in a patch of abundant grass.

Hit with a sudden whim to repair the broken corral herself, just as she would have done in Mexico, she took stock of available materials. The woods around the cabin would provide plenty of small, straight trees for rails. Old spikes could be dug out of the rotted rails. She could straighten them and use them for the new rails. She even had an axe.

Her good sense said she should leave Tom-tom on a picket line. Why repair a corral no one used? Nevertheless, old habits still dominated her. When something broke, she fixed it, and she usually had no money available to make the job easier.

In the nearby woods, she found a straight poplar that would yield two eight-foot rails. It would only have to be dragged about twenty feet to the corral. Of course, a green, sturdy tree required more chopping effort than a rotted log lying on the ground. It took half an hour to put a score on the side of the tree facing the corral to assure it would fall in that direction. When she started in on the other side, she had to constantly remind herself to be patient.

It took a couple of hours to get the tree down, trimmed, and cut into two eight-foot poles. After she dragged those poles to the corral, she found another tree that would yield two poles and a smaller tree that would yield one. She started in on the larger one and soon had it creaking on its stump. A gentle push sent it toward an opening where it could fall free between two trees, but the tree exhibited a will of its own. It pivoted as it fell and landed against the tree she intended to cut later. It hung up in the tree's upper branches and couldn't be budged. A month ago she would have dragged the trunk of the tree back, inch by inch, until the top came free from the other tree. She had muscled out many a tree that way in Mexico. Angry and frustrated at her helplessness, she threw up her hands in despair and walked off to find another tree.

She grew so intent on her quest, she forgot all her woes for a couple of days. When she wasn't chopping down trees, she was notching the ends of rails or straightening six-inch spikes or nailing on new rails or cutting up old rails for firewood. She felt proud of how well she held up under the hard, physical toil.

By Thursday evening, she knew coming to the cabin had been a good idea. The task of surviving had helped her to block out worries about her health and about the villages. Those worries had been draining all the energy from her already-weakened body. She knew that. Now she reveled in the sunshine, the fresh air, and in being with Tom-tom again.

When she called Fred that evening, she didn't have to fake.

"Fred, I'm eating like a pig. I can't get enough food. I wish I had a two-pound steak to grill. I've been fishing, eating fish every morning and night. I had your favorite the day before yesterday, fried bass."

"You're making me cry. Can I visit this weekend? Do you have an extra rod?"

"Better bring your own gear. There's a rod here, but it doesn't look so hot. I've been using a cane pole. I found plenty of night crawlers behind the cabin where we used to dig them."

"I'll come Friday evening, bring you anything you need, but I may not be able to stay."

"Has Dad, or anyone, said anything about my being gone?"

"Nary a word. He's waiting for a big bill from some expensive health farm and will be all the angrier when he finds you thumbed your nose at his money again."

"I don't mind money, Fred. If I had some, I'd buy a steak and some fish worms."

"And then you'd send the rest to Mexico or to some other cause. Wish *I* could be content with just steak and fish worms."

"Ugh! You make it sound like a meal, Fred. I think I'm going to be sick."

"I'll call tomorrow. Have your shopping list ready. Goodbye."

"Fred ..."

The line went dead. She meant to ask about mail, though deep inside the thought of news scared her. Surely by now there would be some word from Mexico, but could she face a bad report?

In the morning, she chopped the rest of the broken rails into firewood and stacked the wood by the front door. Fred would think someone had delivered wood. City-boy Fred would never notice the logs had been chopped with an axe, not cut by a chain saw. Nor would he notice that some rails in the corral had been freshly replaced. Jim now, he would know in an instant. She looked sadly down at the logs and wished she could stop thinking of him.

By ten in the morning, she'd finished the work and put the place in good order. The fireplace awaited the strike of a match to send it into a welcoming blaze. Fred would think she only lazed around.

At noon, she took a bath in the lake, followed by a long nap. While waiting for Fred's arrival, she mixed biscuits and cut up the few remaining apples, stewing them with sugar. Stewed apples over biscuits had been a favorite of Fred's, and it pleased her she had some to offer. Before long he bustled through the door with twice the groceries she expected. He explained he couldn't stay except to eat. He brought in a bucket of fried chicken, which they devoured along with the apples and biscuits.

"You look better. You do. You've more color. You stand straighter."

Anne confided to herself, *He doesn't know what effort it requires for me to stand straight.*

"I nearly forgot. I have a letter for you."

Her heart thumped slugging blow after slugging blow. They racked her chest and left her breathless. Her hand's trembled as she tore open the envelope, but she couldn't read it. She covered her face with her hands and shuddered.

"I-I can't. I'm not ready. I ..."

"You don't have to read it. I'm sorry I brought it, but you seemed so anxious for news. I'll take it back. You're in no shape for this."

"I'll read it. It might be g-good news," she gulped, but in her heart she didn't expect good news. She knew the villagers, and she thought of a hundred things that could be wrong. The responsibility weighed heavily on her again.

Resolutely she picked up the letter. Her hands shook uncontrollably.

"It's from Padre Juan," she said after a minute. "Two villages came down with sickness, Capaso and Padre Juan's home village near the farms. Tutlu has only a couple of cases."

She read further, her heart frozen within her.

"Oh, no! Not Him. Little Pacal became ill and ... and Isdel d-died. Poor Zafrina." Tears burst from her smarting eyes, blistering the letter as she read. "And another worker from Tutlu, Marco Vakak, was brought home with the same illness. They don't know if he'll recover. He seldom came home, maybe once a month. Fred, it's the same as what I have. I'm certain of that. The sickness started all at once, right when mine did, or maybe the day before, but there have been no new cases since then. He says there have been a number of deaths, and many who are still gravely ill. None of them can afford medical care. Fred, it's been a month since I became sick. That means these people have been sick all that time."

"Is it flu?"

"He doesn't say what's wrong with them. He didn't mention virus or flu," she said, rubbing her eyes dry.

"What did your doctor say, the new doctor, I mean. You never told me."

She sank into the sofa and couldn't face him.

"He didn't say. He didn't have all the test results yet. And after he gave me my prognosis, I didn't much care about anything else.

"Anne, what was his prognosis? Were you supposed to go back to him? What about those test results?"

She couldn't keep tears from again filling her eyes. "He wasn't through. He asked a thousand questions. He especially wanted to know if there had been more cases. I didn't think there were."

"Now you know. You should go back, at least for the sake of all those sick people who can't afford a good doctor. You'd serve them as surely as if you worked for them. And it's seldom I get to do anything worthwhile. Let me pay for it, please."

"I'll go back. I'll call for an appointment and show the doctor this letter."

"Should you be here alone? People have died from this. Aren't you taking a terrible chance with your life?"

"There's no chance left to it, Fred. I'm not supposed to live. My lungs are ruined, becoming worse. *Irreversible* was the medical term he used." She said it as bravely as she could.

"Anne!" he said in shock. "You should have told me. I didn't know. We'll try another doctor." Ann had never seen him so serious.

"No. Dr. Logan's good. And I'm here at the cabin to ... to try ..." The look on Fred's face caused her voice to break, and she couldn't continue, but Fred finished for her.

"To try and live. To try and make a liar of these so-called medical experts. And I'm here to help."

"Don't tell anyone. Please. I couldn't bear that."

"I'm good with secrets, Anne. Just try me. Just watch me. Now what can I do for you?"

"I'll see the doctor, and you can pay. I'm going to get stronger. I need another week here, but, worse than that, I need to do something for the people down there. If I knew more about this, it might help the doctor to understand what's wrong with me. I, in turn, might be able to help the villagers."

"I'll learn what I can about the situation, discreetly. There's been some kind of stir in the office ever since you got back. Angel's been having some kind of problem with insurance claims in Mexico. It's likely something to do with this, though so far they've kept me in the dark. Let's keep it quiet about how chummy we are. I'll try and get on Dad's and Angel's best sides for a while and see what I can find out. I'll do anything you want, if it will make you see the doctor and keep you out here longer. You do look better. Now don't let anyone know we even speak to each other. If they ask how you got out here, tell them you took a taxi or something. Meantime, call me every day, and keep doing whatever you're doing."

Anne couldn't sleep that night, though dreadfully tired. Padre Juan and Pacal and Marco and Zafrina paraded through her half-conscious mind. Finally, she stared at the dark ceiling of the cabin, wide awake, and knew she needed to be back in Mexico where she could help. The situation didn't make sense. Why had only two cases, besides her own, occurred in Tutlu? It didn't sound like an epidemic. Why hadn't it spread to more villagers? Why were there no new cases? And yet Padre Juan had intimated there were many, many who were ill in his home village and in Capaso.

How could she help them without becoming an added burden? She wondered if any other children became ill besides Pacal, dear, gutsy, little Pacal. Thoughts rolled around in her brain until she finally attained a fitful sleep.

Chapter 10

Saturday she awoke with a sense of urgency not felt before. She must do something. Her little vacation would have to end. When she tended Tom-tom, she realized she must ride him that day or never. If she could stick on him, he would probably stick on the grassy trail that wound around the lake.

With sudden determination, she saddled and bridled him. Too soon for her confidence to kick in, she sat high in the saddle, atremble all over and not even remotely certain she could handle him. He bent his rubbery neck around backward and bit the toe of her boot to show his impatience. In spite of her misgivings, she loved this spirited, contrary side of Tom-tom. She held him in until they reached the trail and then eased up on the bridle. Misreading his cue, he lowered his head to graze on a nearby patch of grass. She laughed and was content to sit astride and rest a few minutes. At length, she pulled his head up and gave him a slight dig with her heels. She was ready when he bolted. She leaned forward to let him break the wind for her in case he decided to run, and run he did.

Through half-squinted eyes, she watched the landscape blur past while she pressed her face hard against his hot neck and gripped the reins tightly. His flying mane stung her face, and the thunder of his hooves drowned out the hard thumping of her heart. The dense line of trees and brush bordering the lake trail turned it into a regular race track and made control unnecessary. That helped immensely, because she needed all her strength to stay on.

Unpredictably, his pace slackened slightly. She glanced ahead through watering eyes to confirm they had about circled the lake and neared the cabin again. When she saw Jim standing in the path ahead, she felt a glow of pleasure, followed by immediate panic. Could she stop Tom-tom?

"Move! Move aside!" she hollered, but the words didn't carry even to her own ears. Sometimes Tom-tom exhibited an ornery streak. He played stupid and ran into obstacles in his path, especially human-type obstacles. It seemed he had chosen this very moment to render those obstinate proclivities. She sensed it through every fiber of the throbbing horseflesh beneath her. On the other hand, it was nice Jim would see her astride and seemingly healthy, before Tom-tom trampled him into oblivion, she thought philosophically.

Urgency gave her a modest boost of strength. She pulled hard on the reins, attempting to stop him and turn him at the same time, but, in spite of her efforts, only his head and neck turned. He allowed her to pull his head back sideways, to where he stared at her leg, while he galloped merrily on, straight ahead. He looked up at her with wide, rolling, ludicrous eyes. She let up on the reins, so he could at least turn his head forward and see where he was going. Maybe, just maybe, he'd leap aside when he got to Jim.

Horror gripped her, and she wanted to close her eyes but couldn't. At the last second, Jim stepped aside and grabbed Tom-tom's bridle with such an iron grasp it set the horse on his haunches. Tom-tom recovered quickly and jumped forward a step to get his balance. Her strength gone, Anne slid off over his rump in a most ungraceful display, rolled to the side to avoid his hooves, and sat on the ground humiliated. The horse took it all in stride and started cropping the grass beside Jim's feet while Jim held the bridle and looked amusedly at her.

"I should have expected something like this."

"You can put him in the corral, that is, unless you want to ride," she said sheepishly, hiding her exhaustion.

He didn't reply but took Tom-tom to his corral. When he returned, he dropped down beside her on the grass.

"If I'd known you'd try something as foolhardy as this, I'd have come back, job or no job."

"How did you find out I was here. Did Fred tell you?"

"*You* told me. You mentioned once about a cabin you could come to. I know how you think. I had no trouble locating it."

"If you knew where I was, why didn't you come sooner?"

"I was touring Mexico with Angel. Company business. But Fred's kept me posted. He just didn't tell me *where* you were. And you didn't tell me you own a cell phone now."

"Fred got me one to use while I'm here. You and Angel went to Mexico on company business?"

"Yes, and Daddy came down for a couple of days, too."

"What on earth type business would Angel have in Mexico?" she baited, and hoped to learn if it concerned the illness down there.

"You forget, she handles the company insurance claims, and that includes Mexico and anywhere else they have offices or workers or sell products or whatever. It's a big job, and she's all business, at least most of the time."

Anne didn't ask what they did the rest of the time.

"Did you see my villages while you were down there? Did you hear anything? I had a letter from Padre Juan yesterday. He told me about all the sickness. Isdel died, another farm worker from my village, Marco Vakak, was brought home near death, and ... and Pacal caught whatever it is. Do you know anything about this? Do they know what caused it?"

For a long time he didn't answer, just sat there beside her on the ground. His arms rested on his knees, and he stared at the ground between his legs, apparently deep in thought.

Finally Anne grew impatient. "Did you know about all this?"

"That's why we were down there. Many of the sick work for your dad."

"It's not like Dad to care about sick workers, not unless he's liable. With Dad it'd be 'tough luck,' and he'd hurry away to find some more desperate farm hands to hire. There's no shortage of workers down there."

"Someone intimated the illness might have been caused by chemicals used on the fields."

"What about my sickness? I'm certain it's from the same cause, and I wasn't anywhere near his fields, never have been. Chemicals don't drift fifty-five miles. Did the illness strike children and people who don't work in the fields?"

"As far as I know, you're the only sick person who didn't work at the fields."

"Don't forget Pacal. He has the same symptoms. Of course, Angel flew down there to help all those unfortunate workers file their claims."

"You know why Angel and your dad went there. They'll crush this, keep it out of the news, and not pay a red cent. I have to admit, Angel's good at it. And the very fact that you're ill furnished Sumner their most effective defense."

"If they knew about Pacal, they'd doubtless use his case, too. Do you think this illness stems from a virus or from something to do with chemicals? Can't they test the fields and workers?"

"They haven't gotten as far as the workers, yet, but a government agricultural representative went out there to investigate. They took him out into the fields to check the soil. Your dad and Angel insisted he test. He found paraquat and pesticide residue, that's all. The levels registered moderate, well within the legal limits."

"Those chemicals can cause lethal consequences if someone gets careless with them. Sumner might be charged with negligence in some other way."

"I'm sure Sumner will try to pin all the illness on a virus and use your illness as proof. If that doesn't work, they'll pin it on the pilots who sprayed and pay as little as possible in claims. Sumner, of course, can't be found at fault and suffer damage to their reputation. Your dad plays hardball. He as much as told me it'd be better for me to go under than Sumner. The trouble is, I like my flying license, and I'm not guilty of any error."

"Who else was flying?"

"Just Fritz."

"Could he have blundered?"

"No, not even Fritz. Though Anglin would let us both go under to keep Sumner out of trouble. I have my own license for spraying chemicals. I don't use his company license. I needed it because I spray for other companies as an independent contactor. But, when I fly for your dad, I work as an employee, so he'd still be liable."

"Surely you have thoughts of your own about all this."

"I'm not sure. I'd like to go back and check some things, without Angel or Anglin along."

"Soon? May I go? I've gained physically since I've been here."

"Anne, have you? Honestly?"

"I chopped firewood, swam. I carry water. I fish."

"You even ride horseback, sort of."

"*Fred* said I looked better."

"You look fine, now you've rested long enough to get oxygen back in you. You looked white as a ghost clinging to that wild horse."

"Tom-tom."

"Okay, Tom-tom. What would you have done if I hadn't stopped him?"

"Maybe I'd still be racing around. It felt glorious. But actually, he fully intended to stop for a grass break. I know him."

"What if he didn't stop in time? You were about gone, admit it."

"I admit nothing. I thoroughly enjoyed my first ride in years. Nothing compares to sitting high on a horse's back. You become sort of ... egotistical. It changes you, somehow, to sit astride a horse and look down at all those people eating dust."

"Why do you think I fly? It's the same feeling, only I'm higher."

"I never thought of that. You do understand."

"I can tell you've gained physically or maybe just mentally. You're fighting now. But how well do you breathe?"

"I-I don't know. I've learned to pace myself."

"Does anyone know you're here, besides Fred?"

"Homer, from Dad's stables, brought Tom-tom out."

"Did you mend those rails in the corral, or did Homer repair them? I saw fresh stumps."

"I did it. It took a long time. I only replaced a few. I intend to replace more."

"Where's the axe? I need to redeem myself after my last wood-cutting exhibition."

Anne laughed. "No redemption needed. Everyone in the village knew what a feat you performed, even the children."

"Just the same, I could use the exercise. Afterward, you can take me fishing, and maybe I'll swim. Now what trees can I cut?" He picked up the axe and headed toward the woods.

"Any tree straight enough for rails and not too thick. I have six-inch spikes. I pull out the old spikes and straighten them."

"There's a tree already down. It looks straight."

"It's hung up on that other tree, which I originally planned to cut, too."

Jim pulled at the hung-up tree, but it had wedged solidly in the other tree.

"I'll cut the tree it's hung up in and let them both fall."

"That's dangerous. Too unpredictable. Trees make strange moves when two become caught together like that. Just walk this one's trunk back a ways. It should come loose."

He ignored her and chopped low down on the other tree.

"Notch the tree on the side where you want it to fall. You're cutting the wrong side. It can't fall that way because the other tree's leaning against it."

"Okay. I'll notch the other side, if you say so." He went around and started applying vigorous blows to the other side.

"But it's too dangerous now. You've cut halfway through from the other side. And you should chop that notch below the other cut, not above it."

"I'll be careful." He continued to apply massive blows.

"It's falling! Get out of the way – run!"

"They're just trees, Anne." He rained blows on the defeated tree, ignoring the movement and creaking above him.

Whoosh, the trunk of the smaller tree leaped in the air and struck him in the side, knocking him to the ground. Both trees came down on him, smothering him in a pile of trunks, limbs, and foliage.

Anne rushed to the spot where Jim struggled to extricate himself.

"Are you hurt?"

He eventually freed himself and rose, covered with leaves and twigs and wearing an indignant look on his face.

Anne hesitated, then laughed. She lay face-down on the ground and laughed wildly. When she ran out of breath, she gasped her amusement and fought for oxygen at the same time. Jim came over and looked helplessly at her, obviously wanting to help, but he read correctly the warning look in her eyes and said nothing. Instead, he sat beside her on the ground and pretended to ignore her struggles.

"It's good to hear you laugh again," he finally said when she began to gain control.

"It's ... the hardest thing I do. Laughter ... takes so much oxygen. But there seems to be more of that out here than at Sumner's."

"Oxygen or laughter?"

"Both." She pulled herself to a sitting position beside him. "Is Angel serious over you?" She hadn't meant to blurt out her thoughts, but she needed to know, even if she sounded jealous. She faced eternity. Things like jealousy and pride had dropped in importance.

"She asked me to move in with her."

Anne looked at him gravely. She wouldn't ask the next question, the obvious one, though she desperately wanted to know. Jim said no more.

"Shall we fish now?" she finally asked.

"No. Not until I put up some rails. We'll fish after that."

He went to work with the axe, removing old rails, and committing himself to replace at least those.

"I'll straighten the nails when you get them out," she offered and set to work on the large spikes while he chopped and fitted rails. When he'd nailed the last rail in place, he set aside the axe and looked over at her.

"Now I want to fish."

"There's an old rod here. You can use that or one of the cane poles. I'm using a cane pole. We'll see who catches the most fish."

"I'll use a cane pole, too. I want this to be fair."

"I'm out of worms. You'll have to dig us some. I'm saving my energy for fishing." She said it like a joke, but only she knew how little strength she had left. "There are cans and a shovel behind the cabin. You'll see where I've been digging."

Intending only to rest, she fell asleep and didn't awake until he dangled a worm in her face.

"Let's go, lady. Here's your can of bait. I kept the biggest ones. I picked up one of those cane poles, so show me where to fish."

"Fish wherever you like. I'm going to fish over here so I don't have to walk so far," she stated facetiously.

She intended to win and knew she could pull it off if he'd fish somewhere out of sight. Anyway, her spot couldn't be beat for fishing, especially since she had thrown meal and bread crumbs into the water there every day to attract the fish.

Jim started off around the lake, and within five minutes she saw him land a fish. The next time his back was turned, she baited the four hooks of her trotline and slung it out into the water. A short distance up the bank from it, she fished with her cane pole and soon landed a bream. When Jim looked thoroughly engrossed in fishing, she checked her trotline, took off a catfish and bream, and rebaited the hooks. She slid the stringer through their gills and left them in a brushy spot of water where Jim couldn't tell what she had if he came by.

Soon he disappeared around a curve at the far side of the lake, and Anne got down to the real business of fishing. Jim stayed out of sight, and she guessed he had found a good spot. She slid a nice bass onto her stringer and leaned over the water's edge to bait her trotline. Hands dug into her sides, and a voice growled, "Gotcha." Traumatized, she plunged head-first into the water.

"Did you think I'd ever trust you again after that firewood-chopping trick?" he taunted and pulled her from the water, sputtering. "I guess illness hasn't taken the fight out of you anyway."

She coughed and gasped and wiped the water from her face with her hands.

"Are you all right?" he asked, at once repentant.

"Okay," she choked. "I swallowed ... a fish, I think."

"You can't count it. I have six nice, fat specimens. Let's see what your cheating gleaned you."

"Ten."

"You don't win yet. Let's see how big they are. It's the weight that counts."

Anne's eyes grew large when Jim brought out his fish.

"What a whopper! Where did you find him? How did you land a bass that size with a cane pole?"

"I used the rod. I slipped back through the woods and got it. Set the cane pole with a cork while I casted with the rod."

"You monster. Oh, but that's a wonderful bass. Where did you catch him? I didn't know any bass of that size inhabited this lake. Tell me where?"

"Nope. My secret."

"What did you use for bait? An artificial? A bream? Not a worm, I'll bet."

"Don't remember."

"I'll clean the fish if you tell," she tempted.

"Nope. You rest. You can come in the water when I swim, if you like. But I don't want you too tired to eat our dinner or to enjoy the fireplace with me tonight."

"I'll rest. Wake me if I fall asleep."

She lay back and looked up at the sky. This was her element. In spite of her weakness, she felt less like an invalid and better able to hold her own. She could joke about her weakness and admit to being tired without it hurting her pride so much.

"Anne, did the doctor ever explain anything to you about your illness? I mean, did he say how bad you were? Did he say anything about how long to full recovery?"

A guillotine had just dropped and severed her ability to think or speak. She rose to her feet and stood trembling, holding a tree for support.

"You mean Dr. Wildermuth from the hospital, the king of vagueness?" she finally asked. "He told me nothing. He implied nothing."

She silently waited for Jim to say something, anything. When he didn't speak, she grew ashamed of her dishonesty.

"But I found out about my condition, in spite of him. I have major lung damage. I'm not expected to live. I'm expected to become w-worse."

She had managed to speak the blunt words with hardly a break in her voice. It tore her up inside, but she did it. She had no right to keep it from him. Cheating in their fishing contest could be called a joke, but she couldn't cheat in this, even if it threw him into the arms of rich, healthy, beautiful Angel. She dared meet his gaze but wasn't prepared for the look on his face, so intense, so white, so desperate.

"I'm s-sorry, Jim," She could think of nothing more to say. Tears brimmed her eyes. "I'm sorry."

"Anne, don't. Don't apologize." He came quickly to her side.

"You're not worse," he said quietly, more gently than she had

111

ever heard him speak. "Where'd you get the idea you'd die, if not from Dr. Wildermuth?"

"Another doctor. He told me straight out. But Dr. Wildermuth never said I'd get well. He avoided saying anything."

"Did this doctor explain your illness? What caused it?" His eyes burned into hers. His face had a tortured look, his lips hard-set.

"He was waiting for more test results. He asked a m-million questions, especially about my work in Mexico. He asked if we'd used any chemicals of any kind. He especially wanted to know if anyone else had become ill. I told him about Isdel, that my symptoms were the same."

Jim groaned and shook his head.

"I'm supposed to go back to him," she hurried on, breathlessly. "He may know the cause of my problem by now. He hadn't run many tests when I first saw him. I promised Fred I'd go back. I-I'll call for an appointment."

"I'll take you. I'd like to go in with you and ask some questions. I've been down there, you know. I've seen some of the sick. I might be of help."

"Come if you like, if you're not flying Angel or Dad somewhere. It might help the villagers if someone knew for sure what happened to them, though it may not be the same problem as mine. And nothing will help me. He said as much. He said, *irreversible*. That w-was the word he used." She hated it that her voice stumbled again, but she faltered on anyway. "My lungs ... he said I had pulmonary fibrosis, proliferation of connective tissue in my lungs. I had him write it down. There's no reversal in a case as bad as mine."

"Never?"

"Even in milder cases it's extremely rare. Mine isn't mild."

"All right, Preach, where's your faith?"

"Maybe my time has come. I prayed to be healed, but, if God wants me to suffer through this, to die, then it's okay. I asked to be healed according to God's will."

"If you think it's God's will for you to suffer, why do you take pain killers? Why do you try to find a more comfortable position, so you don't hurt so much? Those actions prove you lied when you said it was okay if God wanted you to suffer. It's obvious you're trying *not* to suffer. And didn't you sort of lie when you asked God to heal you according to His will? Did you ask what His will was, or did you go ahead and try to cure yourself?

See, it's all lies. You *want* God to heal you, no matter what, don't you?"

"Oh, shut up. Okay. I'll pray 'Lord, heal me, and if it's not your will, please reconsider.'"

"That's better. Have faith it's not God's will for you to die. At least be honest."

"I am. I will. I'm trying to get well."

"Are you? Or are you trying to kill yourself quick because you can't stand the thought of being an invalid?"

"Maybe I can't. Maybe you're right about that. But that doesn't mean I'm not trying to recover. I'm trying with every fiber in me to get well. I push myself to the limit, and sometimes I push beyond. I rest and try again. I don't feel worse for the effort, nor better either. But I'm still here, and I'm not so scared."

He took hold of both her hands and held them fiercely. "Promise me this. When you need help – I mean oxygen or wheelchair or me or anyone – don't turn your back. Don't turn your back on help."

"You said I should have faith I'd get well. Where's your faith?"

"I've never had any, except in myself. And it's failed me. Now I'm trying to borrow from you."

"God hath dealt to every man the measure of faith."

"Is that from the Bible? It's not in Psalms."

"The Bible is more than Psalms. You should read on."

"I have. Don't rush me. I like to understand things."

"If you're still reading Psalms, you must have memorized them all by now, with a memory like yours."

"Working on it."

"I'm glad. But don't tell Angel. That subject won't enthuse her."

"You're saying she's not all her name implies?" He grinned. "I wasn't born yesterday, sister. I've been around."

"Now that's what she told me, her words exactly, about you."

He laughed heartily. "Are you jealous, I hope?"

"I only hope she doesn't corrupt you."

"I'm disappointed. I hoped for more. Rest now. I have fish to clean."

She stretched out on the brown carpet of pine needles, intending only to rest, but the next thing she knew Jim was brushing her nose with a leaf to wake her.

113

"Time to swim. Do you want to come in?" he asked playfully.

"It's getting late. I'd better light a fire in the fireplace if I intend to swim. I mustn't become chilled, though pneumonia would end all my concerns most efficiently."

"The fire's lit in the fireplace and cookstove. I got water, fed and watered Tom-tom, cut a pile of firewood, and prepared our dinner, most of it, that is."

"All that? Oh, how I miss being able to work hard and fast. I'll be with you in a minute. I have to go change."

She donned her swimsuit, out of date but still flattering, and walked down to the lake. Jim stood in the shallow water when she reached the shore.

"No! You can't be ill. You lied to me. Leeching sympathy."

"That's it. I wanted a free airplane trip to the States. Now that I'm here, I've got to figure how to get a free trip back." She waded into the water to where he swam.

"I'm taking you back tonight."

"Tonight? Tonight!" she shouted.

"Yes, I'm making tortillas to go with the fish. We'll have a fiesta."

She threw water right in his face, and he instinctively returned the barrage. She gave in and turned away coughing. He rushed to her and put his hands on her shoulders.

"I'm sorry. I keep forgetting. Are you all right?"

"I-I just swallowed it." She coughed some more. "I'm okay."

"Well, it's time to go ashore."

He helped her to the cabin in spite of her protests and proceeded to towel her dry.

"Can I help you dress?" He leered mischievously.

"I'll manage, thank you. I'm changing in the bedroom. Go find your own spot."

She changed into navy blue shorts and a soft, yellow sweater and left her wet suit on the front porch. Jim wasn't around, so she sank onto the sofa and had almost fallen asleep when he came in.

"I hung both our suits to dry on the top corral bar."

She gasped and jumped up from the sofa. "Run, quick, and get them! Tomtom ..."

"They're safe," Jim laughed. "But I made the mistake of changing clothes beside the corral, and he ran off with my towel. He dragged it through the dust while I chased him. When I finally caught him, he slung it around in the air. It was white, once."

Anne laughed and settled back on the sofa while Jim fried tortillas and fish. He soon set a platter in front of her, along with a bag of assorted fruit, the very fruits they ate at the fiesta in Mexico. To top it off, he handed her a small box of fudge.

"Now our fiesta's complete."

"You're making me homesick." She reached for the fudge, but he pulled it away.

"That's for dessert."

"I thought I'd never eat another piece of fudge. I got so sick of it down there. But it sounds good now. Isn't that strange? Everything looks good."

"Even me?"

She started to wisecrack, but, seeing his earnestness, she looked him squarely in the eyes.

"The fiesta wouldn't be complete without you."

Jim kept the fire blazing high while they ate. When the food was eaten, she stretched out her feet to the heat and slid down into her corner of the couch. In the grayness of dawn, the sound of an axe awoke her, and she knew Jim had stayed. A quick glance out the screen door told her he had been at it for a while. He had stacked an enormous pile of firewood by the door and now worked in the nearby woods.

She lit a fire in the cookstove and put on the coffeepot. Into one cast iron skillet she sliced potatoes, and in another she fried bacon. When those where both cooked, she slid them to the back of the stove and made a batch of biscuits. Those baked in the hot oven while she scrambled a pan full of eggs. She was setting out dinnerware when Jim walked in, his eyes alight with pleasure.

"When do we eat?"

"Soon."

He poured himself a cup of coffee, snitched a slice of bacon, and sat down on the front porch.

In a short while, Anne brought out two generously-filled plates and sat down beside him. They ate in silence for a couple of minutes.

"Good biscuits. I guess you're still good for something," Jim finally said.

"Gee, thanks. Nice view, isn't it, the sun on the water?"

"I'm afraid it's got your pond at the village beat all to pieces."

"That's because God made this one, and man made the other."

"Don't you mean *woman*? Ruben told me you dug the entire thing yourself, rising early, staying up late. He said they never helped until you were ready to fill in the last section of dam."

"I didn't go down there to make their lives harder and more toilsome. They had enough to do every day just to survive. And I wasn't sure it'd work. It's rocky there. The water might have all seeped out into some underground crevice. There was no way of knowing until the dam was finished and the water began to back up into the area. The spring might not have been strong enough to fill the pond, or maybe the dirt-and-rocks dam wouldn't hold. I was toiling at an experiment. But I let them help the last day, so they could feel proud about it if it did work."

"That's how you go through life. You count yourself, your efforts, as nothing. Your entire life is give, give, give. You should ask more of others, allow them to do more, make them do more."

"The dishes?"

"Dishes? Oh, I walked into that one, didn't I?"

She handed him her plate and leaned contentedly back against the post. He took the dishes down to the water's edge and scoured them with sand and water. When he returned, he refilled their coffee cups and sat beside her again.

"Would you like to ride Tom-tom?" she asked after a while. "The exercise would be good for him."

"Not sure. I saw how well he behaves. Coming down that home stretch, he looked like a cross between a camel and a demon. Didn't he rest his head in your lap while he ran? Strange horse."

"I should have called him Rubberneck, instead of Tom-tom. He's not strong on obedience, but I love him that way."

"So you want *me* to get killed?"

"Have you ridden before?"

"A tad. I'll take him for a spin around the lake, if it'll keep you grounded."

She noted the confident way he saddled Tom-tom and the ease with which he mounted. He had Tom-tom on the run before he had found his seat in the saddle. Instantly, she acknowledged he rode superbly. A smile spread over her face. She knew right then she loved this man. Her illness, the thing that crushed all her hope, had also slowed her down enough to recognize her strong feelings for him. But Angel would be the ultimate winner, and she must keep her feelings in the background. When he returned, she threw her arms around Tom-tom's neck.

"That was beautiful. I'd forgotten how great Tom-tom looked when running. His tail was up, his mane flying."

"Hey, lady." That hug, those compliments, should be for me, not some old nag."

"You did okay, for a tenderfoot." She laughed her tease. "So, you've ridden before." It wasn't a question.

He grinned as he unsaddled Tom-tom and turned him into the corral. "Would you like to walk in the woods before I cook the steak I brought, or do you want to rest?"

"Let's walk." Resting sounded good, but she had to convince Jim she could handle a trip to Mexico. She would soon have to leave him in Angel's arms, but the villages were her responsibility, and there would be no Angel to take them over after she was gone. Their survival rode on her shoulders, and her shoulders had little strength left in them. She must stop dreaming and keep her priorities straight.

"How much would it cost to hire you to fly me to Mexico for a day or two? I'll have another paycheck soon. I want to see things for myself."

"You don't want to see. Believe me. You couldn't help, and it'd only distress you. You've finally got some spirit back. If you went down now, you'd lose it. You're not strong enough yet."

"If I knew what caused my illness, maybe the information would help the doctor with my case."

"No you don't. You're lying, baiting me. You already said it made no difference in your case. You're thinking of your villagers, your *sick* villagers. You think you can help them by going down there."

"And what's wrong with that? If I haven't much time left, wouldn't it be good if I could help in some way? If they have the same thing I have, the knowledge might give one of them the chance I don't have."

"Don't you think anyone else is trying to help them?"

She sat silent for a minute, full of thought.

"No. No one is trying to help them," she finally answered with assurance. "No one with power or money is trying. Maybe Padre Juan or Rev. Sergio or the villagers themselves, but no one else. I can see by your face, you know it, too. You forget, I've lived down there. I know how things operate or don't operate." After another long pause, she said with decision, "I'm going back to the office tomorrow. I'm no good to anyone here. It's time I got back to work. I've learned how to pace myself. I should do better now."

"You don't need the smog and the worry. You should sit right here. I don't believe your doctor. I think you have a chance. God can heal you, can't He? In spite of what the doctor says? Don't go back and kill yourself. I won't stay and watch that."

"If you're my friend, you'll have to watch it. If it's going to happen, it will happen whether I go or stay. And I have to go down there. I see that now."

"Wait till you see the doctor. Maybe the two of us can convince you to stay here and rest. You're better. I'll bet he finds improvement. You have a chance. Don't throw it away. I'm pleading, Anne. What's the doctor's name?"

"Do you think I'd tell you that now? You'd bribe him or convince him to lie to me and give me false hope, the same way Dad must have paid off the other doctor to hide the truth from me."

"I'm sure this doctor can't be bought. I doubt your other doctor was. Maybe he was fooled or lied to. Don't think everyone is like your dad. *I'm* not." The heat in his voice startled her, and she wondered how badly Jim's relationship with her dad had been strained lately.

"I'll stay here until I can see the doctor, but only if I can see him tomorrow or Tuesday."

"If you can't, I'll think up another persuasion."

"I'd stay here longer if I could get to Mexico for a day and look things over."

"Now who's trying to bribe and corrupt me? You *are* your father's daughter. I'm not playing a game. I'm trying to save your life."

"I'm sorry. I'm so helpless."

"Anne Sumner has never been helpless. But maybe it's time you trusted someone else to do something. Maybe it's time you were honest with me."

"Here's for honesty. I want to go to Mexico and find out why the villagers are ill, before Daddy sweeps evidence under the carpet. If evidence proves Sumner caused the sickness in those people, then Angel shouldn't be allowed to cheat them. I want to go down and investigate for myself. But I also want to find out what happened to Pacal and me. I want to know if it's all caused by the same thing or if ours was caused by something different. It won't help me, but I want, I *need*, to know. Maybe it'll help Pacal. Maybe he's not so bad. Sometimes I wish I'd played Daddy's game and had his approval. With all my Sumner power and money, I'd fly that doctor down there to look at Pacal and some of the others." She stopped, not for lack of words but for lack of breath.

"Look, I'm flying your father's jet. I've been flying it ever since I brought you here to the hospital. My plane's still in Mexico. If I thought it might save your life, I'd steal the gosh-darn jet and take you anywhere you wanted to go. I've a mind to do so anyway. Right now my only way to get down there is to fly Anglin or Angel. I'd gladly pay someone else to take you, but I wouldn't trust someone else to know how to take care of you, and I might not be able to get away and come along. Besides, I doubt that anyone else would be able to land in the spots you need to see. I've wanted to go myself, but I can't get away. Yesterday, I stole a few minutes for myself, but they may call me any moment. I'm surprised they haven't yet. And to be honest, right now it'd be difficult for me to afford an airplane ticket to Mexico. I haven't exactly prospered lately. I've got a nice position, but I've seen little green stuff. It's all been talk so far. If I don't play my cards right, I'll need to borrow on my plane to pay an attorney."

The anger of his voice disturbed her. "What's going on, Jim? What's wrong?"

"Nothing. I'm just talking, trying to get your sympathy. Instead, I made you worry. Forget it, please. I'm in fine shape. Dad and Angel love me, and, if I do as they tell me, life will be great." It was a bad combination, his smiling face and bitter voice.

"I know you. You won't be obedient for long. Come to me when you need help. We'll figure something."

"Only if you'll do the same."

She didn't answer but solemnly shook his hand, her eyes answering his.

"I've been trying to build up my body and morale. Now I need to build up my faith. That's where I should have started. It seems my faith became sick along with the rest of me. But I understand things better now. Always before, when I'd try to help the sick, I'd marvel at their lack of faith, at their constant whining about their misery. Now I know that faith comes easier when you're well. Thank you, Jim. You've been a help to me. You don't realize how much. I'm stronger now. I have some fight left in me."

"All you are is fight."

Jim's phone cut into their conversation, and he was summoned back to Sumner.

"What did I tell you? Now, if I don't get back or if you don't hear from me, I'll most likely be in Mexico. Otherwise I'll call. But give me your cell phone number."

"What about our steak?"

"Eat the entire thing tonight while it's nice and fresh. If it doesn't cure you, I'll send another."

"I'm sorry you have to go."

"I'm amazed I could stay so long. I only expected a couple hours of reprieve when I came yesterday morning. I wanted to check on you and stay long enough to grill that steak. But I enjoyed the fish more." He started to leave but turned back and drew her close for a kiss.

Long afterward, thoughts of that kiss lingered. It was the second time he'd kissed her, not exactly a passionate kiss but not a kiss of sympathy either.

Chapter 11

Monday morning she decided to head back to the office. She could accomplish more from there than from her hideout in the woods. Obediently, she called Dr. Logan for an appointment but found he would be gone for a week. The nurse offered the services of an associate, but she declined. On the one hand, she welcomed the reprieve, but she did want to know if he had made any findings that could shed light on the problem with the villagers. Jim's information had started her thinking. She quickly made arrangements to leave her retreat, though with regret.

Back at the office, she at once felt the slimness of oxygen in the city air, but at least she now knew how to police her use of energy. No one knew of her late-afternoon arrival except Fred. That pleased her. She could snoop around and possibly learn much about the villages, maybe even learn what troubled Jim.

At nightfall, she slipped down the hall to Angel's office. The door stood open, and she hurried through to the back room where they kept the insurance records and claims. The room also housed a deluxe printer, which Anne sometimes used for special projects. Now it would give her an excuse for being there if someone came upon her unawares. The room's back window looked out on the parking lot below, so she could watch that avenue for unexpected visitors, too. She spread some bogus printing work on the table by the printer and proceeded with her spying.

Angel's neat, orderly desk came first. Anne envied such tidiness. Her own chaotic work area generally resembled a tornado's path. A quick search turned up nothing pertaining to the problem in Mexico. Before she could check in the drawers, she found a briefcase under the desk. There she found the information she wanted. Leafing through a file titled *Mexico*, Anne came across a list of eighty-four names, arranged in alphabetical order. Beside each one, Angel had listed the name of the village where that person lived, their age, the date they were taken ill, and the seriousness of their condition.

A pencil notation at the top of the page stated: thirty-eight recovering, twenty-four seriously ill, seventeen critical, five deceased. She recognized names and felt immediate sorrow for the families. When she saw Isdel's name listed with the deceased, she realized Sumner considered all these cases related, in spite of the time lapse between these new cases and Isdel's. Finding her own name listed, and with a *critical* grade beside it, startled her. It looked so cold and lonely, sitting there on the printed page. She shivered and wondered if Angel actually knew it belonged in the critical list or if she put it there to help Sumner's cause.

Checking the list again, she noted that eighty-one of the workers became ill on the same date. Her own illness happened the following day, Pacal's the day after that, and Isdel's happened quite a bit earlier. Pacal was listed as seriously ill. Tears slipped out unbidden, along with a degree of thankfulness that he wasn't listed as critical. Marco Vakak, the only other person from Tutlu, was listed critical.

She found more sheets. Some listed the same names but gave more detail. In most cases, Sumner's medic had been the attending medical person, and no claim was filed. A few names had a note by them stating that the ill person might make problems. Anne even found a description of the symptoms in each individual case. She studied the lists again and saw that Pacal was the only young child listed and the only one, other than herself, who didn't work at the farms. Most of the ill were either from Padre Juan's village, close by the farms, or from his mission village, Capaso. She made copies of all the papers and stuffed them into her folder.

Digging through the briefcase in search of more information, she found a drawing of Sumner Farms in Mexico. It displayed every field

Sumner controlled there, showed each field's size, the crop, the date it was last sprayed, and the chemicals used. It also showed when each field needed another spraying. Each field had a "letter" name, and the fields in question appeared to be fields A through E. Fields B, C, and E each had a list of numbers on them. She saw immediately that the numbers represented workers from Angel's list and showed where each person worked when the illness hit. It further listed the exact time of day the fields were sprayed and the exact time workers were in the fields. Fields A and D had the word "test" penciled on them but no numbers. Evidently there had been no workers in those two fields. At once suspicious, she realized these papers were meant for Angel's eyes only. They revealed too much and told a story of something obviously not an epidemic.

Anne copied those new sheets, plus some soil test results on fields A and D. The tests were dated and signed by a government official. They listed the herbicide paraquat as the main chemical and also showed a trace of another chemical, a commonly used pesticide. Either could, of course, do great damage if someone got in the direct path of the spray. The tests didn't expose any wrongdoing or error, but why did they test fields A and D when all the sick people worked in fields B, C, and E?

Finding nothing else relevant in Angel's briefcase, she hurried back to her office and began an Internet study of agrichemicals. She knew somewhat about them, but they hadn't been her area of expertise. Anglin employed a full-time chemist to take care of that end of the business.

She centered most of her research around paraquat, since it was the chemical listed on Angel's sheets. She already knew it was used to kill weeds and defoliate plants, like cotton and potatoes, before harvest. Now she needed to delve into its toxicity.

One study showed that death related to paraquat usually came from ingestion, a scant teaspoon's worth considered the lethal dosage. Usually the person died of lung failure within weeks. The chemical would concentrate in the lung tissue and cause oxygen-exchanging cells to die, only to be replaced by connective tissue cells. The victim would ultimately suffocate to death. It could also affect vital organs like the brain, liver, kidneys, even the heart. It all sounded so much like what the doctor had said about *her* condition.

The study went on to say that paraquat also produced problems when absorbed through the skin, especially in cases of heavy exposure or exposure for an extended period or if the victim had any skin lacerations, sores, or such. However, this form of exposure rarely caused death.

She found no antidotes listed for paraquat poisoning. Survival depended on the amount ingested and how quickly paraquat was removed from the person's system. Little had been written about treatment, except regarding immediate measures like emptying the stomach of the chemical or removing it from the blood. It stated that oxygen should not be administered at the beginning because it could accelerate the injury to lung tissue. She thought about Isdel's airplane trip to get medical aid. He had been given oxygen, and she vaguely remembered Jim giving her oxygen in the plane on the way back to the states. She wasn't sure what treatment the hospital had rendered. Had she been treated for a virus, or did they have knowledge unknown to her?

Her first physical symptoms were identical to what they listed for paraquat poisoning. She had experienced the burning of throat, abdominal pain, nausea, vomiting, and shortness of breath. And yet possibly a virus could cause those reactions, too. Even as she studied and noted the numerous similarities, she still doubted her problem had been caused by chemicals. The fact remained that she had never been exposed to any.

It was growing late, but she called Jim anyway.

"Jim, are you in a place where you can talk?"

"Shoot."

"I wondered if some chemical, maybe some herbicide like paraquat, could have been dropped accidentally near my village the day or night I became ill. I've found new information. If it turned out the illness with the workers was caused by chemicals, could my illness be from the same cause? My symptoms are the same. It might be easy to tell, in my case, if it's from something like paraquat. There'd be yellowed, dead plants somewhere near my village if there'd been an accidental drop."

"I thought of that long ago. I checked every square inch of the area, from the air and from the ground. There's not a sign. I knew for sure I didn't drop any, but I wasn't sure about Fritz."

"I'm just grasping at straws. I remembered that you flew over the night I became ill, about ten o'clock. Can you think of any way I could have come in contact with the chemical that night?"

"I didn't fly over that night. Thursday night you mean? I flew over once in the early evening, it hadn't turned dark yet, and once Friday morning."

"I just guessed it was you. I awoke to a noise and ran outside in time to see a plane's lights heading away from Tutlu, heading in the direction of the plant."

"Not me. Fritz sprayed that night, though. Do you think chemicals caused your problem and not some disease? Don't be afraid to say. I want to know as badly as you."

"I haven't seen the villagers who became ill. But I believe I'd know instantly if I could see them, talk with them."

"If you proved chemicals caused all this, your dad and Angel would burn you as a heretic. All Angel's trips have been to prove chemicals had nothing to do with the illness."

"Let them light the fire then. If you can't take me down there, who can I get? What will it cost?"

"I'll try and take you, somehow. But wait till you're better."

"I may only get worse. I need to know."

"We'll have to be discreet, downright sneaky, to get you down there without anyone here finding out. Give me time to plan, to figure things out."

"I don't want to cause you more problems. It would best for me to take a bus."

"You'll go with me, or I'll find a way to block you. Give me time. I left my plane down there. Your father was down there when I flew you to the plant, and he insisted I fly you in the jet to a Houston hospital. Maybe I can find a chance to get down there and get my plane. Then I won't be so dependent on Sumner. Just wait. I'll do something quick, I promise."

Anne wearily went to sleep, but two hours later Jim woke her, kneeling beside her in the dark.

"How do you feel? Strong enough to take the trip now?"

She nodded and groggily rose to a sitting position on the floor.

"Listen up. Your name is Jose Lopez, my helper. We're flying down to get my plane. Put these on and try to look like a man. Stuff your hair up in the hat."

"I'll try."

"Do your best. It's late. No one should be around. We ride in the cargo area of one of Sumner's commercial planes that leaves for Mexico shortly. We won't have much time down there, maybe enough for a quick trip to one village. I hope I'm doing the right thing by you. We'll come back tomorrow night in my plane."

Anne changed quickly into the clothes. She pinned her hair up and slid on the cheap straw hat he'd left, pulling it down over her eyes. The light jacket he'd brought helped disguise her figure, and the pants were loose and ill-fitting. One look in the mirror told her she could pull it off.

Jim came back and laughed when he saw her. "That will work but not if you carry that purse."

"I have an oxygen tank in it," she admitted.

"So, *that's* how you do it. But I knew that. If you have any extra bottles, throw them and your purse in this sack."

Fortunately, they didn't come into contact with anyone at the hanger. Jim rushed her on board the plane and fixed her a place to sleep, not comfortable, but adequate. Sometime later, when they were finally airborne, Jim came back and went to sleep beside her. In the dim light preceding dawn, they landed at the Mexican plant and hurried across the runway to Jim's plane.

"Do you want to go now? Are you ready for this?"

"Scared, but ready as I'll ever be."

They soon dropped down over Tutlu, and she had to blink rapidly to keep the tears back. Only Ruben waited to greet them when they landed. The villagers, even the children, hung back in uncertainty. Anne, without hesitation, rushed to Pacal's house. When she felt herself gasping for air, she slowed down.

Pacal had always been a slim little urchin, but now he looked fragile as he sat on the dirt floor playing with a toy car Anne bought for him long ago. She looked up at Malinali.

"When did Pacal become ill?"

"The next day, after you left," she said in Spanish, too concerned to attempt the broken English she usually used in talking with Anne.

"Did a doctor see him?"

"Ruben took him in your truck to see the farm doctor. The doctor said he has a virus, the same as Isdel's. He said he caught it from Isdel. He gave him medicine."

"Farm doctor? You mean Amos? The medic? Was Pacal only seen by the medic?"

"Yes, but Pacal grows stronger, I think. I don't think he will die. Do you?"

The mother turned aside to hide her tears when Anne sat down beside Pacal. Anne felt his forehead and found no fever. Other than his accelerated breathing and his obvious frailty, he seemed normal.

"How do you feel?"

"I'm not sick now." He looked up at her with shining eyes. "I would like to go fish or swim."

"He gets tired so quickly," Malinili broke in. "Yesterday I let him sit outside. He's not ill like Marco. Marco can't sit up."

Anne soon said goodbye and went to visit Marco and his family. Angel's paper had listed him as critical, and she believed it as soon as she saw him. She recognized the symptoms, oh, so well.

"I need to ask you some questions, Marco. Just nod or answer as shortly as you can. I don't want to tire you."

Marco's eyes lit up. Obviously, he was pleased with her visit, in spite of his condition. And it was just as obvious he was traveling the last mile of a downgrade to eternity.

"I know Amos said you have a virus. I'm not sure he's right. Did the plane spray while you were in the field?"

"Sprayed ... at night. In the morning they say ... okay to work ... but everyone get sick."

"Marco, look at these pictures of the farms. They show the different fields and the crops planted in each one. Look at it for just a minute. This is important."

He studiously examined the papers she held out.

"Where were you working when the illness started?"

He raised a trembling finger and pointed to field B.

"Did anyone working in this field here become ill?" she asked, designating test field A, next door to his field.

"No. Not time yet ... for that field."

"And this field?" she asked and pointed to test field D.

127

"Not ready either. No workers there."

She glanced up at Jim, who studied the papers over her shoulder, his eyes blue-gray fire, his face white.

"Thank you, Marco. You've been a big help. I'll try to get you medical help, and we'll pray. You won't forget to pray, too?"

"Have bookmark."

He touched a soiled bookmark she awarded him some two years earlier when he was still a child at home. He had saved it, obviously cherished it. She felt tears come and hid them by stooping to kiss his forehead. She managed a quiet, broken prayer, followed by another kiss.

She hurried from the tent, tears streaming down her face, and went straight to the plane. She didn't want to know about the fudge. It didn't matter. She crawled into the plane and leaned over sobbing. When she felt Jim's hand on her back, she turned to find him beside her with questions in his eyes.

"Would you get my sh-shawl from my tent and a-a new bookmark for Marco? Get one that ..."

"Hush. Rest. I'll know which one to get."

She had recovered by the time Jim returned with her mantilla. It seemed like centuries had passed since Jim had first given it to her, but the sight and feel of it brought back too many memories, and her tears tried to come again. She held them at bay and buried her face in its rich folds.

"I gave him the Twenty-third Psalm. Okay?" he asked gently.

"Yes," she choked. "Jim, I want so badly for it to be a virus. That would be much simpler. Why does everything have to be so complicated, so much work, so many decisions, and I'm so tired. Why couldn't it be a flu epidemic?"

Jim remained silent.

"Could we go to Capaso? Can you land there?"

"We'll go. But you're going to rest here for an hour. I'm going to walk around and see if I can learn anything. You sleep."

"I will."

It seemed only seconds later he climbed aboard. When he made a bumpy landing at Capaso, she looked out at the village and sighed.

"Anne, listen to me. I saw those papers you have. I don't know where you dug up your information, but I know what you intend to do.

Give me the papers and stay here. I'll ask the right questions."

"I stole the information. I got into Angel's briefcase and copied her papers. Best be discreet in your questioning. I want to keep this quiet until I know what it's all about."

"You think they inspected the wrong fields and on purpose."

"If a couple more people confirm what Marco said, I'll be certain. I didn't expect something that devious. But, if it's true, this illness, all this illness, was brought about by something other than a virus. The fields they tested, A and D, showed some paraquat and insignificant amounts of other chemical. They showed evidence of being freshly sprayed, and the levels of chemical residue in the soil were normal for a field just sprayed. Paraquat could cause this illness but only if it were somehow misused. If there's any evidence of any kind, it's in fields B, C, and E, the fields that *weren't* tested. Are you following me?"

"Loud and clear. In other words, why would they test the wrong fields unless they were hiding something in the correct fields?"

"Also, why did the tested fields show moderate amounts of chemical when they weren't even due for a spraying and hadn't been sprayed for some time? I checked the papers here, and they show that A and D weren't supposed to be sprayed again. "

"But A and D *were* sprayed, right after the sickness hit."

"They were?" she asked in alarm. "But how do you ..."

"Because I sprayed them. They had one of their little feather lights ready for me, and I sprayed with it."

"Why?"

"Thursday evening the factory called and wanted me to hurry over and spray fields A and D. They told me not to use my plane, that they had one of their little planes all ready for me. I didn't think anything much of it at the time, because I did sometimes use their planes, and they did sometimes call me in to do unscheduled spraying. They said the fields couldn't wait for their regular spraying, and that Fritz would meet me and put in the chemicals I needed to use."

"When were fields B, C, and E sprayed?"

"Fritz and I sprayed them Wednesday night, mainly with paraquat."

"Angel's papers say that the workers started to become ill about ten o'clock Thursday morning. That same morning they worked in fields B, C, and E. Have you sprayed with your plane since?"

"No. It sat over at the warehouse where I left it when I flew you to Houston in the jet."

"Maybe there's some residue left of the last chemical you sprayed before everyone became ill. Maybe the plant mislabeled the container, and something else was used."

"Accidents like that don't happen in a reputable chemical company. And I know for sure I sprayed paraquat, Anne. I didn't make a mistake about that. I wouldn't lie. But I agree with your thinking. If there's any spray left, we can have it checked."

"How about Fritz? Could he have made an error? Was he spraying the same fields?"

"The same fields and the same chemical. I helped every time we filled the tanks. Stay here, and I'll see what I can find out by asking a few friendly questions."

An hour later Jim woke her. He didn't wait to talk but took off immediately.

"Something's funny," he finally said, after they'd been in the air for a while. "I've been trying to put this all together. The farm workers started getting ill Thursday morning while working in fields B, C, and E. Correct? And we sprayed paraquat Wednesday night, late that night, in the unplanted halves of those three fields. I had Thursday off and wasn't supposed to work for Sumner again until Friday. But it was Thursday evening Sumner called me in to spray fields A and D with their own plane. Later that night Fritz told me there was some sickness there. He acted like it wasn't anything much. He was already working on something when I came to spray that evening." Jim sat thoughtfully for a minute before continuing. "And then you came down with sickness on Friday morning. It *must* be the chemicals. It doesn't make sense otherwise. I'm going to land at a small private airfield near here and check my tanks and spraying apparatus for residue. If I can find a few drops of liquid, I'll have it tested. That will at least give us a starting point."

"Don't touch the stuff or breathe it. I don't want you ..."

"I'll be careful, you can be sure of that. But remember, I filled my tanks. I didn't touch any chemical, but I breathed fumes, especially when I sprayed."

He landed at a small, level field with no buildings or people in sight. Anne sat on some nearby rocks while he checked the hopper that was bolted onto his plane. Later she saw him examine the sprayers mounted under the wings. Finally he motioned her to come back.

"There's nothing. I'd guess my hopper and spraying apparatus have been cleaned. And they're bone dry. Let's get out of here."

When they were again in the air, Anne asked, "Is that a normal procedure, for them to clean your spraying apparatus?"

"Ha. Not in my lifetime. When I got there Thursday evening, Fritz was agitated. He said he'd been there all day. Said he hadn't been able to spray that day because they'd had him doing other stuff."

"So your own plane sat there at Sumner's until you took the payroll on Friday?"

"Yes, and there weren't any workers around on Friday either. I see it clearer now. I'm going to drop by the plant and remove all this spraying equipment, the whole works, before we head back to the states. I'll get you back before dawn, so you can slip into your office before anyone's there. Everyone will think I went down alone to get my plane."

"Make it as early as you can. I want to snoop around some more in Angel's papers. I'll make up some printed forms with maps of the different fields, dates, anything pertinent, and take them back to Mexico. I need a signed statement from everyone on Angel's list, and I have to work fast. It could save someone's life, if they started getting the proper medical treatment. Could any of this cause trouble for you?"

"You wouldn't let that stop you, would you?"

"You can't be implicated, can you? You said there were no workers in the fields."

"We sprayed at night. They might have gone in first thing in the morning. The boss often jumped the gun to get things done and to get the workers into the fields. But they didn't work in the area we sprayed. That side of the fields hadn't been planted yet. They worked in the planted sides of those three fields, and their only contact would have been when they walked through the sprayed area on their way to the planted side.

"But that wouldn't cause this kind of devastation."

"No. But I can always be implicated by big, powerful Sumner. They have money, which they intend to keep, and high-powered attorneys who are paid to help them keep it. I can be drawn into this on Sumner's whim if it helps their cause. I hope it doesn't. But with what you've dug up, you can force them to admit to the world that the workers became ill from a chemical, not from a virus. Then the game will change, and anything can happen in the next round."

"I don't know what to do."

"Of course you do. You've told me. You'll make up your forms and get your signatures, no doubt in the face of hell itself, as long as there's breath in you to do it. But let's try and keep it quiet that I took you down here."

Jim's face was set hard and tight when he dropped down to the plant's runway.

"You rest. I'll be a while removing all this stuff. Best to stay in your seat. I'll keep a lookout and let you know if anyone shows up. If they do, I'll throw a blanket over your head or something."

"Gee, thanks."

She dozed fitfully as Jim clanked around the plane, removing the spraying apparatus. He left the equipment in an old storage building and climbed back into the plane.

"That's my own equipment. I hope it's safe there. It's expensive, but I can't tote all that stuff around with me. There's more room for you to lie down now, if you'd like to sleep on the way back. You look bushed."

"I'd like to sit here. It's nice at night."

"Glad to share my favorite ride with someone."

"I like to ride Tom-tom at night, too."

She sat in silence beside him. They had been flying over the Gulf of Mexico for a while when Jim pointed out at the night vista.

"He made darkness his secret place ... round about him were dark waters and thick clouds of the skies."

He squeezed the back of her neck and gave her a quick, grim smile.

Chapter 12

She eventually fell asleep in her seat and didn't wake until they landed at the Houston complex early in the morning. When finally alone in the building, she went straight to Angel's office. No handy briefcase sat out for her investigations this time, and digging into Angel's other files would take too much time. She returned to her own office and formatted claims forms. One form stated information she had already investigated and confirmed as accurate. A form like that would only require signatures of the workers. Then she prepared another form with more blank spaces. It would be for individual workers to state their grievance and press their claims. She would have to help most of those on the list with that. She printed a good quantity of each and stashed them away.

It was nine o'clock in the morning when Fred came into her office. "Work all night?"

"Near about." When concern swept across his face, she added, "I'm fine, Fred."

"You haven't been to the doctor."

"He's on vacation this week. I didn't want to see an associate. Maybe it's better to wait anyway. Then it will be easier for him to tell if there's improvement or regression."

"Rather a feeble excuse."

"Shouldn't you slip away before Angel or Dad sees you here? We'll ruin your plan."

"Not this morning. They're ensconced behind closed doors with Sumner's imperial attorney."

"Eric Zieker, you mean."

"Looks serious. I imagine it's to do with the Mexico problem. They haven't included me in their confidences yet, but I imagine I'll be let in soon. Dad ordered me to meet him at noon today."

"I'd better warn Jim, I guess. They may try to drag him into it."

"He's in there with them now."

"Oh," She couldn't think of anything more to say, and Fred looked at her strangely.

"You look tired, more so than at the cabin."

"I need sleep. Been up longer than usual."

"I'll lock the door as I go out."

Anne awoke in the late morning and wondered why she hadn't heard from Jim. She stepped out to look through a hall window and saw Jim standing beside his plane. He was conversing with Angel. Evidently the Zieker meeting had ended. She watched them for a while and was about to leave when Jim helped Angel into his cockpit. She felt only relief this time. It would give her opportunity to work in Angel's office, undisturbed.

She gathered up a stack of graphics material and carried them to Angel's printer room, spreading them on the cutting board. With the door unlocked, she went straight to the file cabinet and searched through old claims from the past year. On many of them, she could read between the lines and see the highhanded way they had been handled, but she found nothing pertinent to the present situation. She closed the file drawer and investigated the rest of Angel's office. The desktop looked unchanged, but a bottom drawer contained a folder on one of their foreign buyers in Honduras. The buyer claimed personal injury from Sumner chemicals. The letter, even though translated to English, showed the writer to be unsophisticated and uneducated. But she couldn't help but recognize similarities to the present situation in Mexico. Of the three chemicals involved, paraquat was listed as the one at fault, and the workers were ill in the same way as the Mexican workers. Some had died. The workers had used hand sprayers in this incident.

Sumner claimed the chemical had been incorrectly applied. Anne copied every page in the file and took them back to her office.

She wanted to talk with Jim but couldn't call him when he was flying with Angel. She pushed aside her impatience with more hard work and settled in to studying the collected materials. When she had committed most of Angel's papers to memory, she went on to more in-depth study of chemicals, especially paraquat. It made her wonder if Anglin's chemist, John Le Grand, might be of help since he advised their buyers regarding safe application of the chemicals. When in Houston, he usually worked at his lab in the back of Sumner's largest warehouse. He experimented with chemicals and tested products at that laboratory. She didn't know him well but decided to risk plying him for more information. He surely knew of the Honduras problem. Likely he was aware of the Mexican problem also, since he spent a good deal of time down at the Sumner operations where they developed their own chemicals from natural resources.

She took a roundabout passage to his lab so no one would see her. His outside door stood open, and she found him in the lab at the back.

"How are you, Mr. Le Grand? I wasn't sure I'd find you in the States. Been here long?"

"Three months now. I prefer it, of course. I'm surprised to see you here. Not working in Mexico anymore?"

She took a clue from his innocence. "I wanted to visit home for a while. But I'm still trying to help the people down there all I can. Right now they're sadly in need of more farming land up in the hills by their villages. It takes them so long to clear an area. I'm considering purchasing some kind of herbicide, strong enough to help them in the task. I could have someone at Dad's warehouse arrange for an aerial application. Any suggestions on what product would be best? You know what that area looks like."

"Yes, I know ones that would be effective, but I wouldn't recommend doing it right now. They're having health problems down there and are laying the blame on recently-applied chemicals. This wouldn't be a good time."

"Oh, do you mean ..."

"I don't know. I heard they'd been hit by a flu epidemic and that some of the people were claiming they became sick from chemicals the planes applied. I don't know anything more about it."

She could see he *did* know much more about it but had grown wary and wouldn't give out any more information.

"I'll take your advice and wait. Maybe I'd better forget it all together. I'd hate to have a problem like that."

"That might be wise." He shut his lips tight after that.

"Well, thank you. You've saved me from making a mistake. I'll arrange to have equipment brought in and clear the area they need. It sounds less risky, and it's more satisfactory in the long run."

"Yes, they won't have to cut trees or wait for roots to rot."

She thanked him for his advice and left quickly so he wouldn't notice her difficulty in breathing. He obviously knew nothing of her plight, though he apparently knew plenty about the Mexican situation. She regretted visiting him. He might mention it to Angel or Anglin. He would be on Sumner's side, of that she had no doubt. She read his face like a book and wondered if her face could be read so easily. Deviousness depressed her. The whole mess gave her a dirty feeling. Still, if she wanted to save lives and see justice, she had to keep on.

At a nearby library, she checked out a pile of publications and set to work digesting material only a chemist would understand. Little by little, she assimilated knowledge, and, the more she read, the less likely it seemed that such a catastrophe could happen by the chemical in question. No one could deny its lethal qualities. The history of paraquat usage showed cases of sickness and death, but much of the information sounded vague and inconclusive. The extreme cases were mostly isolated. Often the investigator blamed the deaths on probable suicide attempts by ingestion of the chemical. She wondered how correct the assumptions were. At least her father couldn't use *that* defense.

Reading on about symptoms, she grew more dumbfounded. She had experienced most of the symptoms related to paraquat poisoning, right down to the yellowed fingernails. She had applied polish so no one could tell.

She spent the remainder of the day and into the night typing more forms with a variety of statements that could apply to any situation she might encounter in Mexico. She stowed them away in her briefcase, locked it, and slid it under her desk.

Without taking time to rest, she started work on her Sumner publicity projects. Time passed swiftly. It was past ten when her cell phone rang.

"Anne, I can only talk for a second. I wanted you to know that Angel looked at your computer history today and found you'd been studying chemicals. She thinks you're up to something."

"How could she have done that? She left with you in the plane this morning." Anne could have bit her tongue for letting him know she was keeping track of him.

"We were only gone a couple of hours. She did it whenever you left your office. It wouldn't take long to do that, would it?"

"She has a key to my office."

"She also knows you didn't go back to Dr. Wildermuth again. She even knows about the new doctor you saw."

"How would she know that? Only you and Fred know. Neither of you would tell."

"She told me she called every doctor in Houston and pretended she was you checking to see when your next appointment was scheduled."

"Industrious, isn't she, and devious."

"It's obvious you're sisters."

"Jim!" she said, offended deeply. "I'm sneaking to save lives. Her sneaking ... How can you compare us?"

"You aren't sneaking. You would have done the same right in front of her, if necessary. I only meant your industriousness. You both have that. Angel's not without talent, whatever she lacks in principles and morals."

"Is she using her talents on you right now?"

"Always. And so far she doesn't know about our trip to Mexico. But we don't dare take another. I have to go now. She's on her way. Next thing you know she'll be sneaking my phone out of my pants to see what numbers I've dialed."

"Does ... Would she do that – put her hand ..."

"Anne, I'm flying again in a few minutes. I'll be back late tomorrow. It might be better if we don't see each other for a while. Too risky. Meantime, you watch your back, and I'll watch my pants."

Anne's retort died on her lips when the line went dead. The immediate future looked bleak. She'd have to accept the fact that Jim got on well with Angel and vice versa. She'd also have to accept the fact he couldn't take her back to Mexico a second time. But those forms must be signed, and there were things she should investigate, things she should have investigated the first time but lacked strength and time. Suddenly, her fighting spirit came to the fore. She would make a way. If she couldn't fly with Jim, she would find a way to go by herself.

Buying a plane ticket would be too expensive and complicated. She would need some sort of conveyance from the airport to the villages. Swiftly she came to the only decision possible: she would drive. She had enough money for gas, barely, and could use a company car. Any car available would do, and she could leave a message that she was going away to rest for a few days. The company vehicle keys used to be kept in the receptionist's office. She hurried down to see if they were still there.

Four keys hung on the board. She grabbed them all and hurried to the shelter where vehicles were housed. From the frugal choice of offerings, she decided on a compact truck, faded white, with no company name on it. Dusty and dilapidated, it would work perfectly – if it ran. It obviously wouldn't be missed if she took it. It started readily, and she drove it back to the office building. The tires should last the trip, and it had half a tank of gas. She found a jack, a spare tire, and an up-to-date registration and tag. She decided not to mention she appropriated it. Instead, she left a note at the front office desk, stating she would be away from the office for a few days and would be in touch. She left the same note on her own desk.

She remembered the route to Tutlu from back when she made the trip in her old truck, now being used by the village. If she drove like mad, didn't have any problems, and didn't stop for rest, she could make it in twenty-four hours. A few months ago she wouldn't have batted an eye at such an undertaking, but now, just the thought made her tired.

She brought her briefcase, a small bag of clothes, and another bag of offerings from the office kitchen. At least she wouldn't starve for a couple of days. She would be traveling with no expense margin for food, repairs, or anything else. If the truck died, she would have to sit there and die, too. With no illusions, she grimly started off.

Rest snatches became imperative during the trip, but she made the farms in thirty-two hours. Eight o'clock Friday morning she arrived. She wore the "Jose Lopez" disguise Jim had given her.

Cautiously, she drove within sight of the farm's main entrance. The big, rambling house of the foreman sat near the dusty highway, while the smaller houses of the crew bosses sat on the opposite side of the entrance, near the equipment barn and the crude runway. All of a sudden she saw Jim's plane. Driving on to a spot where her truck would be hidden from view but where she could still observe the situation, she parked under the low branches of a tired-looking tree.

She would have to wait until he left before she could investigate anything. She leaned back in the seat and finished off a bottle of lukewarm Half-and-Half. Too tired for anything else, she dozed. A bee buzzing around in her cab brought her totally awake a short while later.

Jim's plane was being fueled by one of the mechanics. Fifteen minutes later, Jim and Angel came out of the superintendent's house. They laughed, and Jim held Angel's briefcase in one hand and Angel in the other. Even at that distance, she could see Angel beam. Jim helped her aboard his plane, and Anne felt actual physical pain at seeing him treat Angel as he treated her.

Instead of crying, she pounded her fist on the steering wheel and told herself to brace up. What did it matter anyway? She couldn't have that much time left. And before she was gone, these people would have justice, even if it brought down her whole family and Jim, too. The thought of dying wouldn't hurt so much if she didn't have to think of Jim falling – falling to Angel's level and to the tune of Angel's whims. She knew how much he loved his plane and loved flying, and that excused some of his actions, but he seemed too easy in the situation. It looked like Angel held him under her power, and he didn't mind being there.

Within minutes they took off, and her time had come. Ignoring the dusty, difficult-to-breathe air, she set out to meet the workers in the fields and ask as many questions as possible. She must first find out if any of the forty-one, not-so-ill workers had gone back at work.

A man worked on an old tractor by the equipment barn. She approached him and named three names from the list, but he only looked at her vacantly. Finally, he motioned toward the fields and went back to his work, ignoring her presence completely.

In the distance, a truck drove alongside a newly-cultivated field and dropped off poles to workers on foot. They worked close by the paved road, so she got back into her truck and drove as close to them as possible. Again she concealed her vehicle and went so far as to remove her license plate in case someone noticed it.

The truck driver saw her walking in the field and stopped until she caught up. When she showed him the list of names, he explained he couldn't read. She read the names, clearly, one by one, while he slowly shook his head at each name. On the nineteenth name, he halted her and said the man had become ill and couldn't work. On name number thirty-four, he pointed to a young man setting a post some fifty yards across the field.

Anne immediately approached him and asked him about his health. She confirmed what Angel's papers had stated, that he had been working in field C when he became sick. They were working in the same field right then.

"But how could you have been working here? It's just been cultivated. There would have been nothing here to work on? There's nothing planted."

"They plowed the field after the sickness hit. They said we must start the field over new."

Anne showed him the picture of the five fields in question.

"Is anything growing in any of the other fields?"

"Only A and D. They have beans."

"You mean the two test fields?" When he looked at her vaguely she realized he was unaware of the test.

"Were watermelons the only crops in fields B, C, and E?" Anne asked to further investigate the information on Angel's papers.

"Yes, watermelons on the planted sides of the fields. The unplanted sides were just weeds. But both sides are turned under now."

"Had the melons just sprouted?"

"No. Spreading out."

Ann had to think for a minute about watermelon production. When the plants started spreading out, workers usually went in with hoes to take out the weeds closest to the plants. That must have been where they had gone to work the morning they became ill.

Anne thanked him and left. Thus ended any opportunity to test fields B, C, and D for chemical residue. Fields A and D were no doubt blinds, like a salted mine, to show only what the owner wanted seen.

When she reached her truck, she decided to check out fields B and E anyway. The map showed a dirt road bordering each of the fields and one bisecting them. She turned down the road between B and E and drew to a stop. The fields had been plowed and cultivated. A bottom plow would have buried all evidence maybe eighteen inches below the surface. She also knew that the clay in the soil would have absorbed the chemical and rendered it inactive. It would be next to impossible to find out if there had been too much spray or too high a concentrate or if some other chemical might be the villain.

Anne decided to risk talking to the foreman in the big house that Jim and Angel had vacated. He hadn't seen her in two years, and their acquaintance had been slight. In her disguise he shouldn't recognize her, anyway. Pretending to represent an insurance company, she asked the man at the door if she could speak with Chester Lorry.

"Gone. He left last week to work in Guatemala. I'm the new foreman," he stated with some degree of pride.

"Do you have his address? His phone number?"

"No. I never met him. I've been here only three days."

"Is there anyone here who could give me information about the spraying? About the sickness?"

"You call this number. They'll tell you."

He gave her Sumner's number. Disappointed, she was leaving when he called her back.

"I need your name, please. They want me to get names."

"Jose Lopez," she answered and went back to her truck before she could be stopped again.

Not bothering to rest, she drove on to Padre Juan's village and found him in his study. He looked wearier and sadder than the last time she'd seen him. She couldn't understand the strange look on his face when she greeted him. Finally, she realized he didn't recognize her.

"It's me." She removed the hat.

"Incognito Anne!" He grinned widely. "Come in."

"I'm sorry I've not been back."

"I know you have been in bad health. I can see that you suffer with illness."

"I guess there's no disguise to hide that. But I came to help. I need to find these people." She showed him the long list. "I want to make sure they've been taken care of, that they received a doctor's care and medication and money."

"No one receives anything. No one goes anywhere or sees anyone. I talked with the men at Sumner Chemical, but they say they cannot take responsibility for a virus. I went also to a doctor I know, and he says it is not a virus, but it is from the farm chemicals. I went back to Sumner again and told them this, and they tell me the workers didn't follow instructions. But the workers did as the foreman told them, and now the foreman's gone. We can do nothing. I can do nothing. People die. My own lungs work poorly, have never worked well. I understand that kind of hurt. But these people suffer something worse, something much, *much* worse. I feel healthy next to some of them, next to you. No?"

"You'll outlive us all, Padre. But you must take care of yourself. We'll work together to get help for these people. You do look tired, Padre."

"Too much tired. I have given up. I feel useless and cowardly, just an ineffective old padre who accomplishes nothing. Nothing."

His discouragement hurt. Anne felt depressed talking with him.

"Padre, we must keep on. See, I've brought papers. I need to see the people on this list."

"You are sick. You should be in bed. *I* should be in bed."

"I'm one step away from eternity," she told him bluntly. "I'll find my bed after I've taken that step. In the meantime, I must get these filled out and signed, as quickly as possible, and I must hurry back to Houston. Can someone help me find some of these people? No one must recognize me."

"They will recognize you if you are with them for more than a minute. You are much loved, and love sees through all disguises," he said in his quaint speech. "I will get Jock to help you. He can even drive for you. You remember him from Capaso, no? He stays here in my village now."

Tears coursed down Anne's cheeks, and she couldn't speak for an instant.

"Is he here now?" she finally asked.

"Yes. His father died, and his younger brother has sickness. He will help."

They sent for Jock, and his smiling, homely face nearly brought back Anne's tears. She graciously accepted his help and soon discovered he could drive — fast and poorly. It might be difficult to explain some of the new dents in the truck when she returned to Houston, but she didn't much care. She actually managed to doze through hairpin turns on no-shoulder roads with steep drop-offs.

Jock soon proved his mind was sharper than his driving ability. She questioned two workers in his presence, and he caught on to what she needed. After that, he became her voice. By Friday night, Anne barely held on, but she had twenty-six signed statements. Fourteen of the statements were signed by the actual workers, while the other twelve were signed by family members of the deceased, and each statement was witnessed by two other signatures. She had also taken pictures of the ill workers and attached a print to each of their statements. Anne felt well-satisfied. These statements would prove the sickness was caused by the spraying. But who should be blamed? Did one of the pilots, Jim or Fritz, make a mistake in the mix or in the spraying? Did the foreman send the workers out into the field too soon? She wanted to know why they plowed under those fields. Was it only a safety measure, or were they hiding something? Too many questions had no answers.

She turned to Jock. "Jock, I'd like to dig in fields B, C, and E tonight. A soil sample might have some residual spray in it. It might even be wise to take a sample of fields A and D for comparison."

"Not safe. Field cursed."

"I'll work carefully. You're to drive, just drive, and stay on guard in the truck while I take the samples." She felt unnerved about the idea herself. "I'll use rubber gloves and put the samples in canning jars. We can find those in the village."

"I'll help. I'll use gloves, too."

"Thank you, Jock. This may take a long time. We need at least three samples from each field, all from different spots, to be sure we get some chemical."

The area looked deserted when they drove there late that night. Anne knew exactly what to do. Once she took core samples at Tutlu in order to get recommendations about what the soil needed for growing crops. She brought along a map of the fields and wrote down the exact location of each sample she took.

Standing at the actual site, it more than mystified her that such devastating illness could occur from a single spraying. Wouldn't the workers have needed to physically eat the chemical to become so desperately ill? The chemicals didn't cause such harm when merely contacting healthy skin. She knew all the facts now, yet she still harbored some doubt that her own ailment had been caused by the same chemicals.

Padre Juan was waiting for them when they returned at eleven o'clock. She showed him what they'd collected.

"Padre, if you're ever in my village, please visit Malinali. Please tell her to not be discouraged and try to carry on. The village needs her intelligence and strength. She can help them keep the fudge going, too. You mustn't become discouraged either, Padre. You're sick, the same as I am, but you, of all people, know how important our efforts are. Maybe you are just an ineffective, old padre, as you put it so humbly, and maybe I'm just an ineffective ex-missionary, but we're not either of us cowards, and we're not useless as long as we have God. I remember those were your exact words the night we had the fiesta in your honor."

"Yes. Thank you. We will be strong together, through Christ – you in your country and I in mine. We'll pray and be strong. Thank you. I don't often sink so low."

"I stay low. When you feel sick, it's hard to rise above low. I've learned that hard lesson."

"You must rest here. Sleep all night, all day, before you attempt the trip back."

"I'll rest a while in my truck, but I want to leave while it's still dark. Call me if there's any news. Here's my cell phone number. If you can't reach me that way, call this other number, my brother's number. Fred will let me know if you call, and it's safe to leave a message with him. I'll leave a list of sick workers with you. Maybe you'll see some I couldn't find. And here are extra copies of forms. Jock will know what to do with them. Goodbye and thank you, Padre."

Anne slept in her truck for a while, but at three in the morning she began the tedious journey homeward, realizing it would probably be over thirty hours before she got back to Houston.

The drive seemed endless, and even though she felt dead tired, she rejoiced when she neared the first large city in Texas. She turned her cell phone back on, and within minutes it showed she had messages. Fred had called twice and Jim had called three times. Both asked her to call back. She turned the phone off. She didn't want to talk with either of them. She might give something away. She gritted her teeth and drove on to Houston. Nine thirty in the morning she neared Sumner and turned her phone back on. It immediately beeped another message, this time from Jim, and it had been left only an hour ago. Her heart froze in her chest as she listened.

"The word's out that you've been in Mexico snooping around. Daddy and Angel are concerned, or I should say furious. They know you have the old Dodge, and Anglin said he was going to report it stolen. Knowing him, I'm sure he did. I hope to goodness you get this message. Get back to the States. If you have anything valuable to your cause, put it somewhere safe, quick. Delete this message as soon as you hear it. I can't help you. Take care of yourself."

Chapter 13

"I've always taken care of myself," she said bitterly as she deleted the message and turned the phone off again. At least they had no idea she'd almost reached Sumner. They couldn't know about the soil samples or about the extensive pile of signed documents she had in her possession. She wanted to thumb her nose at them and go away somewhere, but she had no money left, no place to stay, and no way of checking on how the insurance claims were being handled if she parted company with Sumner. And now she didn't even have a vehicle. She felt incensed about them claiming she had stolen the truck. They had offered her a company vehicle when she first started work there.

The humiliation hurt deeply, but she couldn't stop now to consider pride or feelings. She must work quickly and cautiously. She stopped at a printing place and made copies of the signed statements, bought Ziploc bags at a grocery, and headed to the nearest mini-storage facility. After renting a four-by-six space, she divided each soil sample into two bags and put one of each pair in her briefcase along with the extra copies of the documents. The original, signed documents and the duplicate soil samples she left stored.

At Sumner's she parked the truck in its appointed place and hung the key back on its peg with a feeling strangely akin to parting with an old friend. Once behind her locked office door, she heaved a relieved sigh. It being Sunday, no one had seen her come in. Maybe she could bluff them, convince them she had never left the country. Maybe they were unsure. "Maybe, maybe," she kept saying to herself as she sat down at her desk, tired enough to bawl. Her eyes studied the few papers left out. Whoever had been in her office had not searched discreetly. It afforded her immediate relief there had been nothing available to give her away.

It would be necessary, henceforth, to keep anything valuable hidden, and she must also remember to erase her computer history each time she did any private investigations. At least her blanket and pillow hadn't been in the office while she was gone. Maybe Angel and Dad didn't know yet that she lived there. She laughed out loud again at herself. In the face of all that had happened, and all that might happen, she still worried about something so trivial.

The trip had taken its toll. Her spirit had gone on its merry way with her flesh dragging along behind as an unwilling guest. Now, that same flesh dreaded facing any trouble, and she wondered how much her father and Angel knew. She would tread lightly at Sumner for a while, and she would get those samples tested quickly. The results might enlighten her on what to do next. She had nothing more to go on, but maybe what she had accumulated would scare her father into using his insurance money to help those people. In the phone book she found a place where the soil samples could be tested. She hid that information away in her briefcase along with everything else.

Totally beat, and more than scared, she set to work in earnest to finish her public relations effort for Sumner. They will need it, she thought dismally. In spite of troubles, her adrenaline began to pump at high speed, and she worked inspired. Eventually, she fell asleep with her head on her desk amidst her newest efforts.

A sharp rap on her desk startled her awake. She looked up to meet the cold eyes of Anglin Sumner. He stood close, scowling down at her. The shock felt like a dash of ice water, this first, face-to-face meeting with her father in over two years. Not physically or mentally prepared for it, she pushed her hair back from her face and tried to sit straight, very straight. Inside she breathed a prayer for divine support.

"You're a fine sight! You're as gray as that smog out there. What are you doing now? Looking for some new way to destroy the institution

147

that's keeping you alive?"

"Thanks for the paychecks, Daddy, but only God can keep me alive. I took a vacation, and now I'm making up for it by working overtime. I'm doing good work in spite of my appearance. No one needs to look at me."

"No one will, nor listen to you either. Since when did you appoint yourself Sumner's conscience and watchdog? What were you doing sneaking around down there stirring up trouble – with my money, my truck, and my time?"

"I used my money, and you won't pay a cent for the time I spent down there. Anyway, I was told to take any available company vehicle if I felt up to driving. I felt up to it. I wanted to look in on my village."

"Well, you can leave *my* villages alone. You caused some crooked attorney to go there and stir the people up. You're creating major trouble for Sumner, simply because of a flu epidemic."

"Like in Honduras, Dad? Another flu epidemic? Flu doesn't hit like that. Not with everyone sick within hours. All the symptoms sound like paraquat poisoning to me or possibly some other agrichemical. But I sent no one to any of the villages. I don't even know any attorneys except yours."

"When did you become an authority on this? I've been in this business since before you existed. If you know so much, tell me why you're so sick? You didn't work in the fields. Don't you have the same symptoms?"

"How would you know what symptoms I have?"

"I paid your doctor, remember? And it was a charity, because you weren't employed at Sumner. You picked up the same disease they have, by living in the filth and squalor they thrive on. That is, they thrive on it until a disease strikes. You've only yourself to blame."

"I've never blamed anyone, and you'll be paid back for my doctor bills. I didn't ask to be taken to a hospital and treated. How could someone unconscious ask anything? But, if a farm chemical caused the trouble with those villagers, I *will* ask for them to be treated. And I still won't blame anyone. Accidents happen all the time. But whether it was the foreman's fault, the pilot's, the warehouse's, or even the workers' themselves, Sumner *will* pay the bill and take responsibility."

"Just because you've wasted your time preaching to peons, that doesn't make you God. To me you're the last of three mistakes and by far the most ungrateful. At least Fred and Angeline still do what they're told."

"Thank you for allowing me to be brought into the world, Dad. Soon I may thank you for sending me back out of it."

"You can't blame me for that. If you're killed, you did it yourself. I warned you about living down there, and I'm warning you now to stay out of my business."

She stared at him dry-eyed. Fury and indignation burned hot within her. Pride told her to get up and walk away from Sumner, but responsibility chained her to her desk. She answered him nothing.

Angry and puzzled, he stood and looked at her for a long minute.

"While you've been down there building your little huts for humanity, your sister bought a new townhouse," he said in a kinder voice. "You could have had the same. What a waste. What a pitiful waste." He left and slammed the door behind him.

She trembled all over but felt relief that they didn't know she was the snooping attorney they were worried about. Her disguise had at least held them at bay for a while, but she hated subterfuge. If he ever asked her straight out, she would tell him exactly what she did, and that would be that. But it would be helpful to earn a couple of paychecks before she removed herself from his sight forever.

Through the rest of Sunday and all Sunday night, she worked on Sumner's project, napping often. Monday morning she patted herself on the back over her accomplishments. If she didn't do another thing, she had earned her pay. The entire project would be finished before Sumner's annual banquet, Friday of the following week. It would, no doubt, be the last work she ever did for Sumner. Anglin wanted the materials on display for all Sumner's shareholders, buyers, and business associates to view at his grand affair.

She wondered why she was working so hard to build up and destroy Sumner, all at the same time. If those claims went against Sumner, they would drain the self-insurance fund, and Anglin would have to go to his supplemental policy. And, if the claims in Honduras weren't settled yet, it might give those people new ammunition if they heard about this trouble.

Monday morning, briefcase in hand, she brazenly showed up at the downstairs office and demanded a company car to drive. After the secretary made a few phone calls, Anne was given the keys to a compact not being driven at present. The secretary apologetically told her the car couldn't be taken beyond the Texas line. Those were the conditions of its use.

Anne felt humiliated that a daughter of Anglin Sumner could be given orders by a mere secretary in her father's company. While she stewed over this insult, the secretary handed her the paycheck she hadn't been able to pick up on Friday. She hadn't expected pay for the last week and would never have asked for it. Now, staring at it, she hated the fact this same secretary knew how much she was paid. Maybe the secretary made more money than she did. The thought entered her mind that she could be one of the big bosses at Sumner, could have people bowing to her, rendering her due respect, instead of being advised by an underling not to misuse the worn-out, little, company car. It hurt for a while, until she got her perspective in place and could smile at her Sumner conceit. After all, they were all just employees, not much different from the workers in Mexico. They did what they were told because they were afraid to lose a job or a paycheck. They weren't, in actuality, free to act as they wished.

The thought sobered her again. She wasn't free either. She belonged to her charges in Mexico. She might have to humble herself to help those people, humble herself to survive so she could keep on fighting. But at least her position held a semblance of dignity. She didn't work for personal gain.

In a nearby warehouse, she found her wheels. The dreary, little compact ran like it had less life in it than she had in her. It definitely wouldn't survive a trip to Mexico or even a journey to the Texas line. She drove to a chemical analysis laboratory with her samples, and they promised results in a day or two. She doubted they would find anything. Too much time had elapsed, and it was a long shot at best.

Tuesday, noon, she drove back to the lab to see what they had turned up. The cost didn't uphold the results. They had listed the chemicals. None of the levels were excessive, and none warranted a threat. Slight differences between the test fields, A and D, and the suspect fields, B, C, and E, showed up in the form of mildly higher levels of paraquat in the test fields, but that was natural since it was sprayed later. They did find some chemicals in the suspect fields that didn't show up in the test fields, but they told her those chemicals posed no threat.

She took the expensive data with her, gravely discouraged.

The workers knew, the padre knew, and she knew that chemicals were responsible. But the evidence didn't uphold it. It would be necessary to go ahead with only the worker's statements. At a phone booth, she called Padre Juan's number. When his quavering voice came on the line, she choked up inside.

"No, nothing is done. Two more have died. People are afraid to work in the fields, but they must work or starve."

"Padre, I'm going to mail you copies of all the signed statements. If I can't convince Sumner to help these people, you will need to take the papers to the authorities or to an attorney. I will call if that is necessary. I'll mail them the fastest way I can. Do you have a safe place to keep them?"

"Yes, I will keep them safe, but I do not know any attorneys or any officials. I will do my best if you fail, but you must try. Talk to Sumner first. You try that first."

"Yes, I will. Goodbye." She sighed.

The panic in his voice disheartened her. Why couldn't she lay the whole mess in someone else's hands and forget the matter? She was a United State's citizen and sick to boot. She did everything she could. Why couldn't they just use the papers and let her rest? She finally cried, unashamed, as she climbed back into the car. The weight of the world had settled on her and was crushing the breath out of her. And now she had to face her father and Angel, all of them, and threaten them with the papers. It would be like fighting a giant with a toothpick.

When she reached her office, she made up four separate packets, each containing copies of all the signed papers. Two she left in her briefcase, a third she enclosed in a heavy envelope addressed to Padre Juan, and she slid the last one into a folder and hunted up the powers at Sumner.

Angel was the only one she could find. Both she and Jim lounged in Angel's plush office chairs, sipping drinks and talking. Anne didn't flinch or apologize for interrupting them but laid the folder on the arm of Angel's chair. Standing as painfully straight as she could, with shoulders back, she waited.

"What's this, the material for the promotion? Dad said you were hard at work on it."

"Not exactly. This is another matter that publicity won't be able to help much, a matter that needs to be taken care of quickly, before the banquet, before anything."

Angel stared at the papers, confused for a minute, and then totally absorbed in their content. The realization of what damage they might do was reflected in the expression on her face.

"What am I to do with these?" she asked, her voice high-pitched and irritated.

"Sorry. I would have taken them to Dad or his attorney, but I couldn't find either. My contact in Mexico has copies of all those, and he waits for word from me before he takes them to the proper authorities. I must call him by this coming Friday afternoon, if I'm to stop him."

"So, you haven't been a sleeping dog, have you? I must commend you on exceptional acting. You convinced Dad anyway."

"Dad believes what he wants to."

"Where can I reach you? In your office?"

"I'll be there, off and on. I have my cell phone with me if I'm not there."

All during their little tête-à-tête, Jim sat still without saying a word. Anne didn't have nerve enough to meet his eyes but could still see his face clearly. His eyes registered excitement, and a sort of half-grin played around his mouth. Where had she seen that look before? Suddenly it came to her. It was directly after he landed on that bumpy air strip the first time and again when he split that last piece of petrified wood. She was looking at pride. Didn't he realize this information, this mess, could land right in his own lap? Dad could blame him, probably would, and ruin him. How could he sit there and grin with his chest puffed out like that.

Anne waited another minute while Angel sorted through the papers a second time.

"Who holds the originals? That attorney who was snooping around? Did you bring him into this?"

"I have the originals in a safe place. I've talked to no attorney, as I already told Dad. The person holding the duplicate copies in Mexico is a trusted individual whose honesty will be recognized. He has nothing to gain by it. I must go now. I'm sorry to leave you with this bag."

"Oh, no problem. I'll enjoy it."

Anne was closing the door behind her when she heard Angel say, "Jim, we may be flying again; better go service your plane. No, come to

152

think of it, better service the jet. I hate flying in that uncomfortable little bird of yours."

Anne drove to the post office and mailed Padre Juan's package, not trusting the office mail. Finding nothing more to do, she returned to her office to work and await developments. Prepared for the worst, she settled in to writing the best copy she could create. Her last efforts for Sumner would be superb.

She worked into the evening hours. No one came to her office, and no one called. Feeling too nervous, too vulnerable, to lie down on the floor and sleep, her tired mind told her she behaved more like a horse than a human. Only a relaxed, well-treated horse would lie down and sleep with humans close by. Tom-tom could always be counted on to drop down and sleep anywhere. He had never been hurt, had always been protected and babied. On the other hand, her dad's favorite horse, Caesar, trusted nobody and wouldn't lie down unless far out in the pasture or alone in his stall.

Anne mused over Caesar's behavior, wondered how much of it he had inherited and how much he had learned. His cruel, exacting master always demanded perfect obedience. When Anglin rode Caesar, the big gray seemed to take on her father's personality, the pride, arrogance, and a degree of viciousness. Caesar had sideswiped or kicked Tom-tom more than once when Anne had chanced to ride too close, and it always amused Anglin when Tom-tom nervously sidestepped out of Caesar's path. Though he gave Tom-tom to Anne as a gift, he ultimately took a dislike to him, accusing Anne of ruining him, of turning him into an undisciplined animal.

"Tom-tom acts too much like me, and Dad holds that against him," Anne reasoned, and knew there were times when she hated Caesar for being too much like her dad. "And now I'm becoming like Caesar, too untrusting of everyone to sleep here in this office."

Anne felt a kinship to Caesar, in spite of her dislike of him. He was only a horse. She, on the other hand, wasn't a helpless animal. She shouldn't allow fear and hurts to change her and cause her to feel defenseless. In spite of her rationalization, she couldn't stay there that night. Her thoughts had only served to make her want to see Tom-tom. She carried suitcase, briefcase, pillow, and blanket down to her car and drove to the stables. She had the place to herself. Homer had gone home, and most of his house lights were out. She knew he couldn't see her car from any of his windows.

She petted Tom-tom while his lips searched for goodies or affection; either would do. Finally she made a bed of hay bales and prepared to spend the night. When she stared up at the stars, she felt so alone it hurt. She wished for her little tent in Mexico. It seemed a better place to die.

A couple hours later, she awoke stiff and chilled. Her hay bed irritated her lungs, and she coughed uncontrollably. Too miserable and restless to go back to the office, she drove toward the Gulf. She couldn't count on Jim's promise to take her back to the beach, now that Angel had so thoroughly entered the picture.

In less than an hour, she stood barefoot on the white sand, breathing in the rich air and listening to the rolling surf. The moon and stars dazzled like day, and she studied their lighted pathways across the water. When she stepped into the Gulf's swirling night mysteries, emotion welled up in her.

She wanted to pray, but after a desperate, "Oh, God," nothing more came out. Words, chained inside her, begged for release, but she didn't have the key. She kneeled in the rolling surf and wept silently, letting the waves rock her about. Soon the words were there, flowing freely past her trembling lips, quiet words, half buried in the sound of the surf.

"Lord, you know my desperation and hurt. You see the trouble that surrounds me on every side. Like these waves breaking all around, the flood of humanity washes over me, and every ripple in its turbulent surface is a face of someone I know. They cry out for justice, and yes, for mercy, too. And I'm drowned in the weight of their sorrow and agony. Their tears wash over me and pull me outward in an undertow as strong as death. Will I, too, become one of these faces, swept to and fro by the elements? Or is love truly as strong as death, and will it be my anchor?"

A long hour later, she rose from the surf and walked along the beach until the early morning sun lightened the sky. Stealing one last look at the coloring sea, committing its face to memory, she left to tackle the job ahead of her.

At an all-night department store, she purchased a lightweight nylon bag with a shoulder strap. If, at some point, she had to leave Sumner premises on just her own two feet, it would be difficult to carry a cumbersome suitcase, bedding, and a briefcase all at the same time. The new bag would serve for all three.

On the way back to the office, she stopped at her storage place to drop off any goods she didn't absolutely need. The remaining items, clothing, insurance forms, and her blanket fit nicely in the new bag.

She entered her office at eight o'clock, early, but not too early. No one could accuse her of sleeping all night in the office, and no one would know she totally depended on Sumner. And yet she did. She was afraid to think what would happen if she were kicked out right then.

Agitated again, she bowed her head and silently prayed for guidance and strength:

Lord, please show me what to do. Should I plan for the future, in case I'm suddenly homeless and moneyless, or do I ride this through to the end? Will you be there, Lord, to pick me up or take me home, when all hell breaks loose?

All that day and most of the night, she worked on the Sumner project. It only lacked a few graphics when she put it aside at three in the morning. She considered it the best work she had ever turned out. Why had such inspiration never come to her back in the days when she believed in Sumner?

Anglin would love what she wrote and hate what she meant to do. She felt terribly sorry he had to pay for a mistake not his fault. She understood, perfectly, how he would feel. He would never speak to her again when it was all over, this strong, powerful man she loved and hated and worshiped and condemned.

She didn't feel tired in the least. She had written the entire thing while lying on the sofa, propped up with cushions. Now it needed to be transferred to a computer. She should borrow Fred's spare laptop and lie back on the sofa for that, too, but it had been so long since they'd talked, she felt shy about approaching him. He and Jim still avoided her, supposedly to learn more about the situation and to protect her. She had begun to believe they did it for their own protection. They were afraid. Everyone would be glad when she left the scene permanently. Even some of the villagers had become standoffish about being helped, afraid of losing their jobs.

After a short nap, she typed the work at her desk computer and finished the graphics. The project included itemized plans for the upcoming year's promotions, so her completion of it more or less completed her job at Sumner. Anyone could handle it henceforth.

Come evening, she downloaded the project to a disc and made printed copies besides, so they could view the actual presentation. She took the entire layout down to the conference room table on the first floor and spread it out in exhibition form. It looked like an art show, an attractive, miniature display filling the surface of the table. Now it could be presented at next week's banquet. Maybe it would help them understand she wasn't fighting Sumner. Why couldn't anyone else see things from both sides? She hated to stand against her family, but the ill workers should be helped.

Friday morning she sat at her desk in a state of unease. Sumner had until afternoon to take action, or she'd be forced to call Padre Juan. She fiddled at unnecessary tasks and waited. The past days had taken their toll on her body, and she had hit rock bottom. Just the chore of sitting there exhausted her. She was tired of breathing, and the air she drew in never satisfied her. Her hand trembled when she picked up a pen. Finally, she desisted trying to do anything. Folding her hands in her lap, she sat still and stared at her office door.

By noon she could do nothing but worry. If they didn't come to her, she must go to them, a thought she abhorred. Minutes later her phone rang with a call from Anglin's personal secretary.

"I'm to inform you that the matter in Mexico is progressing. The insurance fund has already settled a number of claims.

"Did ... do you know which claims have been settled?"

"I have no further information. That's all Angel told me."

Anne felt tremendously relieved. They must absolutely hate her right now, but that didn't matter if the ill people received aid. She would leave Sumner. It didn't matter where she went to finish out her life. After she picked up her last paycheck, she would find Angel and get the particulars. How she shrank from that chore.

The news brought such relief, she put her head down on her desk and sobbed brokenly, "It's over! It's over!"

Chapter 14

"Yes. It's over. You've done your worst," Angel said sarcastically, close by Anne's desk.

Certain she turned scarlet with embarrassment, Anne hastily donned a semblance of dignity.

"Angel, can you get me a list of who's been taken care of and what's been done for them?"

"We've only begun. First claims, of course, had to be paid first. Sumner's company fund is depleted. That should make you happy. We had to pay off some large claims. We haven't yet started on the claims you brought us. Those will have to wait until the supplemental insurance kicks in. The insurers will want to make their own investigation and that will take time. I hope you realize this can't all be finished overnight."

"But ..." Anne caught herself before revealing she knew the names on Angel's list, had talked with many of them, and had presented claims to Sumner from those same people. Of course, she'd only reached half the people on Angel's list. Maybe the ones paid were from the other half.

"We need your signed statement that you'll drop this now and will also notify your Mexican contact to cease and desist," Angel demanded haughtily.

"I'll need to see the names of the people who were paid off. I ... I've been given more names than those people who signed statements. I'd like to see how many of them have received assistance."

Angel grudgingly got out a list containing seventeen names. Anne only recognized two of them as being from her list, and those two were not from the critical category. Something rang false.

"Do you have papers showing the settlements given to each of these? I'll need statements about their claims and illnesses, something concrete to send down there."

"I don't have all seventeen with me. Some are still at the attorney's office. You can copy the ones I have, eleven, I believe."

"How about addresses on these people?" she asked while she made copies of the papers. She hid her surprise at the immense sums paid out to the eleven workers.

"I only have what you see there. Our attorney took care of the transactions. I believe most of these claims were paid to day laborers. The foreman had brought them down from Mexico City. They may not have addresses." She laughed. "Of course they stayed at the farm while they worked, but they've all left now. Only the ones who had claims stayed to collect, but they're gone now, too. And they could have gone anywhere they wished, considering the payoffs they received. Sumner gave generously. Millions of dollars have gone out. Of course, these were the desperately ill cases and had to be taken care of first. I believe they worked in a different area of the farmlands from where your villagers worked."

"They might still be in hospitals."

"I have no information on that. These were cash payoffs. The people agreed to arrange their own treatment as they saw fit."

Anne bit her tongue. She had investigated extensively while in Mexico. No other area of the farms was involved, and there were no other workers. Nothing had ever been said about outside labor being brought in. But even if laborers had been brought all the way from Mexico City, they would have lived somewhere back there, and most of them would have had families and relatives.

"Something else the matter now?" Angel asked impatiently. "You're not satisfied with what you've caused?"

"Sorry." Anne smiled and tried to look pleased. "I was thinking of Lino Ortega. You have his name listed here. I know him and his family well. They must be pleased. You don't have a payoff paper on him. Do you remember what amount he received?"

"The attorney still has his papers. Like I said, I don't have any information on those other six."

Anne smiled again, hiding her thoughts. "By the way, I've finished the promotion campaign for the banquet, and I made up next year's campaign, too. I'd appreciate it if you'd let Dad know it's ready. It's in the meeting room. I won't be here. I need to rest ... now that it's over."

"Over for you, maybe. I just spent six hours with our attorney, and now Jim and I have to jet back to Mexico this evening to finish mopping up. I don't know how you stood it down there. It's all right on the coast, in a resort with air-conditioned rooms, but not in that God-forsaken area where you stayed."

"I'm sorry you have all that drudgery ahead of you. I'm giving you my sympathy now, because I intend to leave Sumner at once."

"Look, you stay with Sumner until after the banquet next Friday, Dad's orders. Word's leaked out about this, and Dad wants you to be there doing your job. You're Sumner's Head of Public Relations, at least till after the banquet."

"My presence wouldn't help."

"Dad insists. He said you opened this bag of woes, and you'd see it through."

"I started nothing."

"Look, I had the situation covered down there, until you sent that attorney to snoop and cause trouble. I know you said you didn't, but it happened while you were there, and I'm convinced you orchestrated it."

Anne wondered what Angel and Anglin would say if they found out she was the supposed attorney.

"I'm no asset to the company right now. I've finished my work here. Tell Dad I'm through."

"He needs you at the banquet. He figures that a sick Sumner might be strong enough to appease the shareholders, if he has to explain anything to them."

"But my illness isn't the same thing. It can't be."

"I'm not sure how Sumner intends to present your illness, whether it's to be flu or chemicals. But if it serves Sumner's image for you to be suffering from the same problem the workers have, then that's what's wrong with you. Listen, you seem exactly like them. I've been in their miserable, little shacks. I've heard them breathe and explain their symptoms. It doesn't take a doctor to convince me you're suffering from the same thing. But, like I said, Sumner will decide what's wrong with you."

"I'll stay a few more days."

"You'll attend that banquet. That's what you'll do. That's Dad's demand in return for the demands you made on him." Angel turned and left without another word.

Anne closed and locked the door after her. It humiliated her for Angel to catch her crying, but she had more important matters to be concerned about than that. She must call Padre Juan. He would know if other workers came from Mexico City.

She didn't want to call from the office, so she drove to a nearby park and called the padre on her cell phone. He didn't answer, and she couldn't think of anyone else to contact down there. On a sudden whim, she called Dr. Logan and found him anxious to talk with her.

"You didn't keep your appointment, and you left no way to reach you. The address and phone number were incorrect."

"I wanted to be unknown."

"You never called for the last test results. They definitely substantiated that you had a reaction to chemicals."

"Paraquat?"

"Then you knew you'd been exposed?"

"No. I have no idea how I was exposed. I can't figure it out for the life of me."

"Such damage makes me lean toward the possibility of your having ingested some of the substance."

"Impossible. We can't afford chemicals, and in the village we eat only our own meat and our own organic vegetables, plus a small quantity of vegetables and fruits we buy from another village. We all eat the same thing, and no one else in my village became sick when I did."

"I'm not talking about residue in food. It'd have to be more than that."

"There's no spraying anywhere near the village, and we're on a higher level than surrounding areas, so it couldn't be from water runoff. I thought of a thousand possibilities, but nothing works. Could you tell me one thing? If the doctor I first saw had known what ailed me, could he have saved me from this? Would it have made a difference?"

"I'm certain the doctor knew what was wrong and treated you accordingly. He evidently didn't think it'd help you to know the particulars. He couldn't have done any more than he did."

"Thank you. I ..."

"Come into my office as soon as you can. You won't need an appointment. Just come in. I'll make time for you. We'll see how you're progressing."

Anne said goodbye without committing to an appointment. When she dialed the padre again, she reached him.

"Anne, how are you doing? I have waited for your call. Were you successful?"

"I was given a list of names and told that claims have been paid. The payoffs were awarded to day workers the foreman brought in from Mexico City. Those people supposedly had the first claims and were paid first. It seems they received rather hefty sums of money. There were seventeen people in all, according to this new list. The only names I recognized on the list were Lino Ortega and Carlos Navarro. I didn't receive any information about how much they were paid."

"Yes. Lino and Carlos were both seen by the doctor, and they each were given two hundred dollars in return for signing the insurance release. I told them not to sign, but they needed the money. What were the other names? Do you have them?"

Astounded at the trifling amount paid the two workers, Anne carefully read the list for him.

"I know none of those names. And no workers were brought in from Mexico City. Maybe sometime in the past they have done that but not recently. I'm sure of this."

"Padre, tell everyone not to sign, not to settle, until you or I give them advice. Something is wrong, very wrong. I'll try to do something."

She stifled the sob in her voice when she said goodbye. Devastated to find her work still far from being done, she wondered how she could go on. Was there no easy way out? She must go back to Mexico, and it began to look as if she would die there.

If the Sumner compact could survive the trip, she knew she would attempt it in spite of Sumner's distance limitations on the car, but the little car barely ran and had four bald tires. She wasn't even sure she could physically handle a long drive in her present state. A plane or bus would use up too much of the money she had left, and she couldn't run to Jim. He was flying Angel to Mexico that evening. Instantly a daring thought came to mind. She would stowaway in the plane if they hadn't left yet.

When she arrived back at Sumner's, she parked her car in a building where it might not be noticed for a few days. Office workers had gone for the day, but the jet hadn't left yet. Unceremoniously, she stuffed the list of names and the rest of the papers from her briefcase into her pants pockets. She put her cell phone, the rest of her money, and a few incidentals from her purse into another pocket. She looked wistfully at the oxygen tank before leaving it behind.

Hurrying to the jet, she found it unlocked but heard voices from inside the hanger's office. Quickly and silently she entered, only to find no satisfactory hiding place. The cabin was too open, and the storage area would be out of the question because Angel would definitely bring bags. While still searching frantically for a solution, she heard voices outside. She slid into the restroom, closed the door, and waited. The voices continued, but no one boarded the plane.

The plane shook slightly, and she could tell it was being fueled. Ever so gently she sat on the commode lid and waited. Maybe she could stay there. Maybe no one would use the restroom. Soon Jim's and Angel's voices could be heard, and she felt movement as they boarded the plane. She could tell when Jim put something in the cargo area.

When the engines came alive and the plane lifted off, her heart thumped so loudly she feared they would hear it. Discovery might come any second. If they didn't detect her presence during the trip, what would happen when they landed? She had found no time to make any plans, and now no plans were possible. She would have to wing it.

Snatches of conversation traveled through the thin wall of the room she occupied.

"I don't trust her, Jim. She acted too sweetsy-sweetsy about it. I saw doubt on her face."

"What did you expect?" Jim mumbled.

"I expected a normal human being. Listen, we both had the same parents and the same education. Where does she get off trying to save the world and dusting us off her boots like she's some queen?"

Anne didn't hear any answer and assumed there wasn't one. Shortly, Angel spoke again.

"What are you doing? Going to let me drive?"

"I've set the autopilot. Watch things. I'll be right back."

Anne pressed her ear close to the door and jumped back in shock when it was snatched open. She would have cried out if Jim hadn't put a hand over her mouth. He slid in beside her and whispered in her ear, "Sit still until I come for you, no matter how long."

He left, just like that, and shortly she heard conversation resume. She sat still and tried to calm her fluttering heart enough to where she could hear what they said.

"Something wrong with the john. Guess I'll hold till we land. I'd advise you to do the same. Needs a deodorizer in there, too."

Anne smiled to herself. Jim knew Angel, that was for sure. Angel definitely wouldn't use the restroom. She sat back less tense but wondered what lay ahead. Jim hadn't given her away. He must have known, all along, that someone occupied the restroom. He had once told her he could tell if someone put a gallon of water in his plane, he knew the feel of it so well. She hadn't thought he would know the jet so well.

Before long, she doubted the wisdom of coming. The oxygen in the little room had grown slim. She saw the switch for the fan but feared Angel would hear it. She grew more beat by the minute and eventually couldn't force herself to sit up any longer. She struggled to the small floor and sat with her back against the commode, all the time feeling weaker and weaker.

"Anne. Anne!" The words came from a distance, and the room shook. Slowly her cloudy mind cleared, and she realized she lay on the floor in the passenger part of the plane. Jim was shaking her.

"Did Angel see me? How did I get here?"

"I carried you out. You were unconscious." His eyes bore into her like two burning fires. "No, Angel didn't see you, but does it matter? It was madness for you to try something like this. You should be in a hospital."

Anne felt tears well up in her eyes. "I only fell asleep. I sleep soundly, especially when I have to breathe such stuffy air."

"Don't lie to me."

163

"Can I get away from here without Angel seeing?"

"Do you have a plan? Where are you going?"

"To see Padre Juan."

"Why?"

"Sumner supposedly made seventeen insurance payoffs in Mexico, *big* payoffs, which have depleted their insurance fund. I'm talking about millions of dollars. Angel showed me some of the amounts paid out, and they were generous. She also gave me a list of the claimant's names. No one has ever heard of any of them, except for two men whom I know personally. Padre Juan informed me those two men received two hundred dollars apiece. There's a lie somewhere, and I have to find it."

"Did you think someone like Anglin, or like Angel, would sit back and peacefully pay out big money to a bunch of destitute workers? They'll fight to keep every dollar, and they'll use every trick in the book. Didn't you expect them to fight back?"

"I never did. I-I never did. And I'm sorry for what I'm causing you. I don't want them to ruin you to save Sumner's reputation."

"I can play their game."

"I don't want you to. Not stoop to their level."

"If I don't, I could lose my license, maybe even my plane."

"I'll find a way to help you. I'll think of something. I have to help these sick villagers, but I'd do as much, no, I'd do *more* for you. Don't let them use you."

"What do you want me to do?"

"Don't tell anyone I came on the plane. I'll find someone to drive me to Padre Juan's. I'm going to fight. I may not make it back to the United States again. Don't sell your soul to Sumner, and I'll help you with the last breath in me."

"Listen," his voice sounded thick with emotion, "I'll hide you somewhere until I can get rid of Angel for the night. Then we'll learn what we can."

"No."

"You'll do as you're told, or I'll send you back to Houston. Come on with me."

He hurried her over to a small plane and helped her aboard.

"Stay down until we're in the air, no matter how long it takes. This will have to be done tonight. I know what to tell Angel. I have a plan that should give us until noon tomorrow. Rest."

Within fifteen minutes he was back and had them in the air.

"What did you tell Angel?"

"I told her I was checking out something that might save Sumner. I didn't explain, but I told her I'd try and be back by noon."

They soon faced a sleepy, but cordial, Padre Juan. After pouring each of them a cup of coffee, he got directly to the business at hand.

"May I see the list of names you read me over the phone? Maybe one will make me remember."

He studied the list for a couple of minutes.

"The addresses are listed as Mexico City. Mexico City is not an address. It sprawls and sprawls. Many people live in less than shacks. Some barely survive. Those are the places where they would get day laborers. But I have asked everyone here, and no one has seen any outside workers, not that day, not in the last six months."

"You were in Mexico City for a long time before you came here. Don't any of those names look familiar? Maybe the family name?"

"This one, maybe. Though names mean little."

"Would you know where to reach him? Do you remember what parish he belongs to?"

"Not a parishioner. He was a drunk, a beggar. He could not have worked in any farm field, not for a day. The city, she is a vast place. Many come and go. Many die. Many are lost to family and friends. Many, many have the same names."

"The attorney's paper says they paid him five hundred and fifty thousand dollars. He's supposed to be irreparably affected, in critical condition. It seems to me he'd be in a hospital somewhere, but the paper says nothing of that. Sumner says they've depleted all their insurance fund and have to apply to the company's supplemental insurer, which will take time, more investigation, and more delay for those who need help. Of course, that insurance company will also try to prove they aren't liable. So my efforts, all my efforts, weren't enough to get them the aid they need right now."

"You have tried so hard."

"I'm not through trying. If you can find even one of these men, maybe there is a slim chance. Or maybe you could find a friend or relative. Could you call or write to anyone who might know, maybe to the churches there?"

"I will try."

"I'll be back later to help you. You may keep all those copies. I have more. Now I have to see Malinali and Pacal. Maybe someone there will know more or even recognize one of those names."

It had turned daylight when they landed at sleeping Tutlu. Only Ruben came to the plane. He greeted her warmly and hugged her for a long second – something he had never done. Anne walked to her tent, carefully examining the area in and around it. Jim followed close beside, saying nothing.

"Jim, how could I have been exposed to chemicals? I've gone over what I ate, what I did. I can't find the answer."

"You didn't bring anything from the farms? From the other village? Something no one else had?"

"Nothing. And I've walked over every square inch of space that I might have touched those last two days." She stood there and shook her head in uncertainty. There were not enough answers for all the questions she had. Finally, she looked up at Jim. "I'm wasting time with this. I'll go see Malinali and Pacal now."

"Go ahead. I'll check around some more and talk with Ruben."

Anne couldn't stay long in the little hut. It hurt too much. Pacal still appeared frail. Even if the insurance paid off, he'd receive no aid unless they could prove he was exposed to Sumner's chemicals.

She wandered, slightly dazed, back out into the sunshine. Jim still talked with the villagers, and she was too tired to hurry him. Why hurry, anyway? Nothing mattered any more. Sadly she gazed at the tranquil water of her little pond. Such happy memories lingered there, especially the times she swam with Jim.

An urge to step once more into that water suddenly became a passion that wouldn't be denied. Time and duty stepped aside in the strength of her desire to relive a less-troubled past, maybe for the last time. Emptying her pockets, she walked into the water, remembering a night she swam the silver pond in the moonlight. She hadn't been alone like she was now. Its glassy waters had been full of mystique and fragrance and hope. Now it was all gone.

In the face of her discouragement, the pond lost its magic and became only a bleak stretch of water lying under an unkind sun. She could tell it had been a hot summer. The level had dropped lower than usual. When the water came up to her waist, she slid to her back and floated on the warm surface. The sun beat down hot on her face. When she stayed on her back, the water didn't press so strongly against her chest, and she could breathe more easily. She paddled her hands slightly and floated over to her favorite spot. After a while, she stood and waded toward the edge where the fish traps were stacked. They looked as if they hadn't been used for a long time. Pacal had been the only one to take care of them when she couldn't. They made a forlorn heap of rusted wire.

Standing there in waist-deep water, she could feel her legs tremble under her. Jim came toward the lake, and she knew it was time to leave. She lingered a minute more. She couldn't bear the thought of stepping back onto solid earth and feeling the pull of gravity dragging down on her.

"Are you ready?" he called from the other side of the lake.

She stepped carefully toward shore, sliding her feet along the slick muck of the bottom to avoid stepping on the stubble of the small trees she cut during the lake's construction. When her right foot came against an obstruction, she lost her balance and plunged forward into the water. She landed against a slippery object, submerged a couple of feet below the surface. Pushing herself upright, she slid her hands under the water and investigated the object that had tripped her. It felt like a rounded container of some sort. She reached further down to free it from where it was imbedded in the bottom.

"What are you doing?" Jim called from nearby.

"I took a swim, a last swim." She reached again into the water and pulled on the object. "There's something in the water here, and I want to see what it is."

"They may throw their garbage into the lake, now that you're not here to watch them."

"It's big. A drum, I think. See?" She managed to roll it over into shallower water where a gray edge of it protruded above the water's surface. "It looks like an old, broken container of Sumner's. Throw me one of those fish trap cords. I'll tie it to the handle, and you can pull it out."

She heard an enormous splash, and Jim came beside her in the water. He pushed her out into the center of the lake.

"Close your mouth. We're going to the spring." He dragged her ashore and over to the spring that bubbled out a foot and a half above the pond's surface. He poured bucket after bucket of icy spring water over both of them.

"You're freezing me, drowning me," she sputtered.

"Anne, that's one of the containers of mix that were brought over in the helicopter. Fritz must have dropped it into your lake, and it burst or something. Did you swim that night? You said you did, didn't you?"

"What night? Oh, yes. Some kind of noise woke me, and I heard an airplane. I went outside and saw its lights as it departed. I thought it was you. When it didn't come back, I went in for a swim to cool off. Did the plane drop it? Is that what happened? Why? Was it an accident? That end of the lake has stumps and sharp stubble on the bottom. It must have landed on one of those."

"No accident. Barrels don't just fall out of planes into remote ponds in the middle of the night."

"That's what has been wrong with me. I must have gotten some in my mouth. I did swim to that side. Oh, no! Pacal tends the traps. The tears poured out in a flood. She pulled away from Jim and rushed toward the center of the dam. In a frenzy, she threw rocks and limbs aside, then stumbled back to her tent for a pick.

"Anne, stop. You're killing yourself," Jim hollered, pulling her away.

"Leave me alone," she cried, wrenching herself free from his grip and rushing past him to the dam. She drove the pick deep into it and ripped away dirt, rocks, and debris. Jim grabbed her, and she tore away from him again.

"Stop," he commanded, taking the pick from her trembling hands when she stumbled in the slick mud.

"I made this pond. Now it's killed me. Maybe Pacal, too. I've destroyed the people I came to help. It was all for nothing," she cried as she continued to rip away debris with her hands, tears raining down hot and furiously.

Jim picked her up, ignoring her protests, and carried her aside. He went back with the pick and worked until he'd made a foot-wide cleft all the way to the level of the bottom of the lake. The water washed through in a torrent. She saw Jim's glance continually travel to where she lay on the shore, her cheek pressed against the earth.

When villagers gathered around, he called out, "Stay away, and don't take any fish. Stand back."

Ruben sent them away and helped Jim finish the task, after which they both washed off at the spring. Anne still lay silently but stared up at Jim through half-open eyes when he returned. She couldn't talk, could barely breathe.

"Rest awhile. Ruben and I will investigate. There shouldn't be any danger, but I flooded us with water as a precaution. It's been too long to still be harmful."

Jim hooked onto the handle of the drum with the pick and dragged it ashore. In surprise, Anne watched him drag ashore a second container, the same size, a Sumner twenty-gallon chemical container. Shortly, he came beside her again.

"Can you sit up now? Are you okay?"

She couldn't answer. She could only lay there hating herself for what she'd caused.

His voice grew urgent. "If I help you up, can you sit?"

"Not yet," she heard her voice say, as if someone else had spoken the words.

"Listen then, and rest. That container explains your problem. It's the same chemical that we sprayed at the farms. You must have the contents analyzed. There might be residue in the broken container, but the other one is unbroken and full. It should tell you where the fault lies."

"But they might ... blame it on you."

"They *will* blame it on me. My spraying license has already been suspended. Now it's my pilot's license I fear for."

"No, I won't let ..."

"You'll do exactly what you planned. You'll have this analyzed, and you'll do whatever's necessary. If it's just paraquat, that would be enough to cause your problem, because you evidently got some in your mouth. But, if it is just paraquat, then I can't understand why Fritz dropped off those containers. And, if it is just paraquat, why did the workers become so ill from being in the fields?"

"Angel's waiting for you."

"Not yet. We have time. I owe you this."

She didn't want to be owed anything. Couldn't he see that? Was he too dense to understand?"

"I'll take a sample from both containers, Anne. There may be some diluted chemical left in the broken one."

"Be careful. Malinali will get you something to put it in. Why are you doing this to yourself?"

"I'm not. You are." He patted her on the back and walked away.

The next thing she knew, Jim was carrying her to the plane. She had no strength to even hold on.

"Please leave me here," she said close to his ear. "I'll rest a few days and come back when I'm better."

"The two barrels are hidden in the woods. Ruben helped me cover them. I have samples of chemical here in the plane, ready for analysis." He lifted her to the passenger seat. "Ruben, stand by till I take off."

"Jim, take me to Padre Juan's. I'll take the samples back to Houston and have them analyzed. The padre will put me on a bus. Is there time for you to fly me there?"

"I'm not leaving you in Mexico. We'll go back. Let your dad and Angel rant and rave. You can sue Sumner now for a few million."

"I'm not ready to face anyone yet." She couldn't stop the tears or the gasping. She tried to sound harsh but only succeeded in sounding desperate. "Take me to the padre's."

"No, we'll face Angel together."

Upon hearing Angel's name, the dark folds of suspicion enveloped her and helped her have strength of purpose.

"Why are you so worried about me now? You've hardly spoken to me lately. You've been gallivanting with Angel."

Jim looked at her angrily but only said, "Yes, Anne?"

She couldn't stop the flood she'd started. Though sincere in her grievance, she had to make him angry enough to leave her at the padre's, and she was too weak to fight on even ground. No matter what it took, she mustn't let him get in any deeper by helping her.

"Yes! Why now? Now that I'm worth a couple of million and might only last another couple of weeks, do I suddenly look better than Angel?"

Jim looked furious, and that was what she wanted. She didn't know where the words came from, but they were accomplishing their purpose. "We could marry and sue Sumner, and you'd never need to work again. You wouldn't need a pilot's license. But with that kind of money you could get it back." She finally ran out of breath and out of will to hurt him.

When he still didn't flinch from his resolve to take her back, she snatched the two bottles of chemical and climbed out of the plane. She would have collapsed on the dirt below, except for Ruben's arms. He caught her and took charge of the samples.

"Ruben," she said weakly, ready to faint. "Ruben, does the truck still run? Can you drive me to Padre Juan's?"

Ruben looked at her helplessly. He'd heard all their words. He liked both these people, but his allegiance belonged to Anne if he had to choose sides.

"I will take you."

"You won't need to. I'll fly her to his village." Jim had climbed from the plane and stood there with folded arms.

"No. I don't trust you. You'd take me back." She clung to Ruben in her desperation. "He's lying, Ruben. He'd take me back."

"I might at that." His face looked a mask of tense cords, his eyes glinted like steel. "But you realize, don't you, that you can help everyone more quickly if you just trust me?"

"Help who? Help you? Help Angel to protect Sumner? Why should I trust you? What have you done to help in this matter, besides fly Angel around so she can cover up facts? Why trust you?"

"I don't think you trust anyone but yourself."

"There's enough of 'myself' left to finish this," she retorted and stumbled to the old truck, afraid to face him, afraid she might weaken. Ruben put the containers in the back and headed for the driver's side while Anne struggled with the heavy, ill-fitting door on the other side but couldn't open it. When she saw Jim coming to help, she exerted more and managed to wrench the door open and climb onto the seat. When Jim closed the door for her, she turned away to hide the tears that were flooding again.

Chapter 15

After a few attempts, Ruben managed to start the motor and pull away. Anne had to grasp the seat to keep from falling, as Ruben started off down the bumpy road. After the first bend in the road, she said, "You may drive slower, Ruben. Could you inch along for a while? I'm sorry."

After they had gone a ways, Ruben looked over at her with sympathy in his eyes.

"Do you hate Jim?"

"I don't want him involved. They might try to blame him. And he wasn't to blame. This whole thing may hurt him terribly."

"So you want to hurt him, too?" He looked at her, his uncertainty written on his face.

"I didn't hurt him. I made him angry. I made him happy, too. Because now no one will know he brought me here or that we found the chemical samples."

"You hurt him to protect him?"

"I made him angry to protect him and this evidence. If he took me back, someone might take the samples away before they could be tested. Especially if the results could be injurious to Sumner."

"So you will do what's right, no matter what happens to you or Jim or the company."

"Y-yes. I didn't realize you understood."

"I didn't. Jim said that is what you would do."

Anne turned her head toward the window, afraid the tears would start again.

Finally, she turned back to him. "I stayed here mainly to find evidence for Jim's protection. Please don't tell anyone. Jim would never have let me stay."

"I understand. I will help all I can."

Ruben drove along at a snail's pace, finally stopping so Anne might take a nap on the front seat. When he woke her, it had grown dark.

"Why did you let me sleep so long?" she asked, rising to a sitting position.

"I called. You didn't wake. But it's better to go after dark."

When they pulled into the padre's yard, a neighbor came and told them Padre Juan had left for Capaso earlier that evening to hold an early mass in the morning. Ruben carried the chemicals and a small canvas bag into the padre's dwelling.

"Oh, I'm glad you brought a bag. I wondered what I'd carry them in."

"Jim put it in the back of the truck as we drove away," he explained simply.

"Thank you for bringing me, Ruben. Please hurry back and tell Malinali I might be able to get aid for Pacal. Here, this is my cell phone number. If an emergency arises, please drive somewhere to a phone and call me. Goodbye."

She curled up on one of the padre's rugs and fell asleep, not waking until the gray light of morning filtered through the small window. Still groggy, she fell back asleep. Sometime later she was awakened by someone kneeling beside her. Slightly dazed, she mumbled, "I have the evidence," and fell asleep again. When she awoke the next time, she discovered she lay on a cot. Someone must have lifted her onto it. She didn't remember doing it herself. When she pulled herself to a standing position, her legs shook violently. Holding onto the wall, she walked to the room's doorway and on into the small kitchen. No one was about, so she dropped to a seat at the table and waited. In a few minutes the padre came in, surprised to see her up.

"Padre, where are the bottles I brought?"

He hurried into the next room and brought back the canvas bag and containers of chemical.

"I must get them tested. Can I have it done here in Mexico?"

"I don't know who is trustworthy. Word has gotten out about the drums of chemical."

"But who would tell? Not Jim or Rubin, surely?"

"I think one or more of your villagers. Some went to town. They drink and forget themselves. They talk, and they don't remember what they say. The news spreads swiftly. I think you should leave soon. Take the samples back to the United States. I don't trust things here. Someone may take them away from you."

Anne didn't know if he wanted her to leave for his own safety or hers. Instantly she reprimanded herself for being so untrusting. Jim had been right about that. She couldn't trust anyone, not for the present anyway.

The padre broke into her thoughts. "We will get you to an airplane. I will find someone to drive you there. You must hurry."

"I need a bus. I can't afford a plane. But I need to see farm workers first, as many as I can see, sick or well. I came here for that reason."

"Wait here. I'll get someone."

In ten minutes, the padre arrived back in a dusty, dented, little car. Jock was the grinning driver.

"Here, take these. You can be Incognito Anne, again." He handed her a priest's robe and black hat. "Put them on over your clothes. Be safe while you do what you must do. I will hide the chemicals until you return, and then someone will drive you to a bus."

She quickly donned the strange garments and climbed into the car with Jock. While he drove, she looked over a small sheaf of papers she had printed before she left Houston. They were somewhat crumpled from being in her pocket but were at least legible. She and Jock spent two grueling days seeing workers, until Anne finally said she had enough and would go back to the States.

When they returned to Padre Juan's, he advised her to wear the priest's garments until safe at the bus stop. He brought her the chemical samples and Jim's canvas bag and told her to make haste. When she opened the bag to deposit the bottles in it, she found a hundred-dollar bill lying in the bottom. Astounded for a minute, she thought first of Padre Juan or Ruben but immediately knew they hadn't put it there. If it had been their money, it would have been much less, and it wouldn't have been American money. It had been Jim. She slid it into her pocket. She'd give it back to him, she told herself.

When she went out again to the little car, she was surprised to find Padre Juan in the driver's seat.

"I will take you to Mexico City. It is safer for you to get the bus there."

Gratefully, she settled back and slept most of the way, changing out of the priest robe when they neared the bus station. Soon, she was waving goodbye to the padre, who had appointed himself her protector and had refused to leave until she was safely on her way. She smiled to herself. Little, feeble Padre Juan was protecting her and the bottles. One didn't cry on a public bus, so she slid down in her seat and closed her eyes.

She slept in spite of the uncomfortable ride and arrived at the Houston bus station Wednesday night. From there she took a city bus to her storage area and stashed the bottles. Too tired for more, she curled up on the floor of the small locker and went to sleep with the door slightly ajar for oxygen.

Although stiff, sore, and still tired the next morning, she wasted no time on self-pity. Within minutes she had two sample bottles of chemical ready for testing, reserving only a tiny portion for emergency. At the same lab she used before, she arranged for the tests, explaining to them their importance, that the results might be used for court evidence. When they understood fully what she required, it became necessary to bring out Jim's hundred-dollar bill to help cover the expense.

I'm using Jim's money to ruin him, just as I'm using my father's money to ruin him, she thought to herself. But Jim had given his willingly. She had worked for the other.

With only seventy dollars left in her pocket, she arrived at her office that morning. She would concede to her father's demands and stay through the banquet the next evening in return for the aid he gave the workers. What workers he had helped was still an uncertainty, but it appeared money had been paid out. She would hold to her post and hope no one at Sumner knew about the chemical samples or about her trip to Mexico.

She had been at her desk only thirty minutes when Angel stormed in.

"For someone supposed to be sick and broke, you get around. You look awful."

"Thank you. I'm fine."

"You were in Mexico. I thought Dad said you weren't to leave the States."

"The company car wasn't allowed out of Texas. It's been sitting down in the warehouse. I agreed to stay through the banquet if they started paying off insurance claims. I'm still here as you can see."

"How did you make the trip? I know you went down there."

"By bus." Angel needn't know she jetted one way. A moment of perverseness tempted her to say, "I rode with you, Angel," but for Jim's sake, she kept silent. It didn't matter what they did to her anymore. "By the way, Angel, it seems that two of the workers on your payoff list, Lino Ortega and Carlos Navarro, received only two hundred dollars each."

"That's a fortune to them, and they were hardly ill. They were happy with the money. Why aren't you? I've been killing myself cleaning up this disaster you created."

"I imagine you know as little about being killed as you do about cleaning. You're simply riding around in a luxurious jet, working hard to bury an embarrassing, costly incident."

Anne walked past Angel and out of the office, only to be met by Anglin's secretary, Ms. Phelps.

"You're wanted in the conference room for a meeting."

"Thank you. I'm on my way."

Anne hurried past her and took the elevator down, not bothering to hold its progress for Ms. Phelps or Angel. No need to arrive under hostile escort. She took a deep breath before entering the room.

Eric Zeiker, her father's top attorney, sat at the table with a sheaf of papers in front of him. At first, she thought he was the only one in the room but then saw Anglin standing at the window with his back to her. Her heart jumped in her chest. It had been doing that often lately, and it left her breathless for a few seconds. She knew, then, that she was afraid of her father.

The attorney sat leafing through the papers, his head down, saying nothing. It was a power stance, meant to intimidate her. She recognized it for what it was and was able to recover her nerve. These two men couldn't be faced timidly.

She walked to another window and stared out. She remembered reading that silence was a great tool of intimidation, that most people couldn't stand silence and would try to fill it. Stubbornly, she decided to utter no sound until someone spoke. It became a game with her and helped. She would remain standing, too. How could they intimidate her when they couldn't look down at her? Zeiker had possession of the only high-backed chair, and she refused to sit lower. A long century later, Zeiker's well modulated voice came across the room to her.

"Miss Sumner, please have a chair."

His condescending tone burned her up inside. Who was he to tell a Sumner to take a chair? She would enjoy breaking one over his sleek head.

"I'm aware of the chairs. It's my lungs that are affected, not my eyes."

She heard a soft chortle from her father and could tell, from the corner of her eye, that he now faced her. Leisurely she approached the attorney. Again there was silence, and she refused to break it. Finally he looked up.

"I have some papers to go over with you."

"By all means. Don't be timid." She knew he was anything but that. He was as ruthless and arrogant as her father, and she couldn't help goading him. He colored slightly under the remark.

"The parties of the first part, Anglin ..."

"Please feel free to economize on words. I don't have as much time left as you."

He stubbornly started again, "The parties ..."

"Tell her what it says," boomed Anglin, "short and sweet."

"You may even leave off the sweet," she added.

"You have been disinherited," he stated. His face glowed with pleasure, but his mouth never changed expression.

Her father broke in, "I told you long ago, back when you quit Sumner, you weren't to come crawling back to me with all the lice, fleas, and diseases of Mexico on you."

Anne stood silently for a second, then started to laugh. It was so absurd. She tottered at death's door. Was she supposed to outlive Anglin? She laughed on even louder, hysterically, until she became mortally afraid her breath would be gone before the ordeal ended. She crushed her hilarity and looked her father in the eyes, ignoring Zeiker.

"Please excuse my laughter. I'm sorry I'm not up to this solemn occasion. You might have Mr. Zeiker add to the proclamation that I can no longer be employed by Sumner, as of right now."

"On the contrary, you agreed to stay through the banquet. I hold you to that. You will be paid for this week, whether you show up for work or not."

"The money never meant anything to me, you know."

When she turned to leave, he called her back.

"I'm not through. You're a pathetic sight. If your mother were here now, I'm sure she would laugh at me. I asked for someone to carry on my name, someone who could stand on their own two feet. Instead, she gave me a whimpering, gutless, play-baby son, a sneaky, greedy, conniving wretch of a daughter who only knows how to 'take,' and last of all, her biggest joke, a fanatical do-gooder with no loyalty to her family. A traitor who drags my good name down into the squalor of ..."

"I must go now."

"You'll listen. I said I'm not through," he bellowed. "You're only a tiny flame that I kindled. I can blow you out just as easily."

"Blow my way and you're liable to fan this tiny flame into a fire that will consume you and all you stand for. Remember, even the biggest wind eventually blows itself out."

"Read her the rest, Eric."

Zeiker had a look of real satisfaction on his face when he spoke. "You will no longer use Sumner's stables or any of the equipment and horses. The horse you have been riding, Tom-tom," Zeiker looked embarrassed pronouncing the name, and Anglin sniffed with derision, "is no longer available to you."

"Tom-tom belongs to me. He was given to me on my fourteenth birthday. I'll move him immediately."

"He's moved. I sold him to Just Carriages, the place you've always admired," Anglin said maliciously.

"You can't sell him. He's mine," was all she could think of to say. Shock waves rolled over her. Just Carriages was the company she once wanted to report for cruelty to their horses. Her father was well aware of that. They were the company with the tired, bony-looking horses that were overworked and not watered enough. Many times she had watched them tie the animals out in the hot sun, when a few more feet, and some consideration, would have put them in the shade. She had told her father more than once of how they mistreated their animals and broke their spirit. Goosebumps traveled up her spine. Her father knew exactly what he was doing. Faintness threatened, but Anglin's harsh words brought her back.

"Tom-tom was always a rowdy horse. They'll teach him discipline," he laughed. "After a few weeks on a carriage he might actually be worth something."

Anne saw Jim in the doorway, but he was a blur.

"You can't do this. I can prove he's my horse. Angel and Fred were both there when you gave him to me."

"Do you think either of them would cross me?"

"I'll buy him back."

"Not a chance," he interrupted. "Do you think I'm stupid enough not to think of that? I have an agreement with them. They're not to sell, except to me."

Anne knew what Anglin expected. He wanted her to beg and promise to give up her investigations. That would be the price exacted for Tom-tom. She was sinking into the very floor. With nothing else to say, she turned to the door and nearly stumbled to her knees before she caught the doorknob. Jim jumped to help her, but Anglin stepped between.

"She's not down yet."

Anne recovered her balance and hurried from their presence, embarrassed by her weakness but more concerned about finding Tom-tom. Anglin seldom bluffed. If Tom-tom had been bought by those people, his spirit would be ruined. She couldn't bear that. Hurrying to the building where she left her car, she found the warehouse door locked. Instantly, she knew why. She walked on until she reached a bus stop. The tears she had held at bay while facing her father now streamed down her face in a torrent. She must hurry to the stables.

"Anne. What is it?" Jim had come beside her, his hand on her arm.

"He's taken Tom-tom and sold him to a carriage place, the *worst* carriage place. They're hard. H-He'll lose his spirit. He's *my* horse. He's *mine!*"

"This will all be over soon. We'll find a way to get him back."

"I want him back now, this instant! I can't let him endure that." When Jim had no ready answer, she tried again to make him see the seriousness of it. "I've always let Tom-tom run barefoot. That carriage place uses metal horseshoes that draw up heat from the pavement. Think what that could do to him? But worst of all, think what they might do to his spirit. How long does it take to ruin something? How long, Jim? He might never be the same again."

Jim looked at her helplessly. When he continued to say nothing, she pulled away.

"Go back to them," she called and stepped aboard a bus before it closed its doors.

The bus ride lasted interminably as she suffered for Tom-tom every inch of the way. When impatience got the best of her, she got out her cell phone to try to find the number of the carriage place. Before she could dial information, she noticed a message had come for her earlier. She dialed in to check it, and, when she heard Ruben's voice over the phone, her heart did a somersault. His message came off short and halting, like someone new to leaving phone messages. He said he took Pacal to the hospital in her old truck there at the village. She replayed it three times to be certain he hadn't said more. Her hand shook so she could hardly hold the phone. She tried to call Padre Juan for more information but got no answer. Tortured with the thought of Pacal in worse health and Tom-tom at the mercy of Just Carriages, she closed her eyes to stop the tears. Anglin had caused it all, including her own hopeless condition. Everyone and everything she loved, destroyed before her eyes because of the greed of one man, her own father.

When she finally disembarked from the bus, her emotions were a raw sore that bled. She crossed through the half mile of woods behind the stables, careful to keep under cover. At the barn and corrals, she made a thorough search but found no sign of Tom-tom anywhere. Her blood ran cold. She had hoped it wasn't true. Caesar had been saddled and waited in a small, outside pen, pounding back and forth, pawing the dirt in impatience. There was no Tom-tom.

Panic seized her. She checked in the tack room's dusty phone book and found the number of the carriage company. She stood there, shaking too badly to call the number and not trusting her voice to hide her agitation if she reached anyone. How could she find where they had taken Tom-tom? Just Carriages worked horses both in the daytime and evening. She would have to go to each spot and see if she could find him. If that was unsuccessful, she would find where they stabled their horses during the night. But it might take days to locate him.

"Homer, call me if she shows up," shouted Anglin's big voice from nearby, startling her so badly she dropped the phone book. "Call me, even if I'm riding. I have my phone on me."

Anne hurried around the corner of the stables, hiding tight against the wall. She barely escaped being seen.

"I will, sir. How's her horse taking it?"

"*My* horse."

"Y-yes, sir."

"They said he acted balky and frightened but that he'd settle in."

"So they're already using him?"

"That was our agreement. They were to have him on a carriage every day, starting today. I hope they do break his confounded spirit. He's a wild, rebellious nag. After a few days of real discipline, he won't be holding his head so high."

The vehemence in his voice made her shiver. She knew she represented the "wild, rebellious nag" he, in truth, wanted to hurt. It told her how much he hated her and hated what she had done. Dry-eyed and unsteady, she watched him approach Caesar. Caesar pawed his way across the pen, taking his time. Anglin reached for him, and he pulled away nervously. Anglin delivered a swift blow to his flanks, and Caesar stood still — stiff and obedient.

Anglin mounted, and, when Caesar started to bolt, he brought the quirt down hard, jerking him around. He spent a good ten minutes making him walk back and forth in a tight area, then around and around, circling the small pen. He behaved like a well-trained horse when Anglin rode him, but even Homer hated to exercise him because of his vicious nature. Caesar never accepted petting or brushing and would bite if

181

he had opportunity. He trusted no one, but he obeyed Anglin, and, if Anglin loved anything, it was his big, gray horse.

"This is how a horse should behave," he announced proudly to Homer. "After a week on the carriages, I'll take Anne to see her horse." He snorted and continued putting Caesar through his paces.

Homer made no reply and looked extremely uncomfortable. Anne felt dizzy and numb all over. Her breath came in short gasps. When Anglin started to ride out of the pen, she hurried around the back of the building and through the open back door in fear she'd be seen. The door to Anglin's private tack room stood open, and she rushed into it.

Searching for a place to hide, she found Anglin's gun instead. His target guns were always kept on a rack in his tack room, and one gun had been set out, no doubt for a practice bout after his ride. She remembered other days, days when she and her father practiced shooting together. They could both laugh back then and enjoy the keen competition. She had forgotten those days, but she hadn't forgotten how to handle firearms. She seized the gun, checked its load, and found it ready. Leaving the tack room door open, she stumbled to a nearby window that opened onto the riding area. Shock raged through her when she saw Anglin directly in front of her, sitting astride Caesar like some king. He gazed out at the trail, totally unaware of her presence. She dropped to one knee on the wooden box in front of the window, and the gun went automatically to her shoulder. Shaking like a leaf, she tried to align the bead with Anglin's head but couldn't hold it steady. She gulped audibly and lowered the gun to where it was supported by the window sill. When her hands grew steady, she pressed her hot cheek against the cold metal.

Her vision blurred, and Anglin's head was replaced by pictures of a spiritless Tom-tom pulling a carriage over hot pavement, of a frail Pacal playing with his toy truck, of Marco's trembling hands holding his worn bookmark, of Jim laughing with Angel. The man she'd aligned with the long barrel had brought about all those scenes. Her work in Mexico had been destroyed, and all her charges were in a more pitiable state than when she had first come to them. All her hopes were gone, along with her strength, but she had enough strength left to pull a trigger.

"Tom-tom," she sobbed aloud, then slowly, with deliberation, lowered the gun and aligned the bead with Caesar's broad shoulder. She knew the real way to hurt her dad. She understood exactly how he would feel, his big, grand horse ... gone. It seemed like centuries she kneeled there, staring at her mark, working to steady her aim, rubbing the tears from her streaming eyes. Her finger throbbed against the trigger in time with her thumping heart. Without warning, someone shoved her so powerfully she landed flat on the dusty floor. Before she could recover, Jim had pinned her down."

"Don't ... stop me. Get off. Let me ..."

Her words were muffled as she fought against Jim's hand over her mouth. He wrestled the gun away, dragged both her and the gun into Anglin's tack room, and closed the door on them.

Still she fought him for possession of the gun, bawling, "Why did you stop me? Why? I wasn't aiming at Dad."

"I know what you were aiming at. That isn't the way. Not his horse, Anne." He held tight her struggling arms. "Where'd you get the gun?"

"He's destroyed Tom-tom and Pacal. He's destroyed me. I can't bear it. I hate him. Let him mourn something he loves," she cried, but Jim's hand muffled most of the sound. With his hand still over her mouth, he hung the gun on the rack and dragged her away from the stables. She kicked and fought him all the way into the woods. When they were deep into the brush, a good distance from the stables, he took his hand from her mouth.

She jumped to her feet, furious. "Leave me be! I'll kill him, Jim. I'll kill him." She sobbed brokenly, gasping for breath. "You know I'll do it."

"Not that way, Anne. Listen, your work's not finished. You still have work to do."

"I don't care about the villages or anyone. I want Tom-tom."

"Who else will help them?"

"I-I can't," she sobbed. "I'm going to go get Tom-tom."

"This isn't the way."

"There *is* no way. There's no time. It will be too late. And Dad will have won. I can't let him win."

Speech failed her, but she was still conscious when Jim picked her up and carried her through another piece of woods, laying her on the leafy earth under a tree.

In spite of the silence all around, she knew Jim was still there. She waited for strength enough to speak. "You had no right," she finally choked as she sat up and looked at him accusingly.

"No, I didn't, but some day you'll be glad I stopped you."

"Jim," she could barely talk above a whisper, but she forced her eyes, her entire body to plead her cause, "Jim, if you can feel any pity, if you were ever a friend, leave me now and don't come back."

"Would you throw away all you believe? Would you let Anglin destroy your faith, too? If it were me, or one of your villagers, who sought revenge, wouldn't Anne Sumner, missionary, say something like: 'Don't fret because of the man who bringeth wicked devices to pass. Cease from anger, and forsake wrath: fret not thyself in any wise to do evil. For evildoers shall …'"

"Don't you dare quote Psalms to me," she barged in angrily.

But he'd gotten her attention and drawn her back from the edge, where she tottered.

"It's good to see your eyes can still flash. Don't give up. You're about there. What else can he do to you?"

She sighed, and by her silence told him he had won.

"Will you wait here? My car's close by. Anglin hasn't seen me. I'll get it and pick you up here. The road's right over there. Promise you'll wait."

When she didn't answer, he shook her. "Answer me. Promise me. You know this is important to me, too. I want to know what's in that container."

"Why? You put it in your tanks. Didn't you know what was in it?"

"I thought I did."

"Would you spray something on a field when you weren't sure what it was?"

"I guess I did."

"How? Why?"

"I sprayed paraquat, only it was a weaker concentration, only half-strength. I figured Anglin was having us use lower-dosage paraquat to save money. Labor is cheaper than chemicals down there, and weeds can be pulled by hand if the spray doesn't get them all. But that would make it safer than regular paraquat. The only other thing in the solution, besides water and paraquat, was some additive we were supposed to use, three ounces worth to every twenty gallons of concentrate."

"I thought you said you did everything the same as usual that night?

What about this additive?"

"We'd been using it for a good while. We've used the same formula for over two months. Nothing new happened that night. Not that I know of, anyway. I didn't lie to you about that."

"Who told you to use the additive?"

"The factory foreman said it was Anglin's orders."

"Didn't you consider it might be harmful?"

"I figured the opposite. They told us it would improve the spray coverage and the sprayer's performance. I thought it was some mechanical fluid that would affect the fineness of the spray or something like that. I didn't think it had anything to do with farm chemicals. I still think the same, but I want to know for sure."

Anne looked at him aghast. "Anglin has lied before."

"Anne, if it's something to do with that additive, then your father has made me a murderer. I have to know if I'm to blame for what happened to you. I poured it into the tank."

"You didn't drop it in the lake."

"No, but if I'd had any suspicion it was dangerous, I would have refused to use it. I never had the vaguest concern it might be harmful. Do you believe me? Once I asked the field foreman if the fluid was toxic or hazardous in any way. He laughed at me and said it was harmless as soda pop. And the only reason I suspect anything now is because Fritz dropped those cans in the pond.

"Remember what I told you about that night, that I was spraying fields A & D, the two fields they tested later, but Fritz couldn't help me because he had to take care of something else for Sumner that night? Fritz, no doubt, knew the seriousness of the sickness and lied to me about it. And Sumner must have been worried about possible trouble and told Fritz to carry off the evidence – those drums in your lake that already had the additive in them. I recognized them, remember preparing them. It's funny, too, that they still had me use the half-strength mixture of paraquat on A and D but without the additive. If I'd only used my head. I begin to understand. It has to be something like that, something to do with the mix. When will you know about it?"

He talked fast, excitedly, not like his usual self. Anne saw through him. He meant to make her forget Tom-tom and think about the job at hand. But he revealed more to her than ever before.

"Do you realize that if it's something in that spray mixture, then not Angel or Anglin, either one, will care if I'm a likable guy? They'll drop it all right in my lap. Every witness has disappeared. They've spirited away the field foreman and the factory foreman. Angel no doubt pretends to like me to keep me from running off. They need me for a scapegoat."

"You mean Angel is using you? I thought you were using her."

Jim's eyes became gray flashes.

"We've both been using. But Angel couldn't love anything enough to put it before money."

"Oh, and you could? You mean she doesn't genuinely return your affections, and I'm supposed to sympathize with you? You haven't lost anything like I have."

"I've lost more than you could ever know." There was both sadness and anger in his voice. "My plane will go next. Then there will be nothing left for me. When that happens, I won't go after your father's *horse!*"

His words shocked Anne out of self-pity and jealousy.

"Jim! No!"

"Jim, yes!" His eyes said he meant it.

"If you harmed Dad, everyone would be against you. Angel would hate you." Even as she said it, she realized she had been ready to commit the same deed herself, and, if he had come in thirty seconds earlier, he would have seen the gun aimed at its first target. She must never let him know how far she had been ready to go, and he must never be allowed to destroy his future because of Anglin.

"I wouldn't let you. I'd prevent it," she said, suddenly strong again.

"How? How would you prevent it?" He looked at her with amusement, scorn.

While she searched for the right words, he spoke again.

"If you quit, Anne ... the day you give in ... I'll do what I just said."

"I might not be able to keep on."

"Then you'll be too weak to care what I do. Let me explain something to you. There's no one more dangerous than the man with nothing left to lose."

"Don't. I can't fight you, also. I'm too tired."

He laughed harshly. "Those weren't the magic words to stop me.

186

You didn't look so tired a few minutes ago when you fought me like a she-devil. One minute you hate Anglin, the next you want to protect him. Who are you, Anne?"

"I'm not the girl you met in Tutlu."

He looked at her for a long moment.

"You're the same girl. You've just been through hell. I ... I don't ..." His voice trailed off, and he stood there with the saddest look in his eyes she'd ever seen. They stood like that, facing each other, for what seemed like an eternity. Finally, he shook his head. "I don't see any difference in you, but I miss the bruises on your legs, the smell of wood smoke in your hair."

When he walked away, Ann became chokingly aware Jim was more important to her than the villages, than Tom-tom, than anything. With whatever time was left to her, she could love him with all her strength, as deeply and honestly as she chose. Her love came like a flood breaking through an embankment. It uplifted her, carried her out of herself. It would sustain and keep her until she could finish the fight. Her life had been devoted to loving and serving others. That was a weak, faded love, compared to what she now felt. She loved him in spite of his weakness, in spite of his devotion to Angel, and she'd find a way to save him and still do what had to be done for the villagers.

Chapter 16

She gulped down a sob when she thought of Tom-tom. Was he to be sacrificed along with everything else? She could see his gentle, trusting eyes, his lovable quirks, his childlike playfulness. She could never forget him. He would be a fire eating away inside her as she dutifully tried to keep priorities straight. But she'd do what she must.

"Jim!" She ran after him, unable to call a second time. He turned when he heard her gasps for breath and drew her behind a patch of brush. With his arms around her for support, she fought for air. "I g-give up Tom-tom," she finally stammered. "I'll not ... think about him. I-I'll fight ... I'll help you." She tried to quench her sobs before they used up all her wind.

"It's all right, Anne. Breathe. I know you've given up everything. I know you've been fighting. Just breathe now. Don't give that up." His voice had a desperate ring to it.

Minutes passed while she fought for oxygen. Finally, she managed a husky laugh. "I-I lost my shoe."

"I see it. Sit here while I get it."

"I can ... stand. Got my ... wind now."

"You sound like it," he grinned and went back for her shoe.

When he returned, she was clinging to a tree limb. "Jim, don't give me away, whatever you do. Dad and Angel mustn't see I'm concerned about you. Dad would use you against me, like he did Tom-tom."

"Sell me to Just Carriages?" He laughed. "I don't much care what Angel or Anglin think or do anymore." She took the shoe from him and slid it on her foot. When she looked up again, he stood close in front of her. He gently pushed a strand of hair away from her wet eyes. "Come on. I'll help you to my car. It's right over here. Let's go see your chemist." When they drove away, he laid his hand over hers. "Maybe soon we'll know where we stand."

"It won't make much difference in the long run, will it? Dad will either claim you used the wrong mix, sprayed in the wrong place, or something else. It will all come back to blaming you, won't it? If he's gotten rid of all the witnesses, he can lay the blame on your error and let his insurance company take over and pay the rest of the claims. I've not accomplished much of anything, except to cause you more trouble."

"You don't understand, do you? You don't realize what havoc you've wrought. Let me explain to you like Angel might tell it. First of all, they were hoping to pay nothing and say that everyone had the flu. They were getting away with that. The people are too poor and backward to complain, and your dad sent his own medical person in to hide things, on the pretext of giving them free medical aid. As an extra snow job, Sumner acted like they wanted to cover every aspect in regard to the workers. They immediately called in a government tester to further affirm that Sumner was not to blame for the illness, just in case something came up. They, of course, had him test the wrong fields, but first they had me give them a light spraying so nothing would look suspicious. In the meantime, they turned under the other fields and cultivated them. Finally, you started getting signed papers, and his entire plan fell apart. He had to start paying claims from his fund."

"But that seems suspicious, too, Jim. I can't find the people he paid off. They're like phantoms. Of course, the other insurance should start helping soon, no matter what happened to Sumner's insurance money. Considering the workers' desperate circumstances, there should be no delay."

"Yes, but you're still not thinking. What if your father did something illegal or used something not approved for usage, which caused these illnesses and deaths? Wouldn't that make it a criminal act on his part? It wouldn't matter to the insurers if Anglin thought it was harmless when he did it. They would institute proceedings to take all your father's assets, every penny, and use up those funds to pay the claims. If there wasn't enough money in his corporation, they might be able to confiscate his personal funds."

"You don't think it's something like that, do you?"

"I think it must be. I've been with Angel. She talks ... plenty. When you found those drums, everything fit together. At first they tried to save their reputation and insurance fund. Now I think they're trying to save Sumner. Anglin could face criminal proceedings, even a jail term."

"I never considered ... Why your life isn't worth a plug nickel if that's what it's all about."

She said it so seriously, Jim began to laugh. Finally, she laughed with him.

At length she asked, "You know, don't you, that there was another incident in Dad's farm holdings?"

"In Honduras?"

"And with paraquat. In that incident there was no aerial application. The workers used hand sprayers. Sumner first blamed the sickness on the flu. Later Sumner accused the workers of carelessness and of not following instructions in applying the paraquat. I'm sure Dad's still involved with that trouble, too. I saw Angel's files. Do you think it might be the same thing? It happened about a month and a half before the trouble in Mexico."

"If it is, it means your father may be more responsible than you want to believe. Don't forget Isdel and the sickness that hit the farms at that time. We were spraying paraquat, and it did have the additive in it."

"I know my dad's terribly hard and ruthless, but it's still difficult to believe he'd do something criminal."

"Is this the first thing you've ever noticed? Weren't you suspicious of that fire in the apartments next door?"

"I was, but I don't think so now. A man died in that fire, a homeless man."

"And you don't think Anglin could be a murderer. Yet you told me my life wasn't worth a plug nickel?"

"I don't know. I don't want to think."

"You don't have to. Do as you've always done and be honest. It's the only way for you."

"It's more difficult now. I'm not as strong as I thought."

"Don't you dare compromise. You're still a missionary – the one who 'sweareth to his own hurt, and changeth not.' Don't fail me."

"You're using my scriptures against me. I wish I could remember words that way."

"Piece of cake. I told you I can memorize anything. I remember things I'd like to remind you of – if I really believed you've forgotten." The look he gave her was so deep and searching, she couldn't meet his eyes and turned away to stare out the window.

At the chemist's laboratory, Anne received another shock. The chemical was gone.

"But you weren't to give it to anyone. I paid for it. I told you how important it was. Don't you have any of it?"

"It was picked up."

"I paid for it," she said again in disbelief. "Where is the report?"

"We hadn't finished the analysis."

"Return my money," Anne demanded, close to breaking down.

"We can't refund in a case like this. Work had been done on it."

"You gave my samples away. I flew all the way to Mexico for those."

"I didn't sign it out. Here's the order on it. It says you picked it up."

"Would I be here now if I had? Didn't you ask for identification?"

"Security measures such as that were never necessary here."

"I want my money, and any report you have finished, and any chemical you have left."

"I'm sorry. I have no power to do anything like that. You can call the owner tomorrow. He's out of town today."

When she got back into Jim's car, she was so angry she could hardly speak.

"My father, or Angel, has been there. It's all gone. The place said I'd picked up the chemical. And there's no report because the analysis wasn't done yet. They refused to give my money back, too. I'm nearly broke. I used most of your hundred dollars to help pay for what they didn't do. I let them bully me because I'm a big baby and don't have any time left or any money left to sue them." She wanted to bawl.

"Do you have any more chemical?"

"A tiny bit."

"Don't worry. We'll take it somewhere else. I still have some Sumner money left. Where'd you put the stuff?"

"It's in my storage locker, not far from the office. But where can I have it analyzed now?"

"There's only one party you can trust."

"What one? How do I find an honest company?" She turned her palms up in uncertainty.

"Think. You'll have to think as mean as Sumner if you plan to do this. And I didn't say *honest*, I said a place you can *trust*, a place that can't be bought out by your dad."

She thought for only a second before she realized what he meant. "The insurance company, of course. They have the most to gain. But what if there's nothing harmful in the samples?"

"They'll still thank you for having their interests at heart, if gratitude is that important to you. I think I saw some of Anglin's fighting blood in you a while ago."

"I'm not like him. I don't enjoy hurting people."

"Isn't it right that the insurers not be penalized because of your father's criminal act?"

"I'm not ready for this. I still have doubts."

"Do you now?"

"I-I'll do it. I'll tell them to analyze it. Maybe they'll be able to tell me what benefit someone would gain by using it agriculturally."

"Let's go. Oh, by the way, after you drove off in the truck with Ruben, I went back into the woods, where the hidden containers are stashed, and got two more samples. I took them to a university student here in the city the day I got back. He's deeply into that stuff. He didn't know how soon he could get to it, but we have a slight chance of learning something from that avenue. He doesn't charge as much as these companies, either."

"You're not making so much you can afford to do all this, are you?"

"I have one of Angel's credit cards, since I'm helping Sumner in all of this. She thinks I'm stupid enough to put my neck in their noose and jump off Sumner's corporate headquarters, trusting them to catch me before I hit ground."

"I guess you must have helped her believe that," Anne remarked, looking down at her lap.

"Helped her? I compelled her to!"

They rode in silence to her storage place and picked up the samples. She dreaded going alone into the insurance company, but, when they finally arrived there, she wouldn't allow Jim to accompany her. He had enough trouble of his own.

It took two intensely awkward hours to divulge all her information and clarify the situation adequately for the insurers. She tried not to sound condemnatory of Sumner, but that proved impossible. Consequently, honesty won, and the insurers arranged for the chemicals to be tested.

"If their tests show that Dad's guilty of wrongdoing, I'll be a traitor to Sumner," she said to Jim after she got back into his car. "My actions might put my father in jail, might take away Angel's and Fred's livelihood. If it's true, I don't want to live and have to face my family." She looked up at him seriously. "Angel won't be able to protect you."

"Anne," he looked angrier than she'd ever seen him, "you're becoming more like a Sumner every day."

"I-I *am* a Sumner, a disinherited one, but a Sumner just the same. I'm ashamed to admit it. Would you let me off here? I don't want anyone to see us together."

"Where are you going?"

"I have a place. It's better not to tell anyone. You can phone me on my cell phone. They haven't taken that yet."

"Don't you even trust *me*?" He looked shocked at the realization, as if it had just hit him.

"I'm staying in my storage locker tonight. I didn't want to tell you because you're so stubborn you wouldn't let me stay."

"That locker where we picked up the sample?" he asked matter-of-factly, not acting the least bit surprised or shocked. "Not enough oxygen. And Sumner might catch on to it. Why not stay at the office?"

"I'm scared to. And I don't know if I'm allowed."

"You work there until the banquet, don't you?"

"Yes, how did you know?"

"Angel. Anglin, too."

'Sounds like you're one of the family."

"Will you take some advice?"

"Sure, I need it."

193

"Go to the office, and use it like before. Rest all you can. You've got some hard days ahead."

"I can't face them after what they did to Tom-tom. I can't stand for them to gloat."

"Please trust me. It's important for you to be at that office for the next couple of days. Make sure they all know you're there, even that you're there all night. I know what I'm asking, and I don't think I could do it myself. But it will throw them off the track and allow me to check things more freely. They're not yet suspicious of me. Can't you trust me?"

"Of course I'll stay. I'll flaunt myself. I'll be brazen about it, until they have me thrown out on the sidewalk. Maybe I should buy a new dress, something befitting a Sumner."

"I like you better in those," he signified her khaki shorts and tank top. "It makes me think of Mexico and better days."

"I like them best, too, but I have to go to that Sumner banquet. I can't wear shorts."

"Well, don't ape Angel. Look like what you are – a missionary, an outdoor girl."

"A h-horse woman?" she asked and felt the color drain from her face.

"Yes," he smiled and laid a warm hand on her shoulder. "So, you need something to wear to the banquet?"

"I know the dress. I saw it in a window. I could go on safari in it."

"That's the one. Let's go get it. This one's on ..."

"Angel?" Anne smiled. "Is she going to buy me this new dress with her credit card?"

"I believe she is." His eyes filled with unspoken humor.

"Then I must be sure it's high quality. Angel has impeccable taste. Remind me to send a thank-you note."

Within minutes they were at the exclusive shop, and Anne tried on the ensemble she'd admired earlier. The well-shaped jacket fit closely around her hips with a wide belt to cinch in the waistline. It gave a curvaceous effect, while the multitude of pockets made it look like it belonged in the wilds of Africa. The khaki skirt also fit perfectly but showed enough leg to seriously hinder missionary work.

Jim saw her and looked his approval.

"Do you think maybe there's some magic in this dress?" she asked happily.

"No magic. The magic's in you, but the dress helps bring it out."

When he came over and placed a soft kiss on her cheek, she drew away. She might use Angel's credit card, but she wouldn't borrow Angel's boyfriend.

"Let's get on with this," Jim said, walking back to the car. "Remember to stay at the office. I'll check on the chemicals and find a way to contact you when I know something."

"Let me off a few blocks away so no one will see us together."

"I have a better idea." He drove into a parking lot and got out to make a cell phone call. After only a few minutes wait, a Town Car pulled up nearby.

"Your chariot."

"No. I can't arrive in that. I don't want to be chauffeured to the front door. I want to sneak through a back door and hide. Don't you understand?"

"So, you're going to hide now? Listen, I know it'd change anyone to go through what you've been through. But it mustn't change Anne Sumner, not the plucky girl I met in Mexico. Too much depends on her. She's not allowed to change."

"But you can?" she asked bitterly. "Is that fair?"

He didn't answer, but walked with her to the Town Car. "Promise you'll stay at the office tonight?"

"I'll try." She wouldn't commit herself. Tom-tom must be found.

"It's important, and we're running out of time."

She nodded acceptance. Everything she loved would be sacrificed.

"Okay, I'll be there, if they don't throw me out."

"They won't dare."

"Murder me?"

"Possibly."

She meant it as a joke, but he answered so seriously she shivered involuntarily.

The Town Car did its work well. If she hadn't been fully herself before, she became the old Anne when she stepped from the plush vehicle. She would be true to herself and her morals, and true to Jim, no matter what the consequences. She would hold her head high.

She disembarked in front of Sumner's main building at the exact moment her father came down the front steps. He eyed her departing limo with some degree of surprise.

"Good evening, Dad," she said, with as much dignity as she could muster.

"I hear your fool horse nearly wrecked a buggy today," he stated bluntly without any greeting. "I told them to hook up some extra restraints to him until he understands authority. It won't take long now."

She wasn't ready for attack from that quarter yet. His words hit her harder than if he'd struck her. For a second she reverted to her vernacular of childhood. "Daddy, why are you doing this? You always loved horses. I got my love of them from you."

"If you did, then it must be the only thing you got from me. You say you love horses? Well, prove it. Tom-tom is working there because of you. Did you think you could ride roughshod over Sumner without any consequences? Sure, I know what you feel. I know what's going through your head. But consider this – you could be back up on that horse before nightfall if you started acting like a Sumner."

For a long minute, a silent clash took place between two monumental tempers. Anne's face shone with righteous anger as her blazing eyes locked with his cold, reproving ones.

"Did you know I drew a bead on Caesar today? I had his big shoulder right in the crosshairs of your gun scope," she said finally, with a softness, terrible in its intensity.

"I wondered how my gun got back on the rack after I'd set it out to use. I guess you didn't inherit *that* trait from me. If you had any of me in you, you'd have pulled the trigger. I've never stepped back from anything I've started. Don't expect me to now. If you don't call it quits on this insurance fiasco, remember, it could become much worse for Tom-tom."

"I'll be at my desk until the banquet. After the banquet you'll never have to look at me again."

Anglin brushed past her in anger. She felt like a mannequin as she walked inside the building. At her office door she trembled, afraid of the inevitable breakdown when she closed and locked the door behind her. Promise or no promise, she couldn't stay there, not with Tom-tom out somewhere needing her. Anglin had at least given her the information she wanted, that Tom-tom had worked the daytime shift. It was the worst time, but it also meant he would be stabled that evening.

Before she could turn around and leave, Fred came from his office. She hoped he wouldn't notice her. It would be embarrassing for them both if he tried to make a lame excuse for avoiding her. But, in spite of that, she wanted to warn him about the impending future. He walked right toward her instead of to the elevators.

When he passed by, he said, "Wait while I see if the road is clear."

He studied the parking lot below from the hall window. When he came back, he caught her arm and started to lead her down the hall. She resented it and pulled back, prepared to do her duty by him before she left.

"Fred, things will get worse shortly. Don't be seen with me." She hoped no sarcasm had crept into her voice and knew Jim had been right. She acted like a Sumner.

"Everyone has gone for the day. Didn't think they would ever leave ... I heard about Tom-tom."

"That's why you can't talk with me. You might find yourself haltered to a buggy." She meant to sound funny, but her undependable voice broke and spoiled it. She turned her back to him, afraid the tears would fall. She tried to laugh. "I seem to spend a good deal of my time crying. I think it's becoming a bad habit."

"Come into my office." He had hold of her arm again, urging her, half-dragging her.

When he closed the door, she asked, "Does everyone know about Tom-tom, Fred?" She didn't know why, but it humiliated her terribly. It felt like the entire company delighted in her misery. And why not, she asked herself. She had become the enemy. People would lose fortunes, lose jobs, and stocks would be worthless. For the first time she wondered if she should have kept quiet, forgotten the villagers, and just gone away and died in private.

"Jim told me about him."

"Do you know a-about the containers of chemical I found at my village in the lake?"

He nodded with no expression on his face. "Jim told me about them too."

"I don't know what may be in them, but, if they were hidden for some reason, it might hurt Sumner immensely. Angel says the company fund is gone. Sumner's other insurers might investigate before they start paying claims. They'd take every cent Sumner has if they found dishonesty."

"Do you think there's dishonesty afoot?" He looked at her keenly.

"I didn't. But Dad and Angel are convincing me otherwise."

"You always were sharper than them."

"Fred, do you hate me for what I'm doing, for what it might mean to you?"

"You mean I'll be too poor to buy a beer? Is that why you're doing this to us?" He grinned this time.

"I never thought of that."

Too restless to sit still, she walked over to Fred's window and looked out.

"You have a magnificent night-view from your window. Better than from Angel's or my office. If this were mine, I'd be at the window all the time."

"I don't think I've ever looked out. What's the sense of going through life looking at a beautiful view unless the beautiful view spurs you on to do beautiful things? You are, in point of fact, only looking at time passing by with a pleasant face. I'm sorry. I didn't mean to sound grumpy. Come over here, and let's play computer games. We'll make a night of it. You finished your public relations project, didn't you? Now you've got to hang around, wait for your paycheck, and for the rest of your family to wallow in public disgrace."

"Fred!"

"I'm joking. Do I look broken up?"

"Only because you don't think anything will happen. But it might, Fred."

"It will. I'm certain of it. Come on, lay back on my couch. Take this laptop, and I'll introduce you to medieval times, or would you prefer something else?"

"I've lived in medieval times for the last two and a half years. You don't stand a chance."

"You've only been farming and surviving. Now you'll face armies."

"Bring them on. Just tell me what to do."

Chapter 17

At two o'clock in the morning, Anne awoke to a dark room. The laptop sat on the table beside her. She must have fallen asleep, and Fred had moved it. Fred leaned over his laptop, the light of it glowing on his serious face.

"Still at it, Fred?"

He pushed a couple of keys as Anne pulled herself up.

"I didn't mean to make you shut off your game. You look like you need sleep."

"You ought to come see this. It's uncanny." He pointed to his laptop. "I've been staring through the red rim of my reading glasses at those two tiny little lights on my laptop. See them?"

"What lights?"

"These one's, that tell me I'm not only turned on, but I'm connected to a full source of power," he said eerily.

Anne could tell he was moderately drunk, but she humored him. "So, while I slept, you've been turned on and running."

"Yes, but those little, green lights glowed a ghoulish yellow through the red tint of my glasses. It was as if the eyes of Satan glared out at me and mocked me in my nightly vigil. And ... and I realized ... though fate might guide my fingers, Satan ever watched over my shoulder, or in this case crowded in front of me, probably sat in my lap, just to see what I was doing." He snickered as he continued to stare through the rim of his glasses, now perched halfway down his nose.

"Too many games and too much drink. Maybe you should buy some brown-rimmed reading glasses."

"The red ones are easier to locate when I lay them down."

"Maybe it's not the red rim that causes the hallucinations. Maybe it's your red eyes."

"I'm not drunk, only groggy from lack of sleep. I've worked hours and hours."

"Killing barbarians? Here, you take the sofa, and I'll go back to my office now."

"Stay here. I'll send out for food, and we'll play another game."

"When will you sleep?" she asked, impatient to get away while there was darkness left.

"During office hours, at my desk, like I do every day."

"But I promised myself a good cry, and I've put it off long enough."

"A couple more hours won't hurt."

"I thought I might go out for a while."

"Jim said to remind you of your promise. There's nothing you can do. You have an important deal going down. Don't risk it. I know what you want to do."

"Do you, Fred? I was just going to have a look see."

"You've started something. See it through. You're the prime player in this event. Don't get sidetracked."

"You're in cahoots with Jim. You've purposely kept me here."

Fred picked up his ringing cell phone. He didn't talk, only listened and turned it off.

"Got to run downstairs a minute. Wait here."

Within minutes, he returned bearing a small envelope. He handed it to her with an air of secrecy.

"Better take it into your office and digest it. Jim said to destroy it as soon as you read it. Get some rest, too. Morning's about here, and the banquet's tonight. That will be a hellish occasion."

Anne closed and locked her office door before taking the pages from the envelope:

200

Anne,

I've been all night at the university. The student and his professor evidently started in on our project right after I dropped off the samples. They definitely took the issue to heart. They tried some experiments on plant and animal reaction to the paraquat containing the additive as opposed to their reaction to a concentration of plain paraquat. The paraquat with the additive acted far more aggressive to both plant and animal tissue. The additive seems to increase the effect of the paraquat enormously, and at the same time accelerate its reaction time. They used test mice and test plants, and gave equal portions of each chemical. The plants with the additive died startlingly quick compared to those with plain paraquat – even when they diluted the paraquat to one half concentration. The test mice with the additive mixture all died with massive hemorrhaging of the lungs. The plain paraquat mice are still alive, but have some damage. Now they're trying new tests with an even lower dosage. More students have gotten involved with the project in order to speed things up, and I'm to have the insurance company get in contact with them so they can compare findings. The additive, though it appears to be a complicated molecular formula, also appears to be inexpensive to create if someone had the exact formula and process. They're breaking down the formula as much as possible.

This isn't concise proof, but the very fact your dad used an unapproved product will be enough to put Sumner liable and get money flowing to the injured. The insurance company should begin payoffs immediately and collect the money from Sumner when they prove their case.

Destroy this paper and destroy the student's phone number after you memorize it. I told him you might call for more information.

Jim

P.S. I've enclosed a reminder, so you don't try to quit on me now.

Anne turned to the second page of the note and found it was the sheet she had written in the hospital. It seemed so long ago now. Jim had kept it all that time. He'd even circled the line: "And you go on ... and on ... and on, because you must."

Anne shoved that second sheet into her desk drawer and burned the page Jim wanted destroyed, all the while considering what this new information might mean. Surely her dad knew about this. He knew about it from the beginning. She understood the chemical business better than Jim. It took her only a minute to realize the value of that formula. Anglin wasn't using it to save money on *his* crops. He was thinking much bigger than that. He was testing a formula that would be worth an unbelievable fortune to the person who held the patent. An immense amount of paraquat was shipped around the world, billions of tons. Apparently, this additive was cheap to produce, and a diminutive amount of it would replace an enormous amount of paraquat. Anglin could replace fifty percent of the world's paraquat with his additive. Buyers would rush to buy something that would save them half of their paraquat bill and also cut their shipping expenses in half. Anglin could charge a good price for it and make a mammoth profit. He was definitely playing for high stakes.

It was enough to turn a naturally greedy man moderately insane. She wondered if he had applied for a patent on it yet. Feeling sick over the whole thing, she finally curled up on the sofa and went to sleep.

Midmorning, she awoke with a feeling she had overslept and missed something important. She didn't wait to eat breakfast but hurried away from the office to call the university student. Maybe he could answer some of her most perplexing questions, now that they had some definite results in their testing. She had him on the line immediately.

"I'm so thankful for your prompt and conscientious work. You can't imagine how much it means to me or what it may mean to all of those who are still ill."

"It's an exciting study. I'm glad we're part of it."

"I need to ask you a few questions. I know it takes a long time to ascertain whether you have accurate results, but maybe you can tell me something based on what you believe you've discovered. If a field was sprayed with paraquat combined with this additive during the night and the next morning someone walked through the field, could it cause such devastating results as we've seen in Mexico? Strictly from dermal contact? Paraquat usually has to be taken internally to cause the horrific results some of the victims experienced. Usually assimilation through the skin is not enough to give such massive damage and death."

202

"I understand what you're getting at. I'm well-acquainted with paraquat and its capabilities and risks. This new mixture is far more toxic. It greatly increases the assimilation of paraquat though the skin of the mice, just as it did with the plants. It'd be especially dangerous if the mixture were still wet, or if, for instance, the mixture had dried but the mice were wet. For a parallel we might consider that if a worker was sweating and got against sprayed plants, there would likely be dire results. This product is highly absorptive by the skin, aggressive in its penetration of cells. These are just preliminary tests, of course, but are still pretty conclusive.

"We've only tested with mice and plants at this point. The test mice, exposed only to dermal contact, developed problems comparably severe to the ones that imbibed it. We are working now to establish how low a dosage we must give in order to *not* kill the test animal. It's indeed lethal."

"I see. Has the insurance company contacted you yet?"

"I'm meeting with their representative this afternoon."

Anne thanked him again and went back to her desk, leaving her office door open wide. She wondered if her father felt the least bit of guilt about what he had done to her. Swiftly she put the thought out of her mind. Self-pity time would have to come later. She must brace up for the banquet. All the shareholders would be there, as well as some of his biggest buyers. She would try to survive that before she tackled more worries.

At least by tomorrow, it would all be over for her. She could give her pile of claims to the insurance company, and, from that point on, the villagers could take care of matters. She'd done what she could for them. She'd also done what she could for Jim's protection. It had taken her and Jock a horrendous amount of work to accumulate evidence for his defense. Now, hidden safely away in her locker, were signed statements to prove Jim never sprayed in the wrong fields, that there was no wind when he did spray, and that there were no workers in the fields. Accumulating that information had cost her, physically and mentally, more than she wished to admit to herself. But, hopefully, those papers would protect him and his license. No doubt Fred and Angel had enough put away to keep them in luxury. After the banquet, her job should be done.

Too nervous to sit still for long, she went downstairs and picked up her paycheck, knowing it would be her last one. The thought worried her, but this wasn't the time to think about her financial future. The banquet presented as much future as she could handle right then. She'd felt enormously weak lately. Maybe the excessive work and the smog had triggered it. In some ways she wanted to be worse, wanted to be too sick to go to the banquet, too sick to think about Tom-tom or Jim and Angel.

Near quitting time, Angel dropped by to leave Anglin's instructions. Anne should arrive at six and say nothing to anyone about anything.

"And what will he do if I tell the truth?"

"He said you knew what would happen if you tried anything."

"What more can happen to me, Angel? My work has been destroyed, my health ruined, I have no friends, my horse is gone, my family hates me, and I have no earthly possessions."

"You're still alive. And so is Tom-tom."

"I'd rather he were dead than to be where he is now. Death would be an improvement for both of us. Someone once told me, Angel, that there was nothing more dangerous than someone who had nothing left to lose. Maybe you should tell Daddy that for me. See if he still wants me at his banquet. I could step out of his life this instant."

"I'll give him your message. Don't go anywhere."

"I'll be right here."

Within an hour, Angel called and delivered Anglin's ultimatum. He would make sure her horse never lifted his proud head again if she didn't behave appropriately for a daughter of Anglin Sumner.

When it neared six o'clock, she donned her khaki suit with a queasiness that made her weak all over. Why hadn't she bought a different dress, any dress but this one? It would certainly make her stand out, and that was the last thing she wanted to do. Why had she listened to Jim? She might as well have a sign on her back, "Safari Anne." Could she muster enough pluck to pull off the evening in that getup?

Angel came in just as she was leaving.

"You're not wearing that, are you? I mean it looks nice, looks expensive, but, no jewels? No glamour?"

"Maybe it'd be better for Sumner's appearance if none of us overdressed tonight."

Angel looked at her questioningly and finally added, "You have a point, but I'm not changing a thing. We have no reason to bow in the dust and grovel. We used our entire insurance account to be generous with those who filed claims. And now, because we were so generous, we've got a passel of totally false claims from greedy people after money." She looked straight at Anne. "That's Sumner's position. Don't forget it. Dad said he'd find a specialist to get you back on your feet. And he spoke of buying Tom-tom back."

"I've been to a specialist, Angel. Thank you. I get the message."

"There's a limo waiting to escort you to the banquet. Try to look like the invalid you are."

"Tell the limo to get lost. I'll be there."

After Angel left, Anne rushed to the window in time to see Angel's Lincoln pull away from the curb. It looked like Jim in the driver's seat. Of course, he would escort Angel, she told herself. Her own escort would be her two, slightly-undependable legs. Determination was her only asset. It must carry her through an evening destined to be difficult. She would somehow follow Jim's orders and swear to her own hurt, no matter what that hurt might be.

Maybe she and Tom-tom would meet again, she thought, feeling some of the hurt already. After all, didn't the Bible say there were green pastures in heaven? Naturally there would be horses to feed on them. Somehow she couldn't derive any comfort from the thought. The situation with Tom-tom wasn't the sort of thing she could accept sitting down. Just as she had made monumental efforts to protect Jim, she would do the same by Tom-tom. Through phone calls, she managed to locate where some of the carriages worked and where the horses were kept. Hopefully Tom-tom was stabled with the rest of them. After the banquet, if it ever ended for her, she would find Tom-tom and somehow set him free. Dry-eyed, she hurried down to catch a bus.

She crept though a side entrance at the banquet facility to avoid notice and came upon Jim and Angel in an embrace. Startled, she ducked back out and leaned hard and flat against the outside wall. In spite of her rejuvenated will power, that scene shook her and took away both her breath and courage. With her back against the cool stucco of the building, she tried to regain a semblance of calm. Within minutes, Jim plunged out the doorway and headed toward the parking lot, never seeing her. She waited a few more minutes before entering the building again.

Her Sumner displays had been set up directly inside the door. They took up an entire corner of the room and drew the interest of many a guest. She derived some degree of pride from that. Some of her work had been blown up into giant presentations, much more impressive than her little sheets. She quietly passed through that area.

A good many of the guests hovered around the cocktails but no one she knew. Upon review of the evening program, she saw that the next two hours were devoted to talks about new products and services. Those would take place in designated rooms and were being presented for these earlier guests: the buyers and other agricultural people.

The big-money people, Anglin and the stockholders, would arrive closer to dinner time, which was set for eight-thirty. When Anglin felt they were all sufficiently fed, suitably impressed, and plied with enough liquor, he would address them with his usual speech about the company's prosperity and about all the good they were accomplishing. She saw that her posters had been placed strategically near the podium. He would no doubt refer to them in his talk.

She wondered if he would address the problem in Mexico. Some stockholders would have heard about it. If it were mentioned at all, Anglin would no doubt downplay it. He would turn their thoughts to the subject of how much money they would make in the upcoming years, especially due to their expanding international market. She knew him too well and could predict the entire evening, minute by minute, except for a few small gaps of uncertainty. Those gaps kept her in a state of panic.

Across the room, Anglin conversed with two other well-dressed gentlemen while Angel sipped a cocktail with another man. They'd arrived earlier than she had expected. Anne didn't want to be noticed any sooner than necessary. She couldn't afford to waste energy circulating. It would be difficult enough to sit through the long dinner and speeches. The whole affair would last until midnight or later. A small orchestra had set up on a balcony. Even now they played subdued background music. Anglin never scrimped when it came to show. Sumner looked prosperous, always. No wonder she embarrassed them.

In a nearby lecture room, she took a seat near the middle of a row where it would be difficult for anyone to approach her, yet she was fulfilling her part of the deal. She wondered what price they meant to exact for the return of her horse. It would, no doubt, be divulged before the evening grew old, but she knew it would be higher than she could pay. The voice of the lecturer droned monotonously, and finally she dozed, sitting upright, until the sound of people leaving the room awoke her. The lectures were at an end, and she must face whatever ordeal awaited her.

Her ornate name card sat inevitably on Anglin's table, the last place she wanted to be. She had been placed on Anglin's right, between him and Fred. Angel would sit across the table, on Anglin's left. Trapped, she thought, amused slightly at Anglin's playing the good father role. She felt sick to her stomach but vowed to show no weakness in front of him. Surviving this night would be the hardest thing she ever did. She sat in her chair and held onto the table edge to steady herself.

Words surged through her mind, familiar words. They rushed one upon another, and she prayed silently: *Oh Lord, the sorrows of death compassed me, and the floods of ungodly men made me afraid. Be not far from me, for trouble is near, for there is none to help. Deliver my feet from falling. Be merciful unto me, Oh God, be merciful unto me, for my soul trustest in thee. Yes, in the shadow of thy wings will I make my refuge, until these calamities be overpast.*

Encouraged and a bit calmer, she sat there and somehow knew she would upset Sumner's applecart that night. Sadness filled her, along with pity for her father. She had always wanted to please him but had failed miserably, and that knowledge drove her to do the bravest thing she could think to do. She rose from the table and walked straight over to Anglin where he conversed with other guests.

"Hi, Daddy. I've been in the lecture hall becoming educated." She said it simply and generously, as a child might. She kissed him lightly on his cheek and walked away. She didn't turn back to look at his face. They both understood she wasn't begging his favor or asking a quarter. It was the last time she would ever kiss him, she told herself, and then wondered if it was the first time also. Had there ever been another kiss?

"Some getup, Anne," Fred announced, coming up to her before she reached their table again. "I heard a couple old dowagers admire it and your figure. I'm not sure which they envied more."

"I hoped the outfit would blend me into the background, not make a sensation." She gazed around the room and found other eyes upon her. "I'd better sit down before someone comes over to talk."

"Are you sure that skirt has a *sit-down* mode?" His droll expression made her blush.

It wasn't long before everyone took their seats, ensuring she'd not have to converse with any of the curious who might know of her illness. It was one advantage, anyway, of having family on each side and in front of her. Zeiker and his wife sat at the other end of the table, and Jim's name decorated the card beside Angel. He had yet to put in an appearance. When he did, she would endure that along with the rest and show no weakness.

The conversation around her stayed totally away from Mexico, chemicals, horses, and her. She appreciated that, anyway. After a few minutes, Anglin turned to Angel.

"Where'd Jim disappear to?"

"He'll be back shortly. He called and said the jet had a mechanical problem, but he should be finished soon. We're going to Mexico after this shindig"

"Glad to see you're still working to iron out this mess."

"Work? Ha! I play tonight. We'll hit the resorts. I'm sick to death of all the misery I've waded through."

"That's fine at this table, but don't let on to anyone else how heartless you are."

"I'll be meek as Anne tonight."

"Meek? That's hardly the word I would have used."

They talked back and forth as if she wasn't there, and no one made eye contact with her. She minded her business, smiled, and ate. The table grew silent as dinner progressed.

"Let them be uncomfortable," she thought, and looked down at her plate. "I'm used to silence. It doesn't bother me."

A few minutes after ten, Anglin made his way to the front of the room amidst a round of applause. He came off confident and personable, and Anne experienced a degree of pride in him. He spoke naturally, his subject matter well-chosen and uncontroversial. He enumerated the many plusses of Sumner, emphasized its growth and prosperity, and ended with a pat on the back for all of them because of the good work they'd accomplished around the world. He mentioned nothing of the recent catastrophe.

Anne wondered why she grew more and more nervous. Her skin felt clammy, and she was cold. Didn't anyone notice the chilliness of the room? Zeiker's wife took off her wrap and complained about the warmth. Anne gripped her hands tight together and tried to conceal her anxiety, but her feet and legs persisted in their restless fidgeting. She reached for her coffee cup for the third time and for the third time found it empty and set it back down. Suddenly, her attention was caught by a question from one of the shareholders.

"Anglin, I couldn't help hearing about that little problem down in Mexico. I know others here share my interest. Is it a real crisis or a false alarm?"

"Grace, it's totally real, but no trouble of any magnitude. I'll admit Sumner made some slight errors. We trusted people too readily and gave too freely, against the advice of our attorney I might add. You see, we've hardly ever had to touch our insurance fund in the past. When we were recently faced with what appeared to be legitimate claims, we hurried to pay without instigating extensive investigations. Though there were some doubts as to the legality of the claims, we decided it'd be best to honor them and do our investigations afterward. We didn't want to be responsible for someone not getting prompt medical aid."

Anne couldn't keep back an audible gasp at the bare-faced lie. Her attention intensified as Anglin continued his suave explanation.

"It was a mistake on our part because claims started to come out of the woodwork. And you can hardly blame those poor devils down there for seeing an opportunity and grasping it, especially when you look at the squalor of their lives. I might add that Sumner has immensely helped those very conditions by supplying good-paying jobs for many of the people. But it's only natural to expect some greed and dishonesty to creep in."

"But weren't there deaths associated with this?" another shareholder asked, over the low rumble of voices in the room.

"We now believe all of those resulted from a flu virus. We know of no one who had serious problems from chemicals. It turned out, after investigation, that many of the sick had been exposed to a virus. My own daughter, Anne, contracted this same virus over fifty miles from the farms. The symptoms are identical with those in these other claims."

Fred put a calming hand on Anne's arm, and she realized she had been ready to jump up, had risen halfway out of her chair. She settled down again to listen attentively.

"But the newspaper implied that some of the claims appeared to be legitimate," another voice stated.

"Yes, there were some real claims. One of the pilots made an error and sprayed a field on the wrong day. But workers affected by that incident had only mild symptoms and were immediately treated. Sumner took responsibility for the pilot error. However, we can't help all those who are ill with disease, no matter how philanthropic we feel. Even my daughter, who was flown here gravely ill, didn't receive Sumner insurance money, simply because a virus, not chemicals, caused her problem. She was working among the people down there, helping them better their lives. Thankfully, she has recovered enough to be with us here tonight. With her help, we will work hard and put this behind us, so we might continue to ride prosperously. My pity runs deep for those who suffer, no matter what the cause. But I can honestly say, as it was said in Psalms so long ago, that 'Mercy and truth are met together; righteousness and peace have kissed each other.'"

Anglin smiled broadly at the large round of applause, accepting it graciously.

"He's using my scriptures," Anne said in surprise, loud enough for Fred to hear. He turned to her and grinned.

"Jim told him to. He gave him that one to use in his speech."

"Then Anglin intended to talk about the problem?"

"Sure. Grace, the lady who asked the first question, was told what to say. She's a friend of Anglin, has a crush on him, I think."

"And Jim gave him that scripture? Why?" she asked in Fred's ear.

"He said he wanted to see how you'd answer him," Fred said quietly.

"I'm not going to answer anything. I won't be speaking."

"You must, you know." Fred said it without looking at her, his fingers drummed softly on the table.

Chapter 18

Now she understood her terrible apprehension. She had been afraid she would have to speak to that room full of people.

"I'm leaving, Fred," she whispered. "I don't know where Jim is, but tell him goodbye."

Anne rose and hurried to the side entrance behind the displays. The door was cracked a few inches and someone watched through the gap. She opened it anyway and was surprised to find Jim.

He grabbed her arm. "Where do you think you're going?" he asked in the gruffest of voices. The yellow, outside light revealed his disheveled appearance.

"You're a ragamuffin. You're filthy and bloody and ... and Anglin is selling you out. He said you sprayed on the wrong day. He's put the blame on you."

"Two days ago I received orders to appear for questioning next week regarding my flying license." He said it haughtily.

"Oh! What will you do?"

"I'll tell the truth ... like you'll do tonight."

"I can't do anything. I'm afraid to go back in there. I'm scared to death."

"Is it because of your horse? Are you afraid to speak because of Tom-tom?" His expression looked cool and distant.

"Of course not." Scorn coursed through her with a vengeance. "I've given up Tom-tom. I've given up everything. All I have left is my integrity. I won't give that up."

"I counted on that, but to be sure you wouldn't weaken ..."

"You smell of horse!"

"You should have seen him, Anne. He fought like the devil. He has enough spirit for ten horses, as my appearance proves. He's saved. He's hidden for you until you can see him."

Anne looked at him dumbfounded for a minute. She couldn't quite absorb his words.

"Tom-tom?" Her voice trembled in her uncertainty and came out a whisper.

Jim nodded his head seriously.

"Tom-tom?" she shrieked, and grabbed hold of his jacket, shaking him in her excitement. "Tom-tom, Jim?"

"What other horse?" he grinned wryly.

"How? How, Jim?" She held onto him for support while she tried to grasp the enormity of what he'd just said.

"I rode him, flew him. There's no time now. Get in there, and do your part. I'll be here watching, listening."

"Tell me about Tom-tom. I'm not part of this fiasco. I'm not scheduled to speak."

"You will though. Wait and see. Go sit down." He shoved her lightly back into the room.

Anne had crept along the wall a couple feet when a voice from the back of the room addressed Anglin.

"We'd like to hear about the conditions down there first-hand, Anglin. Could your daughter come up and speak to us for a few minutes? Maybe answer some of our questions?"

"Yes," another voice seconded. "I'd like to hear about her work."

"Anne's still a sick girl. But her sister, Angeline, has been down there constantly since the incident. I'm sure she'd be glad to answer your questions."

"I know everyone here would like to hear about Anne's work," a third person responded. "Could she humor us for a minute? She could sit while she talked."

More affirmatives popped up around the room. Anne shrank back toward the doorway, but Jim still blocked it.

"Anglin thought he had you over a barrel, that you'd obey. Now he's not so certain," Jim gloated excitedly.

She started to push Jim out of the way, but the look on his face arrested her, like he searched her deepest depths. He stepped inside the doorway and joined his voice with the others, "Let Anne speak. We'd like to hear from a real hero."

"Jim," she whispered loudly, "you're embarrassing me. I can't."

"If you can drive all the way to Mexico, fight me like a wildcat, and try and shoot your father's horse, then I know you can find strength to stand up to Sumner."

He gave her a vigorous shove into the room and started clapping. Someone in the back took it up, and the others joined in at once. They had spotted her. Anglin spotted her last of all. The expression on his face was not good to look at. He stepped down and waved her to the stage. She stumbled twice on her way there, her legs busy trembling when they should have been supporting her. She gripped the stand in a death grip and stood there staring at the full room.

What could she say? Maybe there would only be a few questions, ones she could answer easily and get away. But the room waited in silence, and no questions came. Anglin stood nearby and didn't hide his impatience. She breathed a silent prayer and asked for the right words, but no words came.

"Th-this is difficult for me. I have, by the grace of God, been sustained to this hour."

She could think of nothing more to say. Her mind stuttered, like Jim's speech, and wouldn't work properly. In terror, she glanced over at Jim, still standing inside the door. Straight away she thought of Psalms. She could follow Anglin's example and quote Psalms.

"With your permission, I'll follow my father's example and quote scripture: 'He weakened my strength in the way; he shortened my days. I said, O my God, take me not away in the midst of my days.'" She bowed her head for a brief second to catch her breath. "'O spare me, that I may recover strength, before I go hence, and be no more.'

"I ask only that He spare me until my father's words are fulfilled,

213

until mercy and truth are met together, until righteousness and peace have truly kissed each other." She looked around the room for strength to say what she must say. Anglin's face appeared tense and hostile, as did Angel's. Angel had turned around and now stared at her. Fred sat tall and nodded to her as if telling her to go on.

"But how can there be a kiss when there is no breath? And how can there be mercy when there is no truth? I have been closer to this situation, or I should say *tragedy*, than any other person. I have new information that even Sumner hasn't received at this time, but this is not the time or place to discuss it."

The room came alive with conversation as she paused to get her breath. She glanced at Anglin and was shocked at the look on his face. The corners of his mouth were drawn down in such an expression of hate it unnerved her. She quickly looked away and placed her gaze on Fred, who now smiled.

"This much I can tell you. There is no flu, not even one case of virus, connected with this situation. But there *is* much illness, terrible illness, such as I have been dealing with in my own body, and there is death. It was all caused by one factor — chemicals."

The general buzz rose to a roar, and people called out questions from different parts of the room. She wasn't ready to answer questions. They must all hear the truth while she still had breath.

"I can also assure you that no pilot error occurred. I have in my possession twenty-eight documents, signed and witnessed, that prove this conclusively."

The audience grew livelier, and one man at a front table called out in a booming voice, "Who gave you these documents? How do you know they're real?"

"Because I collected these statements myself on my last trip to Mexico. They show clearly we cannot lay the blame on any pilot. The fields in question were sprayed during the night. No workers were present."

She all of a sudden felt bolder, like she could finish the job if she only didn't look in Anglin's direction again, if she only could keep her legs from buckling. As soon as she told the whole truth, her work would be done.

"Although we can't lay the blame on either virus or pilot, a culprit has been found," she rushed on, her mouth close to the microphone to make sure her voice carried. "This devastation was caused by a chemical additive that was mixed with the herbicide paraquat. It made the paraquat more lethal and more readily absorbed, especially when it was still wet or when it came into contact with wet human skin.

"If you know anything about farm labor at this time of year, you know a worker's skin will be wet with perspiration. On that dreadful morning of illness, many of the workers walked through dew-wet fields of weeds that had been sprayed the night before. And some workers only touched weeds with dried chemical on them, but, because their skin was wet, they, too, were affected. I have many more signed statements and documentation attesting to these facts."

She glanced at Anglin. He looked incensed and was headed her way, but the room had all at once become surprisingly quiet. Her strength drained, she rushed to finish.

"I have personally given a list of the ill workers to Sumner and to their insurance company. I know most of these workers and their families." Her voice suddenly carried with a wonderful clearness as she forgot herself and thought of Pacal and the others. "Yes, they are poor. They work for next to nothing, are mostly uneducated, and many live in squalid conditions. But they have bodies, just like ours, and feelings and hurts and joys and children they're proud of. They don't fake illness. They haven't found that necessary. It's true that some have only minor sickness, but some are terribly ill, and some are already gone."

"Your dad said you were fifty miles away from the farms," shouted the man with the big voice, yet still barely able to be heard over the excitement and noise of the agitated audience. "How did you become exposed? You said there was no flu, didn't you?"

"There was no flu, and I'm a victim of the same chemical mixture. I'm sorry, but I can't discuss the circumstances that lead to my exposure until the testing is complete."

"Nor did I wish to discuss it," broke in Anglin, beside her now, "but I'm afraid she's made it necessary." He shoved in front of the microphone and applauded Anne as if she were dismissed. "Anne," the malice showed raw across his face, "you'd best go lie down. You look exceptionally weak. I'll finish up here. We asked too much of you for your condition."

215

She found herself waved away, as surely as she had been waved forward to speak a few minutes earlier.

"I have to admit to all of you that I let being a father get in the way of some small bit of truth. Some of you know of this, but for those who don't, I believe it will clear the air if I explain. You see, my daughter had been laboring in Mexico beyond her ability and strength. She recently had some drastic setbacks. With physical and mental state deteriorating, she attempted suicide by means of oral ingestion of paraquat."

Anne staggered as the words penetrated her consciousness. She turned and stared at him, wide-eyed and horrified. When she saw the effect of his words on his audience, she wanted to sink into the floor or turn and run. Half the room looked at her as she stood listening in disbelief, halfway between the podium and the side door.

"I have the doctor's report here for anyone's investigation," Anglin said, drawing most of the attention away from her. "We flew her straight to the United States, to our family doctor, the minute we learned of it. The doctor has been aware of it from the beginning. Possibly some of the illness and death of the workers stems from this same cause. Paraquat has been used before in suicide attempts, as those who work with these chemicals are well aware."

Unable to stand there any longer, under the assault of Anglin's lies, Anne rushed toward the door in an agony of humiliation. Jim stopped her, pulled her outside with him. She fought him to get away, but he held her tight.

"Did you hear him? He lied! He said I tried to commit suicide, that I took paraquat. He said that to everyone. Maybe from the beginning, he's told people that. He knew all along what caused my illness. He knew it wasn't the flu!"

"Anne," Jim shook her urgently. "Did you expect him to sit back and take it without fighting? Grow up, Anne. If you shot a bear in the foot, what do you think it would do? Go back to your table, you little fool. You've unleashed hell, now be ready to fight. I'll clean myself up and be there in five minutes."

"I can't. It's too big for me. It seems too big for God." She stared wildly at the seemingly hostile room.

"Baby, didn't you feel the earth shake and tremble? He heard. He's flying on the wing of the wind this minute. It's about time for me to do some flying, too. Brace up, and go sit down. You're white as a sheet. Don't faint now. I need you here." His hand held tight on her arm, his eyes pleaded.

Like a robot, Anne walked back to her table and only half-realized when Fred pulled out her chair. Like someone in a dream, she sat, facing straight ahead. Angel conversed with Zeiker and his wife. People talked all around her, and she heard her name spoken more than once, in spite of Anglin's rambling voice that was trying to lead his audience back into the realm of safe nothings.

When she heard a man at a nearby table say something about her sharp-looking outfit, she found herself struggling hysterically between laughter and tears.

"You should go home and to bed," Angel said, turning to her.

Anne ignored her. *What home, what bed?* she thought desolately. Let them talk on. She was busy staying alive. She'd do her talking to God. Lines of scripture and prayer ran through her mind in a seemingly endless flow: *I am like an owl of the wilderness ... I am as a sparrow alone on the housetop ... I have eaten ashes like bread, and mingled my drink with weeping ... my days are like a shadow that declineth ... put thou my tears into thy bottle.*

Words spilled over words and cried out from the depths of her heart, but she sat there expressionless, with dry, hot eyes and mute tongue. Angel looked at her strangely, half-mocking, half-questioning. Many faces were turned her way. She could see the white blur of them, but she continued to stare straight ahead at nothing. She wondered how Fred felt about all of this, but she couldn't turn toward him. When she saw Jim approach the table, she prayed silently, *Oh Lord, give me the strength to see this through.*

He sat down and pulled his chair close beside Angel's. Anne could see a smile pass between them. Suddenly, Anglin got back on the subject of pilot error, and Anne found herself quaking within.

"Now to make this matter clearer, we have one of our aerial applicators present here tonight. I mentioned, earlier, there had been a slight reaction to the spraying, mild and mostly in the form of skin irritation. It lasted only a day or two. That situation was caused by a simple misunderstanding that resulted in our pilot spraying the wrong field. He'll come forward now to explain about this, and about the chemical itself, so we can put all this to rest, once and for all. After we hear from him, we'll end the speeches, and the music will begin for those who are waiting to dance. Jim Orr, come to the microphone, please."

Anglin had a self-satisfied look on his face as he worked his way back toward his table, stopping on the way to shake hands with the occupants of the various tables he passed. Anne refused to look at Jim as he haltingly rose. She could tell his face had turned toward her, but she was afraid to meet his eyes. She wanted to warn him: *Dad's giving you an ultimatum. You have to choose sides, right here and now. If you go against him, you had better be ready to run to the ends of the earth.*

Anne felt him study her. She heard his mocking laugh, like he had heard her silent message. She looked up in time to see him turn to Angel. "He's punishing me for giving him that scripture idea for his speech. I guess Anne did him one better."

"Hardly. He fixed that neatly. Now it's your job to finish it. Remember we have our insurers here and some other interested outsiders. Get it done quickly, and then let's go somewhere."

"Fly?"

"If you've got that problem fixed on the jet. I won't go in your bird."

Anne's body tightened as Jim headed toward the podium. Every nerve in her had tensed. She was literally scared to death, not for herself, not for the villagers, but for Jim. What were they making him do? It would be better for him to run out of the place and never come back. Anything was better than this. She couldn't bear to listen, and yet she was riveted to her seat.

Anglin took his seat at their table as Jim stepped up to the microphone. Jim seemed confident enough, though she couldn't read his face. He gazed casually around, then placed his gaze on Angel and smiled at her.

"I want to tell you a story," he began, his brogue only slightly pronounced. "Tonight I see a strong, beautiful woman who has worked tirelessly to iron out the difficulties in this trying situation. She has flown back and forth between here and Mexico to make sure every tiniest detail was taken care of. She compiled accurate lists and talked individually with each of the claimants and their families. She had tests conducted and left no stone unturned in seeking the truth. She has been loyal to family, to company, to those who are suffering, and to me, her friend. But most of all she has been loyal to her own principles."

It was obvious Jim had his audience. Smiling, interested faces now turned toward Angel. Anglin breathed deeply, a contented sigh, and settled back in his chair with a complacent smile. Anne ached for Jim, through and through, as her anger mounted toward those who forced him to go against his conscience. She suffered torment as each of his words cut through her like a knife point.

"She, of all people, could tell you what took place the night that hell fell from the sky." Jim paused and nodded toward their table. "I was in the sky earlier that night. And I know she's the one who should be speaking now, not me. But I've been there beside her. I have personally flown her back and forth to the little villages in lower Mexico where she's worked diligently to find a fair and equitable solution to this problem. I know, for a fact, there were times she was too tired to keep on, but she forced herself because she deemed it necessary."

Anglin beamed at Angel, a bit nervously, and Angel looked as if she might be capable of blushing. Anne could see both of them, without looking at either.

"Would you like to know what this woman, this grand lady, was doing the day before the illness struck Mexico?" He paused again and looked around before continuing. "She was doing what she'd been doing every day for two and a half years – working hard, laughing with the sun on her tanned face, and delighting in the fact her two little mission villages were doing so well. She was at a wonderful stage of success. The villagers all loved her. Their education had been improved. Their life styles, their morals, and especially their economy were on an upswing. It was a wonderful time of rejoicing and festivity in her villages."

Bewilderment hit the room like a cyclone. People jabbered confusedly. Angel seemed to be in a state of shock, and Anglin sat rigid as a post. Anne looked around in alarm, until Fred dug her in the ribs and brought her attention back to Jim.

"That day, the day before the illness struck, Anne's smile flashed in joy as she prepared for festivities to celebrate her villages' new prosperity. She was the picture of health and happiness." Jim smiled and looked straight at Anne.

"There was a small lake in her home village, a lake she'd dug for

219

them with her own two hands, working hard with shovel and pick against earth and rock. Any of us would have hired a bulldozer for that kind of work. She often swam in that lake at night to cool off. I once swam with her in the cool night hours and shared with her the mysteries of Mexico's flower-scented nights.

"It was on another flower-scented night that two twenty-gallon drums of paraquat solution, combined with the additive Anne mentioned earlier, were dropped into her lake by my fellow pilot, Fritz Farley. No one knew of this except him. That night, only minutes after he'd dropped them, Anne swam in her lake. The next morning she was deathly ill, but still cheerful, thinking only that she had a bad cold or virus. I flew her here to the hospital in a semiconscious state."

It was obvious Anglin would have already attacked Jim, if there hadn't been a roomful of people to witness it. He started to stand, then settled down hard in his seat. Jim had a mocking expression on his face, daring him to interrupt.

"Does that sound like someone who would try to commit suicide? Anne Sumner is the sanest person I've ever met. These beautiful displays up here are all her work. Do they look like they were done by an unstable person? Why would someone tell the doctor she'd tried to commit suicide? Only the villagers and I were present when she became ill."

"Let me read you something," came Angel's voice from her table, where she now stood. She had no microphone, but Jim had so captivated his audience the room was totally quiet. Angel's high-pitched attempt to be heard pierced the silence unpleasantly. "I'd like to read something written by Anne. You judge whether this was written by a sane person.

"'It feels similar to how it is when you've driven for a long, long time, and your eyes won't stay open, no matter what you try. And the back of your neck, your head, your entire body becomes numb with drowsiness.'"

Anne listened in startled disbelief. It was her own note to Jim that she had placed in her desk that morning. Angel must have stolen it when no one was there. Even as she listened, outraged, she was thankful Jim's name wasn't on it. Angel had no way of knowing she wrote it to Jim. Angel's voice shrilled on, interrupting her thoughts:

"'You think how delicious it'd be to close your eyes for an instant, to let happen what may. Even if you slammed over an embankment or smacked into a tree, you wouldn't feel anything because you'd already be deep in sleep. And the temptation lingers. It travels up around your groggy mind.'

"Now I ask everyone here, doesn't that sound like someone with mental problems?"

The audience swung back to Anglin's side, nodding and mumbling agreement.

"Let me finish that letter, Angel, since it was written to me," said Jim in a voice that cut through the room. He looked the part of a white nemesis, standing so straight behind the podium. Suddenly his brogue was gone and he stuttered, but his voice remained loud and clear.

"'The t-temptation lingers. It travels up around your g-groggy mind – until you suddenly r-remember your duty.'"

Anglin laughed out loud and looked his ridicule. Angel looked too astonished to speak. Jim closed his eyes, took a breath, and started speaking again, only more slowly.

"'You remember the p-passengers, who trust you with their lives, and you remember those in the other vehicles, whom you might endanger.'"

His stutter disappeared as his voice rang out with conviction, even passion.

"'You remember the friends and acquaintances of those people, who would also be affected if you gave in to your weakness. And last of all, you remember the ones who love you, if you are so lucky, the ones who would sorrow over your passing.

"So you struggle on, and slap yourself in the face, and look for a place to pull over and snatch a few minute's rest before you go on. And you go on ... and on ... and on, because you must.'

"Anne wrote that to me right before leaving the hospital, to describe her condition. For those here who haven't been informed, it's pulmonary fibrosis. She was never expected to walk out of that hospital. Her dedication to others lifted her from what should have been her death bed and drove her to go on – and on."

The roar of the room suddenly drowned out even the microphone. Jim silently waited. Most of them had chosen sides, and Anne was the victor. Truth had spoken for itself.

Angel showed her fury. "The nerve of that dirty traitor!" She looked straight at Anne. "I'll fix it so he never flies again. I'll see him behind bars." She started to rise, but Fred reached across the table and pulled down ungently on her arm.

"Be still. You bore me, Angeline. She's won this round. Let it be."

Angel looked to Anglin for support and started to rise again, but Anglin waved her down.

"You've made enough scene for one night. Be still and smile, or I'll disown the entire lot of you."

Fred plastered a wide grin on his face while Angel scowled. Anne looked around in wonder, only halfway registering what had happened. But her heart kept slugging inside her to the tune of: *My letter, he memorized my letter. Every word of it.*

Suddenly, Angel echoed Anne's very thoughts. "He memorized the whole stupid thing. Who'd have dreamed?"

When the room grew silent, Jim continued, "I've watched Anne carry on, never daunted by any obstacle, trusting God to carry her through, having faith she can change the world with her own two hands, with her unbelievably tough will, and with her totally unselfish heart.

"I haven't much faith, not like Anne's faith. I can't do like her and walk on the wings of the wind. I just fly ..."

He stopped and hurried toward Anne, who had struggled to her feet and had turned to leave the room. She knew she could only hold back the tears a few seconds more. Jim's speech had taken her breath away far more effectively than a mile run would have done. The outside door seemed like a speck in the distance, but she couldn't let herself collapse in that room, not in front of all those people – and Jim.

The sea of faces between her and the door were all turned in her direction, many smiling, all sympathetic. Some had tears streaming down, and she wondered if her eyes were still dry. She saw people stand and start toward her.

Struggling hurriedly on, she had just passed the last table when she felt her knees give way, then consciousness.

Sometime later, whether minutes or days, she wasn't sure, she found herself lying on the grass. Jim bent over her. She looked up at him, tried to raise her hand, but no strength came to her. Her eyes felt dry and burning as she stared into Jim's concerned gaze. Full consciousness returned like a whirlwind, and she remembered what had happened. She looked around and saw they were in the park adjoining the banquet facility.

"Talk to me, Anne. Talk to me. You can still do that, can't you?" She heard the desperation in his voice.

"Jim, w-what have you done? Angel and my dad, they'll ..."

"Did you think I'd let you face hell alone?"

"Did I fall in there?"

"No. I got to you. You were standing. I think you were unconscious before you made the door, but you kept on. We made it, together. But listen to me. I know I'm responsible for all this, too. I never demanded to know about that additive."

"Who would have? I would have done the same as you and thought nothing of it."

"But it's not just that. I gave you oxygen on the plane, when I first took you back to the states. Oxygen can make the reaction worse if it's given right away. I didn't realize. I know you've researched paraquat recently, the same as I have, and you know that, don't you? You understand what I may have caused with that oxygen?"

"Of course I've run across that information. I never gave it another thought. How were you supposed to know something like that? I told you I had the flu."

"I thought you hated me for what I might have done to you. And last weekend, you hardly had strength to stand when you left my plane and went with Ruben. And you killed yourself getting all those statements to protect me. You never told me why you wanted to stay. You fought with me to hide what you planned to do."

"If a guilty conscience, or indebtedness to me, has caused you to desert Angel and Dad, if that's what holds you here by my side, I release you. I never, ever, even for a second, blamed you. Of course I knew about the oxygen. It would have made little difference in my case. The doctor said as much. You can tell Dad and Angel what you just told me. Tell them you felt responsible for my condition. Angel will understand. She'll forgive you. I think she had feelings for you. I saw you with her ... before the banquet."

"Hush. You don't get it at all. I couldn't take two days with your sister on a full-time basis. I know what it'd be like. I've been around."

"Angel said you'd been around. I've told you that before."

Jim laughed harshly. "A person can be around and see things, dirty things, but they don't have to become soiled if they don't choose to. I hope I'm talking about myself. Now take Angel. She enjoys the dirt, literally wallows in it."

Suddenly Anne sat bolt upright. "I smell it on you!"

Jim looked confused, then dumfounded. "Angel's p-perfume? I couldn't help that."

"Horse! I smell horse on you again. I'd forgotten. Was it true or a dream? Did you ..."

He grinned at her as if he were holding a box of chocolates behind his back.

"Jim, my heart won't stand s-so much."

"Tom-tom runs free. I left him with friends, far-away friends. Anglin will never locate him."

"How? How, Jim?"

"That night Fred kept you busy for me, I wasn't at the university *all* night. I spent half the night searching for where they'd stabled Tom-tom. Tonight I went back and freed him."

"Wasn't he locked in?"

"Locked up tighter than Anglin's conscience. I climbed through a window too small for me and made it look like Tom-tom kicked his way out. I broke wood, trampled wire, and made sure I left some of his hair on it. The fool stables had barbed wire. I got it worse than Tom-tom did, but luckily it's in a place it won't show. I rode him bareback through two suburbs. Dogs barked like crazy, and he threw me once. I had a devil of a time getting him to my friend's helicopter."

"Helicopter?"

"Yeah, that's when he got unmanageable. He didn't like the noise one bit. You can't believe how indignant he looked, nearly human, rolling his big eyes and showing the whites. He bent his head around backward to see what we were doing when we tried to strap him into some makeshift slings. He got tangled every time I'd think he was about ready, and he went wild with that helicopter hovering above him. I finally climbed on his back, held the rig straight, and signaled my friend to go. Some ride that was. He was as happy to land as I was, and he'll for sure buck you off every time he hears a plane."

Anne laughed and cried at the same time.

"When we landed, he wasn't one bit shaky, no tremble at all. He smelled other horses, whinnied, and pranced off as soon as he was free. He didn't even wait to say thanks. I've been kicked, shoved, stepped on, dragged, and once he fell down and rolled on me."

Fred was suddenly beside them, casually smoking.

"How is it in there, Fred?" Jim asked

"Dad's white hot, and Angel's burst into flame. We had an abbreviated family conference before we parted company. We plan to frame you, to say you're covering up your own scheme to get rich. It will be like this. We'll say you and a chemist friend of yours developed this formula to make paraquat go further. Anglin's got it all figured. He remembered you at times sprayed other places and bought the chemicals from Sumner. Well, you'll find all your receipts gone, compliments of Angel. Meanwhile, Dad has pulled all the copies of your orders. He'll say you had left-over chemical from Sumner's jobs because of using the additive, and that you sold it to those other places you sprayed to make a bigger profit."

"You know what, Fred? That would work. I did supply the chemical and charge places for it. If I have no receipts to prove I bought the chemical from Sumner, he could lay it all on me."

"Sumner will pretend innocence of knowing anything about this additive. We'll say you did it on your own, and we'll act horrified about it. Of course, Anglin still hasn't found a way to get out of being liable. You were given paychecks, and they can't hide that fact. And since they hired you, they are responsible. You'll have to work fast, Jim. Dad's gotten rid of everyone who knew anything. He's been liquidating and getting his money out of the country as quick as he can."

"Switzerland?"

"Offshore account. Sumner's expendable, but his money isn't, and he doesn't intend to go to jail."

"You guys better be careful," Anne warned. "Don't either of you tell me anything more, because I'll use it to Sumner's hurt. You've been staying away from me so you won't have trouble. Don't blow it now."

Fred looked at her in amusement. "You little blockhead," he said tenderly. "Yes, Jim and I both had to be convincing, or we couldn't have gotten away with anything. And since there are a few items to tidy up, we'll continue this charade for a while yet. *I* will, that is. Jim is now a fallen angel, simply because he hasn't *fallen for Angel*. He's no longer under grace. Take care of him, Anne."

Fred faded away as silently as he'd arrived.

"Jim, what about Angel? And your future with the company?"

"We're all weak, Anne. Not even your father has your strength. But I thought you knew me better than that. You were so self-sacrificing. You inspired me to try my hand at it. I've never done anything meaningful. I thought it'd please you, my infiltrating them."

"Me? Strong? Never! I'm not strong. I don't care if the whole world dies right now. I'm selfish, and little, and you make me almost hate my own flesh and blood. But you forget, now I'm a mad-woman, and you're a murderer. I don't mind about myself, but you've still got a life ahead of you."

"I'll have to get what proofs I can, before I'm jailed and can't do anything. Luckily I left my plane in a safe spot. At least they won't get hold of that. Let's get out of here before someone stumbles on us."

"You go. I don't want to move again. I'm so tired. I see no path, only a maze of trouble. I'm sinking in a swirling caldron of trouble. I'm not strong at all. I've fallen flat on my face."

"That's what I expected you to do"

"You expected me to fall on my face?" she asked surprised and offended.

"Yes, fall on your faith."

"I think you have a slight lisp."

"I stutter. I don't have a lisp. I know what I said. And so do you."

"But can't I hide, just for a moment?"

"I'm sorry, this isn't the moment. Let's fly, Anne, while it's dark. Let's fly to Mexico."

Chapter 19

With blurred eyes, Anne stared out the window at the dark Gulf below them, thankful and afraid and overcome by memories. She felt terribly tired, but it was good to be in the air again and good to sit beside Jim.

"Sleep if you can."

"I don't want to sleep anymore. I don't want to miss anything. I want to look out at the sky and the sea."

"We're halfway to heaven, Anne."

"I believe I'm more than halfway," she said drolly, turning toward him.

"You know what I mean."

"Jim, your speech tonight took me by surprise. And my letter, you memorized my letter, and other things that I've said, too. I thought you ..." she couldn't find the words she wanted.

"I've listened to everything you've ever said. I thought you knew that."

"I didn't. I don't know anything. Women like to hear things."

"So do men."

"You were with Angel. You deserted me, like Fred did. You both deserted me when I needed you."

"You never said you needed me. You made me think Tutlu and

Capaso were the only things important to you. You don't trust anyone, Anne, not your villagers, not me, not Fred, not anyone, and sometimes not even God. I know. I see. You were so terribly worried about those illnesses. I thought I could help more the way I chose."

"Was that the only reason you were with Angel – to infiltrate Sumner?"

He didn't answer, and they sat in silence for a long time. She thought he would never answer that question, but the quiet finally broke.

"At one point, when I believed you didn't care, I c-considered chasing, just to see where it'd lead me. The challenge intrigued me. When I realized I could have Angel, and a chunk of Sumner to boot, I also realized they didn't interest me. Only a spunky little missionary held my attention. But I learned far more than I ever expected, and I stayed to learn more."

"Why didn't you tell me? Was it because you knew I m-might die, will die?" It frightened her to say it.

"Not because of that. I've faced death before. That couldn't bother me. It was your goodness. I didn't think I could live with that."

"And now?"

"Now, I know I can't go on ..."

He didn't finish it but reached over, unfastened her seat belt, and pulled her to him. With his arms wrapped around her, he held her tight against his chest, his body shaking all over. She didn't know if he was crying, but she knew she was.

It seemed ages they held to each other close, only feeling, never speaking. There was nothing to say. There was only that minute and maybe a few more after it. But it would suffice.

"You understand what you're letting yourself in for, don't you?" she finally asked, her cheek still pressed against his shoulder, her eyes still full of tears. "You definitely haven't considered your future."

"You've shown me a new future. It doesn't matter how much time we have left together here, does it? We'll get married when this is over. That's all the earthly future I need right now."

"I'm afraid of what we have yet to face."

"We'll face it together. Even if we drop into those black waters down there, we can swim to eternity together, can't we?"

"It sounds like fun, the swimming I mean," she said flippantly, to

228

hide the deep emotion his words engendered. "Are we closer to the States or to Mexico?"

"Halfway."

"So, we're either halfway to heaven or halfway to Mexico. I wonder if there's some significance in that. I guess you'd better try to stay airborne. I want to see Tutlu one last time. Will that be possible?"

"We'll see Tutlu. I promise you that."

She slid down into her seat, and he strapped her in.

"But how will you know what my dad's up to while we're down in Mexico? We won't be able to keep an eye on him."

"Fred will keep me posted."

She felt satisfied for the moment, but something else came to mind.

"Now I remember what I wanted to ask you. Your speech, there at the banquet. Your stutter went away. I mean near the end, when you didn't use an accent. How did you manage that?"

"The same way I always do, by acting. I pretended to be the man you wanted me to be, full of virtue, faith, and unselfish. I played a hero with no stutter." His eyes laughed at her.

"I think you played yourself."

She drifted off to sleep, and the next thing she knew, Jim was shaking her awake. They were circling Tutlu in the morning sunlight. Anne wasn't prepared for the flock of villagers who surrounded them when they landed on the bumpy runway. It was difficult to climb from the plane in her too-tight, too-short, banquet clothes. Ruben rushed to her aid, smiling comically.

The villagers, who had always been shy around her, seemed to see something different in her face. They came up, one by one, and embraced and kissed her. Pacal ran to meet her, and she could see his improvement. The children took her hand and led her, practically pulled her into the village, where they pointed to a neat stack of boxes, each filled with fudge. It wasn't an enormous amount, but it was proof they had gone on.

Anne looked questioningly at Malinali.

"We take it in the truck, Capaso's fudge, too. We sell it to the stores and come back and make more."

"And the men who always drank the profits?"

"They are still here. They still drink. But now we put our feet down flat. Some men help and even the children. Both villages do better now. We help each other."

Anne looked around with interest and all at once noticed the lake had water in it. She stared at it aghast. Ruben grinned at her, reading her mind.

"We fixed the dam. A government man came and checked the water. All the chemicals have washed away. We had much rain."

Anne could only stare at the shimmering pool of water, riding at its original level. Tears filled her eyes. "I wish we had time for a swim." She looked longingly at Jim.

"We'll come back," he said simply.

Weary, but happy, she climbed aboard the plane and sank into a short nap while Jim flew on to Padre Juan's home. In a short while the plane bumped to a stop behind his rectory.

Anne found it an ordeal to face the padre. What could she say with the situation so uncertain? Would aid ever come, or would Anglin's sharp attorneys and the insurance company's attorneys find a way to beat these poor people out of the care they needed so desperately? A feeling of helplessness came over her. Somehow the university tests would be annulled or ignored, the way everything else had fallen through. Big money had such power. She felt totally low as she walked up to the padre's small, flower-bedecked cottage.

Padre Juan rushed out the door like a small whirlwind, his face bright and smiling. He embraced her and chattered so quickly in Spanish she could hardly make out what he said.

Grasping her confusion, he slowed down and started again.

"I tried to call. I just got back from Mexico City. I've been there working most of the time since I took you to the bus."

"You've been working there as sick as you are?"

"Yes. I worked, but I had much help. I told myself, if Miss Anne can work with her sick lungs, then I, by the grace of God, can do the same with my tired lungs. I learned much, very much. I found an attorney who will help us and not charge. He went with me. We searched for names on the pay-off list. We checked all the churches, the doctors, and the hospitals. We found only one man from the list, Sandro Caldera."

"I remember his name. The paper said his illness was terminal.

They paid him eight hundred thousand dollars."

He laughed. "In truth, they paid him eight hundred dollars, and he was to leave the country. He had family in Honduras and was to go back there. But he didn't go back, and we talked with him. He told us he'd gone to Sumner farms a short while ago to look for work. He told the people in charge that he'd worked there before, that he knew Anglin personally. A lady took him aside and gave him papers to sign, gave him money, and told him to leave for Honduras immediately. He, of course, signed the papers. Though he can't read, he wasn't going to pass up a chance at eight hundred dollars. The man was not ill, and he hadn't worked for Sumner in over six months. He showed us an airplane ticket the lady had given him the day after their meeting. It had expired, and our attorney has it now. We have not learned much, but that may help."

"It's enough," Anne said, angry but elated. "It's strange anyone would do something so risky. Will the man stay in this country to be a witness?

"We have arranged for that. Also, we have more good news. Jock located Chester Lorry, the old foreman of the farms. He knows some of Chester's relatives, and they told him Mr. Lorry had gone to Guatemala. Our lawyer will try to get him back here where he can tell the truth about the spraying."

Anne sat down totally overcome.

"Miss Anne, can you wait and speak with this lawyer? He will meet me at Capaso tonight to finish all the claims. You could help him. I would like for you to talk with him."

"We'll be there, but not till after dark," Jim promised. "We can't stay now. Sumner is attempting to frame me. The law in both countries may soon be after me, and I may need an attorney, too, but right now we have business to take care of. We may be as late as eight or nine tonight, maybe later."

"We will wait for you."

Jim flew to a level strip, surrounded by trees, where they could safely rest for a while.

"After dark we'll go to your dad's factory. I still have my keys. I'll fill up on fuel and look around for any chemical that might still be there."

"Is it safe? Won't they watch?"

"No place is safe now. But we can't stop for that. You want to see this through, don't you?"

"I still have my keys, too. I'll snoop around inside."

"Don't bother. I'm sure they left nothing incriminating. But you could go in there and empty out the Sumner larder. Let's prepare for a long haul."

Later, as they surveyed the factory from above, it appeared dark and deserted.

"Jim, there's usually a guard."

"I'm hoping it's Carlos. He'll keep quiet. I'll just send him to the opposite side for an hour."

"Can you trust him? He may have orders."

"I helped him out of a scrape. We're friends. I trust him, and he trusts me."

When they landed, there was no sign of a guard or anyone else. Jim pulled into the shadow of a building.

"Wait until five minutes after I'm gone before you go to the office kitchen. I'll meet you there when I'm through. If anyone shows up, turn on the big, front-office lights. I'll see them. Don't leave till I come, no matter how long I'm gone. I'll check every building here. It will be my last chance to do that."

An hour later Jim came into the kitchen.

"I was getting scared. I was ready to go out and look for you. Here's a pile of food. Wish I could have found some clothes to change into. This getup wasn't made for the jungle, in spite of its safari appearance."

"I think it's perfect." His expression made her laugh in spite of herself. "I filled my fuel tanks and put in two extra containers for emergency."

"I take it you didn't find any of the additive."

"No. I searched every inch. If there's any left, it's labeled something else. A chemist would have to test every barrel, and even then I doubt there's any still here."

"That doesn't leave us in a great position, with the evidence and the key players missing. All that's left is this insane missionary, who rides around with a thief, who sells illegal chemical for his own profit."

"Looks bad, doesn't it?"

"Yes, but I've been thinking. There's someone else missing. How are you supposed to know about this chemical? You're not a chemist. You would need to have a chemist accomplice. Who will they accuse of creating this compound?"

"You're right. Maybe Anglin's chemist in Houston created it."

"If Le Grand were involved, Dad would be afraid he'd talk under pressure."

"Any chemist might talk under pressure, but Anglin might buy their silence by making it look like he'd protect them. It's not illegal for a chemist to experiment with a chemical. Maybe I stole the chemical from the chemist. No, I guess that's not possible. According to that university student, it'd be too complicated for me to make it by myself, and there has obviously been a good quantity produced. Any chemist involved, Le Grand or whoever, would have a tough time talking his way out of this. And Anglin would never let him be questioned. That would be much too dangerous. I'll call Fred and see what he thinks. Hand me that phone, my cell phone has no reception here."

Anne didn't need to ask Jim what Fred said. Fred's voice came loud and clear over the receiver. Le Grand had disappeared. He attended the banquet but left after Anne mentioned the additive. Anglin was looking for him, and Fred had hired his own private investigator to locate him first. Jim hung up the phone and looked at Anne.

"Le Grand. Running scared, but lucky to be running at all. If your daddy finds him first, he won't have to worry about ever testifying again."

"Dad would never go that far."

"He can't afford to let him be questioned. That's much too dangerous. Surely you don't still think your father would have any qualms over eliminating a mere chemist, if his existence put Anglin's hide and money at risk."

"I don't know. I'm not sure I know my father at all. And there's something else I don't understand. Fred said they destroyed all records of your buying paraquat from Sumner, but how could Angel get hold of your personal receipts?"

"She has a key to my place. Evidently went straight there from the banquet. I think she felt a wee bit vengeful last night. Worse yet, I stupidly handled all my dealings with cash. It will look exactly as they planned for it to look, like I accumulated excess paraquat by using the additive, and that I sold it to the other places I'd sprayed. It's easy to find out that I don't make much money, and that those small amounts of profit would be helpful to me. It's just penny ante enough for some poor crop duster to try. Let's get out of here before someone we don't want to see shows up. Get in the plane, and I'll load the goodies."

They were soon soaring across the night sky in the direction of Capaso. Anne sat and stewed over the impossible situation for Jim.

"Perk up. Don't look so glum," he said, reading her mood. "You've had some of the best news ever today. We'll lick this."

She lifted her head and managed to smile. "Wasn't Malinali great? The whole village surprised me. They're going forward."

"I don't know how you feel about it, but to me that bit of spunk they exhibited seems worth more than any improvement you could have accomplished."

"You're right. The real benefit had to come from inside them. They always had it in them."

"They needed encouragement. They used your courage to find their own. Look at Padre Juan. That's not the sick, droopy, dejected, little priest I used to know. And who knows, maybe his attorney can also help clear me, that is, if I can stay free for a while longer."

"Maybe Fred can locate that chemist. And that's another thing, Jim. I can't believe about Fred. I-I'm proud of my brother. He always seemed weak and more or less useless. His whole life added up to a computer game and a bottle of beer."

"Things aren't always what they seem."

"I think I understand. He used those things to escape from what he saw around him. He couldn't give up the benefits, so he blinded himself. Such a waste. Fred's smart, too."

"Smarter than you realize. He's a genius with a computer. He can do anything."

"Yes, I've played computer games with him. I know his talent in that direction."

"Games, nothing. I mean he infiltrated all of Sumner. He can find out anything – in minutes – about the company, about every employee's private files, about everyone's home computer, even Anglin's and Angel's private computers, and about other companies."

"I didn't realize, but then he was always sort of a hacker."

"He doesn't play games half so much as you'd think. He uses them as a cover up. I've caught him, and he's confided in me. Said he did the hacking for his own amusement. But lately he's been studying you. He admires you, Anne. You've worked your influence again, like you did on me. Look around. Everywhere you go you influenced people to be better, to do better."

"If that's true, then it makes me more than happy. I never hoped for that much. But I'm so tired. I wish I could sit back and enjoy it."

"You have to bring down your dad. You know that, don't you?"

"The bitter drop. I've always looked up to him in so many ways. What made him go so far?"

"Uncontrollable greed for money and power. He went deeper and deeper, until anything seemed all right."

"I'm fearful he did have something to do with the burning of that warehouse."

"I knew you'd come to that eventually."

"If he orchestrated that, can you imagine his horrible shock to learn someone died in that fire? That would be enough to change someone for the worse, make them go downhill."

"I'm sure he fell long before that. Don't feel sorry for him, or you'll never be able to finish this."

"I will feel dreadfully sorry for him and love him in spite of what he has done, but I'll finish this come what may."

"Look, there's Capaso. I wish they hadn't put out landing lights. And that big bonfire shows up too well. I appreciate their thoughtfulness, but I'd rather they'd left it dark. They might as well have hired a skywriter to advertise I'm here."

"We'll be quick."

"I don't think they'll let us. I smell a fiesta."

"Oh, what will we do?"

"We'll eat, dance if you're up to it, and then fly like all hell is on our tail. We'll find a place to hide and weather this thing out. I'd leave those high heels in the plane if I were you."

The village came out in force, with a young man dressed in business

235

attire and Padre Juan in the lead. The padre introduced him as Lupe Rodriguez, the attorney who was helping them. Ruben was there also. He ran and put out the landing fires.

"Ruben, have those fires been lit for long?" Jim asked concernedly.

"When we heard your plane and saw your lights, we hurried to light the fires. No one had time to see the fires."

"Great. Then we can stay awhile."

"I see Malinali and others from Tutlu. Reverend Sergio came, too," Anne said excitedly.

"Well, let's get the business done, and maybe we can party a few minutes before we have to fly out of here."

"Yes," she said eagerly and turned to the attorney. "Mr. Rodriguez, we'll tell you all we know, everything we've learned in the last couple of days."

"Thank you. Any information will help. I made copies of the papers you gave Padre Juan, and I've collected other information. We have a strong case. I'm certain we'll win."

They went aside with the attorney, and between them they gave him the complete story, including how Sumner would attempt to frame Jim. He showed interest and excitement over the revelations. He took down the phone numbers of the university testing the chemical and of the insurance company involved.

"I'll help you also, Jim, but it isn't safe for you yet. Try and find the chemist, and force him to tell the truth. I'll try to confiscate the Sumner records in Mexico. Even if your receipts have been destroyed, they probably haven't adjusted the financial records yet. This Mr. Sumner wouldn't want to tell a bookkeeper about this, and I doubt he'd know how to fix the books himself. A good audit could show much. If we can prove any dishonesty in the company, it will help greatly. Try to remember purchases, jobs, dates, anything that might be pertinent. In the meantime, be cautious. I'd better go now. Good luck."

Jim and Anne found a seat by the fire and were soon loaded down with food. Anne laughed out loud when one of the children brought her a chunk of fudge. Padre Juan soon came and sat with them.

"I have seen much in Mexico City. I am glad I am here and not there. The place has changed, sad to say, for the worse. I sometimes wish

236

I could go back in time, back to when I did my circuit by horseback. Even with weak lungs, I was able to take care of four churches. I don't know if I could handle a horse now."

"It might depend on the horse," Jim remarked dryly and couldn't resist telling Padre Juan the story of Tom-tom's rescue.

"I don't think Tom-tom or I will ever forget our trail ride in the sky," Jim finished to the tune of Padre Juan's merry laughter.

"What a grand horse. I am glad he is free. Yes, I see it now. I see the future. My villages, your villages, Miss Anne, will be like your horse. They will be full of spirit and pride, with their heads high. You have unhooked their harnesses and set them free."

Out of the darkness, a teenage boy rushed up to where Jim and Anne sat talking. He shook Jim's shoulder urgently.

"Motor comes. Two miles, maybe three."

The padre explained, "They take turns and watch the trail. You had best go quickly. It may not be a friend, I regret to say."

Anne and Jim were running toward the plane before he had finished his sentence. Jim grabbed Anne up in his arms and sprinted the last of the distance. Ruben helped lift her into the plane, and they were in the air before she could fasten her seatbelt.

"I know this territory. I don't need lights right now. There's the vehicle, down there. He's not as close as they thought. His engine might drown out the sound of our motor. I'd rather no one knew we were in Mexico. Are you all right? You shouldn't have tried to run."

"It felt good, for a second or two anyway. I'm all right."

"Close call for us. Fun though, wasn't it?"

"Glorious! A fitting end for the day."

"What, the fiesta or running for our lives?"

"Both! I loved both."

"I believe you did," he laughed. "Now, here's what we'll do. We'll cross that mountain range and head straight for the Gulf and home. I'll leave my plane at the ranch where I took your horse, and I'll try and find that chemist, if he's to be found. Rodriquez and Padre Juan gave me hope I can be cleared."

"Yes, we can do it. And will I see Tom-tom?"

"You can ride him if you feel able," he laughed again, and then his smile vanished as he studied his instruments.

With set lips he made quick adjustments, gravely shaking his head after each one.

"Engine's hot, too hot. Have to kill it, or it'll freeze up."

"There's no place to land here. Just mountains, trees."

"Look hard. We have a few seconds."

Anne felt a great sense of panic when the sound of the engine ceased. She looked excitedly at Jim, unable to voice her fears.

"It's all right. We'll float in. If we can't find a landing strip, we'll take a bushy tree top."

He'd grinned, tried to sound reassuring, but she knew better. She strained to study the area below.

"Quick, Anne. See that bare spot down there?"

"Too small. It's a cliff, a steep cliff with a tiny, tiny shelf of rock."

"It's our landing strip, baby. While I circle, you check for holes, stumps, and rocks."

"Check, check, check," she shouted excitedly as Jim drew close to the ragged cliff.

"You mean it's clear?"

"No," she screamed, "Holes, stumps, rocks – all over the place!"

"Hang on, honey. This is gonna be bad. I can't afford another pass. I'll try and find my spot as I come in. I know this place now. They burnt it off for corn once, long ago."

"We're thousands of feet high. Somewhere down below there's got to be a better spot."

"No, I know this area. This is it. There's nothing better down there."

"How, Jim?" was all she could say, her heart in her throat. She knew enough about airfields to know it was too short, far too short.

"Did you feel that updraft? That's going to help us or kill us."

He never looked at her again as he made a wide sweep of the area, dropping lower with every passing second. Scared to death, Anne closed her eyes for an instant but opened them as he ended his sweep and approached the cliff head-on. It seemed they were hardly moving, and yet the cliff suddenly sat directly in front of them.

"You're too low. You're going to hit the edge!" she screamed.

"A gamble. Need every inch for a short landing."

Only the seatbelt kept her from becoming airborne in the small cabin as the wheels touched the jagged rock. A shower of debris poured over the windshield and made it impossible to see anything. They stopped with such a jolt her restraints cut into her.

"Piece of cake. Open your eyes."

"I can't. Are we alive? Is the plane alive?" she asked, half in shock.

"I'll know in a minute. Heck of a spot to take off from though. Wait here. I'll have a look." Minutes later he came back. "You must have been praying."

"I-I forgot to."

"Propeller survived. Tires too. That's hard to believe."

"What's wrong with the motor? Why'd it get hot?"

"No oil. Someone tampered with the oil line, probably back at the village. I can fix it, but I need oil. I only have a couple of quarts with me."

"How far are we from Capaso?" Anne asked.

"Maybe a few hours walk, but there wouldn't be any help there."

"My truck may still be there. Reuben brought half of Tutlu to the fiesta in it. It drank gallons of oil, so I kept a good supply on hand. There should be a couple cases of oil in the back, if you can use auto oil. And if the truck's still there, Ruben will be there, too. He could help you."

"I'd better get going fast, or he'll leave before I can catch him."

"These mountains are treacherous at night. You'll get lost, fall into a declivity, or maybe walk into a trap if you make it to Capaso. Someone, somewhere, expects your plane to come down."

"In this mountain range, they don't expect a survivor, and they wouldn't know where I came down. They don't even know what direction I headed. It'll take daylight to find us, unless they get lucky. I'd better go quick, or we won't get out of here before morning. I know the lay of the land. I think I can find it."

"What can I do to help?"

"Sleep and build up energy. This isn't over. I'll move some of this stuff so you can lie down. Hey, these aren't the containers I brought."

"The oil?"

"The extra fuel. These aren't the tanks I put aboard back at the factory." He unscrewed the top of one. "I'm pretty sure it's the additive we used in the paraquat. The odor's familiar."

"How? Where? Someone means to frame you with the evidence."

"You mean kill me, with the evidence on me. They did a darn good job of it."

"Was it during the fiesta?"

"The fuel line had to have been done there. I'm not sure about the tanks. Could have been when I searched the warehouse or could have been at the fiesta. Doesn't matter where, though. I'm sitting here with enough evidence to send me to prison for life, or worse. One way or another, I'll fly out of here."

"You can't take off from this spot. It's too short, too rough."

"Sure I'll take off. I'm going to drop this chemical right in your dad's lap. You rest and don't worry. I'll be back."

He disappeared into the darkness and left her with a feeling of helplessness. The old Anne could have gone with him, kept up with ease, and maybe even passed him by. She climbed down from the plane and looked the situation over with a small flashlight she found. The plane's prop rested less than a foot from a large tree, so the plane couldn't go any further forward. Following the path it had made as it landed, she was amazed at how many times the tires were within an inch of disaster. How would he ever get off that cliff? He would have to take the same path he came in on, and it wasn't long enough, she saw that right away. But the shelf inclined uphill from the cliff's edge to where the plane rested. That rise had helped him stop. Would the drop help him gain momentum for a takeoff?

One thing for sure, he would have to taxi the plane around, and there was no way to do it unless someone cleared the area. Clearing was a task she knew well. She couldn't work fast, but, if she worked slow and steady, pacing herself like she did at her father's hunting cabin, she might be able to accomplish something. Jim would have no time to clear it when he got back, *if* he got back. Daylight would soon be upon them, and Jim had a long walk ahead of him.

In her search for tools, she found a hand axe behind Jim's seat and an old grease rag she could kneel on. She looked down at her clothes. After all she'd been through, the beautiful suit still survived. She couldn't crawl in the dirt and ruin it now. Whether they escaped from their precarious perch or dropped into that dark abyss below, in what better attire could she be dressed? Without more deliberation, she discarded skirt and jacket. Finally, tossing modesty to the winds, she folded away the thin blouse. Only rocks and trees would witness a lone female, in her underclothes, crawl across the rocks in the moonlight.

She started work at the cliff's edge and couldn't help shuddering when she looked down into the depths below. A strong wind blew up at her, chilly because of the altitude, but she was soon sweating from her work. She removed rocks and wood, piece by piece, shoving them aside as a border for her narrow runway. With the axe she broke off jagged edges of rock where necessary. A few small trees had made a start on the rocky bench and had to be chopped away. She filled holes and depressions with dirt and tamped them with a rock.

In the hurry of working, she lost all reticence and could laugh at the ridiculous picture she must make in her strange work clothes, or lack of work clothes. Twice she thought she heard the sound of an airplane or helicopter but never saw any lights and never lost a minute's labor because of it. When she finally declared the runway finished, it was a narrow path indeed, but it was the best she could do.

She didn't stop to rest but went back to where the plane sat. The debris covering its wings and windshield made a perfect camouflage. She could leave that like it was. But the plane still needed a large area cleared so they could jockey it into position for takeoff. That would be a big job, since the area near the edge of the woods had more brush and trees. She struggled at clearing the landscape until her unprotected body was covered with scrapes, bruises, and dirt, but she finally had the job done to her satisfaction. Too tired to walk back to the plane and too tired to care about anything, she stretched out on the ground and fell asleep.

"Anne. Anne!" At first she thought it was a dream. Then she was being lifted. "Are you all right?"

She screamed and struggled so violently he dropped her on the ground. She jumped up, screamed again, and ran for the woods.

"It's me. I just got back. Didn't mean to frighten you. It's me and Ruben."

"My clothes," she gasped.

"I should have known you'd go native on me if I left you here in the woods for long." Jim could barely suppress his mirth, and Ruben laughed deep and fully.

"Throw my clothes over here."

"Would you like a tub of water?" he called.

In the moonlight she could see the grin on his face.

"Hot water and a big, fluffy, white towel, some scented soap, and some bubbles."

"I have a gallon of cool water."

"I'll take it. Go work on your plane so I can get my clothes."

"Use all the water. Any you don't use will be dumped to lighten the plane. And take your time. We have plenty to do." She watched him walk over and study her primitive air field. He soon turned back toward her. "I see you've been up all night finishing the fudge again. Nice runway." He said it matter-of-factly, as if he'd expected it of her. When she slipped up near the plane to get the jug of water and her clothes, she was sure she heard Jim laughing.

Behind a large tree she had her bath, pouring the water slowly over her head and making it accomplish as much as was possible with the limited amount of it. With no fluffy towel for drying, she stood naked in the woods letting the wind do the job for her. The chilly breeze made it an unpleasant wait, and she was glad when she could finally put her clothes back on.

When she emerged from the woods, she saw that Jim and Ruben had repaired the broken line and were now taxiing the plane around. Too tired to offer help, she sat down and watched. When the plane was in position, they worked to lighten it, even drained the gas tanks until there was barely enough fuel left to get anywhere. Jim walked over to where she rested.

"I'll never make it out of here unless I'm close to weightless. I'll have to leave the tanks of chemical. It's better not to risk it anyway. The odds of getting off this rock are only about fifty-fifty. I'd hate to crash with that chemical on board my plane. I'd accomplish exactly what they want. Ruben said he'll hide them if I smash up."

"What's all this *I* business?"

"After you rest, I want you to go back with Ruben. I'll pick you up later."

"I don't weigh much. I hardly ate anything at the fiesta. Besides, I only brought high heels." Her voice sounded close to tears.

Jim looked at her searchingly for a minute. He walked to the cliff's edge, gave one quick glance down, and jogged back to the plane.

"Come on, Ruben. Help me find another one hundred twenty pounds of weight, even if we have to throw out my seat. Anne, get in and strap yourself tight."

The lump in her throat, when she climbed into the little cockpit, mocked her reserve of bravery. She had looked over that ledge one time too many. After adjusting the seat belt, she tried to fall asleep, eager to be unconscious when they passed that last foot of earth.

Jim soon climbed in beside her, took her hand in his and squeezed it tight for an instant. She pretended to be asleep.

"Come on, Anne, don't sleep through this. This is our minute."

Chapter 20

"*Y*ou devil. I'm tired. I don't want to look."

"I'll be lonesome all by myself."

His final appeal revived her spirit. She sat straight, eyes on the darkness ahead.

"How far can we go with the gas we have left?" she croaked.

"Good girl. We'll try for Sumner's warehouse. I can get gas there again, but if necessary we can go further."

"You'll go right into the arms of the law if you go there. I guess it's better if we drop off this cliff after all."

"If anyone is looking for me, they think I'm back here. Didn't you hear the search planes? I'm hoping to find the plant deserted."

The engines suddenly made a terrific roar, or was it her own head, she wondered. When Jim released the brake, the plane leaped at the short runway, and then abruptly the runway ended. She felt the drop and waited for it to turn into a dive. They bounced, terribly, as if meeting constant obstructions, and she wondered if they had already crashed and were bounding across uneven ground but instantly knew the ground was too far below for it to happen so soon. She dared to look out and saw the shadow of trees reaching their arms up. She started to cry out. With her unvoiced scream still in her throat the erratic drop turned into a gentle upward sweep, and the trees were left below, far below. Anne sighed audibly and released her tight grip on the armrests.

"See? I knew you were lying. You didn't want to die back there. You want to see what's going on at the factory."

Anne groaned. "I'm more afraid of that than anything else in the world right now."

"It's the only safe place to get fuel. I can't stop at an airport. They might have been notified. It'll be a few more minutes. Try and rest."

"Now you want me to sleep. You wake me so I can be scared to death leaping off that cliff, and now you want me to sleep during the safe part."

"You can sleep while I'm fueling, too."

"Ha. Wish I could."

Shortly, they approached the Sumner warehouse, and it looked deserted. Jim cut his motor and was preparing to land when all of a sudden he pointed over at the furthest building.

"Your dad's jet! Wonder who's flying it. Wonder who's here. Let's go say hi."

"Let's leave. They'll report you."

"I'll find some way to scare them out of it. I want to see if your dad or Angel came."

Instead of using the runway, he dropped down behind the biggest building and taxied the plane around to the pumps.

"I'll fill up, and, if no one comes out, we'll take off. That's all I can promise. Hey. There sit the fuel tanks I filled earlier. So, they were exchanged here. At least that will save me time." He hefted them aboard, taking a second to smell the contents and make sure it was fuel.

He had finished the job and boarded the plane when a husky figure left the main office building and started across the runway toward the jet. The man never looked in the direction of the small plane hidden in the shadows. Jim's entire body seemed to leap erect when he spotted him.

"Fritz," he hissed and started to climb back down.

"He doesn't see us. Maybe we can still leave."

"Not a chance. And I've been waiting to see him." The menace in Jim's voice warned her of what to expect.

Jim leaped to the ground and trotted toward the man before she could try to stop him. He moved fast and no doubt silently, because Fritz never saw him until Jim's arm shot out and spun him around. From where she sat, Anne could hear the force of Jim's first blow, and she watched in horror as a terrible fight ensued.

She couldn't sit there and be a spectator when she might be needed. Weak she might be but helpless, never. She looked for the axe, but Jim had evidently left its weight back on the cliff. She climbed shakily down anyway, armed only with the small flashlight, but determined to be a buffer between Jim and anyone else who might show up.

Dizziness assailed her as soon as her feet touched the concrete, and she had to hold onto the plane for a long minute, but her eyes never left the scene in front of her. Fritz had height and weight on Jim. His arms looked amazingly long and brawny, but he couldn't use them to advantage while Jim pummeled him close in, a constantly moving engine of destruction.

Stumbling across the runway toward them, she saw Jim take blow after blow on his face and chest, but he never gave an inch. Somehow she knew Fritz was no match for his frenzied assailant. She couldn't picture Jim losing any fight. It wasn't in him to lose. Jim was meting out terrific punishment to a whimpering, staggering Fritz. When Fritz fell to the ground, Jim was on him.

"Jim, you've won. Let's go, quick."

"He dropped the chemical in your lake."

"I know."

Fritz turned away his bloody mouth, a hand held up to protect his face. "I knew nothing. Just followed orders. I didn't know it'd hurt to drop it in the water. They told me to hide it quickly. I followed orders to keep my job. I still don't know what or why."

"Who put that tank of it in my plane, Fritz?" Jim asked menacingly.

"I did. Anglin ..."

Jim struck him again. "Following orders, huh? And who cut my line?"

"Felipe and I. I followed you when you left here. When I saw where you landed, I flew on to the farms, left the plane, and drove back."

"Why didn't you do it at the factory?"

"You came out too soon."

"Are you flying Anglin somewhere right now?"

"No, I'm ..." He suddenly stopped and wouldn't say more.

Anne saw the dark face at the window of the jet. She grabbed Jim's shoulder and pointed.

"Who's in there, Fritz?"

"Le Grand. He won't do anything. He's scared stiff," Fritz said in disgust.

"Fritz, we have enough evidence to put Anglin away. You're his accomplice. The law can get you and Anglin both for murder. And I can press charges against you for sabotaging my plane. That's a charge of attempted murder."

Fritz looked thoroughly scared as he tried to speak. "You know I didn't murder. I did my job."

"I'll tell them you planted evidence, too. You dropped those drums in Tutlu's lake. Anne will back me up."

"I've got to leave the country."

"Did Anglin pay you to leave?"

"He told me to take Le Grand with me. Said he'd come for the jet later."

"You don't take the jet or Le Grand. You go to the police.

"You know I didn't murder anyone. I'll help. I'll testify."

"I haven't time to mess with you now. Give me your word, and I'll let you hide out until I need you."

Fritz quickly nodded his acquiescence.

"Tell Anne where we can reach you if we need you. Maybe we can keep you out of it. But don't try and contact Anglin unless you want to face what he'll face. Right now I have to tend to Le Grand."

When Jim hurried away to board the jet, Fritz turned his bloody face to Anne and gave her an address and phone number where he could be reached. She felt he told the truth, but with Le Grand's testimony Jim wouldn't need Fritz. Just the same she wrote a quick line or two of testimony for him to sign.

"I-I'm sorry about the lake. I didn't know. And I didn't know you were on Jim's plane last night, either. Your father must not have known."

He left hurriedly, and Anne turned back in time to see Le Grand thrown from the jet. He landed hard on the pavement below and didn't try to move. Jim jumped down and dragged the half-conscious man toward his own plane. The chemist started to shriek, but Jim smacked him hard across the mouth, then ruthlessly shoved and dragged him across the field and aboard his own plane. By the time Anne reached the cockpit, Jim had Le Grand in the cargo area, trussed up tightly.

When he started to cry out again, Jim pointed to the containers of fuel.

"Here's the additive that Anglin planned to frame me with. How would you like to take a bath in it?"

"It wouldn't harm me. It has to be mixed with the paraquat to do harm."

Anne took pad and pen and wrote what the man said.

"You dirty murderer. You knew. Wait a minute, Anne. I'm going to go get some paraquat."

"No one knew what it'd do."

"You invented it. You're responsible."

"No. No, another chemist formulated it. I worked with him at Grome Chemical. He discovered it."

"Where is he?"

"He became ill. Blamed it on his experiments with these chemicals. He quit, and I never saw him again after he left his job. But I knew what he was working on. A great discovery. So I continued his work."

"Stole it, you mean."

"He wanted nothing more to do with it. Was scared of it. He didn't care if I continued. He said so."

"How'd Anglin become involved?"

"I needed money to get it tested, to get a patent, to produce and market it. I told Anglin. We tested a small amount."

"Yes, in Honduras. I know."

"Not just there. We tried it in other places. Nothing happened until Honduras. Anglin didn't believe the chemical caused it."

"But you did?"

"The workers had the same symptoms I saw in Briggs. I told Anglin."

"Briggs?"

"Arron Briggs, the sick chemist I just told you about.

Anne knew that name. She'd heard it somewhere. She wrote it down and stared at it. Within seconds she pictured the name in newsprint.

"Arron Briggs. He was the homeless man who died in the

apartment fire," she said excitedly.

"What fire?"

"The one next door to Sumner, remember? The newspaper article said the homeless man found there was identified by a medical tag around his neck."

"Maybe he wasn't homeless at all," Jim stated grimly.

Even Le Grand looked startled. "When? When was this?"

Anne gave him the date.

"That was after I ..." He groaned and turned his back to them. It was obvious he'd say nothing more.

"After what, Le Grand?" He grabbed the man's arm and shook him. "After what?"

"That was when I was in South America."

"Were you working for Sumner then? Did Anglin know about the chemical yet?"

"He knew."

"Jim, let's get out of here before someone comes."

"Sure, as soon as Le Grand signs a statement."

"I wasn't there. I didn't know. You're speaking of murder."

"We're talking about signing what you just told us. If you don't, we'll give you a bath in your brand of paraquat and let you deal with the Mexican government. I'm sure they won't be overly lenient, after they realize how much death and illness you've caused. In the States you might strike a deal."

"Was Isdel's death from the same thing?" Anne asked.

Le Grand turned away and wouldn't look at her.

"I'll sign," he finally said and sighed.

Jim untied his arm and watched him shakily sign the statement. Anne made a second copy of it and added a statement to protect Jim. When Le Grand had signed the second paper, Jim tied him down again, and Anne climbed into her seat.

"Fly! Fly fast!"

"Fast and low. We stop for no one. Put that paper in something waterproof. If we're shot down, the world will still know what happened."

Her eyes wide, she looked over at him, and he grinned back.

"Just kidding. We'll make it now. When we get there we'll call the district attorney and arrange to turn over Le Grand."

They heard a soft groan from Le Grand, but they neither one turned to console him.

Anne turned her attention to the dark waters of the Gulf. The white froth of the waves below loomed close. Jim *was* flying low and fast, and his face was a tight, stern mask that didn't invite questioning. She realized he flew low to avoid detection or pursuit. His joking had been for her benefit. She slid further down in her seat and let tiredness roll over her. The last day had been impossible. She didn't want to ever move again.

When she awoke, the plane was parked in a grassy field and was opened up to let the breeze blow in on her. Directly below her stood Tom-tom. He looked up at her and rolled his eyes ludicrously. She started to climb down, but Jim had to help her to the ground. She threw her arms around Tom-tom, petted the sniffing muzzle, laid her cheek against the soft, red mane, and cried silently into it. When she finally looked sheepishly up, Fred and Jim both watched her.

"I-I'm ready to call the DA now." She couldn't keep her voice from breaking. "You should hide until you're cleared, Jim. I'll drive Le Grand to the authorities."

Fred stepped up to her and smiled.

"It's all taken care of. Jim and I handled it. Relax. Le Grand's been picked up. Jim isn't under suspicion anymore. The villagers will get aid, immediate aid."

"The courts are slow. The insurance company may be slower."

"We'll start the ball rolling with Sumner's insurance fund."

"It's all gone, Fred."

"It *was* all gone, but it came back again and grew somewhat."

Anne looked at him blankly.

"Dad had me set up an offshore account for him. By making false insurance payoffs, with a couple of legitimate ones for the sake of show, he managed to get most of the Sumner insurance fund into an offshore account. He also started drawing more and more money out of Sumner, after you caused more and more problems, and deposited it in the same account. You had him worried, Anne."

"But then it's gone."

"Not exactly. I also set up an offshore account for myself at the

250

same time I set up Dad's. Dad's been depositing all the money into my account, unbeknownst to him. I have his account card in my pocket."

"How could you manage something like that?"

"I admit it got tricky a few times, but I got away with it. I just had all the money transferred back to Sumner's insurance account. I put it through this morning, right after Jim called me."

Anne stood there stunned, not sure she heard right. Fred grinned at her.

"I've been patting myself on the back and waving goodbye to my money, both at the same time." There was something immense about Fred as he stood there with a comical expression on his dependable face.

"Fred, you're safe, aren't you? You can't get into any trouble?"

"I'm totally fine. But Angel may need a good attorney or a villa in Honduras. She got stupid or greedy, likely both. Dad gave her eight hundred thousand dollars and told her to do some actual payoffs while she was down in Mexico. He wanted a few legitimate deals to help cover up his false ones. But she tried Dad's trick in order to feather her own nest against a possible Sumner disaster. She made only one payoff with the money, a false payoff to the tune of eight hundred thousand, to a Sandro Caldera. I believe that's the name. She paid him eight hundred dollars and arranged for him to leave the country while she pocketed the balance. She apparently didn't know that Anglin had invented names for his payoffs. He hadn't let her in on that part of it. Anyway, she found a real person and thought she could trust him, or maybe she was afraid Dad would find out if she invented someone. Apparently, she used this Caldera because she figured Dad would remember him as a worker.

"Oh, Fred, I can't believe all this."

"You'd better." He looked at her sadly. "It's always been like this. I'm darn glad to be through with it. I'm just sorry for what it did to you."

"Where's Dad?"

"In his office the last I heard. He'll be picked up for questioning, and they'll no doubt charge him. He doesn't know yet that his plans all blew up and that Le Grand is in custody. He'll face a first-degree murder charge, at least for Arron Briggs, before this is over. Maybe more before it's finished."

"Why? Why did he do it, Fred?"

"Enormous money, gargantuan opportunity to become ultra, ultra wealthy. It might tempt me, now that I know what he was about."

She turned to Jim. "I want to see Dad," her voice broke, but she finished unashamedly, "before they get to him."

"You're hardly steady. You've clung to that rail ever since you left the plane. I've been standing here waiting to catch you when you fell."

"I'll never see him again, if I don't go now. I know. I feel it."

"He'll insult you, spit on you, or worse."

"Yes. But I'll not be a coward and hide from him. I caused this. I'll face him."

Jim turned to Fred, a determined look on his face.

"Fred, Anglin may still be there. Maybe we can beat the police. Can you drive us now?"

"Of course, Anne will want to say goodbye. Step into my chariot everyone."

They all three sat in Fred's front seat, and Anne held tight to Jim's hand. She knew it was Fred's and Jim's shoulders that braced her upright. She couldn't summon her strength back. Perhaps she had left the last of it back on that rocky cliff in Mexico.

She couldn't help but glory in those two great men who sat beside her. It made her proud to be there with them. She wanted to tell them what she thought of them, how magnificent they were to her eyes, but words wouldn't come. Her heart held more than mere words could utter. She rode thus for over an hour, not able to sleep and not able to speak, but only to feel.

When they finally reached the complex, police guards barred entry to the building, and another officer stood at the bottom of the steps in front of the building. The Sumner buildings stood like sullen, grey battlements against the sunny Houston sky and gave the impression of a storm coming in.

"You'd both best stay here. I-I'll go and see him alone."

Fred nodded. Jim only looked at her questioningly. She took a few unsteady steps toward the building, paused, then turned and rushed to Jim who waited with outstretched arms.

"Jim, I love you. You understand that, don't you?" she cried, close to his ear, holding him tight. A nameless fear gripped her heart. She met his kiss with all the passion and love she'd smothered inside her for so long. When she finally pulled away from his arms and met his eyes, it wrenched her through and through.

"I understand everything about you, Anne." He smiled, but behind his smile was a white, mute agony.

She blinked rapidly to stop the tears and quickly turned away, walking unsteadily over to the officer at the bottom of the stairs. "May I go up? I'm Anne Sumner. I need to ..."

The front door burst open that instant, and Anglin came haughtily down the steps with an officer on each side of him.

She stumbled closer, in spite of the policeman, and planted herself where Anglin couldn't help but see her.

He stopped short and stiffened visibly. While they stood there and faced each other, the air around them seemed charged with passion.

"Pity?" He roared. "Don't dare!" He waved her away and hurried on past into the waiting police car. She heard the door shut with a dull thud, and it seemed to slam on her heart.

The sun burned hot on her bare head and made heat waves against the gray pavement. They were thick, tangible heat waves, surrounding her like so many memories, and they wavered like the ripples on Tutlu's tiny lake. She could see Pacal splashing in the water there, and Tom-tom galloping through the shallows, sending up a rainbow spray, but when she tried to look deeper into its shimmering depths, the heat waves melted, and she felt the pavement come up to meet her, hard and rough.

All of a sudden there were words and memories all around her, throbbing through a suddenly dark world. Some of the words were there beside her and some came out of a misty past, but they were all there together.

"Look. She's fallen. Someone call an ambulance."

But there was no sound of an ambulance, only the distant hum of an airplane filled her ears. She knew she had to run and wave him in, but she couldn't make her legs work. Maybe she had stepped into that stump hole again.

"Anne! Anne!" came from someplace close by, and she tried to find the speaker, but all she found was a haunting, *Talk to me, Anne. Talk to me. You can still do that, can't you?* Like a dream, the words tumbled

253

through her soul, over and over again. And she answered them with her heart, because her lips couldn't form the words. *Once I swam a silver pond in the moonlight, and I was not alone.*

Nearby a car door opened, and strange voices cut in, "Sir, your daughter fell. An ambulance is on the way. We can wait a ..."

Another voice followed, close on it, a proud voice. It registered both harshness and awe.

"Not Anne ... not my daughter. She's not down yet. Get on."

Jean James was active in many outdoor pursuits before becoming a full-time writer. She collected live mammals and reptiles for international distribution, collected live venomous snakes for antivenom production, and worked on sundry wilderness construction projects. She's married to WW2 veteran, William James, and they have six children.

Mary James has spent half her life writing and the other half making music. From age five she has written songs and performed as a touring singer/musician. Today, she spends most of her time on the road but is always anxious to come home to her photographer husband and trouble-making horse.

CPSIA information can be obtained at www.ICGtesting.com
Printed in the USA
245123LV00001B/2/P

9 780982 659489